Falls From Grace

Grace Notes
Book 1

Ruby Landers

RUBY LANDERS

Falls From Grace

Cover design by Cath Grace Designs

ISBN: 978-0-6486402-3-3

First edition 2024

This book was written on unceded Jinibara and Gubbi Gubbi lands. I acknowledge the traditional custodians and storytellers of the lands on which I live and work, and where this book was written, and I pay my respect to Elders past, present and emerging.

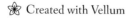 Created with Vellum

Hey. This is for you x

Prologue

TMZ

Twice Struck or Three Strikes? Country Music Superstars' Marriage Implodes!

The king and queen of country music are reportedly calling it quits after the king was caught, yet again, in a steamy clinch with another woman. Cole Corbin was captured on camera groping an amorous fan at infamous Nashville late-night venue, Losers. The woman at the heart of this month's scandal - a veterinary nurse named Amber Lee - wrote on social media in a since deleted post that she believes they had "a special connection," and claimed the encounter was "passionate."

This is the third time Corbin has been photographed in less-than-ideal circumstances, with apparent dalliances with young starlet Huxley Sway and bombshell influencer Anya Amora captured by

1

paparazzi in the last twelve months. It appears that this most recent clinch is finally the last straw for glamorous wife Savannah Grace.

Sources close to the couple report that Grace had previously been willing to give her wayward husband the benefit of the doubt. "He's a handsome guy and a superstar to boot; women are always flinging themselves at him and Savannah trusted him when he said the photos weren't what they looked like."

This third strike, however, is just one too many coincidences for the country star to swallow and she's ordered him to pack his bags. "Savannah is beyond heartbroken," our sources revealed. "She put her trust in him and he burned her like a firework on the fourth of July."

To make matters worse for the singer, her soon to be ex-husband has reacted to his marching orders like a man released from prison. In the week since the news of the split broke, he's been photographed partying non-stop with a bevy of beautiful women, even playing an impromptu gig at Nashville's famed Basement, where he reportedly announced to the stunned audience the launch of his solo career.

As husband-and-wife duo Twice Struck, the pair rocketed to fame with their first single, "Your Heart" hitting number one on the country music charts and number three on the Billboard Hot 100. The talented pair have rarely been out of the charts ever since, releasing six hit albums together and cementing their position as country music royalty. Their most recent release, "Without You" went triple platinum and featured their signature duet vocals that Pitchfork described as "voices matched in heaven, like nothing seen in country music since Dolly met Porter."

"It's a triple whammy," our source disclosed. "Not only has Savannah lost her husband, she's lost her band and her career. He's off playing solo gigs and she's left holding the baby."

The couple welcomed their first child, Tucker Grace Corbin, back in March. He's now just three months old.

Chapter One

This, Brynn knew, would not be rock bottom. If there was one thing she'd learned over the last decade of her life, it was that what you thought was rock bottom was often just a pit stop on the way down. There was always somewhere further you could fall.

This moment right now, however, had to at least rate somewhere in her top three rock bottoms. As she stood on her front doorstep, reeling, Brynn took stock.

The first rock bottom of flunking out of med school in her final year was pretty memorable. It was what her disappointed parents would pick as her rock bottom if they were asked. Brynn, however, would disagree with that assessment. Not because it was a particular life highlight for her, but simply because her parents still didn't know about the next rock bottom in line: the solid year of serious drinking she'd done about it.

Brynn mentally flicked over the complete series of humiliating, drinking-related rock bottoms she'd tumbled down as efficiently as if it were drinking and not medicine that was her true calling in life. It took a moment for her to shake herself out of her shame spiral, reminding herself she'd now been sober for six long years. Was that two rock bottoms or twenty? Who could count?

Since she'd quit drinking, her life hadn't ever shattered that way again, at least not as spectacularly. It hadn't exactly continued on in the upward trajectory anyone had previously imagined for her, but she did okay. She wasn't a doctor, but she still saved lives. Being a life-guard might not be as prestigious or highly paid, but there were more than a handful of weak swimmers still walking this earth because of Brynn Marshall's strong stroke and quick actions.

Her life had been - up until three minutes ago - all around pretty great for the past few years: *chilled, relaxed, calm, easy-going...*all were accurate descriptors for Brynn's state of life. A bit of a theme there, sure, but she'd worked damn hard to get this laid back. And she'd been fortunate. So many others moved to LA and got swallowed up by the scene, dying of unfulfilled ambitions and a life lived at full speed. Not so for Brynn, who'd deliberately kept her expectations low. She'd fallen on her feet in so many ways, the most important of which was finding a solid, nurturing home base.

Her neat, sweet, studio apartment - not owned, just rented, but hers for the last five years - was the center of her life in LA. She'd somehow stumbled onto the one and only freakishly affordable piece of real estate in one of the most expensive cities on the planet. Her landlord, Patricia, didn't say much, but Brynn figured she was like a surrogate granddaughter to the elderly woman, since she'd never once upped the rent to match their surroundings; it was clear she wanted her young lodger to thrive. With property prices rocketing out of reach all around her - and her never-ending student loan bills to pay from her years of pointless study - Brynn knew she would never survive this city without Pat's unwavering support.

She was fortunate, also, to have the support of amazing friends. Okay, specifically, she had the support of one excellent best friend, and a handful of pretty good acquaintances she was working on. But for a town like LA, that was doing okay. Noah Lyman was right this minute ambling up the path behind her, all skinny jeans, man bun and sculpted facial hair.

"What's that?" he asked by way of greeting, noticing her frozen position, stuck staring at the notice pinned to her front door. "Holy shit!" He grabbed for it, tearing the paper slightly. "You're getting evicted?"

———

"That was cold." Noah shook his head, knocking back his shot of green juice from the booth seat opposite her. "I can't believe Pat sold you out so quickly. I thought you two had a vibe."

"Me too," groaned Brynn. "I honestly thought she kinda cared about me. At least enough not to cash up her properties and move to Vegas for the high life the moment she knew she could."

6

Noah snorted.

"It's LA real estate, Brynn... what did you think, she was gonna take care of you, instead? Keep your little *Golden Girls* fantasy going on forever?"

"No," Brynn lied, taking a swig of her kombucha and diverting her gaze out the bistro window. "Of course not. It's just... I'm thirty-one years old and I'm gonna have to go live with a bunch of roommates again. Do you know how much I hate that idea?"

"I mean, sure. Maybe it'll be good for you, though?" tried Noah with a shrug. "You never know. Could get you out of your rut."

"I'm not ready for the toxic positivity spin just yet," she pushed back glumly. "Let me wallow in my depression first." She looked down at the bottle in her hands, desperately wishing it was something stronger.

They sipped in silence for a moment, before being interrupted by the rudely healthy-looking server placing their order on the table between them. Burger and fries for Brynn, kale slaw for Noah. Because Noah had picked the restaurant, the burger was tempeh and the fries were lotus root, but since he was also paying, she took what she could get.

"Wait." She propped her elbows up on the table, popping a fry into her mouth. "You said you had good news to celebrate and I'm here raining all over your parade. What's up?"

"Are you sure you want to hear it right now?" Noah looked up. "We can stay depressed if you want."

"No, come on, I'm sorry. It's fine, cheer me up."

"It's... big." His brown eyes were sparkling.

"How big?"

"The biggest." He shook his head slowly. "I don't even know; I keep pinching myself. It's finally here... the actual big time." He looked a little shellshocked at the words leaving his mouth.

"Noah, what the hell? Tell me!"

He grinned.

"You know how Bella had been calling me and wanting to meet up?" She nodded. Noah was a musician - a pretty successful one, even by LA standards - and Bella was his manager. "I had lunch with her today. She'd had a call, wanting to set up a collaboration."

"With who?" Brynn bounced slightly in her seat with impatience. Noah took a deep breath for effect.

"Savannah Grace."

"Who?" She frowned, trying to place the name.

Noah wilted.

"Twice Struck?" he tried.

"What?"

"Ah fuck, man. Savannah *Grace*. Twice *Struck*. She's an enormous deal. It's because you don't pay any attention to country music."

"Ohhh, *country* music, yeah. Not really my thing," she confirmed apologetically. "But she's big?"

"So big!" He shook his head in exasperation. "They were pretty much the number one act for forever until her band broke up a couple of years ago. Wait, you know the song..." He began to hum. *"Your blood, my veins, your heart, my pain..."*

"Oh." She brightened, joining him for the next line, her voice going high and silly. *"These bones, my cage, your hands release me..."* She stopped and grinned. "Talk about a co-dependence anthem. I hate that fucking song." Noah groaned and threw a strip of seaweed at her. "But her voice is stunning," she allowed, picking nori out of the long strands of her dark hair.

"Look, she's famous as hell, her voice is insane, and she wants to work with me." Noah spread out his hands, his grin wide and goofy. "This is a big deal. She wants to break out of the country music box and I'm who she wants to collaborate with. The fact that she even knows my name is crazy enough, to be honest."

"I'm stoked for you." Brynn reached across the table and punched his slender bicep. "But I'm not surprised. You're kind of a huge deal yourself, you big ole superstar." Noah rolled his eyes, uncomfortable as always at any reference to his success as indie music's newest critics' darling. "What does it mean to collaborate, anyway?"

"Well, in this case, it means I'm leaving LA for a little while," he said. "Could have been better timing, it turns out," he added awkwardly, as he met her eyes.

"It's okay," she lied, trying not to let her face fall. No home, no best friend. A one-two punch. "For how long?"

"Maybe a month... maybe three months?"

"Oh... wow..."

"She has a winter home. You know, celebrities; it's a rich person version of a log cabin." He shrugged. "Just, you know, massive. It's super secluded, somewhere in the woods in Vermont. She's up there to bunker down, get away from everything and just get the right vibe."

"Yeah... the vibe," Brynn said distantly. She was trying not to cry. Three months without her best - and really, only friend - while she would be living god knows where, with god knows who - and, for that matter - doing god knows what. She couldn't afford to stay living in Santa Monica on her salary, and there was no way she'd find a place that wasn't closer than about ninety hours of commuting in the traffic to the beach for work. Which likely meant finding a new job to boot. Three strikes to Loserville, population: Brynn. Suddenly, she felt incredibly tired. A stubborn jerk of a tear forced its way over her lashes and she tried to brush it away before Noah noticed.

"Oh man." He noticed. "I'm sorry. I'm blabbing away about winter homes and you don't even *have* a home." He looked at her. "I'd say you're welcome to sublet my apartment while I'm away, but Jack's already half moved his girlfriend in. You know how he gets. If I'd known, I'd-"

"It's okay! I'm okay." She was not okay. "Honestly, I'll work it out. I'll start looking tomorrow; it won't be that bad." It would be that bad. Her solitude and peace were two pillars supporting her wellbeing and sobriety. Her job with its sun and surf kept her sane. The idea of living with strangers again made her chest feel tight. She'd have to move fast, because without a job, she'd have no references. Shit, maybe she could just move into her car for a while? The AC was broken but with the back seats folded down-

"Wait!" Noah jerked her out of her ever-increasing anxiety spiral. "I have the best idea! You should come with me!"

Brynn shook her head, confused.

"I can't do that," she told him flatly. "This is your big break. She wants you, not your loser friend hanging around."

"First up: not a loser. Secondly, it's not going to be just her and I holed up in the woods. She's a massive star. There'll be an entourage...a manager, assistants, a chef...and like, staff."

"You want me to come as your entourage?"

"No! But she won't even blink if I bring someone. I mean, probably anyway. I'll tell her... I'll say.... ha! I'll say I'm bringing my wife."

"I'm not marrying you, Lyman. You're very pretty, but I'm gay."

"I know, asshole, you don't have to actually marry me. Just pretend. Come on, think about it. We'll get to winter holiday in Vermont! Bella already said I get a whole damn suite to myself as part of the deal." She clearly didn't look convinced because he continued. "Look. We both know you're staring down a scummy rental with five roommates in West Covina." He spread out his hands apologetically while she blanched, knowing his assessment was correct. "Instead, you could be living in luxury surrounded in, I don't know... scenery. It's perfect! I'll be busy writing with Savannah all day and you'll have the place to yourself. It'll just give you time to work out your next move."

"I mean... Noah, that's just... really crazy. Generous and crazy. *Crazy.* I don't know what to say..."

"Then pretend to make me the happiest man on earth and let me be your fake husband," Noah deadpanned. "Come on, Brynn, I'm going to be stuck in the woods with a megastar. She's going to be a spoiled, narcissistic pain in the ass. They always are. Having my best friend there will make it bearable. I'm begging you."

"Because you're kind enough to pretend it's a favor for *you,* I will throw you a bone and kindly consent. For your benefit, obviously."

"Yes! Thank you for saving my skin!"

"And your blood and your veins, your heart and your bone cage," she reminded him.

"Alright, now let's talk about how you're not going to get me fired by mocking the hand that feeds us..."

———

Two days later, Brynn stood in the debris of her apartment with a small collection of cardboard boxes and a much bigger pile of garbage bags. There wasn't any point in keeping a lot of belongings. Storage was expensive and there wasn't much she owned that she treasured. To her left lay an open suitcase as she tried to figure out what - if any - of her Californian wardrobe would translate to late fall in Vermont. Jeans, vests, light sweaters, her favorite leather jacket. To her right, her 'keep' pile. Summer clothes she'd need on her return, a small collection of trinkets, her beat-up guitar, and some books.

She pulled the last stack from the bookshelf, ready to sort. The pile tipped, leaving the hefty volume at the bottom staring up at her. She pulled her hand back as if it had burned her. In a way, it had. *Gray's Anatomy*: the textbook, not the TV series. She remembered pouring over it in pre-med, tracing the shapes on the page with her fingers: the directional flow of blood through the coronary arteries, the pattern of cranial nerves across the face, the sites of oxygen exchange in the lungs. She'd imagined them under the skin of strangers in the street, sure in her belief that one day all this knowledge would translate to her fixing problems, correcting the course of a body going off track. She'd spend her life saving other lives. Being of service. Being useful. Being what her family expected.

Instead, here she was: newly unemployed, having given her notice down at the beach this morning and just about newly homeless. The entirety of her future plan right now was to accept a free plane ticket across the country to hang onto Noah's coattails, eating free food and sleeping in a free bed, mooching around the woods on a celebrity's dime. *Useless.* The word hissed in her mind with the memory of hot breath too close to her ear, the tone sneering.

What did she even have to show for herself? What was her life worth? Shame overwhelmed her as she stared down at the book, remembering what it felt like to have a purpose. Acting almost on autopilot, she tucked the textbook into her suitcase, trying not to think too hard at what that action signified.

Chapter Two

In the middle of the afternoon the following Sunday, Brynn jolted awake as the plane wheels juddered down on the runway in Burlington, Vermont. At Noah's raised eyebrows and gesture, she wiped a little drool off her chin and rolled her shoulders, trying to get the crick out of her neck. Once they'd disembarked and collected their luggage, they were whisked away by a discreet, luxury town car driven by a large, muscular white man who didn't offer his name.

Brynn blinked as they quickly passed through the picturesque town and entered the most glorious blast of red, green, and gold forest she'd ever seen. Fall in LA was pretty much the same as spring and winter: mid seventies and sunny. But *this...* this was fall on steroids. Dappled sunlight teased through the windows as the colors glowed. Views of Lake Champlain, perfectly calm, sparkled between the trees. Settling in for a long ride, she was surprised when within about twenty minutes, they pulled into a large imposing stone driveway with an eight-meter wrought-iron gate.

"Why are we stopping?" she whispered to Noah.

"I think we're there?" he replied, craning his neck around to see as the driver spoke into the intercom.

"I thought we were headed for some private, middle-of-nowhere in the woods? We're barely out of Burlington."

"Yeah, but you're forgetting: when you're rich, you can buy your woods wherever you want them."

Noah was right. After the enormous gate admitted them, they drove for another few minutes through pristine private woodlands before they finally - and yet suddenly - saw their destination. Brynn's jaw dropped. The view before her was almost beyond comprehension.

The land had come to a narrow headland high on a bluff on the shores of the lake. The house was immense, and yet somehow quaint, built from dark stone, almost black, with gabled windows and lush with immaculately tended vines. The forest wove like a red and gold tapestry around it, with the afternoon light reflecting off the water behind it. The view stretched out over the gray lake to the distant mountains beyond.

As they stepped out of the car in front of the stately home, Brynn almost snapped in half at the icy breeze that ran through her, despite the leather jacket she wrapped around herself. Beside her, Noah shivered too.

"Ah, the Californians have arrived," boomed a loud voice, the tone wry. Coming down the steps from the house was a lean middle-aged white man who seemed wildly underdressed for the weather in a crisp blue business shirt and neatly tailored suit pants. He was apparently too rugged to be bothered by the temperature though, leisurely shaking both their hands, waving for them to leave their luggage to be attended to as he led them into the house. "Chester Keaton," he introduced himself. "Savannah's manager. Welcome to Lake's End. We're real pleased to meet you, Mr. Lyman, Mrs. Lyman."

Brynn tried not to twitch at the greeting and Noah's mouth only quirked slightly as they studiously avoided each other's eye contact.

"Whew, it's warmer in here," was all she could offer as they crossed the stone threshold and she took in the bright white interior of the entranceway.

Chester led them through the grand entrance hall into an expansive living room. The floors were polished wooden boards which glowed with the warmth of the large glassed-in fireplace. The furniture was a combination of expensive brown leather and dark gray linen couches, all so cushy and soft they made Brynn want to curl up and melt into them instantly. A grand piano took up the far right corner, making her fingers itch to look at it. One end of the room was floor to ceiling glass, letting in the afternoon light and the view over a manicured lawn, with big white Adirondack chairs set out overlooking the bluff and down to the lake. The water beyond was so limitless it almost looked like the ocean.

"It's only going to get colder, Mrs. Lyman," warned Chester with a twinkle in his eye. "Hope you packed your winter coat!"

"Brynn, please," she corrected him. This *Mrs.* business was going to be the death of her, as she fought off the strained, mildly hysterical giggle bubbling up inside her. "And this *is* my winter coat," she added wryly, shrugging inside her leather.

"Ah. I'll have Remy take you back into town tomorrow so you can start your shopping tour then! Burlington is very well resourced."

"Yeah, that'd be... great." Brynn was not a shopper, and she definitely didn't have the budget for whatever a *tour* of shopping entailed. Chester had stylishly-cut steel-gray hair and dark flashing eyes surrounded by deep crow's feet that made him look perpetually a little worried, despite his cheerful smile. He cocked his head for them to follow.

"Brace yourselves," he remarked, before opening one of the glass doors and leading them back outside into the chill. Later, she would wonder if Chester had been warning them about the cold outside, or something else altogether. Hunching her shoulders, Brynn gestured for Noah to go first, trying to shelter behind his skinny frame as the light breeze sliced through her.

The perfectly trimmed lawn was emerald green and lush, feeling soft under her shoes. When had she last walked on grass? Her life in LA was all pavement and sand. She tried to take in the surroundings, but it almost felt too much. Every tree was spectacular in its individual blaze of color, the lake a sheet of polished glass, the sky a soft blue completely untouched by the smog of LA.

The men ahead of her came to a stop and she stepped around from behind them to see why. Hidden in one of the Adirondack chairs at the edge of the bluff, looking out over the lake was a woman. She, too, seemed dressed poorly for the cold, in skinny blue jeans, ankle boots and a gray knit sweater. Her long blonde hair was pulled up in a messy bun. She wore no makeup and while her cheeks glowed slightly pink in the cold, her lips were blanched almost white, her large blue eyes watering. For a moment, Brynn wondered if they'd surprised her while she was crying, but as the woman's unflinching expression settled on them, she figured she was just cold.

"Savannah Grace," Chester gestured. "Noah Lyman, and his wife Brynn." Brynn started. Not just at the 'wife' word again, but at the realization that this was the megastar they'd come to meet. She didn't look like a celebrity at all, nor Brynn's idea of a country singer. This small, plainly dressed woman? No cowboy boots or big hair? She rolled her eyes internally at herself and looked closer.

Savannah was objectively stunning, even dressed down the way she was: her eyes the exact same shade as the lake, full lips (probably natural, her LA brain immediately assessed), flawless skin and both curves and legs that her plain outfit couldn't conceal. She suddenly realized the gray-blue eyes were watching her back and she felt a flush come over her as she rearranged her own expression from checking her out to one of friendly greeting. *Great wifing, Marshall,* she thought with chagrin.

Savannah didn't get up but reached out to shake both their hands, her fingers icy cool. Brynn fought the urge to squeeze them between her own and rub some warmth into them. Why on earth would you choose to sit out here when there was a delicious log fire inside? How long had she been there, and more importantly, how long would they have to stay out there with her? *Fucking celebrities.*

"Lucille will show them to their rooms, but I thought you'd like to meet our guests first." Chester filled the silence after both she and Noah had murmured their *nice to meet you-s*. Savannah seemed to shake herself, as if remembering that talking was a thing that regular mortals did.

"Thank you for coming," she murmured, the words barely out of her mouth before the phone beside her on the wooden chair interrupted with a piano version of *Brahms' Lullaby*, which frankly was a very creepy ringtone to choose. "Excuse me," she said, before turning her body slightly and answering the call. She listened for less than a second. "I'm on my way," she said to the caller and hung up without saying goodbye. She got to her feet. "I'm really very sorry," she addressed Noah. "We'll talk soon," she promised, as if they hadn't just flown seven hours to meet her. All three turned and watched as she paced across the lawn and disappeared into the house.

"Did we...do something wrong?" asked Noah. Chester shook his head, looking faintly worried as he always seemed to.

"No, no, all is well," he said, his voice remaining cheerful. "Savannah is just a bit torn between responsibilities at the moment. She'll settle down and focus when you two start writing. Oh, my stars, Mrs. Lyman, you look frozen through. Let's get you back inside, shall we?"

Brynn had never been so pleased to submit to old-fashioned chivalry in her life. Once inside in the warmth, an older woman appeared and introduced herself as Lucille, the housekeeper. She led them up an enormous white flight of stairs and along corridors hung with stunning black-and-white shots of a number of musicians in action, none of whom Brynn recognised, although one or two looked vaguely familiar. Coming to the end of the hall, Lucille opened one half of a double door and welcomed them to their suite.

Suite was perhaps underselling it. Brynn's entire apartment could have fit inside it eight times over. As the door closed behind them - Lucille letting them know there'd be pre-dinner drinks served at 6 p.m. - she and Noah exchanged awed grins and high-fived each other before leaping in to explore.

They had their own bright and beautifully appointed living room, with three gigantic sofas and an oversized television, a well-stocked kitchenette complete with a tall bar fridge filled with drinks and snacks. The bathroom was stunning: all soft gray stone with a lush clawfoot tub positioned under a vast picture window facing out over the lake. Finally, there was a luxuriously appointed bedroom with the biggest bed Brynn had ever seen. The bedding was soft, white and fluffy, making it look like a giant cloud. With a groan, she flopped her tired body down onto it and lay sprawling, limbs spread out like a starfish.

"Where are you going to sleep, Lyman?"

"Pfft," Noah snorted. "I could have an orgy on the other side of this bed and you wouldn't even notice."

"Good point." Brynn rolled over about eight times and claimed the right side of the bed as her own. She sat up and gazed outside, mesmerized by the gentle undulations of the lake, framed by the spectacular patchwork of bright trees. "So.... Savannah... was she just what you imagined?"

"I don't know," mused Noah. "Too soon to tell. I mean, we barely saw her."

"Right? She was rude. So very *I have more important things to do than waste time on mere underlings like you*."

"I'm not sure man, she seemed... fragile or something." Noah had hauled his suitcase out and started to unpack his many hair products.

"Ugh please, that's such a gross dude thing to say. She's pretty and she's petite, so you're all *naw, she's fragile*. The woman's a power-house; I'm sure she doesn't need you to sweep her up in your manly arms and save her."

"Doesn't mean she's not human." Noah shrugged as he crossed to the bathroom, likely to take up all the storage space. Brynn rolled her eyes and followed him, her far more humble cosmetics bag in hand.

"You've changed your tune. You thought she'd be a typical celebrity pain in the ass, then after she acts exactly like one, you decide she's a delicate teeny-weeny human. It's got nothing to do with the fact that she's wildly gorgeous, though, right?"

"You noticed that too, huh?" Noah wriggled his eyebrows at her. "Unlike you, since you're a country music philistine, I already knew what she looked like. But no, it's not that. I think she just seemed... sad. And stressed, or something. I hope she still wants to write with me." He looked worried.

"She paid for our flights out, didn't she? I'm sure she'll get her head out of her ass soon enough. Don't worry about it just yet, my friend."

They unpacked together. Noah was a ski-bunny in Winter and his wardrobe was far more Vermont-ready than her own. Brynn wasn't particularly worried. Their suite was deliciously toasty, and she figured it'd be at least a week before she even wanted to get out of the impossibly cozy bed.

"Dude... what's this?" Noah was peering into her almost empty suitcase. "Some light reading?" He was looking at her old anatomy textbook.

Brynn flushed.

"Nothing. Just a whim," she hedged. Noah sat on the end of the bed and cocked his head.

"What kind of whim makes you pack twelve pounds of medical text on a plane?"

"I don't know... I just imagined brushing up on my knowledge again, that's all," she minimized.

"For fun?" Noah looked incredulous. Then he looked shocked. "Brynn, are you thinking about going back?"

"I don't know!" she huffed defensively. Noah was looking at her like she'd casually suggested a cosmetic limb amputation. He stayed silent, waiting. Damnit, that interrogation technique always worked. "Maybe," she admitted. "I just... what the hell else am I doing with my life, you know?"

"Med school nearly killed you," he said flatly, as if she needed reminding. "Find something else! There're all kinds of things you could do if you're done hauling people out of the ocean. Being a doctor isn't the be all and end all."

"I'm sorry, have you *met* my parents?" Noah had, in fact, met her parents. Her mother was an eminent cardiothoracic surgeon and her father the head of neurology at Stanford. "Or my siblings?" Her big sister Anna was a pediatrician, while their younger brother Stephen was completing his training as an emergency room physician. "Jesus, or my *grandmother*, for that matter?" Her Grandma Thea was a legendary infectious diseases specialist and the family matriarch. Being in medicine in the Marshall family was more than an expectation; it was assumed to be the rule.

"Fair point. Your family is legitimately crazy though." Noah shook his head. "Remember when I'd just gotten my big record deal and your ma told me I should consider turning it down to go back to college instead? I think even the idea of an Asian guy without a degree gave her actual heart palpitations," he snorted. "They're very narrow. Plus, you're a grown adult, Brynn; you don't have to do what they tell you anymore."

"I know that!" she exhaled sharply. "But it still sucks being the family letdown. And outside of that..." to her extreme annoyance she was suddenly on the verge of tears. "I'm feeling a little lost right now and you mocking me about it isn't exactly helping."

"Hey!" Noah leapt off the bed and before she knew it, she was wrapped up in a tight bear hug. "I'm not mocking you. Jeez, tiger, I got you." She sniffed and wiped her tears with a handful of his t-shirt. "That better not be snot." He patted her on her back, making her laugh-cry. Great. Hysteria. He pulled back, holding her shoulders and looking her in the eye. "Brynn," he declared. "You're a goddamned rockstar. You're going to find your thing and when you do, you'll be unstoppable."

"Alright coach." She batted his hands away, but she couldn't stop her grateful smile. "I'm good, you pepped me. Is it time for those drinks yet? I'm dying for half a bottle of good whisky. I'm *kidding*," she added, throwing her hands up at his look. She was kidding, but she also wasn't lying. Rock bottom, as always, just over the horizon if you tried.

Chapter Three

By the time she and Noah prepared to head downstairs for happy hour, Brynn was feeling better. She'd showered off the long day of travel in the insanely wonderful bathroom under a showerhead the size of a dinner plate, and changed into something warmer. She looked at her freshly washed reflection in the full-sized mirror and shrugged. Her long dark hair was sleek and fragrant after a dose of the luxury shampoo she'd found waiting on the shelf, and the cold climate couldn't repress her California glow. She knew that her best skinny jeans paired with a red plaid button-up with the sleeves rolled to her elbow wasn't exactly dressed up, but she figured gay-woman and indie-music-wife weren't too distant from each other. Besides, Savannah herself had seemed pretty casual.

She walked back into the bedroom and immediately started laughing. Noah looked back at her, dressed in skinny jeans and a red plaid shirt.

"Jesus," he said. "We've been married five minutes and we're already merged into twins."

"It's because we're lesbians," she sighed. "Alright, you have to change."

"Why me? This is my favorite shirt!"

"You brought twenty shirts. I only have, like, three of them."

"Ugh." He slouched back to their shared walk-in closet and came back out in a V-neck long-sleeved t-shirt that was somehow both loose and flattering to his long, lean frame. "Better?"

"Yeah, you look very *Men's Health* magazine," she told him. "I'm definitely going to steal that from you."

"Wow, marriage is awesome, I can see why my mom is always at me about it," Noah grumbled as they headed out the door.

When they entered the living room, Brynn found herself almost aggravated by how beautiful it was. The tail end of a blazing red sunset still lit the sky beyond the glass wall and the darkening interior was lit by the warm glow of the fire and several extremely tasteful copper lamps. To her surprise, Savannah was already present, tinkering quietly at the beautiful piano in the corner, her golden hair in loose waves down her back. The music wasn't familiar - it felt improvised - and for a moment Brynn found herself wishing they didn't have to disturb her so she wouldn't stop playing. Chester, however, popped up out of his armchair where he'd been furiously typing on his phone.

"Mr. and Mrs. Lyman!" he greeted them cheerily. "I trust your accommodation is sufficient?"

"It's amazing, thank you," Noah told him. "And please, it's Noah and Brynn."

"You won't change him," came the voice from the piano. Savannah had stopped playing and swung around on the seat to look at them. "He's old-fashioned. It took him eight years to call me by my first name."

Now that she was finally talking, Savannah had a soft southern drawl, the aural equivalent of melted toffee, the warmth of which seemed at odds with her stillness. Her tone was dry and it was difficult to tell if she was teasing Chester or instructing them on expected cultural standards. "I'm sorry I had to rush off earlier," she added. Brynn wondered if Chester had prompted the apology. "I'm so grateful to you for coming; I know you're a long way from home."

"Are you serious?" Noah was bouncing slightly on the balls of his feet with the air of an excited child. "I'd have flown to the Arctic to write with you. I'm so honored."

His genuine enthusiasm broke through something in the air and Savannah smiled. The smile transformed her face entirely and Brynn caught a glimpse of the intense charm and charisma routine to a famous person. She could imagine that face on album covers and stadium stages, microphone in hand, crowds adoring her. Hell, she'd be half-tempted to buy a poster of that face herself.

"I'm looking forward to it." That drawl again, pure whisky and smoky mountains. Savannah's eyes - dark gray in this light - sought out Brynn now. "Mrs. Lyman, I hope you won't get too bored while you're here. It's not LA, but I think it has its own charms."

Brynn couldn't stop her slight grin this time. She imagined teleporting Savannah to LA for an instant, to see the life she'd left behind. The wealthy star would be horrified, she was sure of it.

"Believe me when I say I'm thrilled to be here," she said sincerely. "And for the love of god, won't someone please call me by my first name around here?"

Savannah smiled again, and wow, okay, a girl could get used to being the focus of that particular blaze of light. "Sure, Brynn," she said lightly and Brynn was not quite prepared for how her name would sound coming out this woman's mouth. Fine. Okay, consider her charmed. Noah was right. Perhaps Savannah was, in fact, a human. Or maybe she was just really good at being charming when she wanted to be. It was part of her job, after all.

Chester played barman and Noah said yes to a whisky, while Brynn asked for a soda water. Savannah didn't have to ask before Chester handed her an oversized wine glass with a splash of red wine inside. Brynn managed not to snigger as Noah choked on his first sip. She knew he'd only asked for whisky to try to fit in with his idea of a country musician, and there she was, demurely sipping on a merlot. She settled in, prepared to enjoy his discomfort, but Savannah surprised her.

"Would you perhaps try the wine?" she suggested, as if it were extremely important to her. "It's from a vineyard back home and I'm kinda partial to it."

Brynn was pretty sure that was code for *a vineyard that I own*. Noah gratefully accepted, while Brynn regretfully declined. Savannah looked at her for a beat longer but didn't push it, for which she found herself grateful.

Another three people wandered in: a fashionably nerdy white guy with vanity frames and freckles, a stunning, tall, willowy Black woman who looked like a supermodel and another white guy: an honest to god cowboy with a broad chest and boots that made him look like he'd ridden up on his own horse. Savannah introduced them as Travis, Coral and Jed, three members of her band. All three were intimidatingly cool, in a completely different flavor of cool than people in LA. LA cool was always trying to one-up you, to remind you of your place. Nashville cool was less showy and more watchful, letting you come to them. Brynn already preferred it.

Travis instantly gravitated to Noah, clapping him on the shoulder. "I love your album, man," he said straight up. "Savannah introduced me to it and I've pretty much worn holes in the vinyl playing it."

"Oh wow, thank you, that means a lot." Noah looked thrilled. That was the thing about Noah. He didn't do cool. Which somehow made him cooler. He and Travis looked straight up in bro-love already and the two of them took a seat on one of the sofas, happily manspreading and leaping into conversation, most likely about guitar pedals and various extremely niche bands only other cool people liked. Brynn hoped being the wife didn't mean she'd have to join in. She shifted her weight awkwardly from foot to foot, trying to decide.

Coral wrapped her arms around Savannah and kissed the top of her head. Savannah seemed to lose the stick up her butt at her presence, her body looser and more relaxed with her friend at her side. Jed and Chester talked loudly at each other, pouring more drinks and Coral drifted over to argue exactly how a real margarita should be made (*salt, not sugar, what kind of monsters-* Brynn's ex-alcoholic brain instantly supplied, as if it had mattered back then, or in fact, now). She looked up and realized she was left alone with Savannah, who was looking at her with an unreadable expression.

"So-"

"Do you-"

They both spoke at once, then paused, gesturing with politeness at the other to go first. Both opened their mouths to try again, then stopped simultaneously. Savannah laughed and Brynn found herself totally disarmed by her. She tried to remember that famous, beautiful people were professionally magnetic, but she couldn't quite force herself to see the woman before her in that light. Savannah was barefoot, in jeans, still makeup-less with her skin glowing in the warm gold light, her head tilting slightly upward to look Brynn in the eye and Brynn found she did not want to look away.

"You go," said Savannah, shaking her head.

"I was just going to say how beautiful your house is. Your decorator has great taste."

"My decorator?" Savannah raised her eyebrows. "My decorator is me, so... thank you."

"Oh." Brynn felt stupid. "Sorry... just you know LA; even the average pet dog has his own stylist and decorator."

"No, I get it," Savannah said. "I'm famous, so I'm also spoiled and lack my own taste, right?"

"Oh shit, I'm sorry, I didn't mean-"

"I'm teasing you." Savannah reached out and touched her arm, a small smile on her lips. Brynn exhaled loudly and shook her head ruefully. "Do you?" Savannah asked her.

"Do I what?"

"Have your own stylist and decorator?"

Brynn snorted.

"Do I look like I have a stylist?"

Savannah gazed at her, considering.

"I don't know, I'm not from LA."

"You're very tactful, Ms. Grace."

"It's Savannah, please, *Mrs. Lyman.*" Her mouth quirked in a way that Brynn would not hate seeing again. "So... Brynn, what's your story?"

"My...story?"

"Who are you? What are you about?" Her tone was warm.

"Oh." Brynn stalled for time, feeling mildly panicked. Being the lone unemployed weirdo surrounded by famous musicians felt unpleasantly reminiscent of how she felt in a room full of her family, especially when they all talked shop. "I'm really very boring," she hedged.

"Somehow I doubt that." Savannah looked at her steadily. "You seem very..." her words petered out. "I'd like to know your story," she said again, with determination. She really was standing very close. Brynn could almost count her eyelashes. She breathed in.

"Okay, well... I guess I-"

Savannah's attention suddenly shifted. She pulled her mobile phone from her back pocket, and Brynn caught a few notes of the famous lullaby again.

"Yeah, okay," Savannah said to the caller briskly without even waiting to hear them speak, then hung up abruptly. She looked at Brynn. "I'm-"

"You're sorry, you have to go," Brynn supplied for her. Savannah looked back at her inscrutably for a beat and then nodded. "No problem." Brynn blinked and backed away as Savannah turned and slipped out of the room. "*Jesus*," she breathed to herself, as she headed over to join Noah.

For a second, the singer had sucked her in. She'd made Brynn feel utterly like the only person in the room, which was the actual definition of *professionally charming*, she cursed herself. Now she just felt stupid. Thank god she hadn't gotten the chance to babble on about her life, as though Savannah had actually given one single fuck about hearing it.

"You good?" Noah asked as she slouched over to sit next to him. She nodded, flopping down beside him.

"Oh hey, you're the wife, right?" Travis drawled, leaning around Noah to shake her hand. "Nice to meet you. So great you could get to come up and spend this time together." His words acted like a prompt and Noah quickly wrapped his arm around her shoulders, supportive husband style. It was actually pretty nice, feeling like she belonged for a moment, even just as a spouse. "How'd you two meet?"

Brynn and Noah looked at each other. She smiled, as if reminiscing about a romantic moment.

"I saved his stupid life," she said fondly, squeezing his knee.

"Brynn's a lifeguard," Noah explained.

"Woah," Travis looked actually impressed, but Brynn could tell he was imagining her in a swimsuit. Men always did when they heard what she did for a living. Right this minute there was the theme to *Baywatch* playing behind his eyes while she bounced in slow motion down a beach. "You were drowning?"

"I mean... I did swallow a ton of water. Got caught in a rip in Malibu. One minute I was going under, the next she was hauling me out. As soon as I could breathe again, I asked her out."

They'd agreed to stick to the truth wherever possible during this fake relationship adventure and, so far, so easy. They patched over the next part of the story - Brynn saying he wasn't her type, what with how she was super gay - by smiling at each other sweetly.

In real life, Noah had recovered quickly - both from his near drowning and his rejection - and they'd still had a drink after her shift had ended. A drink had led to tacos and tacos had led to true love. Just not the kind they were trying to project now.

"Ugh, that's so romantic." Travis shook his head. "I always wish I had a story like that to tell, but I met my boyfriend on Grindr." Okay, maybe he didn't particularly care about her in a swimsuit. "Of course, I told my mom we met at the library."

"No, man, it's romantic wherever you find love." Noah was such a soft touch. "Particularly when you're on the road all the time, right?"

"Yeah. I mean, we were. We've been in limbo, really, since the whole thing with Cole. And Tucker too, I guess. We haven't been on the road together in almost three years and I miss it. Hoping you'll be what turns that around for us."

Brynn did her best to look interested, but they were drifting back into shop talk. She sipped her soda water, letting their words fade into the background, and watched the room. Coral and Jed were in some kind of intense conversation, maybe even verging on an argument. She wondered if they were a couple. Chester called out to them and they both burst into laughter, whatever it was, forgotten. No one commented on Savannah's absence.

They all wound up sitting around a huge cedar table, eating an incredible spread of what Luis - the full-time chef - assured them was all local, farm-to-table and organic. Savannah slipped back into the room and took a seat without any fanfare, not long after the food arrived. The conversation was already loud and it didn't falter with her re-emergence. Only Coral pulled away from where she'd been talking to Noah and checked in with her, their voices low and intimate.

It was weird...Savannah wasn't like the other celebrities Brynn had encountered during her time in LA. She didn't take charge of the room, didn't act like she was the boss, and there was no deference shown to her at all by the others. It was more like hanging out with a group of friendly workmates or even siblings. If your siblings generally liked each other, that was.

Savannah caught her eye from her position near the other end of the table and raised her drink at Brynn slightly, her expression seeming apologetic, even verging on regretful. Brynn smiled back politely. She would normally tell herself to be on her guard around a woman that beautiful, but after this welcome dinner was over and Savannah and Noah got to writing, she was pretty sure they'd have nothing at all to do with each other, and that was just fine by her.

Chapter Four

By 5 a.m., Savannah had given up on sleeping. Her nights were usually disturbed, and this one was no different. By now she'd been lying awake, staring up at the darkness for what felt like hours. Her brain whirred like a non-stop machine, producing worry after worry until her stomach churned. She slipped out of bed, into her running clothes, and quietly closed the back door behind her.

Outside, it was still night, but the promise of sunrise gave her just enough light to make out the path. She began to jog, her body feeling tight with cold and tension, slowly loosening as she made her way through the trees. It didn't occur to her to feel afraid of the forest in the dark. She'd grown up in the Tennessee woods and the whispering of the trees and the occasional snap of a twig felt like home. Humans were much scarier than anything in nature, but since these woods were both private and protected, she felt even safer out here than if she were tucked up in her bed indoors.

Slowly, the anxieties that had left her wrung out and sleepless began to lose their sharpness as she started to expend the energy inside her body. The low light slowly filtering through the trees felt like a relief, like the darkness had been mental as well as literal. She looped back around the path and down the big hunks of solid granite that acted as steps to the lake, just in time to see the first sliver of blazing rose-gold as the sun slipped up over the mountains. For a few dazzling minutes, the lake was awash with color.

Savannah perched on a boulder at the edge of the small beach and caught her breath. She let herself finally feel present, concentrating on the sound of the water gently lapping at the lake shore, the bird chorus awakening, the soft cool breeze against her heated face as the world slowly lit up around her. She wondered what it would be like to never have to go indoors again, to shed her life like a skin and disappear into the woods forever. She imagined sleeping in a tree hollow like a wild animal, finally at peace.

But that was not her life. She breathed in the cold air and tried to take advantage of these few stolen minutes to herself. They were so few and far between these days she wanted to cry. She didn't want to waste the small time she had by fussing, so instead she began to focus on the day ahead, trying to break things into bite-size chunks she could manage.

Today the band were departing, all three flying back to Nashville to get on with their lives and their other projects. Savannah had nothing for them, not yet, and their return to Vermont depended on what, if anything, she could produce for them to work with. She wasn't used to having sole creative control and she was both extremely thrilled and daunted by the idea. Which was where Noah came in.

He wasn't quite what she'd expected when she'd asked her team to bring him on. His album had first fallen into her lap when she was quietly at her lowest. She was barely showing her face in public and couldn't bring herself to even look at her guitar, let alone sing. Even listening to other people sing felt like suffering a thousand paper cuts. The first time she'd heard Noah Lyman's *Dead Star Ballads*, it had simply blown her apart. It felt like a small cyclone had run through, blasting open doors in her mind she'd never even known were there. Finally, she'd felt a whisper of creativity and hope. It had reminded her of the sheer power of great music, and what's more, it had prompted the epiphany that if she were to truly break with her past and establish a fresh path, it wouldn't be within country music. She was done.

She hadn't read much of the publicity Noah had done for his album, because if by chance the man behind the music that had come to mean so much to her was an aggravating, self-important asshole, she didn't want to know about it. But what she did see, she liked, and she couldn't shake the idea that Noah Lyman was exactly who she needed to help her navigate this next step.

She was thrilled when he accepted, but as the days counted down to his arrival, she'd felt increasingly nervous. Now it was getting real. Not only had she invited an absolute unknown into the center of her world, it was also now make or break time. The tiny flame of an idea she'd nurtured would either blaze into light or sputter into nothing. And songwriting together was an insanely intimate act; what had she been thinking, not thoroughly vetting this man?

Then, all of a sudden, the day had come and there he was. A gangly, handsome, Chinese-American, Californian hipster, with a beautiful wife in tow. She'd felt uncharacteristically shy after her long hiatus from the industry, but he brought a warm, genuine energy with him that felt wildly reassuring. He seemed to tread lightly in a room. This, to Savannah, was a huge relief. She'd had about enough of pushy alpha males in her life.

His wife, too, intrigued her. Brynn was tall and gorgeous, with gleaming chocolate-coloured hair and dark eyes. Her skin glowed with tan and she had appealing freckles across the bridge of her nose and cheekbones. She was casually cool and very hard to read. But she definitely seemed strong, which made her like Noah even more. A rock star who seemed happy to let his wife shine. *What a damn novelty,* she thought bitterly.

She realized the sun was fully up, light spreading higher in the trees, and she jolted to her feet, quickly jogging back to the house, back to her life and responsibilities. No longer a wild creature, but a human woman once more.

———

Later that day, she hugged her band goodbye as they loaded their gear into the van Remy was taking to get them all to the airport. The sky was blazing blue, but the air held the full promise of the coming winter as Savannah squinted into the midday sun.

"It was great to have you here," she said to Coral wistfully. "I wish you weren't going."

"Babe, you got this." Coral tucked a strand of her hair behind her ear for her. "It makes me so happy to see you finally getting back to what you love. It's time to write something that will make the world go, 'Cole *who?*'"

Savannah cringed.

"I don't think I can think about it that way," she denied. "I want that man as far away from my writer's block as possible."

"Oh honey, he is. I just mean...I have full faith in you. I can't wait to hear what Savannah Grace sounds like as a free woman. You're going to blow us all away, I just know it."

"Thank you." Her voice cracked and Coral hugged her tightly before sliding into the van. She wound down the window to look Savannah in the eye.

"Quit stalling and go and get to work with that sexy young rockstar you hired," she said with a smirk. "And don't do anything I wouldn't do. Or, maybe, do."

"He's *married.*" Savannah found herself checking behind her, mortified, in case anyone could possibly have overheard. Coral just laughed and cocked a finger gun at her as the van pulled away.

Savannah hugged herself for a moment as she stood alone in the cold. She felt forlorn, like her last protection against the next stage of her life had been stripped away. Then, forcing herself to straighten her spine, she walked in to try to get said life back on track.

———

"So," said Noah, smiling at her. "How do you want to do this?"

"Well," she said. "I guess..."

Silence grew. They were sitting downstairs in the band room. When she'd bought the house, it had been a large rumpus room, and just three months ago she'd had it soundproofed and refitted. It was big yet cozy, one of the only places in the house that had no view whatsoever. She liked it that way. It felt private and warm, with its dim lighting and all of her favorite well-loved instruments.

"How do you normally like to work?" Noah tried again, and she realized she'd been staring blindly at the floor for some time. She blinked and considered his question. The last song she'd co-written with Cole, she'd been naked, soaking in the enormous bathtub at their home in Nashville, while he lazily strummed his guitar from the tiled floor beside her. She'd belted lyrics at the ceiling and he'd smiled that slow grin of his and jotted them down in his battered notebook between slugs of red wine. She looked back at Noah and found for a second, she literally couldn't speak.

"You know what?" he said, and she braced herself. He'd flown across the country only to work with the broken half of a once hit band.

What a waste of everyone's time. "Let's try something else?" he suggested, asking her consent. When she nodded, he stood up from his chair and gestured for her to follow him. They left the band room together, headed up the stairs and toward the back door. Following his lead and shrugging into her jacket, they headed out into the breeze.

They trudged side by side down the forest path, the cold air smelling like fresh earth and pine needles. A breeze blew up off the lake.

"I'm following you, by the way," Noah said after a minute. She fought off a sense of mild panic.

"I thought I was following you!"

He laughed.

"The blind leading the blind."

"This is exactly what trying to write with me will feel like," she blurted. "Not that you're blind in this analogy. Just me. I don't know how to write with someone else. I mean, someone who's not..."

"Your husband," supplied Noah, looking straight ahead through the trees.

"Ex," she said automatically. He glanced over at her and she shrugged. "Yeah. It's a little weird for me I guess." *Understatement.* "I'm sorry."

"Don't be sorry." He ducked a low-hanging branch and stumbled slightly. He righted himself on the path, unfazed. "It's material."

"What is?"

"This. The discomfort. The confusion. The loss. The weirdness of something new. It'll be our first song."

"It will?" She listened to their footfalls, the crunch of fallen leaves on the path. He nodded. His easy confidence was kind of warming.

"Yeah," he said. "This moment right now in the woods. Both of us uncomfortable... maybe lost." He looked around at the trees and she found herself laughing. "Soak it up for a minute. Just... feel it." Somewhere inside she felt kind of stupid as well as slightly annoyed at the California hippiness of being told to *feel* her feelings, but she nodded, and they trudged in silence for a moment, nothing but the sound of their footsteps and the ceaseless whisper of the trees. She let herself soak it all in.

"I need a guitar," she said after a while, a sense of restless energy tickling at her empty hands.

"Now we're talking." Noah whirled around, the same energy lighting up his eyes. They sped up the pace back to the house and right back into the band room, this time with something firing between them.

Two hours later, he put down his guitar and considered her closely.

"Let's not force it," he said. "We've got the beginnings of something. Like... the vibe."

"The vibe." Savannah wanted to murder him. It must have been obvious, because Noah threw up his hands in surrender.

"I can feel it," he insisted. "Can't you? The song is right... *there*. But we're working too hard and we're new at this and we're blocking it from coming through."

To her surprise, Savannah knew exactly the feeling he meant; she was feeling it too. It was like trying to remember a dream as it slipped further and further away from you the harder you tried. Dreams and songs used a different part of your brain than thinking. They couldn't force their way back into this.

"Let's take a break," she agreed. Noah sprung to his feet like a man saved. They both headed back up the stairs, agreeing to meet back in an hour. She slipped out the door again, this time heading for the lake. The sun was just sinking behind the mountains, the beginnings of darkness creeping in. She took the big stone steps at almost a run, desperate for the solitude of the quiet lake edge and endless expanse of water. She burst onto the small pebbled beach, allowing her lungs to fill with a desperate, heady gasp.

"Shit!" A voice rang out. Savannah whirled around to see that her tiny private beach had an intruder. "God, sorry, you scared me." Noah's wife was perched on a boulder near the water. Savannah's boulder, the one where she always went to think. "I didn't expect to see anyone and then you came crashing out of the woods and I thought you were a bear!"

The tension escaped her in a sudden laugh. Brynn was holding her chest and looking actually frightened. "There aren't any bears in these woods," Savannah told her. She walked closer. "Just cranky old country singers."

"That's even scarier." Brynn widened her eyes. "I didn't mean to crash your beach time or whatever."

"No, it's okay." Savannah surprised herself by hoisting herself up on the boulder next to the other woman. "Make yourself at home. You may be here for some time," she sighed. Brynn turned her head to look at her. Her dark hair was tied back, tousled by the wind, and her eyelashes were so long they cast their own shadows in the fading light. Savannah looked at them more closely. God, they were *real*.

"Songwriting kicking your ass?" Brynn said lightly, as if it wasn't a case of Savannah's entire life and hopes of a career all crumbling before them. She checked her irritation, paused for a moment, and let Brynn's lightness take hold.

"Kicking my ass, kicking Noah's ass, and I'm pretty sure he wants to kick my ass about now," she admitted, tucking her own hair back as the breeze tried to wrap it into her eyes. The cold air stung, the freshness like a balm after the frustration in the band room.

"Huh," said Brynn. "Beware the fury of a patient man," her lips curved into a smile and she pulled her knees up to her chest, resting her chin on them. Everything seemed to go still.

"What did you just say?" Savannah's voice was low.

"Oh, nothing. Just a thing my dad used to say. Noah actually doesn't experience fury; he's made of marshmallows."

"No- please... say it again," she said urgently, staring at the woman's face. Her heart was racing, something flaring deep in her chest at the sound of the words. Brynn cocked her head and looked at her with concern.

"Beware the fury of a patient man?" she asked. Savannah stared at her for a beat longer, the words echoing in her ears. Before she could stop herself, she'd grabbed the other woman by her surprisingly strong shoulders and smacked a jubilant kiss on her forehead before jumping down off the boulder, her boots crunching in the pebbles.

"Thank you!" she called over her shoulder at the woman left sitting stock still on the lake shore as she raced back up the granite steps.

Forty-five minutes later, Noah re-entered the band room to find her, guitar in her hands, notebook open on the floor before her. "Listen to this!" she cried jubilantly and began to sing.

Chapter Five

The morning sunlight was strong enough for Brynn to voluntarily choose to step outside. She congratulated herself on acclimatizing from California, even if she was currently wearing a tank top and Noah's long-sleeved V-neck under her sweater. She'd knocked back the proffered *shopping tour* for winter clothes and, so far, wasn't regretting it. Especially right now as the sun shone, and she dug into a plate of chef-provided eggs, toast, hash browns and spinach, with perhaps the world's best black coffee, seated alone at the big outdoor table on the back patio.

The velvety lawn glowed blindingly in the light and the lake sparkled blue and silver from beyond. Brynn had decided that maybe today she'd venture out and explore the surrounding woods. She'd slept like a baby for the second night in a row in the humongous white bed, Noah not returning from his writing session until well after she was asleep. She'd left him snoring as she ventured out for breakfast.

"Howdy partner." The door opened behind her and out he walked, a modest bowl of something green in hand.

"Don't let anyone hear you talk like that," she hushed him. He sat down opposite her, looking mildly wounded.

"I'm not pulling it off?"

"Nope."

"Huh."

He dug into his breakfast and they chewed in silence.

"So?" Brynn asked him.

"So, what?"

"How was it? Write a hit song yet?"

Noah took another bite, chewed for way too long and swallowed, then took a sip of his tea before responding.

"Well, Savannah did, for sure. Not sure I was much help."

"What do you mean? I thought you were co-writing? She railroaded you?"

"Not exactly." He sipped again, looking thoughtful. "We tried to write together. We were really starting to get somewhere with this one song... kind of a soulful thing about putting yourself out there again after heartbreak," he explained. Brynn nodded. "We were just a bit stuck, you know? So she called a break, went for a walk, and when I came back, she had pretty much fully written this whole other song, entirely without me."

"Oh, wow. Like, a different version?"

"No. Literally, an entirely different song. This blazing, angry, killer of a thing. It's... honestly just an incredible song. Starts out quiet, then just sleepwalks you into this blaze of cold rage. She was just... shredding on that guitar... and oh my god, her voice," he said reverently. "I was blown away."

"Maybe she just needed to clear the cobwebs out," Brynn reassured him, though she was thoroughly diverted by the idea of quiet blonde Savannah *shredding*. "I'm sure you'll get back to writing your song together today."

"I'm not even sure we should." Noah put down his fork and looked at her almost glumly. "I can't even describe this song she made, all on her own. I'm not sure she needs me."

"If she didn't need you, she would have already written that song and a whole bunch of others without having to invite you up here," Brynn argued. "You clearly did something to help open the floodgates."

Noah looked somewhat cheered.

"Yeah, I guess I did. But I already know this album is going to end up named after that damn song last night, I swear to god. *Beware the Fury*," he mused, "Or *The Patient Woman,* what sounds better?"

Brynn stared at him, several belated realizations hitting her at once. She opened her mouth and then thought better of it.

"Beware the Fury," she said instead. "Killer title."

———

Wrapping her leather jacket closely around her, Brynn wondered if maybe she should be leaving a trail of breadcrumbs. A private forest couldn't be all that big, could it? She'd stolen one of Noah's woolen beanies and had a good pair of sneakers, but she definitely didn't want to get lost out here. It was mid-morning though, with the sunlight dappling the path through the trees ahead and the house not too far behind her. She'd pay attention and all would be well.

It didn't take long until her thoughts wandered. Noah had sounded uncharacteristically worried and she hoped that today would be his chance to shine. He was an incredible musician, and, she imagined, a great co-writer. He was patient and generous to a fault. He and

Brynn goofed around and jammed sometimes, and even though she was a rank amateur he never made her feel like one. She hoped Savannah would cool her heels a tad and make good use of the ridiculous music brain he carried around inside his handsome head.

She would tell him, later on, once things had picked up song-wise, about the weird moment on the lakeshore with Savannah. She didn't want to steal his thunder by intimating that it was her who had accidentally inspired something in the singer. It was a throwaway line of poetry that Brynn didn't even really know she remembered having heard until she said it. Savannah's eyes had gone big and dark, focussing on her in that intense way of hers that made the world disappear for a moment, like it was just the two of them under the darkening sky.

For a second Brynn thought Savannah was going to straight up kiss her on the mouth as she grabbed for her, clearly high on adrenaline, but she'd smacked a kiss on her forehead instead and ran away, leaving Brynn both amused and confused. She'd chalked it up to artistic eccentricity, but now she realized Savannah had broken through her writer's block in that moment and was already blasting a new song in her mind.

A bird whizzed low past her head, drawing her attention back. She realized she'd walked a fair way from the house and, craning her head around, she wasn't quite sure where it would be in relation to where she was. No problem, she'd just walk back the way she'd come. There was a rustling in the undergrowth somewhere off the path and she quickened her step. No bears, Savannah had said. But like... wolves? Mountain lions? Brynn was most definitely a city girl for a reason. Damnit, there was a fork in the path ahead and she wasn't entirely sure which one she'd come down. Wait, Google maps! She pulled out her phone, only to find there was no reception. Of course not. Stupid woods.

She started off down the fork to the right, hoping to see something familiar, but it seemed to be looping further from the direction she thought she should be going. She heard a twig crack and froze. This was just creepy. Then, all of a sudden came a rumbling, shuffling sound. Was this how she died? The sound came closer and Brynn realized it was the footfalls of someone running. Some kind of back-woods psychopath? She backed up between the trees at the side of the path, looking for cover.

The runner was in line with her when Brynn recognised the blonde ponytail and realized help was at hand.

"Savannah!" she said with relief. The woman leapt out of her skin, stumbling and saving herself from falling only at the last second.

"What in the fu-!" Savannah caught herself neatly before the curse flew out. She was flush-faced and breathing hard, her lips parted and looking way too attractive in her running gear for Brynn's liking. The singer put her hand on a tree trunk, pausing for breath. "What are doing lurking in the trees? You scared me half to death!"

"You scared *me* half to death!" refuted Brynn. "I didn't know who was chasing me through this creepy forest!"

Savannah shook her head with a look of disbelief.

"I couldn't chase you if I didn't know you were here," she pointed out. "And it's not *creepy*, it's perfectly safe. I always run through here. It's peaceful."

"Not today, it's not," Brynn disagreed. "Bears, wolves, mountain lions." She gestured around her in the now quiet woods. "Psychopaths running through the trees."

"My apologies for scaring you with my routine, everyday jog," Savannah said drily. "Shall I leave you to it?"

"No!" Brynn said quickly, taking a step towards her, fully preparing to run after her, if that's what it took. "I'm actually totally lost," she admitted. Savannah's lip quirked.

"No, you're not," she told her. "This path is a circle. You'd get back to the house either way. I mean, one way would take you about an hour, but you'd still get home." She shrugged. "Also, we're about three-hundred feet from the house."

"No." Brynn refused to believe it.

"Yes." Savannah cocked her head for her to follow, and Brynn quickly complied. Together they trudged down the path, which suddenly felt quite picturesque and lovely, now that she had company. "Were you going anywhere in particular?"

"Just wanted to explore," Brynn told her. "At least, I thought I did. But it turns out the woods are not for me."

Savannah examined her.

"You're missing out," she said. "They're beautiful. You just need a better guide, that's all. You know... I can take you out on a real walk, if you want."

Brynn looked sideways at her. Savannah's cheeks were still pink, wisps of blonde escaping from her ponytail. She looked fresh as a daisy and ridiculously pretty. Exertion suited her.

"That's super kind of you. You don't have to, though." Brynn thought she was letting her off the hook, but Savannah actually looked disappointed. "I mean, you know, you're busy and I'm just a hanger-on here. I don't want to put you out," she rushed to add.

"You wouldn't be putting me out. I prefer being in the woods, honestly. It'd give me an excuse to escape the house for a while," she said with a small shrug. "Evade my responsibilities."

"Oh, this is a playing hooky situation?" Brynn raised her eyebrows. "Then I'm in." She was rewarded with a small, pleased smile.

"Look," Savannah nudged her with her elbow. "The house you lost." Ahead of them the path was opening up to a view of the lawn and the immense, towering, gray-stone house. Brynn raised her eyes to the sky.

"In all fairness, though, it's a very small house," she said defensively, and Savannah laughed out loud.

To her vague alarm, Brynn very much liked making this woman laugh. She seemed a little lighter today, compared with their other interactions. Perhaps clearing the writer's block was the reason. At any rate, her laugh was ridiculously lovely. Brynn wondered if maybe, in some weird world, they could almost be friends. Then: *Brahms' Lullaby*. Again. She fought the urge to roll her eyes.

"Okay, yeah, I'm coming," Savannah said to the caller and hung up. Her phone manner was lacking, to say the least.

"Coke habit?" Brynn asked casually.

"What?"

"Your dealer? Always calling, you're always rushing off."

"You're joking, right?"

"I mean, you wouldn't be the first famous musician in the history of the world." Brynn shrugged.

Savannah gave her a solid glare.

"You really are... kind of offensive?" She didn't sound sure how to take her.

"Am I?" Brynn got a kick out of annoying her too, it turned out.

They were nearing the house now and, to her surprise, she realized she was actually quite disappointed to be losing Savannah to her mysterious life while Brynn headed back to her day alone. Off to their suite to stare at the pages of *Gray's Anatomy* and think about her faltering, sputtering life. Savannah, though, seemed to have other ideas. As they reached the solid stone entranceway, she whirled around to face Brynn, hands on her hips.

"You really think you have me all worked out, don't you?" she said, her tone sharp. "Famous, rich, spoiled, fancy-free...profligate."

"I don't even know what that last word means," Brynn said evenly.

"No substance, control or morality," Savannah said, her blue eyes narrowed.

"Oh, *morality*," Brynn replied. "Is that some kind of a Southern thing?"

Now Savannah looked actually pissed.

"Okay, you know what? Come with me."

Suddenly Brynn's arm was in her grip and she was led in the opposite direction of her and Noah's suite, along a long corridor and up the stairs into what was, to her surprise, clearly Savannah's private wing of the house. They passed a few closed doors and came to one at the end, where Savannah shot her an unreadable look and then opened it.

The room was big, bright and open, with expansive views over the lake, and Brynn could hear a woman's voice, cajoling just out of earshot.

"Baby?" said Savannah, walking toward the sound.

There was a thunder of small feet and a tiny dark-haired boy appeared in the doorway, pausing just long enough to beam a huge smile on his tear-stained face.

"Mama!" he cried, and threw himself forward.

Savannah dropped down to her knees and he flung himself into her arms. He buried his face in her neck and she buried hers back, kissing the nape of his neck.

"Hey darling! You had a good nap, huh?" She pulled back to smile at him. "Then you woke up and Mama wasn't there!" He buried his face in closer and she stood up, snuggling him close, his short, chubby legs clinging around her waist. "I'm sorry, peanut, I came as soon as Megan called me." She broke her attention just long enough to give Brynn a pointed look. Brynn just stared, understanding dawning.

The woman - Megan - stepped into view. She was a young white woman, slightly anxious-looking, casually dressed, with a thin brown braid hanging down her back.

"I'm sorry," she said, her accent crisp and British. "I know you were out running, but he just really wanted you."

"It's okay," Savannah said, stroking the child's hair back. "I always want to know if he needs me. I'm never too busy. Not for my boy." These last words she directed at the little face that had pulled back to look at her.

Remembering there was a stranger in the room, the toddler turned to stare at Brynn. His big brown eyes looked serious and concerned as he took her in, soft smudges of eyebrows and a sweet, slightly down-turned mouth. He had dark chestnut coloured curls. Brynn's first thought was that he looked nothing like his mother. Her second thought was that oh wow, right, Savannah was a *mother*. Her third thought was that weirdly her insides had turned a little to mush because damn, that was a cute child.

"This is Mama's friend Brynn," Savannah told him as he took her in. "She's staying for a little while." Brynn told herself it was embarrassing to enjoy being described as the singer's friend when the audience was a baby, but it didn't stop the pleased feeling welling up inside her. Savannah looked at her now. "This is my son, Tucker. He's two. And I'm very sure he's never touched *cocaine*," she said pointedly.

"Of course not," Brynn said. "Not until he's at least five, hey kiddo?" Savannah did not look remotely impressed with her humor, but Tucker lit up with a big smile at being addressed. He pushed at his mama to be put down, which she obliged, looking mildly incredulous as the child toddled away from her and lurked around Brynn's knees, staring up at her. "Hey buddy," she crouched down. He looked both shy and pleased and then grabbed her hand and began to pull. Brynn followed as he pulled her past Megan, who stood kind of awkwardly in the room just watching, and over to the bookshelf, where he pulled out a book seemingly at random and shoved it in her hands.

"Oh darling, Brynn doesn't-"

"I got it," she interrupted Savannah and sat cross-legged on the floor, turning the book over in her hands. "Oh, *The Little Yellow Digger,* great choice." She began to read and within a page, Tucker had plonked himself in her lap.

Brynn felt extremely squishy on the inside now. It had been a while since someone had just wholeheartedly embraced her on sight. His body was warm and surprisingly heavy for someone so small, and he leaned back on her trustingly as she read. She finished the story and closed the book, but Tucker simply handed it back to her.

"Again," he said.

"Tucker, no, you've already read that one," Megan interrupted, walking over to the bookshelf and picking out another. Tucker and Brynn looked at each other. His serious gaze didn't waver. So Brynn opened the book and started reading it over again. Tucker looked fascinated, touching each page and staring at the illustrations. Savannah came over and sat in a nearby armchair, and Brynn tried not to be aware of her eyes on her as she read. When he handed it to her again, she started a third rendition.

"Megan, why don't you go take a break?" Savannah said to the young woman, who seemed both nervous and relieved to get to leave. As she grabbed her bag and disappeared out the door, Savannah seemed instantly to lose the rigidity in her shoulders.

After the fourth rendition of the story, the child finally seemed content it was done and pushed himself up to pull more books out, spreading them around him in a fan on the floor as he tugged them out in handfuls.

"Megan seems a little uptight for a dealer," Brynn offered, and Savannah rolled her eyes, but couldn't seem to stop a smile.

"I'll take that apology about now," she said wryly.

"Oh, I'm not apologizing." Brynn raised her eyebrows. "It was a logical guess, given the information I had at hand."

"I'm going to ignore that and just pretend you did, since Tucker clearly likes you."

Tucker looked up at his name and smiled his blinding smile. Now he looked more like his mother. Particularly as she smiled back, her face full of love. Brynn wondered what it was like to love someone that much. There was a squeeze in her chest as she looked at the two of them.

"What's his favorite thing to do?" she asked. "Reading books? Or... swimming?" She looked at Tucker, who bobbed up and down, clearly knowing he was being talked about. "Oh, or *ice cream?*" She wriggled her eyebrows at him and he squealed.

He got up and toddled over to a low cupboard, tugged it open and began to pull out toys, adding to the mess on the ground.

"Ugh, he's a cute one," she said to Savannah, realizing she was being watched closely.

"You're good with him," Savannah said after a long moment of quiet. "And his favorite thing is music, actually."

"Of course it is," Brynn said. "Must get that from you, right?"

Savannah smiled at her.

"I mean, both sides, I guess."

"Oh, his dad is musical?" she asked.

Savannah looked surprised and then laughed.

"Yeah. He is."

"What's so funny?"

"Nothing. Just, it's refreshing. You're obviously not a tabloid reader, huh?"

"Uh, no. Sorry. Am I...missing something here?"

"Really? Noah didn't talk about it?"

"Uh...no. I don't think so?"

"My ex-husband is Cole Corbin," Savannah said, clearly watching for her response. When Brynn looked blank, she smiled broadly. Tucker was now playing with a pair of toy dinosaurs at her feet, making little roaring sounds. "We were in a band together. It was big. Then he cheated repeatedly and I was the sucker who believed his lies until I didn't. Now we're divorced and I'm this guy's mom," she stroked Tucker's hair, "and trying to make a comeback on my own."

"That's a lot," Brynn said, nodding her head as several things started to slowly make sense to her about Savannah. "I'm sorry you were married to a douchebag."

Savannah spluttered with a short laugh before shrugging her shoulders.

"Me too," she said simply. "I guess it sounds self-obsessed of me, but I just walk around assuming everyone in the world knows. That I was the stupid, trusting wife. The dupe, you know."

"I didn't know," Brynn said simply. "And that's not what I think."

"What do you think?" The answer seemed to matter to her.

"Well, that he was blind, obviously," her mouth said before her brain could filter it. She decided to brazen it out, looking Savannah clear in the eye and just hoping she wasn't blushing at her slip. "Blind and undeserving of you. And that you must have loved him well to decide to trust him. He was lucky and he abused that."

Savannah gathered Tucker up in her lap and kissed his head. When she looked up, it was obvious she'd been trying to hide tears in her eyes.

"Thank you," she said softly. "God, does Noah have a brother or something?" Brynn could see she was aiming for a joke.

"Only child," Brynn shrugged. "Can't you tell? The man is far too calm and secure to have grown up competing with siblings."

"You're lucky," Savannah said, still snuggling her adorable son, who had tilted his head up to look at her, his small chubby fingers reaching for her ponytail. Brynn watched them together. She thought of her life as Savannah understood it, and then of the reality of it.

"Yeah," she said wistfully. "Totally."

Chapter Six

Savannah felt different as she entered the band room today. She couldn't put her finger on the exact feeling, she just knew her body felt lighter. Her shoulders weren't hunched and her jaw wasn't clenched. Something had lifted.

Perhaps it was her song. *Her* song. Not only her first since the big split, but her first *ever* that was truly her own. Both she and Cole had only dabbled in writing their own songs when they met. Everything that Twice Struck released, they'd co-written. There was a secret terrified part of her that had wondered if it was *only* in combination with Cole that she was a song-writer at all.

And then, last night, it had all just poured from her, the rage, the grief, the shame, all into one explosion of a song. She'd taken Noah aback, she could tell - hell, she'd taken herself aback - but she knew it was a good song, maybe even a great one.

She weirdly had Brynn to thank for it. That phrase, *beware the fury of a patient man,* dropped into her ear in that wry Californian accent at just that exact moment, when Savannah was both frustrated and finally breathing in. It had knocked the wind out of her with its accuracy. Because she was so *sick* with having to be patient: patient with Cole and his struggles and lies; patient at being pregnant while never quite sure if her spouse had her back; patient at new motherhood while the father of her child betrayed them; patient at being a solo parent while her once blooming career withered and died; patient at being the holder of everyone else's livelihoods and dreams while her own were crushed. And having swallowed so much rage just to keep ongoing. Savannah had tried to bury her fury, day after day. The release was sheer bliss.

She couldn't wait to record the song, couldn't wait to blaze through it live on stage. She wanted to release it onto the airwaves, like a howl. *See? Do you see who I am? What I'm capable of? I'm not who you thought I was.* She wasn't sure if the message was for Cole, or the paparazzi journalists, or the music critics or herself, but she was practically quivering with excitement now that she'd finally done it, to see what else she could do.

The lightness in her body was perhaps also slightly due to her unusually social morning. Bumping into a visitor during her run in the woods would normally be a mood ruiner for her; her zealously guarded alone time severed by the need for polite small talk. But Brynn didn't seem to want or need that from her, and instead their conversation flowed in an honest, somewhat spiky manner that Savannah genuinely enjoyed. She could have done without the drug references, but as it turned out Brynn had no idea she was probing a sore spot. To her own bemusement, she cared about Brynn's opinion of her, enough to correct her assumptions about her

70

apparent rock'n'roll lifestyle and to let her in past her usual guardrails.

Tucker had taken to her right away, which was hardly surprising. The sight of the lanky, cool, Californian hipster sitting cross-legged on the playroom floor, patiently re-reading her son his favorite story had cracked her heart slightly. His father hadn't stuck around to read his son stories. Her bandmates made up the bulk of her closest friends and they all liked Tucker well enough, but none - not even Coral for all she and Savannah loved each other - were really into kids enough to interact with him beyond a superficial level. Her family were... well, enough said on that subject. Rosalie - her oldest friend back in Nashville - adored him, but she was the closest thing Tucker had to real family. And as for Megan...Savannah wasn't sure the au pair was working out. She was diligent, cautious, qualified, and kind enough, but the warmth was definitely lacking.

Brynn, however, had lit up at the sight of Tucker. For a moment, Savannah felt slightly teary: almost no one but her looked at Tucker like he was more than a job or a cute inconvenience. She had no one to rave to about her son the way she wanted to rave; there was no one else who truly saw the magic and beauty of his miraculous existence. When she grieved the loss of her marriage, that's what hit her the hardest. She'd never once imagined loving her own child could be such a lonely experience.

It had blown her mind too, when Brynn had turned out to know nothing about her humiliating divorce. The tabloids had been so relentless, the magazine covers so salacious that Savannah went into every new interaction with a hint of defiant shame. She'd assumed since Brynn's husband was there to help pick up the professional pieces of her personal implosion that the other woman had known all the miserable, embarrassing facts of her life.

Brynn's generous and forthright assessment of the situation had moved her. God knows why Savannah cared so much, but the frank admiration and validation from this cool, gorgeous woman had felt like a balm. She'd replayed the moment over and over in her mind - *blind, obviously* - until she was convinced Brynn's tone had been almost flirtatious. It was a while since Savannah had been flirted with - albeit innocently - and the self-esteem boost was embarrassingly welcome.

"Sounding good."

Savannah looked up from where she'd been idly picking at her guitar to see Noah had arrived. He was smiling at her and she found herself smiling back, faintly flushing as she remembered it was his wife whose imaginary flirtatiousness was giving her a slight charge.

"Hey," she greeted him. "I'm just messing around."

"Sounds like the missing piece, don't you think?" He looked bright, picking up his own guitar, strumming back to her the notes she'd been playing. "I think it's our chorus," he demonstrated, as he seamlessly moved into the verse they'd been working on yesterday. This time, as the verse ended, they both strummed the new chords, grinning at each other. It worked. Savannah's mind flashed almost involuntarily, to the sight of Tucker nestled in Brynn's lap, Brynn tucking her dark hair behind her ear as she read to him. Savannah began to hum, and the lyrics started to follow.

———

Their afternoon session had gone well and Savannah hadn't wanted to push it, so after awkwardly meeting Noah's happy high-five at the door, they'd both walked away early and feeling good. The new song was melancholy with a sense of warmth and it left Savannah feeling an ache in her chest, but in a good way.

Noah was the right person to write with; she congratulated herself on her foresight. He was sensitive without being thin-skinned and persistent without being pushy. His hooks were neat and surprising and his lyrics taut. This was going to work! The excitement fizzed in her blood.

She headed upstairs to find that the playroom was empty. Megan must have taken Tucker out on a walk. She felt overwhelmed by a sense of wanting to see her child. She knew childcare was a necessity in her life if she was going to work, but entrusting her baby to a stranger was still hard for her on a daily basis. She dialed the au pair but the phone rang out. Megan was probably just busy with the child, she reminded herself not to stress. She headed outdoors to see if she could find them.

She heard Tucker before she saw him, his screams bordering on hysterical. Fear leapt in her chest and she raced towards the sound. She rounded the corner of the boat house expecting to see blood, but instead she found Tucker strapped into his stroller screaming and Megan pushing him grimly down the path.

"What happened?" she cried, kneeling down to undo the straps.

"Nothing," said Megan, her face a little flushed. She sounded defensive. "He's just out of sorts. He didn't want to be in the stroller, that's all."

Savannah pulled her weeping son out of the stroller and into her arms, where his crying escalated and she cradled him.

"Mama's here," she soothed him. "I've got you." Slowly his hysteria ceased, but her normally bright child stayed cradled close to her, his hot face pressed into her shoulder. "Why didn't you call me?" she asked Megan, her voice tense. The young woman shuffled her feet.

"There was nothing wrong!" she protested. "He's just grizzly. I didn't want to disturb you."

Savannah drew in a breath. "Please call me if he gets upset like this," she said, her tone clipped. "And better yet, if he gets this upset, I'd like you to try to understand why, instead of pushing on with something he clearly doesn't want to do."

"Okay," Megan agreed easily enough, but Savannah wondered if she was just being placated. She let the nanny go for the day and silently battled with herself while she sat on the cold, damp grass cuddling her son. Was Tucker being cared for properly? Was this just how it felt when someone you didn't love cared for someone you did? A constant re-explaining of boundaries? It wasn't like Megan was unkind to Tucker, but still, she wondered.

"Oh, my love." She kissed her son's upturned face, drying his tears. "Mama missed you. Shall we go for a walk together? Maybe go see the ducks?"

"Yeah, ducks," he said softly. She gently talked him back into the stroller and buckled him in, singing songs and making him smile. He was such a little trooper; it broke her heart.

"Wait," she said. "I have another idea."

A few minutes later, she had Tucker propped up on her hip as she knocked at one of the doors at the other end of her house.

"Why are you knocking, dickhead?" called Brynn's voice from somewhere within. "Just come in!"

Savannah entered the suite, standing awkwardly inside the living space, suddenly feeling like she hadn't quite thought this through. Brynn was nowhere to be seen.

"Um, hey," she called back softly.

There was a loud crash, then a thump from the bedroom, and suddenly Brynn appeared. She was wearing a pair of small pajama shorts and a thin baby blue tank top, the outline of her body clearly evident. Her shoulders, arms and legs were all bare, sun-kissed muscles. Her hair was tousled and her expression was something of a deer in headlights. Savannah was pretty sure hers was too.

"Oh god, I'm sorry, I thought you were Noah," Brynn clapped her hand to her forehead. "Sorry about all the..." she trailed off, sentence unfinished. "Oh, hello there young sir!" She drifted closer, offering Tucker a big smile. Tucker leaned into his mother but smiled back bashfully.

"I'm sorry we disturbed you," Savannah said tentatively. "We were wondering if you would like to come for a walk with us."

"Yes!" Brynn fist pumped dramatically for Tucker's benefit, who giggled. "Let me just get dressed."

———

Back out in the air, the three of them headed for the path along the lake. It dipped up and down, high on the bluff and low along the beachfront. The air was chilly and smelled of fresh, clear water and damp leaves. Brynn shivered in her leather jacket.

"You know you're going to have to start dressing for Vermont," Savannah told her.

"I didn't pack well," Brynn admitted.

"Burlington has great winter shopping. You don't have to be this freezing all the time." She herself was wearing a dense wool coat that protected her against the breeze, but within weeks she was going to need to upgrade to one of her real winter jackets. Brynn sighed.

"I know, I know," she said huffily. "I hate shopping, to be honest."

"What *do* you like?" Savannah asked curiously. She knew she liked Brynn, but she knew so little about her.

"Oh." Brynn paused, like the question was too private to possibly contemplate sharing. "The ocean," she said after a moment. "Sushi. Star-gazing - like, the nerdy kind, not the romantic. Other people's dogs. Road trips. Music."

Savannah had a lot of questions. She started on familiar ground. "What music?" she pounced.

Brynn raised her eyebrows.

"Is this a coolness test?" she asked cautiously.

Savannah shook her head with a smile. Brynn rattled off a bunch of artists, mostly hip indie bands, like Savannah had expected she would, along with some old school soul and some mainstream pop.

"Notable genre exception," she responded, though she was unsurprised.

"I'm definitely not an opera fan," Brynn replied. "Or a big classical buff. Unlike Mr Brahms over here." She reached in to boop Tucker's nose. Tucker chortled at her, but Savannah wasn't going to be fobbed off that easily.

"And country music?" she asked. Brynn looked awkward.

"I kind of was hoping you wouldn't ask," she confessed, screwing her nose up and looking out over the lake. "Not really my jam."

"That's fine," Savannah told her. "But I want to know why."

"I don't know... like, I'm sure there's a lot I'm missing," she hedged. "Just you know... everything I've heard is very twangy guitars and *my old dog died,*" she did a quick ho-down motion with her arms.

"I knew it! *Ugh,* I've met your kind before." Savannah had been expecting something like this, but the obnoxious dance move really pushed her over the edge.

"I'm not trying to offend you... wait, what kind?"

"I mean, you're a snob, obviously, but ignorant is what I meant."

"Oh wow, you're not pulling any punches on this one." Brynn didn't seem offended, more intrigued. "*Do* go on," she invited.

Savannah gestured to her to take over pushing the stroller as she pulled back her hair that kept blowing into her eyes and started twisting it into a knot.

"It's typical Northern bias against the South," she began. "Saying you hate country music is a socially acceptable proxy for thinking we're all a bunch of hicks."

"Woah, wait-"

"No, it's true. You haven't even investigated country music. You give these tired old cliches and I bet you can't even name more than three songs, not even by Dolly."

"Oh please, of course I can. *9-5, Jolene...* um, *I will always love you,* and... um..." She held up her hands to ward off Savannah's scoff. "What was that disco one?"

"Amazing," she said sarcastically. "Did you know she has over fifty albums? Country, Americana, Bluegrass, she's literally the biggest, most accessible star in the world - the woman has a goddamn theme park, for crying out loud - and you've not even bothered to take her seriously enough to deliberately listen to anything that you haven't accidentally heard at the grocery store."

"I- I mean, Dolly is cool, no one is disputing that."

"Did you ever hear the album Loretta Lynn recorded with Jack White? She was in her seventies and she still blazed rings around your indie icon."

"Really?"

"You should take a listen, just for an absolute start," Savannah said pointedly. "Country music is *old*. It comes from ancient European traditions. It's African. It was the music of enslaved people, of struggle, of protest. It's storytelling. It has a lot more to say than *my old dog died*." Savannah grabbed the stroller back, since her son was being pushed by a philistine.

Brynn looked actually chastened.

"Okay," she said, wrapping her jacket around her tall frame. "I admit, I haven't really given it a shot." Savannah snorted. "Where should I start? If I wanted to educate myself?"

"Is that not just asking me to do the work for you?" Savannah asked spikily. "You managed to find your way into other genres just fine."

"Fair enough." She spread out her hands in surrender. "Just figured since I was in the presence of an expert, I'd be stupid not to ask."

"What do you reckon, Tucker?" Savannah peered around the stroller, letting her son's sweet face take the edge off her head of steam. "Pizza and a listening party?"

"Yeah!" he piped up, kicking his legs.

"I could clear my busy schedule for that." Brynn smiled.

———

That night, Savannah kissed her baby's sleeping head where he lay peacefully for once in his new big-kid bed and tiptoed out of his room. From her own room she wandered out on the balcony, wrapping herself in a blanket for warmth. She leaned on the railing and stared out at the dark night. She could sense, rather than see the woods and the still lake.

Tonight, she would probably get some sleep. Tucker was exhausted and his little heart was full from the blaze of attention that had been his mama and Brynn combined. He'd been whirled around the living room on Brynn's hip as she danced with him, then cuddled cheek-to-cheek with his mama as they swayed to softer songs, ate pizza on one woman's lap and then the other, forgoing his highchair for being part of the action.

Savannah had to admit that her heart felt pretty full too.

"Listen to this," she'd said, over and over, playing Brynn a selection of her most favorite country artists and, to her credit, Brynn had kept an open mind, asking thoughtful questions and nodding along at times.

"Wait, who is *this?*" Brynn asked about Amanda Shires, about Adeem the Artist, about Ashley McBryde and that was just the *A* section. Savannah started to get an inkling of exactly what kind of country music was going to steal its way into the Californian's soul. She liked being there to see it happen.

"Now you're getting it," Savannah said, as Brynn picked up the record arm and dropped it back for another listen to *Parking Lot Pirouette.*

Brynn gave her a crooked smile and touched her lightly on the hip as she passed her on her way over to attend to Tucker's shriek for her attention. Savannah felt that touch all the way through her body. She wasn't quite sure what was happening, just that the combination of the song, that smile, the casual intimacy of the touch, her child's happiness, all made her feel full right up to the brim in a way she hadn't in a long time.

She wrapped the blanket more tightly around her shoulders as the coldness started to seep into her body. She heard an owl screech in the woods and the trees rustle in the breeze. Somehow, this time, she didn't long to be out in the wild. She turned and walked back inside, ready for once to go to her bed alone.

Chapter Seven

"Hey, where've you been? It's getting late; I was just about to send out a search party." Noah looked up from where he was sprawled on the couch in their living room. Brynn came in the door, tossed her jacket aside and flung herself on the other couch, kicking out her legs and stretching her back. Two-year-olds were *heavy*.

"I was hanging out with Savannah," she said, almost surprised herself as she announced it. "And Tucker. Man, is he a sweetpea." She propped her arm behind her head.

"Oh, wow, you met her kid? Wait, you're hanging out? How? What did you get up to?" He held up his hands and laughed. "Woah, sorry. Just she's a bit of a mystery to me."

"We... listened to country music actually." Brynn sat up, a silly grin on her face. "Did you know some of it is actually kind of great?" She dodged as he threw a cushion at her face.

"I told you, dude." Noah shook his head at her. "But it tracks that you wouldn't take my word for it until a smoking hot woman sits you down and makes you pay attention."

"*Smoking* hot, huh? Noah... you got a little crush there?" For some reason, that idea made her stomach kind of tight.

"No, just objectively, she's hot and you- *wait*. Do *you* have a crush on her?"

"What? *No*," she scoffed, possibly too fast. "And even if I did, she's straight - presumably - and basically your boss, so it would be a teeny, tiny, completely innocent crush, *if* I did, you don't even need to worry."

"I mean, I wouldn't exactly describe her as my boss, but she does think you're my *wife*, Brynn, so you hitting on her would be really, really bad." He gave her a firm stare.

"Got it, got it, one-hundred percent absolutely not hitting on her," she agreed. "Just admiring innocently, and now a little bit of a country music fan." She held her hands up with a grin and he groaned.

Was it a crush? She had eyes so she couldn't help but notice the curves of Savannah's knockout body, the hidden sparkle of her eyes, the sheer biteableness of her lower lip. Uh-oh, okay, apparently she'd noticed a lot. But you could admire someone's beauty without it being a crush, exactly. There was, however, a noticeable buzz running through her after her evening with Savannah, a happy, tingling energy that possibly was a worrying sign.

It had just been a really nice evening, that was all. After Savannah's annoyed lakeside lecture (*hot,* Brynn's brain helpfully supplied) she had invited her back to her wing of the house, requested Luis whip up a couple of big pizzas for them (wood fired, thin crust, authentic) poured herself a glass of red wine (just sparkling water for Brynn, thanks) and sat on her living room floor, pulling out record after record.

She'd lost any of her usual reserve, her voice getting high as she made passionate points, her hands flying as she spoke. Her eyes shone whenever Brynn enjoyed a track until Brynn herself could no longer separate her own aural enjoyment from that of getting to make Savannah look so victorious and happy.

Tucker had clambered all over Brynn, tugging her in all directions, his big eyes bright and his excitement clear. It had felt nice to be so wanted and accepted, the little boy grabbing her hand, jumping into her arms, patting her face and laughing hysterically at her extreme witticisms, such as making his nose beep or tickling his toes. He was just ridiculously sweet and funny.

The combination of good food, increasingly good music and being the focus of attention for both a beautiful woman and an adorable child; it was enough to make anyone feel slightly intoxicated.

Was it a crush if you fell asleep that night with a smile on your lips, replaying a song in your head? Brynn could only hope not.

———

The next morning, after breakfast, Brynn set herself up at the living room table with a third cup of coffee to stare at her textbook again. She was surprised and yet reassured to realize she still remembered her respiratory and metabolic acidosis and alkalosis ranges, which her brain had somehow decided that she, as a layperson, obviously needed to maintain, along with memes from eight years ago and lines from *The Simpsons*. Even as she was pleased with herself, she was frustrated for being pleased in the first place. If she'd stayed on track, that knowledge would be like being happy she remembered how to tie her own shoes and she would have wildly expanded her expertise since then. God, she really was a loser.

Could she really go back? Where would she need to start? How many other thirty-somethings would there be amongst the other med students? Surely, now she had a stack of life experience behind her, she could handle the pressure. Or would it be worse, because she'd already failed once before?

Her family would be happy to hear she was back on track. Brynn figured it would be at least fifteen years of hard slog before she was back at a level her parents would deem acceptable to add her back into the bragging rights they had about their other children. Brynn wondered if she'd fallen out of their annual Christmas letter alto-gether. *Anna has been promoted to associate professor of pediatric medicine, Stephen topped his class for his physician exams and...that's it, all our children accounted for! Petra, our golden retriever, has had a stellar year...*

She slumped in her chair and let her head fall onto the pages of the textbook in front of her. Who was she kidding? This was an exercise in futility. Did she even want to be a doctor, or just to make her parents proud? The thought of being back on the wards still turned her stomach to stone, but she knew it was about more than that. She just wanted to know she had a place in the world, that her life had purpose.

The first few years in LA she'd worked a mishmash of jobs, mostly on film sets in catering and low-level assistant work. She had no real interest in show business though, and the egos and competition she saw there not only bored her, but when compared with the career she'd left behind, it crushed her soul.

For a while, lifeguarding had filled a hole, preventing drownings, resuscitating a few near misses. She'd loved the feeling of plunging into the water and knowing her body was strong, keeping families together and loved ones safe. There was no reason she couldn't go back to that, if she could just find a place close enough to the beach, but the truth was, she'd conquered it. After years of playing it safe, she wanted a challenge again. She had no idea what that challenge was, though.

She pushed back her chair and decided to get out in the fresh air. She still wasn't keen on the woods but she'd enjoyed the lake walk with Savannah and Tucker yesterday. Adding an extra couple of layers of clothing under her increasingly useless jacket, she headed out into the cold.

It must have been the company that had made yesterday's walk so pleasurable though, because today it just felt miserable. The day was gloomy; both the lake and sky were the color of dull steel. What had been a chilly breeze yesterday felt bordering on a gale today; her hair kept being whipped from her ponytail and into her eyes, which were streaming from the chill. Finally, a steady cold rain began to fall, and cursing, she jogged her way back toward the house.

She arrived on the back doorstep just at the same time as Savannah, who was back in her distracting running gear and looking far too bright compared with Brynn's black mood. The sight of the singer was a welcome serotonin hit though: with her skin gleaming with rain and her smile blazing despite still catching her breath, she was the definition of a sight for sore eyes.

"Hey," Savannah gasped, bending down to remove her running shoes. "What are you doing out here? It's hardly the weather for a walk."

"I mean, I know that now." Brynn screwed up her nose as she shrugged out of her wet jacket. "But surely it's not running weather either," she pointed out, tugging off her boots.

"Doesn't matter," shrugged Savannah. "Rain or shine. Keeps me sane."

And fit, Brynn's brain chimed in, trying to keep her eyes away from where they badly wanted to gaze. "Hey," she remembered, as she followed the other woman into the house. "I've got a bone to pick with you."

"You do?" Savannah cast her a low-lashed glance over her shoulder, which honestly, in any other context, Brynn would have interpreted as flirtatious. She blinked and pulled her brain back under control. They entered the main living room where the log fire was burning. Normally she'd be thrilled, but after her own unscheduled jog, it felt stifling. She pulled off all her layers until she was left with just her t-shirt, which she plucked away from her body, fanning herself with it. She felt Savannah's eyes on her.

"Yeah," she continued, shaking raindrops out of her hair. "Yesterday you gave me a thorough run-through on country music, but you left someone out."

"Who?" Savannah blurted, clearly shocked to imagine Brynn knew an artist she didn't.

"You," Brynn pointed out. "I don't know much, but I do know you're a big deal. So what gives? Too modest?"

Savannah was already pink-cheeked from the exertion and the warm room. She had no further layers to take off, at least not without Brynn needing to flee like her head was on fire. Still, she flushed a little deeper at Brynn's question. She looked slightly disturbed rather than pleased, and Brynn found herself wishing she could shove the words back in her mouth.

"I... feel weird about my music," Savannah said. "It's from another life, you know?" Brynn nodded, waiting. "Do you really not know any of it? I mean- I'm not...it just felt like it was everywhere for a minute there."

"Yeah, I do know that one song," she admitted. "*Your Heart?*"

"Ugh, I hate that fucking song." Savannah rolled her eyes. Brynn laughed out loud.

"Wait, what? Didn't you write it?"

"Co-wrote it, sung it, recorded it, released it, played it about a thousand times live," Savannah agreed. "Still hate it. Always hated it. It was about Cole, his addiction, our fucked up marriage. Most of the lyrics are him begging for another shot. Then it was our biggest hit, and I had to sing it night after night, forever. Always made me feel a bit sick."

"Oh," said Brynn. A weird wave of shame washed over her as she heard that Savannah's husband had been an addict, as if she were

90

guilty by association somehow. "Do you...want me to not listen to your music?" she asked. "I won't if you don't want me to."

Savannah looked at her for a long moment. There was something in her eyes that Brynn couldn't read.

"I mean. You can? It's out there forever. I don't know why it makes me feel weird thinking about you listening to it," she said softly. "Maybe because you're the one person I've met in a while who doesn't know me as the other half of that whole... thing."

"Then I won't," Brynn said decisively. "Not if it makes you feel uncomfortable. Mostly, I just wanted to hear you sing," she confessed. Savannah tucked her hair behind her ear. For someone who had fame, money, power and prestige, she looked very small all of a sudden.

"Noah and I are going to lay down a couple of demos this afternoon," her voice was halting. "You could come listen, if you want to. If you don't have other plans."

Brynn stared at her. "Really? I mean...yes! I would love that. If you don't mind." God, they were both acting excruciatingly vulnerable today. She could see why Savannah might feel exposed by inviting her to listen in to new music, but for some reason Brynn felt like she was risking something too.

"I don't mind." A small smile crossed Savannah's lips. "It would be nice to have another opinion. Now that I trust your taste in music a little more."

———

A couple of hours later, Brynn sunk into a comfy couch in the band room. She hadn't been down there before, but she liked the feel of it. It was dim, almost windowless, cozy with low golden lighting and instruments everywhere. She'd asked Noah where they'd be recording and he revealed that the space was wired as a recording studio, with a sealed sound booth and mixing deck off to one side.

When they were ready to record the real deal, they'd have a whole team involved: the band, sound guys, Chester, maybe they'd even head back to Nashville, he wasn't sure. Today they were just laying down early demos they could send to the band for their input, and recording basically involved Noah running from one room to the other to flick mysterious switches.

Brynn tried to make herself invisible. She didn't want to disrupt the process and was acutely aware of how lucky she was to be in the room at all. She had always loved watching Noah do his thing; every time he pulled a guitar over his head, her best friend looked transformed. He was supremely confident whether he was on a big stage or messing about with a riff. Savannah, on the other hand, seemed nervous. She fussed with the setup and spent an age making sure their instruments were tuned. Brynn wondered what it must feel like to be trying to prove yourself on such a high level. She could empathize.

Suddenly though, the fussing and discussions ceased and they both took their place at a microphone. Noah had a bass guitar and sat, while Savannah plugged her electric guitar into an amp and stood. They nodded at each other and Noah counted them in. Any nerves Savannah had seemed to disappear as she began to strum. Her long hair was loose and she looked damn good with a guitar.

Brynn was about ten feet away. She wished it was further because she wasn't quite sure what to do with her face. Neither musician was looking in her direction, but she knew she was in their peripheral vision. Then Savannah opened her mouth and began to sing, and Brynn forgot everything else.

Her voice was unbelievably... well, sexy, was the first word that came to mind. It was sweet but powerful, with the occasional throaty edge. The sound seemed too big for her small body. The song started out slow, then it climbed. The structure wasn't verse-chorus-verse but one haunting ascent. The guitar picked up pace, with the bass thrumming below it and Savannah's words became frenetic, her raging voice breaking at the top. Brynn realized her own knees were quivering slightly at the power of the onslaught of sound. The crescendo was furious, but somehow beneath it, it made you want to move. As the last notes faded into silence, she realized her mouth was hanging open.

Suddenly, both sets of eyes were on her.

"Well, what do you think?" asked Noah. He was grinning, clearly high on the adrenaline of the killer song. Savannah was breathing the same way she did after a run, her chest heaving, and her eyes still reflected the emotion she'd been channeling. Brynn didn't have the words. She instead made a show of slithering from the couch to the floor and laying there, flat on her back, her arms flung over her head. She heard laughter - Savannah's, with Noah's in the background - then the sound of a high five.

"Really?" Savannah's voice had drifted much closer and Brynn looked up to see her standing over her with her hands on her hips. She looked pleased, though. Brynn didn't move.

"Fuck," she breathed. "That was... *not* country music."

Savannah snorted and nudged her ribs with her boot. "Like you'd know."

Brynn sat up for her own physical safety, and reached out a hand, letting Savannah pull her up. She ended up standing slightly too close to the other woman and made herself step back. She looked down into Savannah's eyes. "I don't know what you sounded like before, but that was... you... are incredible," she said, her filter blown to shreds.

Savannah gazed up at her. "Thank you," she murmured. "I owe you for that song." Brynn shook her head, glad Noah had ducked back into the sound booth.

"Nope. That was all you."

Savannah still hadn't stepped away. She started to open her mouth to say something else, when the door opened and Noah returned. The moment broke as Savannah turned away and headed back to the mic, picking up an acoustic guitar this time.

The next song was more traditionally structured, but Brynn wasn't sure she could describe the genre while it was stripped back the way it was. Noah sang backup on the chorus, adding to the richness of Savannah's voice, and Brynn suddenly realized she had a lump in her throat. The lyrics were of loneliness, but the chorus offered the chance of warmth. *You make me wonder,* they sang, *if I could have a home again one day.*

Again, both sets of eyes were on her as the song ended.

"I love it," she said softly. "I love it a lot."

"Yes!" Noah pumped his fist. "It's a good one!" He hustled off to the sound booth again. Savannah stayed where she was.

"You really like it?" she asked. "I'm glad," she responded to Brynn's slow, emphatic nod. "Me too."

———

That evening they all ate dinner together, after Savannah had returned from settling Tucker for the night. Chester had reappeared, apparently after heading back to Nashville to smooth over a few things with the record label. He chatted about it blithely - that the executives weren't thrilled with the amount of time the solo album was taking, their objection to the fact that Savannah was straying from her tried-and-true country roots - and Savannah looked more and more miserable the more he spoke.

"Hey, Chester," Brynn broke in. "Where in Burlington would you recommend for buying winter gear? I'm pretty sure it's not about to get any warmer up here."

"Oh! Well, there are a few good options," Chester started brightly. "Are you looking for fashion or for more of an outdoorsy look?"

Brynn felt Savannah's eyes on her as she gamely led poor Chester to believe she would take his extremely comprehensive and informed shopping advice. Soon enough they moved on to Burlington's other attractions, then the weather generally, including whether or not they'd be here to see some snow. The singer caught her eye and smiled at her, grateful.

After eating, they all ended up having drinks around the fireplace. Chester sat on one of the big cushy armchairs, while Noah and Brynn shared a couch and Savannah lounged back on another, looking almost relaxed. She rested back into the cushions, her legs kicked up in front of her, her sweater clinging to her body, while the wine glass almost dangled from her elegant fingers. Her lip quirked as if she was enjoying a private joke, though her lashes were low and she gazed into the middle distance, zoning out from the conversation in the room. Brynn would have paid good money to know what was going on in her mind.

"Hm?" Brynn asked, distantly realizing that Noah had said her name a couple of times. He gave her a concerned look, and she realized she'd been drowsily gazing at Savannah's reclined form until the rest of the world had slipped away. It was officially time to call it: Brynn had a serious crush.

Of course Savannah was beautiful; she was a goddamned megastar. On top of that, she was intensely charming, with those fathomless eyes and blinding smile that made you feel like you were the only thing that had ever mattered. Spending time hanging out with her and Tucker had only shown Brynn more sides of Savannah, leaving her incredibly aware of how compelling she was; god, all of it had felt intoxicating. But watching Savannah sing had turned out to have been a truly *terrible* idea. Brynn couldn't shake the image of her body behind a guitar, the tilt of her throat, the blaze in her eyes, the ease of her beautiful voice. It was one-hundred percent a crush and it was exponentially worse than it had been the day before.

Clearly, there was no way in hell she could indulge this particular crush. The whole facade of their fake marriage and Noah's huge career opportunity hinged on Brynn leaving this the hell alone. It pained her to realize, but considering how many weeks or even months they might have left, she knew it was definitely time to put some solid distance between herself and Savannah.

Chapter Eight

That week, the weather turned bleak for good. The beautiful bright fall days gave way to dark metallic skies and relentless rain. The wind blew in mournful howls around the house and the cold outside was merciless. Two days in a row Savannah had tried to go for her morning run only to be beaten back by lashing rain and ice, with wind gusts strong enough to stop her in her tracks. She felt restless and caged. There was a small gym on the second floor with a view of the storm and she ran hard on the treadmill, wishing for fresh air and escape, but it just wasn't the same.

She was frustrated, and not just with the weather. After such a promising start, she and Noah had hit a brick wall with a resounding thud. A full week had gone by and they had nothing to show for it. They tossed around ideas, played each other scraps of melodies, tried to write lyrics, but nothing was working.

The band room was starting to feel oppressive, the dim warm space no longer a haven but a trap. They tried writing in the living room in front of the fire, but they both felt self-conscious whenever anyone else was around. Seeing Chester made her feel anxious; the staff apologized and scuttled through as though caught trespassing and Brynn disappeared immediately if she so much as poked her head in and saw them there. There were numerous other spaces they could - and did - try, but they both were coming to the realization it wasn't going to be magically solved by finding the right room to work in.

Something just wasn't clicking. By the end of the week Savannah called time.

"Let's just give it a break for a few days." She worked hard to keep her tone light. "It's been a long week and maybe we just need to have some time away from it and come back."

Noah nodded. He looked worried. "Yeah, totally," he said, scratching his chin. "We'll just chill for a little while and come back fresh."

Savannah did not want to chill. She wanted the same wild, sharp inspiration to hit her as it had with *Beware the Fury*. She wanted a return of the deep sad sweetness of *Make Me Wonder*. She wanted the full and satisfying feeling of music suddenly pouring through her. She wanted to *work,* damnit. And if she couldn't have that, she at the very least wanted to go for a freaking run. Being both cooped up and creatively blocked made her want to climb out of her damn skin.

"Motherfucker!" she cried, her annoyance spilling over as her shoelace came untied and she nearly tripped on the treadmill. She slammed her hand onto the emergency stop button and slid off the back of the machine, breathing hard.

"Woah! Sorry," Brynn stood awkwardly, half in and half out of the room. She was wearing very short black running shorts and a loose red t-shirt, cropped so that when she raised her arm to scratch the back of her neck a sliver of tanned abdomen came into view. She was clearly here for a workout. "I'll come back later."

"No, Brynn, it's fine-" Savannah called to the other woman, but she'd already turned and left.

"All good!" Brynn's voice came down the corridor as she kept walking. Savannah sighed. For the last week she'd seen almost nothing of Noah's wife. Despite the weather trapping them all indoors, their paths never seemed to cross. Only twice she'd seen her at dinner where she'd been polite but guarded, as if they'd never laughed together or passed a giggling child between them, the teasing spark in her eyes fully extinguished. Savannah knew it was stupid to mourn something that had barely existed, but she found that she did.

She wasn't sure what had happened. Maybe Noah was pissed at her over the terrible writing week, so his wife was too? That seemed unlike what she knew of either of them, but then, what did she know? Maybe her writer's block was making her completely miserable to be around, to the point everyone was dying to avoid her and Brynn was simply the only one with the luxury to do so. Or just maybe, Savannah's life was too weird for her to relate to anyone anymore and she was just terrible at making friends. It felt like a tiny spark that had only just been lit was being extinguished. Her shoulders slumped.

She flicked off the lights in the gym and headed back up to her wing to shower. Afterwards, she called Coral.

"I miss you," she told her friend after she'd finished explaining her terrible week. "Any chance you want to change your plans and come back to hang out with a washed-up has-been?"

"Oh honey," Coral huffed. "I heard your new tracks. You're killing it. Any artist would commit murder for even one song as good as that. You're allowed a down week for crying out loud."

"So that's a no, then?" Savannah gazed out through the rain-lashed window to the gray lake. The water was so churned up by the wind that it looked like the sea.

"I would love to. The minute we get through the next sixteen dates we're booked, I'll be there. Nothing will hold me back," she promised. "Even though, for reasons that escape me, you're holed up in literally the whitest corner in the entire of America. *That* is how much I love you honey, that I will come and hang out with you in fucking *Vermont*."

Coral was touring with one of her side projects. The biggest problem with Coral was that she was a powerhouse; she never ran out of energy for hitting the road and performing her ass off. She was a killer drummer and her smoky vocals had her always in demand. Savannah just hoped she could win her back when - if - this writing hiatus ever ended.

"Where are you tonight?" she asked.

"Richmond," Coral sighed.

"Virginia? Text me when you get to your hotel room tonight?"

"Yes, mom." Savannah could pretty much hear her eyeroll, but she knew there'd be a text later. When your best friend was a Black trans woman touring the Bible Belt, worry and safety check-ins became second nature.

"Mama! *Mama!*" Tucker's pleading went from plaintive to shrill, and Coral quickly said her goodbyes, never one for indulging in kid time.

"What's the matter, peanut?" Savannah scooped up her small boy and held him close. He wriggled, pushing against her chest until she let him go.

"Lellow Digger?" He passed her his book, yet again, his face earnest. With a sigh, she cuddled him back close and began to read his favorite - and her least favorite - book all over again. The recitation of the familiar words made her recall Brynn's enthusiastic reading and her son's excitement at another adult paying him much needed attention. The contrast between the sweetness of that moment and the extreme distance from Brynn this morning nagged at her. When Tucker went down for his nap, Savannah couldn't stop herself. She marched to the other end of the house and banged on Noah and Brynn's door.

Brynn answered. She was still in her workout clothes from earlier and didn't look like she'd broken a sweat yet. Her expression was wary.

"Hey," she greeted her. "Everything okay?"

"Have I done something to offend you?" Savannah blurted. Brynn frowned, concern flaring in her eyes. She let the door fall open further.

"No," she denied. "Nothing. Why do you ask?"

"I just-" Savannah tried to laugh, to break the tension. "I feel like you're avoiding me. And it's okay," she rushed on, "if you are. I mean, you don't have to hang out with me just because you're in my house, I get it... I just don't want to have upset you and not know it."

"Savannah..." Brynn's eyes were soft. For a moment, it felt like she was about to reach out and hug her, touch her, something. But the moment passed. "You haven't done anything wrong. I'm sorry if I've been distant. I just-" she paused, and Savannah very clearly understood she was looking for an excuse. "I'm trying to use this time away to focus on study. I've decided to go back to med school." She gestured behind her and there was, in fact, a giant textbook open on the dining table, a steaming coffee cup to the side.

"Med school?" She tried to imagine Brynn as a doctor. She was kind and caring and smart, but something about the picture seemed off.

"Yeah. I'd almost completed it... once. I'm going to go back and do it right, but first..." she grimaced for effect, "I need to figure out exactly how much I've forgotten."

Somewhere in all this, something was missing, Savannah could feel it. The studying was obviously real, but it wasn't the whole truth. Savannah stood, searching Brynn's eyes for a moment, but Brynn just smiled back, not budging from the doorway until she started to feel stupid. Whatever was going on, their budding friendship was clearly over.

"Okay," she said softly. "Well, that's great to hear. Good luck." She offered her own bright - fake - smile and turned to go.

"Savannah," Brynn called her back. Savannah turned, partway down the corridor. Brynn scratched the back of her neck again, the same awkward gesture, the same rise of the t-shirt. "I like you, a lot. I enjoyed hanging out with you and Tucker. You - you're both - wonderful. I just...I gotta focus, you know?"

"Yeah," Savannah said wryly. "Me too, I guess. Catch you around, Brynn." She walked away. It was fine. Something was going on, but it was fine. Maybe Brynn and Noah were having a rough patch. Maybe Brynn was somehow secretly some kind of highly temperamental person, easily taking offence and Savannah had- Whatever. It was all fine. She wouldn't give it any more thought.

She'd forgotten to cancel Megan for the afternoon, and the young woman was already in the suite waiting for Tucker to wake. Savannah wasn't in the mood to interact with the nanny, so she left. She picked over her lunch, her appetite minimal. The wind hurled shards of rain at the windows, but she couldn't stand to be inside any longer. She marched grimly along the lake path in her raincoat, water streaming down her face, soaking her hair and her jeans. When she couldn't feel her fingers anymore, she trudged back toward the house. She caught sight of Chester through the living room window, pacing around with his phone, and did a quick pivot, instead entering via the band room.

She pulled her wet clothes off and sat on the sofa in her t-shirt and underwear. She picked up her guitar, strumming out her mood and, to her surprise, the music began to flow.

———

"It's brilliant," Noah told her, two days later. "It's heartbreaking and melancholy... a real punch in the gut, but kind of twisty? I love it." She smiled at him from her seat in the band room, guitar on her lap.

"Not too dark?"

"Perfectly dark," he said seriously. "So far we've got rage, sweetness and pain... pretty sure there's nothing you can't do." She scoffed, pleased that he liked the new song. His smile faded, though. "I'm wondering though... if maybe I should just... go?"

"Huh?" She startled. "No! Why?"

"You're writing these killer tracks pretty much despite me instead of because of me. You see that, right? We try and try and then I leave you alone and you just suddenly explode with something."

"That's not true! *Make Me Wonder* we wrote together, and it's beautiful."

"I barely wrote on that at all; it's mostly you... your lyrics, your hooks. I was just the glue that pulled it all together. It's okay." He waved his hand as she started to object. "I'm not offended. I'm loving what you're coming up with and I feel like possibly the best thing I could do to help would be to just get out of the way." He was struggling not to look downcast, but he didn't sound bitter or bereft. It didn't seem to be about ego, and Savannah appreciated his honesty. She tried to find the right words to make him stay.

"We have three songs," she said, "and I need at least another nine. This is all part of the process. *You* are a part of the process. We haven't truly hit our stride yet, but I need you, Noah. I really need you. I knew it the first time I heard your album and I know it now. I can't do all this without you." She felt panicked. "Please don't leave now." She knew she sounded a little desperate, but then, she was.

106

"I mean, if you're sure," Noah said uncertainly. "I want to stay. I just want to help rather than hinder, you know?"

"You are," she swore. She wasn't ready to wear the responsibility alone, and she was sure they'd crack the code of writing together soon. "I actually have something else I started, and I wanted to work on it with you."

"Something else?" he said, his smile growing. "You're on a real roll here."

"Yeah," she smiled back. "It's a love song. For Tucker." She started to strum. He picked up his own guitar as he listened and together they started to work.

———

The next day, the rain and wind finally disappeared. The air was freezing and the clouds hung around, but the storm had finally dissipated. At Savannah's encouraging, Megan had wrapped Tucker in his coat and taken him out for a walk in his stroller, while she had finally gotten to go for a real run through the woods. Mud splashed all the way up her legs as she ran down the rain sodden track, but she felt exhilarated and thrilled to finally be free. After her shower, she found she still didn't want to be indoors, so she wandered out to find her son.

On her way around the lake path, she saw the stroller parked on the beach and spotted Tucker and Megan sitting side by side in the middle of the small jetty. Her son was pointing over at the water and chattering brightly. She smiled. Like his mama, Tucker was clearly the outdoorsy kind. She heard voices and turned to see Noah and Brynn walking in from the lake shore path toward her. Noah was rugged up in a big down jacket, but Brynn was still underdressed and looked frozen. She might have looked damn good in her leather jacket, but Savannah had no idea why the woman wouldn't just cave in already and buy a real winter coat.

Her first instinct in seeing the couple was happiness - two people she really liked, in one place - before she remembered the weird distance from Brynn. She straightened her spine, wondering if the coolness would stay in place with Noah there as the glue between them. Maybe it wouldn't? As they got closer, Brynn smiled at her warmly enough, but then her gaze slid past her quickly, a frown appearing.

"Hey!" she shouted. She started to run, shoving past Savannah and bolting for the lake. Savannah whirled around to see Tucker, just as his small body leaned too far out over the edge of the jetty and he slipped with barely a splash into the freezing water below. Her own scream stuck in her throat as she raced toward the lake.

Brynn, though, was miles ahead. Her jacket was already discarded on the lakeshore, her sneakers too, before she plunged into the frigid water. Savannah had splashed up to her knees in the icy lake when a pair of hands grabbed her by both arms and Noah held her back.

"It's okay, it's okay, Brynn's got him-" He resisted her struggling and wouldn't let her go. She stopped fighting him when she saw he was right. About fifteen feet away, Brynn was upright again, Tucker's head on her shoulder and pushing back through the deep water toward them. Time seemed to jump sideways all of a sudden and then her coughing, spluttering, frozen wet child was in her arms and she was crying hysterically and kissing his face, clutching at him, stumbling back to shore, while he cried, big, healthy, angry, frightened wails.

"You're all going to get hypothermia!" Noah's stressed voice was the first thing to break through - after seconds or minutes she wasn't sure - and Savannah's head snapped up to see Brynn, drenched right through and shivering violently on the lakeshore beside her.

"Boathouse," Savannah managed, pointing in the direction of the building that was significantly closer than the house. As they began to stumble up the path in their drenched clothes and boots, Savannah suddenly realized.

"Megan!" she cried, turning around to look.

"She was looking at her phone," Brynn said grimly. "She wasn't watching him."

"She freaked out," Noah told them, looking far more sympathetic than Savannah felt. "She ran off after she saw us all come out of the water."

The boathouse was unlocked but only slightly less cold than the outside world. The inside was dim and mostly filled with a small fishing boat and a collection of canoes, but they were out of the chilling breeze and there was one thing that would help.

"Towels." Savannah pointed and Noah opened the cupboard, bringing over a stack of big fluffy navy blue and white striped beach towels. She gave him her phone and asked him to call Chester while she stripped her son of his icy wet clothes and wrapped his small cold body in a dry towel. She unzipped her jacket and tucked him in against her chest, wrapping him up tight and cradling him close. His sobs began to calm as he warmed and she kissed the back of his neck over and over, her own tears starting again, feeling beyond sick as she imagined what she'd almost lost.

She looked over and saw Brynn struggling out of her sodden jeans, wrapping a towel around her waist and pulling off her wet sweater and t-shirt. Her body was lean, tanned and strong and Savannah was overwhelmed with desperate appreciation for her. Brynn looked up and caught her staring as she wrapped a towel around her shoulders, her wet hair in long tendrils over her back.

"Thank you." Savannah's voice cracked and she could barely see for tears. Brynn walked over and sat right next to her on the low wooden bench.

"Hey," she said, her voice light as she tucked a dark strand of wet hair behind her ear. "You doing okay there, little buddy?" Tucker lifted his head from his mother's shoulder to consider her.

"I saw fishes," he said softly.

"You sure did," Brynn smiled. "Can you do a big cough for me?" Tucker obliged, then sniffed and laid his head back down, pressing his face into Savannah's shoulder. "If you want we can get him checked out to be safe, but he's going to be just fine." Brynn found her eyes. "Okay, mama?

Savannah could only nod, her eyes overflowing again.

"Chester's on his way. He said with a golf cart?" Noah looked nonplussed. Savannah spluttered out a mildly unhinged laugh. Chester to the rescue at five miles per hour seemed surreal. "Little dude okay?" Noah asked, worry lines appearing on his perfect forehead.

"Thanks to Brynn," Savannah said, holding her baby tightly.

Noah sat down next to them and rubbed his wife's shoulders over the towel as she shivered.

"Pretty lucky having a lifeguard on the beach today," he said fondly.

"You were a lifeguard?" Savannah asked, recalling the total lack of hesitation as the other woman had plunged into the water.

"Malibu's finest," Brynn said wryly.

"When?" Savannah had so many questions.

"Up until about three weeks ago," Brynn laughed.

"Oh!" Savannah gazed at her. She could suddenly see it: those long, strong, tanned limbs, her firm shoulders and abs, the sprinkle of freckles across her pretty nose. Brynn would look right at home on a golden beach in a sporty bikini, ready to save lives. She realized she was blushing and had been staring way too long. "Bit warmer in Malibu?" she managed, like an idiot.

"Little bit." Brynn grinned back, wrapping her towel tighter. The sound of a golf cart pulling up was a welcome distraction.

Chester got them home in record time - as far as golf buggies went - and inside Lucille had the fire roaring and a whole tray of hot chocolates waiting. She fussed around with the air of a harried nurse and within minutes they were all installed near the fire, everything cold and wet removed, snuggled up in cozy blankets. Tucker was briefly whisked away and returned with a dry diaper and warm pajamas and his own small milky hot chocolate, which he slurped joyfully. He wriggled out of his mama's lap and did the rounds, grabbing Brynn's knees and grinning up at her bashfully, peering around at Noah, who picked up a cushion to play peekaboo. Apparently, it was the greatest day of her son's life.

At some point, Chester disappeared and then re-entered.

"That was Megan departing," he stated simply. "She said to tell you she's very, very sorry and that she won't be back."

Savannah glared into the fireplace.

"Probably for the best," she said shortly. She had a momentary vision of her hands around the young woman's throat and blinked it back. She couldn't imagine letting her son out of her sight ever again, and the realization that she would have to hire yet another nanny felt sickening. And then there was work. "That's me out for at least a week," she told Noah with a frown. In reality, it would probably be longer. She had an assistant who handled this kind of admin, but there was no way she wanted to trust her son with another nanny without some serious vetting and a supervised trial. "I have no idea how I'll find childcare again at such short notice."

"I'll do it."

Savannah's head snapped up. Brynn shrugged and gave her a small smile.

"I mean... I'm not, like, qualified. But I'm police checked, first aid and CPR certified and I will definitely do a better job than Megan did."

"Are you serious?" Savannah stared at her.

"Why not?" Brynn shrugged. "I'm here. You guys are busy. Me and Tucker have a vibe, don't we, kid?"

"Get up!" demanded Tucker in response, reaching for her. Brynn plucked him from the floor and he settled easily in her lap, looking back at his mama with a proudly smug expression.

"See?" Brynn said. "Tucker's in."

"But what about your studies?" Savannah asked. Noah turned and stared at his wife, who avoided his gaze.

"It's fine," she said. "I mean, we'll have to talk hours, but I could do like, half days or whatever, if it helps?"

"Help? You would be a lifesaver. Again, that is," she realized what she'd said. "You would be my lifesaver." Why did that sound like a come-on? Why were they both blushing? Why couldn't she be normal? "I mean, if you're sure you're sure," she concluded weakly.

"I'm sure," Brynn said simply. Tucker had a chubby fist full of her hair, pulling it between his fingers and stroking it clumsily. Brynn smiled down at him. "We'll start tomorrow. We'll have a blast. No more swimming though," she warned him.

"Go fwimming?" he said brightly, not a care in the world, making the adults laugh. At that moment, Savannah could have kissed everyone in the room.

Chapter Nine

Brynn felt oddly nervous. Not about looking after Tucker; that part seemed pretty easy. Interacting with his extremely attractive mother was less so. It wasn't exactly sticking to the plan she'd set herself to avoid the woman, but Savannah had looked so defeated, and following on so quickly from seeing her distressed and traumatized, Brynn found she couldn't help but want to rush to her aid.

On top of that, she just liked the kid. Tucker was sweet and funny and saving him from the lake had left her with a strong sense of responsibility for him. She burned hot with rage every time she thought of his neglectful nanny and the catastrophe that could have been. Not watching kids around water was one of her biggest bugbears, having retrieved more than one near-drowned child from the ocean due to carer inattention. And Tucker was so *little*.

She'd experienced a moment of true terror when it took more than a second to locate him in the deep water. The relief when she'd grabbed him to the surface and he'd coughed immediately was intense. She couldn't begin to imagine what Savannah had experienced watching from the beach. Seeing the extent of the distress and relief on the other woman's face as she clutched her son to her body had brought tears to Brynn's eyes and she'd had to turn away not to join in with all the crying. Rescuing a child you knew was different, it turned out.

And so when the question of who was to care for Tucker arose, she was damned if she'd let some other young, thoughtless au pair take responsibility for the little boy. The gratitude on Savannah's face said she was relieved to entrust him to Brynn over another - albeit more qualified - stranger and that, she had to admit, felt pretty damn good.

Maybe too good, as a matter of fact. Hopefully, taking care of Tucker only meant a few hand-off conversations with Savannah at most. After all, the point was that Brynn looked after him so she could go away and work. It would all be just fine. There was really no good reason why she was checking her reflection in the mirror for the eighth time before leaving. Toddlers weren't generally known for their strong opinions on outfits and hairstyles, she chastised herself, and left for her first day as Tucker's official caregiver.

———

There were butterflies in her stomach as she knocked on the door to Savannah's wing. Stupid, pointless butterflies, but butterflies nonetheless. The door swung open.

"Hey," Savannah greeted her, and Brynn immediately felt the wind knocked out of her. Savannah was smiling, her golden hair loose, wearing a red knit sweater over leggings, complete with oversized wooly hiking socks on her feet. Brynn knew she had it bad when her brain still read it as *sexy*. Savannah looked objectively adorable, but she had to pull it together.

"Hey," she said back, her smile widening without her permission. They looked at each other for a beat, then Savannah stepped back, welcoming her in. She followed the singer into the expansive playroom down the hall where Tucker was standing in front of a wooden play kitchen, absorbed and chatting to himself as he opened and closed the oven door.

"I believe he's making you coffee," Savannah said, her voice low and warm to her left.

Brynn's face cracked into a smile she couldn't stop as Tucker pulled open the oven to grab out a small wooden cup. He turned and watched her, clutching the cup indecisively, his eyes unsure. She sat down on the floor where she'd stood.

"Oh man," she looked up at Savannah, "I could really go a coffee right now. I'm super thirsty."

Savannah shot her a look of such warmth that Brynn felt it in the pit of her belly, before looking over to her son at his kitchen.

"What do you reckon, baby? Is that coffee ready yet?"

Tucker hung back another second before wandering over, cup in hand. He stopped right in front of Brynn and handed it toward her shyly. She reached out her hand for the cup.

"Thank y-" she started, but Tucker wrenched it back.

"Too hot!" he announced and ran back to his kitchen to shove the cup back into the oven.

"Damn." Brynn looked back at Savannah, whose eyes were sparkling with held back laughter. "So close."

"Can I make you an actual cup?" she offered.

"Depends. Did he get his brewing technique from you?"

Savannah's mouth quirked and she cocked her head for Brynn to follow her. They entered the big, open-plan, kitchen-dining-living space. The immense windows faced out toward the forest, but little light came in today. The sky outside was almost charcoal and the rain that lashed the glass kept alternating into chunks of ice. Wind howled through the trees, sending their bright leaves tumbling through the air and shredding them of their vibrance. Warm copper light fittings kept the room from darkness.

The comforting scent of coffee filled the air and she turned to watch as Savannah moved about the kitchen. Her movements were graceful and practiced, a woman who was comfortable in her own space. She reached up to pull two cups out of a cupboard above her head, her sweater rising with the movement and Brynn bit the inside of her cheek, hard, in self-recrimination for staring at the perfect curve of her ass. She wrenched herself away to go stare out the window instead, worrying that the silence between them was quickly going from comfortable to loaded.

A moment later, Savannah was beside her, extending a big white mug of coffee toward her. Black and strong. Savannah had both observed and remembered how she took it. She murmured her thanks and quickly reverted to talking about the weather, rather than reading into it.

"Is it hailing or snowing?" Brynn asked as they stood side by side, looking out at the frozen drops smushing against the glass. When she dared to look over, Savannah was watching her face, with something - amusement, perhaps - in her eyes.

"Hail is a warm weather thing," she told Brynn. "What you're seeing right now is frozen rain. With a bit of sleet."

Brynn was nonplussed.

"Aren't hail and frozen rain exactly the same thing? Ice from the sky?"

"Different mechanisms." Savannah looked thoughtful. "Hail comes from raindrops that are thrown up by the warm air of storms into colder parts of the atmosphere where they freeze and fall to earth. Frozen rain, on the other hand, starts up high as snow then partially defrosts on the way down," she explained. "What?" she asked, when she caught Brynn's expression.

"You're a *nerd*," she said wonderingly.

"Excuse me?" Savannah's jaw dropped.

"You're like, a weather nerd." Brynn couldn't stop smiling. "How do you know this shit?"

Savannah rolled her eyes, but she was fighting a smile too.

"I read a lot," she said defensively. "It's interesting to me."

"The weather?" Brynn raised her eyebrows.

"The *world*." Savannah shook her head. "I didn't get close to finishing high school," she disclosed. "It wasn't really set up for kids like me, who grew up poor. Not just like a little bit poor-" her eyes flicked up to Brynn's. "I mean my family was really poor. The other kids... well, you know kids. Suffice to say, I didn't fit in." She shrugged, something flashing in her eyes. "Then, you know... I left home by my mid-teens anyway, so I wasn't exactly able to go to school, since I had to survive. But I read everything I could get my hands on. Still do. I don't want to not be informed."

Brynn gazed at her. She'd tried to keep the conversation shallow. The weather, for crying out loud. But instead Savannah had just gifted her with an entire stack of insight into the kind of woman she was. Smart and vulnerable, curious and creative, a self-made fighter. And now she was looking back at Brynn, waiting for a response. *God, you're so fucking hot,* was what she wanted to say.

"Like I said, a nerd," she repeated instead, biting her lip against any further words slipping out, but letting the warmth she felt glow in her eyes.

Savannah rolled her eyes again, but her smile was there too.

"I don't talk about my childhood much," she admitted.

"How come?"

"People get weird about it. I'm not ashamed of it, but people who didn't grow up the way I did tend to romanticize it. I guess because of where I ended up?" She gestured around her.

"Ah," said Brynn. "Everyone loves a Cinderella story." She scrunched up her nose and Savannah snorted.

"Yeah, they do. I just think it's kind of gross to view poverty that way. Like poor people are a nice moral lesson about bootstraps or appreciating what you have."

Brynn knew she had no concept of this. She'd been on the verge of contemplating homelessness in LA, but that was out of pride and a misguided attempt at mental health preservation. She might not want to accept their help, but she had well-off parents to fall back on. She imagined having no protection at all from the economic and social forces that prevailed and it made her feel cold.

"How does it feel?" she asked curiously. "To go from so little to so much?"

Savannah examined her for a moment.

"Weird," she admitted. "Morally complex. I donate a lot. Lots of food programs and housing support in particular. But also, clearly... I keep a lot of it too." She looked up at the ceiling of her immense winter mansion. "It leaves you always trying to make sure you're safe, even when you're beyond comfortable. Sometimes I lie awake calculating what I'd do if my album fails, or my tour doesn't sell. As if Tucker and I couldn't live forever on what I've already got. It's stupid."

"It's not stupid." Brynn frowned. "You're being self-protective and protective of your child. You might know intellectually that you've got what you need, but child Savannah's always going to be in there, working hard to survive. You've got to take care of her too."

Savannah blinked at her. Brynn watched her face, hoping her scrutiny wasn't too obvious. Savannah could be so unreadable sometimes. She hoped she hadn't said something that offended her. Without her permission, her own hand reached out and squeezed Savannah's arm, just briefly. A small smile crossed Savannah's face, a warmth passing over her features before she bit her lip and changed the subject.

"You haven't seen a lot of real winters in your life, have you?"

"Nope. Californian born and bred," Brynn agreed, the subject change giving her mild whiplash.

"You don't travel?"

"Not a lot," she admitted. "My parents are workaholics. Our vacations were usually us kids at summer camps, so they didn't have to take time off. Then I was in pre-med, then med school, so it was all work all the time. Family curse," she said wryly.

"So I guess you're a nerd too," Savannah observed, polite enough not to probe the benign emotional neglect of Brynn's own childhood. Brynn smiled and shrugged. "Why did you leave med school?" Savannah asked softly.

Brynn had various shallow answers for this she'd rehearsed over the years. But the fact that Savannah had said *leave* instead of *quit* and had already been vulnerable with her left Brynn surprised by an urge to be honest for once.

"I pretty much straight up had a mental breakdown," she said simply. She kept her gaze on the dark sky and tumultuous forest outside. "There was a lot of family pressure, a lot of internal pressure. There's a lot of competition and not a lot of support. The work is... well, it's hard." She frowned. "My supervisor was sexually harassing me. I was assaulted by a patient. I tried to tell my parents, but..." she trailed off with a shrug. She risked a glance sideways. Savannah was just watching quietly, no judgment or pity in her face.

"It was about a month before my final exams. I was trying to study and I just... realized I would literally rather die." She didn't go into the horrifying details of it all, but when she met Savannah's eyes again, she saw understanding there. "My roommate found me in time," she said simply. "When I woke up in the hospital, I had a panic attack. Not so much at what had happened, but that I was back *there*. I signed myself out and never set foot in a hospital again."

Savannah said nothing, but her hand slipped into Brynn's and squeezed. The warmth and softness of her skin pulled her back from the dark reminiscence all at once. She took a breath and smiled at Savannah, gently pulling her hand back with regret.

"Damn, you'd make a good therapist." She tried for a smile. "You're kinda easy to talk to, I'm sorry. You probably need to get going. What do I need to know about Tucker? Like, what should I feed him for lunch? Wooden coffee aside."

Savannah looked surprised.

"Oh, I'm not leaving today. I figured it would be easiest on him if I were here while you settle in. I can show you around and explain everything while you both acclimatize," she explained.

Brynn swallowed hard.

"Makes sense," she said. "Thank you." She'd accidentally signed up to hours of time with the one woman Noah's *wife* didn't want to stop gazing at. Happily, at that moment Tucker burst in, coffee apparently forgotten, a small toy digger in his hand.

"Fix it!" he exclaimed, shoving it at Brynn. She sat down in an armchair and turned the toy over in her hand, thrilled for the distraction. It seemed intact. Tucker stared up at her, hopefully, his hands on her knee.

"Uh," she said, making the bucket move up and down. Savannah reached out and took it, their fingers brushing slightly.

"Bzzzzt," she said, pretending to drill the side of it with her finger. "Bzzt, bzzzzt," she turned it around a few times. "All fixed!" She handed it back to Tucker, who jumped up and down, holding it.

"All fixed!" he repeated and ran the digger up and down Brynn's forearm.

"All that, and you're a mechanic as well," Brynn observed.

She didn't have to look up to know the way Savannah's full pink lower lip would move in response to the tease, but she looked up anyway.

———

They ate lunch together, Savannah explaining her philosophy of toddler mealtimes as they did.

"He has to come to the table and we decide the options, but he can eat as much or as little as he wants. If he's hungry, he'll eat. If he's not, he won't. I want him to get to trust his own body and I don't want mealtimes to be a power struggle."

"Seems fair. He'd win, right?" Brynn jested, taking a bite of the delicious potato salad that Savannah had served up out of the fridge.

"Uh, yeah," said Savannah flatly. "Have you ever heard a two-year-old child scream at the top of their lungs and *never* stop?"

Brynn blinked, suddenly realizing what she had signed herself up for. Savannah raised an amused eyebrow as she watched her face.

"Okay, so if that happens, I can just give him whatever he wants until he stops screaming, right?" she tried hopefully. Tucker was swinging his legs in his highchair and looking adorable and innocent. Savannah bit her lip and shook her head wryly.

"Afraid not. I'm not trying to raise a monster."

"So what do I *do?*"

"Well, we're the grownups, so we get to set the limits. He's allowed to be angry about it. He's allowed to be sad. The limits stay, the feelings stay."

"So, what, I just let him scream?"

"No. You cuddle him, if he'll let you. You name the feeling: tell him it's okay to be angry, or sad. You support him for as long as it takes until he moves through it and then you move on together."

"Oh," said Brynn. "That actually makes sense... I think."

She watched Tucker as he plowed his digger into his sliced apple and used the bucket to try to shove the food into his mouth. The apple hit the ground, but undeterred, he tried again.

"Well, yeah," Savannah agreed. "I'm trying to teach him that life isn't about always getting what you want or being happy all the time. That being sad or angry or jealous or disappointed are all feelings it's okay to just feel. And I don't want to gaslight him by telling him he isn't feeling them or shouldn't feel them when he very clearly is."

"Huh."

"What?"

"I just... if I'd learned all that as a kid I probably wouldn't have become an alcoholic," she observed. Oh wow, she was all about the truth bombs today. Now Savannah would never want to leave her child with her.

"I mean, maybe?" Savannah agreed, piling up her salad on her fork. "But I'm sure you know addiction is more complicated than that."

"You don't seem surprised," Brynn observed.

"I noticed you don't touch alcohol," Savannah said. "I figured it was either that or you were pregnant." Brynn almost choked on her mouthful of potato. "And if you are, you're hiding it damn well," she cast her eye down Brynn's body.

"You notice a lot," Brynn replied, as soon as she'd recovered.

Savannah's cheeks went pink. She focused down on her plate.

"I guess I do."

"Six years sober," Brynn reassured her. "Just in case you were worrying."

"I'm not," Savannah looked up, her blue gaze intense. "You leaped into that lake a mile ahead of me without even stopping. I know I can trust you with his life because I've already seen it."

Brynn stared back. Savannah's trust in her touched her deeply. With her child, no less. She swallowed a sudden lump in her throat.

"I've got you," she said quietly, to them both.

"I can't tell you how much that means to me," Savannah said. "After everything. To be able to trust someone." She gazed at Brynn. Both of them seemed unable to look away. "God, anyway." Savannah broke first, her eyelashes dropping. She stood up abruptly, picking up her plate. "I appreciate you, is all," she said from the sink, over the running water, her back turned.

"Up up up!" called Tucker and Brynn stirred herself into action, scooping him up from his highchair. "Wash hands," he instructed, and Brynn carried him to the kitchen sink and helped him wash mayonnaise off his hands and face as he giggled and splashed water absolutely everywhere. She caught Savannah watching with interest.

"I normally-" Savannah started, holding up a small cloth, hesitating. You know what, don't worry. He's having a great time."

———

The next hour passed pretty easily. Tucker was busy and loud, and the two women alternated between joining him in his play and exchanging information about routines and care. There was no time for meaningful smiles or lingering glances or intimate conversation, to Brynn's extreme relief.

Tucker melted down at around one p.m. and Savannah looked at the time, startled.

"He usually takes his naps right after lunch. I guess I just got distracted," she said over his wails.

She took Tucker into his small, lovely bedroom and quickly changed his diaper, then tugged a soft t-shirt down over his head while he wailed. Brynn hung back anxiously, wondering if she'd ever be as competent in the face of a miserable child. He clung to his mama, shrieking, and Brynn's confidence dwindled. Savannah held him tightly, next to his bed and turned to look at Brynn, hesitation in her face.

"What's wrong?"

"When he has a nanny they usually put him to bed here, and he goes down okay, but he won't have a bar of that when I'm here. I usually cuddle him to sleep in my bed."

"Oh," Brynn replied. "Go for it, whatever's easiest."

Savannah nodded.

"It's right through here," she said, gesturing over Tucker's cries. She opened the door on the far side of the room and as Brynn glimpsed through to an expansive master suite and giant bed, she suddenly realized she was being prompted to enter Savannah's bedroom with them. Bawling child or not, this felt like a step she could not bring herself to take.

"Oh no, it's okay, you do your thing, I'll just-" she gestured behind her awkwardly, her stomach clenching. Savannah hesitated, and Brynn understood she was supposed to be learning how to get the child to sleep. God, she needed to get her shit together. Still, there was no way she was going in there. "I'll just wait back here?" she tried, gesturing to an armchair in Tucker's room. Savannah nodded quickly and carried her son into her bedroom.

Brynn perched awkwardly on the edge of the chair, fiddling with the hem of her shirt. In the next room, Savannah tugged off her big goofy socks and pulled down the soft-looking comforter. Her bedding was a soft, dusky pink, more luxurious and feminine than anything Brynn had ever owned. She lay down on her side with her head on the pillow and cradled Tucker against her, holding him tight. He pulled

132

back and murmured something plaintively and she picked up her phone from the bedside table and pressed play on a song.

He settled in and she held him as the song played through hidden speakers somewhere. As soon as it ended, it began again. The song started out with gentle piano but the woman's voice was strong and emotive. It didn't feel at all like a lullaby. It felt like a love song and a fight all in one. Brynn felt it in her bones as she absorbed where she'd found herself, watching Savannah laying in her bed, her golden hair across the pillow, the outline of her hip, her shapely legs, her eyes closed as she held her sweet boy in her arms. Brynn got to her feet and left the room like someone had pulled a fire alarm.

She paced in the living room. It would be okay. It was just this one ridiculously intimate day. After this, they'd be like ships in the night. She leaned her forehead against the window, trying to cool her heated face, but the window seemed at least triple-glazed against the ice outside. Her blood felt like it was fire in her veins.

About half an hour later, Savannah emerged to find her sitting on the couch, calmly reading a book she'd stolen at random from the floor-to-ceiling bookshelf at the back of the room. Savannah's hair was tousled and her features soft and flushed.

"Oh my god, I'm sorry, I accidentally drifted off," she apologized. "We don't always sleep that great at night and the second I lay down it was all over." She took a seat at the other end of the couch. Her feet were still bare. How was it that even her feet were ridiculously pretty? They looked cold and Brynn wanted nothing more than to bring them up into her lap to rub them, or for Savannah to slide them under Brynn's thighs for warmth. "I didn't mean to leave you there on your own while we slept."

"It's fine," Brynn managed. "I didn't want to sit and watch you sleep like some kind of creeper," she said, which was both the truth and a lie. She held up the book with a smile. *Jane Eyre*. "This seemed appropriate to the weather," she nodded to the window where the frozen rain still lashed.

"God, I love that book." Savannah took it from her, turning it over in her hands and smiling down at it like it was an old friend. She felt Brynn's gaze and misinterpreted her silence. "What, you didn't think poor white trash would read classic literature?"

"What? No!" Brynn was horrified. Savannah smirked, and she realized she was being played. "You're an asshole," she spluttered. "Playing on my middle-class guilt. I actually think it's pretty perfect for you... a girl born into poverty grows up and becomes lady of the manor," she gestured at the house around them. "Plus, lots of that cold weather you seem to love."

"That's a horrible summary of Jane Eyre," Savannah scoffed. "Thornfield Hall burns to the ground... she's never *lady of the manor*."

"Right, but you are hiding your mentally ill wife in the attic, so there is that," she joked. "Wait, does that make *me* Jane?" Holy shit, why was she flirting? She was just trying to be funny, but it was coming out all wrong. Savannah straight up giggled, tucking her hair behind her ear and biting her lip in thought.

"If I'm seducing my young hireling I think that means Noah is Jane," she said sensibly.

"Except aren't I essentially your governess now?" protested Brynn, swallowing irrational jealousy. "*I'm* Jane."

"I think you're probably right," said Savannah, a satisfied smile taking up residence on her face, possibly something to do with Brynn zealously defending her right to her fictional seduction. "Oh god." Savannah sat up straight. "That reminds me, I'll call Chester. He'll arrange your contract and all the paperwork."

"Contract?" Brynn asked. "I mean, I'll sign all the NDAs, background checks, whatever that you need, but I don't want you to pay me."

"Of course I'm going to pay you." Savannah looked shocked. "It's a huge undertaking and you're doing me a massive favor. I couldn't work without this help. I *value* your help. A lot. It pays well, Brynn."

"I don't want to be the help," said Brynn simply, feeling slightly humiliated at how much she didn't want this to be their dynamic. Savannah considered her for a moment.

"Is this an ego thing?" she asked. "Because I have to tell you as someone who comes from a long line of janitors and cleaners I'm going to take that poorly."

"No," Brynn said firmly. "It's not. Look. I'm here as a guest, right? Noah's here to work. I'm just a hanger-on. Getting a free holiday. Living in your house, eating your food. Doing this would make me feel like I have a right to be here. That I'm not taking advantage of you being-"

"Stupidly rich."

"Generous," she corrected.

"Noah will be getting paid," Savannah pointed out. "So your logic is flawed."

"Fine. Noah can be the help, then," Brynn said firmly.

"I don't see why it's any different-"

"It's different because I want to be your friend!" Brynn burst out. Then she flinched. What the hell was she thinking? Her bank account was tragic, without any promise of money coming in. A solid few weeks or months of pay would do wonders for her future prospects. And since she was trying not to get close to Savannah, putting a good, arbitrary, HR-enforced boundary between them was exactly the right thing to do. And yet... even though nothing could happen between them, Brynn could not stomach the idea of being so pathetic as to have a huge crush on her *boss*. "Oh wow, I'm such a dork." Her eyes went wide. "I'm sorry, I-"

"I want to be your friend too," interrupted Savannah. She pulled up her legs and hugged her knees, looking very small and human. "I don't want to be one of those dumb celebrities who thinks their paid assistant is their best friend." She picked at a tiny chip in her nail polish. "But I do, in fact, pay *both* my best friends. Coral is in my band and Rosalie runs my nonprofit. And I know they love me, but that's still an undeniable fact."

"Savannah," Brynn wasn't sure if she'd ever said her name out loud, to her face before. She liked the way it rolled off her tongue, the way it made the singer raise her head and look at her. "If you pay me, I will quit. I won't be on your payroll."

Savannah looked at her for a long time. Despite the triple-glazing, Brynn could hear the sound of ice pelting against the windows and the wind howling outside. It was that, for sure, and not the prolonged eye contact, that made her shiver.

"You're something else," Savannah said softly. "I'm very grateful we're going to be friends."

Brynn swallowed loudly. "Me too," she said.

Chapter Ten

Brynn stood in the doorway late that afternoon, but she didn't leave. It was probably something to do with the small child clamped firmly onto her right leg and refusing to let her go. Savannah backed his actions fully. She was just glad Tucker had taken it on, so she wasn't tempted to do it herself. There was something about Brynn's presence that made her feel like she truly wasn't alone, for the first time in years. A warmth buzzed within her and she didn't want it to stop.

With a sigh, she bent down and gently untangled her son from Brynn's long, lean calf. He protested, then shoved his face into his mama's shoulder with sadness.

"It's okay, darling, she'll be back tomorrow." She smiled at the other woman over his soft curls. Brynn reached out toward them and gently squeezed Tucker's arm, her fingers brushing Savannah's shoulder on the way back. A shiver of pleasure ran down her spine.

"We'll hang out soon, little buddy," Brynn promised. She looked back at Savannah, still standing close. Not for the first time that day, she was struck by how dark Brynn's eyes were, and how ridiculously lush her lashes. Her lips were full and pillowy and excruciatingly expressive. She really was unfairly attractive, but the sprinkling of little freckles really pushed it over the edge.

"Goodnight," she managed, realizing a moment too late that it was very much still the afternoon. Brynn didn't even blink.

"Goodnight," she returned, softly.

She raised her hand and gave a small wave, before turning and walking away. Savannah watched her until she disappeared and then closed the door with a sigh.

"Shit," she said quietly. "I mean... sugar," she corrected as Tucker raised his head to regard her seriously. "We really like her, don't we, kid?"

"Weally like her," echoed her son.

The rest of the afternoon and into the evening passed like a long, slow blur. She was only half in the room, playing with her son, singing him songs, feeding him his dinner, bathing him and putting him to bed. The other half was reliving small moments. Stolen glances, a crooked smile, deep admissions, a bitten lip.

"Oh no..." she breathed, collapsing onto the couch where only a few hours ago Brynn had sternly and heatedly refused her money in demand for an equal footing. She let her head fall back as she stared up at the ceiling for a long moment, aghast at herself. She pulled out her phone, her fingers hovering indecisively for a moment before she made up her mind and FaceTimed Coral.

For a while they chatted about how the writing was going and Coral's time on the road. Her side project, Honeybaked, was still in the Red States. Savannah tried not to quiz her too hard on safety, knowing that her friend didn't need to be reminded how fucked up the world was and Coral, knowing *her* friend was a worrier managed to pepper her anecdotes with minor details like the band having her back and security being cool.

"Okay spill, what's up?" Coral said after a while.

"Why do you think something's up?" Savannah hedged.

"I can hear it in your voice, babe, and you look distracted. I know you. Quit stalling and tell me."

Savannah's stomach clenched. She made herself take a breath.

"I think I have a crush on my governess," she admitted after a moment.

"Your... governess...?"

"Yeah. That is... I mean, my nanny, obviously." She felt weirdly flustered even talking about it.

Coral was silent, her face confused.

"I... mean, okay? I didn't see that one coming..."

"Oh god." Savannah suddenly caught up and waved her hand rapidly. "Not Megan! God no, Megan quit."

She told Coral the story of Tucker's near drowning and had just got to the part about Brynn diving into the water like a goddamned superhero to save him when Coral interrupted.

"Let me guess: Brynn's the nanny now."

"How did you-"

"I knew it!" Coral cried jubilantly. Savannah glared at her. "Okay, *that* I saw coming."

"No, you absolutely did *not*."

"Oh, but I did! I don't care if she's married to a dude, that woman is queer as fuck. And I noticed you noticing her, you little minx."

"You think she's queer?" Savannah sat upright even as she cringed at herself for her eagerness to support her own tingling sense that Brynn's warm, frequent gaze was not entirely innocent.

"No grown-ass straight woman wears that much flannel," Coral said flatly. "Nor should they."

"That's just a cliche." Savannah rolled her eyes, disappointed. "God, Coral. This is bad. She *is* married. To my new - and extremely lovely - songwriting partner." She sank back on the couch, feeling excruciated.

"Well, yeah, I happen to think it's perfect," Coral told her. Savannah blinked. "You could do with a good safe crush," Coral continued, leaning in toward the screen like she was about to deliver a home truth. "Ever since you left Cole, you've been acting like you're not the red-blooded woman we all know you are. Getting hot and bothered over someone would be *good* for you, and since nothing can happen here, you can just relax and enjoy it."

"Enjoy it?" Savannah looked up, frowning. It was true that she'd barely thought about sex - or even romance - since the moment she kicked her ex-husband out. The very idea of going back through all *that* all over again had sounded far too overwhelming; it was better just to shut all those feelings down altogether. And it had worked, it really had. Until now.

"Of course! Me? Well, I might find myself a little tempted." Coral raised her eyebrows, her expression sultry. "But you never would. You're so... moral," she teased. "And god, if Noah isn't the hottest man I've seen in miles... you know for sure they've got to be rock solid. *Ugh,* the two of them." She rolled her eyes heavenward at the immense good looks of the couple. The hesitation clearly remained evident in Savannah's face, since Coral huffed in response. "Just enjoy it! Check out her ass when she's not looking. Have a little harmless flirt. Take things into your own hands if it gets too hot for you to handle." She wriggled her perfectly sculpted brows suggestively.

"Stop it." Savannah shook her head, going slightly pink despite herself. "Besides. It's worse than that. I *like* her. I can talk to her. She makes me feel... safe," she confessed.

"Okay, well *that* can't continue." This time Coral was the one to frown. "I like a bit of harmless fun for you, but I don't like the idea of you getting hurt."

"Me neither," said Savannah softly. "But we just straight up proposed friendship to each other this afternoon. And now she's-"

"Your govern*ness,*" Coral teased.

"-taking care of my child every day. I'm going to see her all the damn time and I already just *like* her so much."

"And she's hot as fuck."

"And she's hot as fuck," Savannah whispered, dropping her head into her hand.

"What does Ros have to say about it?"

Savannah looked up.

"Oh, I haven't spoken with her about it," she said lightly.

Coral gave her a look.

"Of course you haven't."

"What does *that* mean?"

"You call me when you want permission to misbehave," Coral told her, "and Rosalie when you need rescuing from whatever situation you've gotten yourself into."

Savannah's jaw dropped.

"That is *not* true!"

"Hm, well, call her then," she said, like it was a dare.

"I will," Savannah retaliated.

Coral just grinned.

"Sure you will," she said, and Savannah shot her a dirty look. Coral smirked. "Look, hon," she advised, "just do what you do best."

"Suffer in silence?"

"Write it out. Feel your feelings... all those angsty, longing, *horny* feelings and write some fucking great songs. Make another billion jillion dollars and let *that* make you feel better."

"I can't tell if that's the best or the worst advice you've ever given me."

"You're welcome, honey. You know I've got your back."

———

The conversation with Coral seemed to have broken something open inside her. Instead of keeping a lid on her feelings, Savannah found they were bubbling out everywhere. It really would have been better for everyone if she'd simply kept her mouth shut and her eyes down.

When Cole was sleeping with every woman in every town, she'd become an expert in keeping her feelings - and her awareness - buttoned down tight. If she didn't look at it directly, maybe things weren't as bad as she deep down suspected they might be.

For the last few weeks with Brynn, Savannah had employed the same tactics. Don't look too close. Don't think too much. Don't lie awake at night wondering. But yesterday, some combination of Brynn's smoldering eyes, fierceness and the way she kept making herself vulnerable for Savannah... a barrier had been kicked down. She could no longer deny that *something* had been growing within her and thanks to her conversation with Coral, she could now admit that something was *lust*.

She *wanted* Brynn. Coral's advice to just enjoy the pleasant friction of wanting someone you couldn't have would have been great if it wasn't for the complication that she also found she was starting to really care about the other woman. If Savannah let herself, she could find she wanted her in more than just physical ways. This was bad news.

She knew what it was to be cheated on. Even if Brynn ever returned her feelings - and Savannah was far from sure she did - there was no way she would ever cross a line that would harm Noah the way she herself had been harmed. It was a hard and fast boundary for her, of that she was sure.

Brynn was only here for a matter of months at the most. She could hold it together that long. But if Savannah was going to come out of it without getting hurt, she was going to have to shut something down.

Losing the friendship - the tenuous but growing connection between them - felt like the worst part to lose. And it was the part Brynn herself seemed to be fighting for. Savannah recalled the low timbre of Brynn's voice as she spoke her name and her forceful tone as she straight up refused to join Savannah's payroll. The shiver down her spine that followed was quickly chased by a flood of warmth. Brynn wanted this connection with her every bit as much as she did. Enough to turn down cold hard cash.

Okay, the physical attraction then. She was not an animal. She could shove that back, deep down, in a little box inside her, just like she'd shoved down far more powerful feelings before. This she could do. She'd turn it off like a switch.

The next morning, when Brynn arrived to take care of Tucker, Savannah gave it a go. No big deal, just a beautiful woman at her door. Smiling at her with dark pretty eyes, and bending down to swoop Savannah's thrilled, giggling child into the air. Ignore the flex of her forearms, the easy strength of her shoulders, that's none of your business. Just smile and offer her coffee and don't look too close. Don't think.

She kissed her son goodbye and - with noticeably less of a pang than usual, in light of his excited face and Brynn's easy warmth - she left him to go meet with Noah in the band room.

She brought with her a new song idea, something that had started low in her belly this morning when she'd opened the door to Brynn. In the heartbeat before she remembered to shut it down, all she'd wanted was to lean in and bury her face in the other woman's neck, inhale her scent and pull her close. Then, just as quickly, she remembered sharply that it could never happen. It was a feeling she couldn't quite put into words just yet, but she could just about hum the first verse.

They worked for hours, Noah pulling together a few prescient lines that only served to remind her they currently shared the same muse. The melancholy and guilt that realization brought to her added a deeper nuance to the song, but the real hooks and a chorus continued to elude them.

They took a brief break, sitting side by side by the fire upstairs, with a drink and a small cheese plate, and whether it was to help her resurrect a barrier or just to torture herself, she asked him to tell her about how he met Brynn.

His fond grin as he recounted how Brynn had saved him from the sea made her stomach churn. She felt the first real stirrings of true jealousy, imagining what it would have been like to have been pulled up out of the salty ocean to your first view of sparkling dark eyes and freckles.

She fought off the feeling. She didn't want to be jealous of Noah; he too was starting to feel like a friend. And besides, jealousy whispered unhelpful things in her ear, like maybe Brynn was a little bit wasted on the beautiful man in front of her, that despite the clear fondness between the couple, there seemed to be an absence of any kind of genuine spark. She'd never even seen them kiss, she realized. Sometimes things could start to fizzle out in long-term relationships, she knew that, but oh god how she'd kiss her if Brynn were hers.

Feeling more ashamed and conflicted than ever, she reentered the studio where they tinkered around a bit more, a few more melancholy longing lines coming to the surface, but the heart of the song still escaped them. They called it a day, and after Noah left, she stood for a long minute in the solitude, taking deep breaths and solidifying her resolve to turn off any non-platonic feelings for Noah's wife.

She reentered her suite to silence.

"Brynn?" she called. "Tucker? I'm home."

Nothing. She frowned, kicking off her shoes and padding down the hall.

"Shhhhh!" she heard from a short distance away. Curious, she followed the sound to the playroom and looked through the open doorway. The room looked empty. Tucker's giggle rang out.

"Hiding, hiding, hiding!" His gleeful voice was coming from the small blanket fort she'd erected in the corner for him.

"Buddy, have some chill." Brynn's low voice from the fort was amused, the wry note making Savannah smile automatically.

"Hmm," she said out loud. "I wonder where they are? I'm sure I left them both here this morning…"

Tucker giggled again, the blanket fort rippling as he wriggled.

"Maybe they're in the toy cupboard?" she mused, opening the door. "Oh! Not in there..."

She pretended to check under the table and under the rug before Tucker ran out of patience and shouted, "inna fort Mama!"

She pulled back the blanket to see her son's excited face from his perch on Brynn's lap.

"I found you!"

"I found you!" he cried back.

She opened her arms for him to come hug her but instead he demanded, "Mama in! *Mama in!*" his voice rising when she tried to protest.

Carefully, she squeezed into their little fort. Brynn was sitting cross-legged, an excited toddler bouncing on her lap. She looked perfectly content, despite the roof of the blanket fort being at the same height as the top of her head, the static cling wreaking havoc on her smooth locks. Tucker looked as happy as she'd ever seen him, waiting for her to cram herself in opposite them before leaping onto her lap.

"Hug!" he shouted, wrapping his arms around her neck. She squeezed him close and smiled across at Brynn, who was only a few inches away.

"How did today go?"

"Great." She grinned. "He's amazing. We had a fun day, didn't we, kiddo?"

"Fun!" he agreed. "Woot woot!"

Savannah laughed.

"Did you teach him that?"

Brynn shrugged with a lopsided smile.

"I'm a great influence. Kid's gotta party."

"Hide!" Tucker jumped off her, landing on Brynn's leg and wobbling. She winced slightly and righted him and he jumped out of the fort. Brynn tried to follow him out but, "uh-uh, hide!" he shoved the blanket back down in her face. "Mama, Bwynn, hide!" He raced away.

"Uh," Brynn looked over at her, "this is the only hiding place he knows isn't it?"

"I think we're stuck here," Savannah acknowledged. Their eyes met and Brynn chuckled, Savannah joining in awkwardly. This was less than ideal. They waited a moment, listening, both faces turned toward the doorway of the fort rather than looking at each other.

"Hiding, where are you?" Tucker called out happily from somewhere in the room. They smiled at each other again. The tiny fort felt increasingly small as she belatedly noticed their knees were almost touching. She shuffled back an inch, but there was nowhere further to go.

The blanket fort was dim and close, lit with a soft glow from a small string of golden fairy lights. The lighting was beyond flattering; Brynn's skin glowed and her hair and lips shone.

She was gazing at Savannah with sparkling eyes and not looking away. She placed one finger against her lips in a teasing *hush* gesture. Suddenly Savannah wasn't in control of her own thoughts anymore. She thought about how easy it would be to lean across and kiss her, right here in their hiding place, where no one could see. She thought about how badly she wanted to take that long lovely finger and bite it, then pull it into her mouth and slowly suck, imagining the sound Brynn would make if she did. God, those were beautiful hands. Savannah knew just by looking at Brynn how strong and capable they'd feel against her body. She swallowed hard.

Brynn leaned in even closer towards her. Savannah got a hit of her scent: clean laundry detergent, honey shampoo and warm skin.

"You okay?" Brynn murmured quietly, her tone unbearably intimate this close. Savannah nodded mutely, her breathing shallow. "You've gone all flushed." Brynn gestured helpfully with that same finger at her throat and face, and Savannah felt hot all the way through her body.

"It's the fort," she reached for an excuse. "It's a bit claustrophobic."

Brynn whipped open the fort for her. She started to laugh.

"I think you can leave." She swiveled her long limbs aside to let Savannah clamber out on wobbly legs to see her son happily absorbed by reading an upside-down book a few feet away.

Savannah pulled her sweater up over her head, feeling a bit like her body might burst into flames at any moment. Pulling at her t-shirt, she swung around to look at Brynn. Was there something knowing in the other woman's face, or was she just being paranoid? God, she was not handling this.

She thanked Brynn briskly, made a time for her to come again the next day and hustled her out the door claiming exhaustion. Brynn looked slightly startled at her hasty expulsion, and Savannah would have felt guilty if she wasn't doing it for the sake of Brynn's marriage.

Another few minutes with those dark eyes on her skin and god knows what she'd want to do.

All evening she tapped out a frantic rhythm with her fingers, against the dining table, her hip, the bathtub, and - after Tucker had been tucked into his own bed - she tapped it against her thighs, the rhythm turning sultry when she slipped her hand between them, and by the time she came, shuddering with her back arching off the bed, the rhythm in her head had turned into a song.

———

"Woah..." said Noah a few days later, staring at her with wide eyes. She looked back, slightly breathless, electric guitar still clutched against her lower abdomen. "That was... um, forgive me, but sexy as fuck." He grinned broadly; she grinned back. Oh god, she was writing about his wife - this was so twisted - but damn, she knew an excellent song when she heard it, and so, apparently, did he. The crush was going to stay innocent and harmless. The song was anything but. "Let's lay it down right now!" he said jubilantly. "It's perfect as it is. I'll just add a little -" he thrummed a slow and dirty rhythm with the bass, "and it's done."

"Okay!" she agreed. Coral's dubious advice was definitely paying dividends. Brynn smirked at her with a teasing crooked grin and a lyric got written. They verbally sparred, leaning toward each other over the kitchen island, so close and yet so far, and a riff sprung into her head. She'd tossed and turned at nights and blushed and held back her sighs in Brynn's presence until this song had teased its way all the way out, a catharsis that was as much about the edging as it was about the pay-off. She'd leaned hard into the agitation of a growing *want* and this was the result. Three-and-a-half minutes of the sex part of *sex, drugs and rock and roll.*

"Hang on a sec." Noah pulled out his phone and held it up to his ear. "Brynn!" he exclaimed after a moment. "Come down, we're laying an awesome track. We gotta hear your opinion.... okay... okay, yep great, see you in a sec!"

"No!" Savannah gaped at him, but he'd already hung up the phone. "I-" she struggled for a reason. "It's not ready. I mean, she's got Tucker with her, it's not really meant for my son to hear-"

"She just said Tucker was asleep." Noah shrugged. "It'll only take a few minutes. Come on, it's our tradition now!"

Savannah sucked in a deep breath. She hadn't bargained for this. Singing about her unrequited desire in front of Brynn herself? This was - the door to the band room swung open - oh god, actually going to happen.

Brynn walked in, looking appealingly rumpled, her hair out and slightly mussed, wearing one of Noah's long-sleeved t-shirts, the white one that offset her warm tanned skin and showcased her beautiful collarbones.

"What's up?" she said, shooting them both a blazing smile. "You got something new?"

"Get ready to drop your panties," Noah said with a grin and Savannah died. "This song is fucking hot."

"Okay," Brynn shrugged. "Turn me on, my little rock stars," she smiled confidently.

Savannah swallowed. The bravado of her was both enthralling and a little annoying. Here was Savannah, silently writhing in discomfort and Brynn was blithely daring her like there was no way she'd even blink if Savannah turned up the sex. Well, fine.

Noah counted them in. Savannah fixed her eyes on Brynn, gripped hard to her electric guitar, and began to sing.

Don't look at me with eyes like that,
Don't rip off my disguise just yet,
You have no right to make me so....
Wait..ing for something I'll never get

Brynn was watching back, her hands shoved deep in her pockets. The line that teased the word *wet* made her rock back on her heels before she righted herself, her gaze wavering just slightly.

You say that we're friends but when our fingers brush,
I can see us as lovers, oh I could make you blush

Slowly, Brynn sat down on the sofa, leaning forward with her elbows on her knees and her hands laced in front of her. Her gaze met Savannah's again, a little less confident now.

You don't want my money and that's alright honey
But I'd give you all I've got to get you in my bed

Color suffused Brynn's cheeks. She coughed, covering her mouth, before she looked up and met her eyes once more. Savannah let the guitar bounce against her pelvis again as she sang the bridge and Brynn seemed transfixed by the movement, her gaze traveling up her body so clearly, Savannah felt it like a touch. She didn't drop her stare, belting out the rest of the hungry, teasing, borderline filthy lyrics with heat.

The final crescendo hit and she let her head fall back as she smashed out the last notes with vigor. As the sound faded, so did her bravado. She was playing with fire and she knew it. Where Coral's advice fell flat was letting your crush *hear* your goddamn horny songs about her. She knew she was flushed and sweating and now she had to meet Brynn's eye. She lifted her head with trepidation.

Brynn wasn't looking at her. She was grinning at her husband.

"That *was* sexy as hell," she enthused to him. "Well done, team. It's a killer song. Can't wait to hear the finished product." Her smiling gaze skipped over to Savannah who was almost quaking with tension, still breathing hard from the song. "I better get back up there in case

Tucker wakes," was all she said, her voice light and her eyes perfectly calm. "Catch you later?"

"Oh? Uh, y-yeah," Savannah stuttered. It was humiliating. The lyrics should have been wildly obvious to anyone who was paying any attention at all. But Brynn, it appeared, was entirely oblivious. The gaze Savannah had felt? Just a thoughtful, friendly eye. All the heat was coming from one direction and one direction only: Savannah. It should have been a relief, so why did she feel so damn crushed?

Chapter Eleven

Brynn walked upstairs on shaky legs. When she finally made the privacy of a closed door, she leaned back against it and took a long wavering breath. What the hell had just happened? She tried to break it down and make sense of it.

Savannah and Noah had written a song. A *sexy* goddamn song. Noah had invited her to listen to it, then Savannah had looked her dead in the eye and spent three minutes turning Brynn on so intensely she had practically melted into the floor. She'd lost all sense of restraint and let her hungry eyes roam, watching Savannah's hips slam into her guitar, the slide of her pretty fingers as she played, the gasp of her breath between notes and the blaze of her eyes as Savannah let herself *want*.

Brynn had finally come to her senses as the song came to an end - way, *way* too late - and jerked her gaze away, forcing herself to grin at

Noah like all was well. Then she'd stammered something and fled, her panties not so much dropped as ruined, her face pink.

That was the last time she would ever set foot in the band room. There could be no more watching Savannah sing. Savannah was one hell of a performer, that was clear, and - fair enough - she liked an audience. But why did it have to be *Brynn* she looked at when she sang words like that? Brynn just wasn't built to withstand it. It was bad enough that she already had a debilitating crush on the woman without now adding knowledge of her as a sexual being to the litany of things she lay awake at night over.

Because on top of the images, those lyrics were going to torment her. The line about someone who didn't want her money had given her serious palpitations. Could it...? *No.* Brynn would not let herself go there, because that way lay madness. Just like Noah did, Savannah would pick up tiny sparks of inspiration everywhere. A snippet of conversation with a friend was fair game.

Brynn had bigger problems right now, like whether she had literally drooled on herself during the performance and whether Savannah had noticed. She was *seriously* failing at this wife business if so.

She was beyond thrilled when Tucker woke up and she could throw herself back into kid world.

"Hey, buddy!" She ducked into his bedroom and raised the blind. His cries stopped immediately when he saw her and he all but leapt into her waiting arms. "Did you have a good nap?" she asked him as he smushed his face into her shoulder. "Are you ready to have some fun?"

"Fun!" he enthused, still clinging to her. So far, caring for Tucker had been incredibly fun. He seemed to love her company as much as she loved his, bouncing joyfully from one activity to the other. They played play dough and dinosaurs, built immense block towers and pretended to be dragons that could fly and breathe fire. They read hundreds of books, Tucker laughing when she did silly voices. They went for walks, sang songs, collected leaves and stones and twigs and made wild messes with paint. Honestly, this had been her funnest job ever. It was hard to think of it even *as* a job, since being around Tucker were some of the happiest moments in her day.

On what had been Brynn's second day with him, Savannah had returned from writing, and after pressing her face into her son's hair and listening to his excited babble, she'd turned to Brynn with a note of caution in her voice.

"You didn't call me," she said with a slight frown, tucking a wisp of blonde hair back.

"I'm sorry?"

"You know you can call me if he's ever upset and needs me there. You're never disturbing me, if he does."

"I know," Brynn replied. "I will."

"I just... I don't want you to hold back. There's nothing more important I'll ever be doing that you can't let me know, if he's upset or worried, or-"

"Savannah." Brynn smiled. "*I know*. If he's ever upset and I can't calm him down myself nice and quickly, I will call you... I'm not shy about it, don't worry."

"You mean... he hasn't cried?" Savannah gave her a strange look.

"No." Brynn shook her head. "I mean, he got mad when he asked for ice cream for lunch and I said no. But we ate pretend ones instead and he thought it was great. Oh, and he gave me a serious pout when it was nap time, but I said I'd nap too and he was fine."

"Oh," said Savannah. Tucker barrelled hard into the back of Brynn's knee, nearly dropping her to the floor, and she quickly scooped him up and hung him upside down from her shoulder while he giggled and squealed. Then she popped him down and he ran on his way again. Savannah was gazing at her, her face soft. "You," she said, her voice low and warm, "are wonderful."

Brynn fought valiantly against a blush and grinned at her.

"He's easy." She watched as Tucker flung himself into a pile of soft teddies. "You've got a great kid."

For a second, she thought Savannah was going to hug her. Thankfully, she didn't. Brynn wasn't quite sure how she'd react if Savannah pressed her body into her arms.

And that had been days before the scene in the band room. Now? Brynn was a straight up nervous wreck. She wasn't sure the best way to play it. Should she be cool and professional and pull back again, making sure Savannah knew she wasn't about to forget herself? Or should she joke it off, tease the woman about her hot song and insinuate that Noah was totally going to get it tonight? Even the thought made her feel a bit icked. Her 'husband' was like a brother to her.

In the end, when Savannah came in the door, the spark from earlier seemed to have been drowned in exhaustion and she seemed entirely oblivious to Brynn's discomfort. That made it easy for Brynn to pick the third option: change nothing. She could be warm and silly and friendly and act as if no one had gazed into anyone's eyes and sang in a sex-drenched voice and no one had ogled and drooled and made an absolute lustful fool of themselves. Everything was *fine*.

———

Back in her suite, she found herself alone. Noah had headed into town for the evening, and Brynn was at a bit of a loss. The weather outside was formidable - cold didn't even begin to cover it - and she didn't have anywhere near enough clothes to consider facing it. She gazed out the window, watching the sky darken as the wind tossed the bare branches of the trees.

What she should do, she knew, was to pick up her textbook and study. Since she'd started caring for Tucker, she'd found more and more reasons just to let the practice slide.

Turning back to the room she almost automatically returned to her new habit. There was a turntable in the living room of their suite and she'd borrowed stacks of records from Savannah's collection. She was working her way through slowly... from the great classics like Patsy Cline, Loretta Lynn, Tanya Tucker and loads of Dolly, to more recent and varied styles, both contemporary country and Americana.

She had started, quite honestly, to make Savannah happy, and perhaps to prove a point. But she continued because somewhere along the way she'd gotten hooked. Brynn had always thought she'd loved music, but something here nagged at her, got under her skin, wouldn't let her rest until she'd absorbed as much as possible. She found great comfort knowing she wasn't the only person who'd drowned her sorrows in all the wrong ways, that she wasn't the only one who wanted the prettiest girl in town - the one she couldn't have.

It also made her feel closer to Savannah, knowing these were her influences, her teachers, her compatriots, her people. She loved the accents, the warm sweetness of the voices, the same accent she heard in her dreams. It felt like learning a new language and finding new friends.

The record skipped into silence and Brynn got up and turned over the vinyl. She lay on the floor as the notes began to swell and closed her eyes.

———

"You alive?"

Brynn squinted as a lamp suddenly clicked on, flooding the room with light. She hadn't even noticed night falling. Noah gazed down at her, amused.

"I don't really know how to answer that," she confessed.

Noah shrugged out of his winter coat and chucked it across the back of the couch. He slumped down into the plump cushions and kicked off his boots.

"What's up?" he asked. "You look... catatonic."

Brynn returned to staring up at the ceiling. She felt certain that if she were to talk about the car crash trajectory she was on, it would somehow hasten the inevitable. She fought the instinct to keep it all inside. Trying to bury her feelings had only ever ended one way: in the need to drown them all deep in a bottle of whisky. Besides, this was *Noah*. Not only was he her best friend, he was the calmest, most grounded person she'd ever met.

She rolled her head to the side, just enough to meet his eyes.

"You were right," she said glumly. "I have a massive crush on Savannah." For a moment, they just looked at each other, Noah's expression unreadable. Then, "*Ouch! Motherfucker!*" She jerked upright, her arms flying up to ward off the volley of couch cushions being lobbed at her head. "*Noah!* What the fuck?"

"Don't *what the fuck* me, Brynn Marshall!" He ducked as she sat up and flung one back at him. "You know better than this! I fucking *warned* you!"

"I know! I know, okay?! *Argh,* stop assaulting me!" Noah faked another throw and she flinched. "I'm not going to *do* anything about it!" she cried. "I'm not stupid, Jesus!"

"Brynn!" Noah flung up his hands, looking wildly exasperated. "Is she... have you-"

"No!" Brynn refuted. The idea was laughable. "Please. Have you *seen* her? She's a fucking... megastar, right? And about three thousand miles out of my league." Even as she said the words, she felt a pang in her chest. On the one hand: *true.* On the other hand, sometimes the way Savannah looked at her was... confusing.

"Ugh." Noah clapped his hands on the top of his head, slightly disheveling his sleek man bun. "I can't believe I'm saying this, but for fuck's sake, Brynn, have you seen *yourself?* I mean, I know you too well to ever think of you that way anymore," he looked faintly horrified, "but the first time I met you, I nearly crapped my pants at how hot you are."

Brynn snorted with an unexpected burst of laughter at the extremely weird expression on Noah's face.

"I don't know what's happening here, Lyman," she told him. "Are you telling me to go for it with Savannah, or are you hitting on me? Because if talking about crapping your pants is how you go about it, I'm finally starting to understand why you're single."

"Fuck you." Noah shook his head, but she could see the laugh he was holding back. Then he frowned. "Also, I'm doing *neither* of those things. I don't like hearing my best friend deluding herself that anyone is out of her league. But Brynn... *me* and Savannah? We're on kind of thin ice." He stared at her, willing her to get it. "This is the biggest of opportunities," he reminded her, his tone pleading. "And on top of that, I just really want to do everything in my power to back her. She's fucking brilliant, Brynn, but she seems to believe she really needs my help. I'm honestly not sure what I'm achieving other than being her emotional support guitarist, but she... trusts me. I don't know what it would do to her - or to the whole process - if she found out I'd made up this dumb lie, but I don't really want to find out."

Brynn swallowed. When she weighed it that way - Noah's big break, Savannah's comeback, Savannah's trust - her stupid crush didn't even rate mentioning.

"It's cool, Noah," she told him. "I'm going to keep it together. It's just a crush. I mean, it's *Savannah*, and I have eyes, and a pulse...that's all," she berated herself. "But I care about you and... I care about *her*," she reminded them both. She sat up straight. Crushes were just... crushes. There was no rule in the world that said you had to act on them. She'd hold it together and then Savannah would go on back to her rarified world and - with Noah's support - fucking *kill* it, and Brynn would go back to her life. Whatever the fuck that looked like.

"It's not, like... serious, or anything?" Noah looked worried. "I mean, I'm not going to stand in the way of-"

"No!" Brynn scoffed. "Jesus, no. Like I said, I'm not deluded. But speaking of delusional. What in the hell are you talking about, with this whole *emotional support guitarist* spiel?" She glared at him. "I don't know where you get off pretending to be anything other than a goddamn rock star. You," she pointed at his chest, "are integral to this whole thing and *Savannah Grace* knows it. So shut your damn mouth." Brynn grabbed hold of a stray couch cushion warningly, and he rolled his eyes.

"For fuck's sake," he muttered. "How did we both turn into total wrecks out here?"

Chapter Twelve

Savannah took a couple of days to lick her wounds. Before, she had wondered endlessly. Was the way they almost flirted with each other innocent or intentional on Brynn's end? What was going on with that gaze: did Savannah imagine her eyes on her ass or did Brynn just check out her body for real? But after the scene in the band room it was beyond clear to her. She'd writhed against her guitar and sung her sexy heart out and Brynn had... mildly approved?

If Brynn noticed the abashed, reined in Savannah that emerged after the band room, she didn't really show it. Her smiles were still warm, her eye contact still prolonged, but Savannah had stopped reading meaning into it. Her new friend was a warm, intense person. And she couldn't be mad about it. She was relieved even; maybe now she could put this crush aside the way she wanted to.

In the following days, Brynn reported for Tucker duty and Savannah had her coffee ready on arrival. They sipped it together and talked easily enough. It felt pleasant and domesticated and warm. Then she'd leave for the studio, to work on what she and Noah now referred to as the *longing song,* dumping all her angst and thwarted desire there.

The song still refused to take shape but she couldn't let it go; some superstitious part of her believed that unless she could cast her feelings into the perfect net of a song, they might haunt her, unresolved, forever. Plus there was just *something* there, some glimpse into the depths of her soul where she wondered if this song might in fact be her greatest, the song that would be her legacy, if she could only make it manifest. It haunted her dreams, but neither she nor Noah could bring it to fruition no matter how hard they worked at it.

By Thursday, she was feeling antsy.

"I think I'm gonna take a walk," she told Noah mid-afternoon. He looked at her dubiously; the weather had been solidly miserable all day.

"Do you want company?" he asked bravely.

"Oh, no, thank you. I just need to blow out the cobwebs on my own," she said hastily, releasing him from the obligation.

She wrapped herself in her big, navy blue, down jacket and tucked her feet into her boots, before traipsing out toward the lake. Her face and hands took the brunt of the icy wind and she shoved her fingers deep into the pockets for protection and bent her head to stop her eyes from watering.

The lake was pale gray with little white peaks of waves. The trees were now fully denuded of their leaves, adding to the sparse cold of the breeze. To her surprise, she saw Brynn in the distance, coming down the path from the lake towards her. She pushed the stroller ahead of her with the rain cover down to protect Tucker from the elements, but Savannah's jaw dropped when she realized Brynn was still only in her leather jacket.

"What are you doing?" she cried as soon as they were within earshot of each other. Brynn was pale and obviously shivering.

"He's fine," Brynn protested, drawing up closer. "He's in about twelve layers and under the rain cover. If anything, I'm probably cooking him."

"I meant *you.*" Savannah reached out and plucked at the inadequate leather jacket sleeve. "Why on earth don't you have a proper jacket? You must be hypothermic!" She took the stroller from Brynn and hurried them back towards the house, ignoring Brynn's steady complaints that she was *fine.*

"You're not fine," Savannah pointed out once they'd entered the house and she'd ordered Brynn towards the fire. Brynn was still shivering, but looked like she was slowly defrosting, the color coming back into her cheeks. "This is ridiculous; we're going shopping."

Brynn looked mutinous, but Savannah held up her hand.

"I can't lose my governess to consumption," she announced firmly and a small snort escaped the stubborn Californian. "Now, I'm buying you a damn coat and there's nothing you can do about it."

She let Noah know they were done for the day, then piled Tucker and Brynn into the town car - each as dramatic as the other about it - and directed Remy to take them into Burlington. Tucker was safely belted into his carseat and Brynn insisted on sitting in the back with him. Savannah sat in the front and listened to them interact, Tucker chatting excitedly and Brynn inventing little games to keep him entertained.

Savannah had never been especially great at making things fun. She tried hard and they giggled together a lot, but she was by nature serious, and had struggled with grief and solo parenting his whole life. She envied Brynn's natural ability to be goofy with him and worried about how much Tucker would miss that when she was gone.

Her melancholy thoughts kept her company as she gazed out at the mostly bare trees passing by outside the window, but evaporated quickly once Remy dropped them off at Church Street Marketplace. The pretty brick street was open for pedestrians only, so they left the stroller in the car and let Tucker run along beside them. Savannah gripped his hand for safety, but he quickly insisted on holding Brynn's too as they walked down the street. In no time at all, Brynn had him swinging between them, giggling wildly, and Savannah's heart filled. These were the kinds of small pleasures her son had missed out on, with only his sad mama and his nannies to parent him. It warmed her right through to see him so happy.

Vermont was Savannah's favorite place on earth, because aside from the beautiful scenery it held one strong perk. For some reason - intentional ruggedness, reverse snobbery, the long winter, who even knew - Vermont residents did not seem to give one single fuck about celebrities. Oh sure, there were sideways glances and double takes as she walked down the sidewalk, but there were no phones pointed in her direction, no random paparazzi, not even an autograph seeker. It was an incredibly peaceful contrast to the rest of the country. Besides, Savannah knew full well that her celebrity status was finally slipping; she hadn't released an album, toured, or made a television appearance in well over two years. Even the tabloids had lost track of what to say about her.

The day was freezing cold, overcast and the light breeze like a knife. Savannah whisked both her charges into the nearest outdoor store she could find. Brynn gravitated immediately to the sales rack, pulling out a jacket with barely more warmth than her current Californian wardrobe. Savannah had to take her by the arm and physically drag her to the real winter section. She pulled a long winter jacket off the rack, with the highest down rating, and made her try it on. It was similar in the style to the one she herself wore, but in black instead of blue.

The Brynn that met her eye in the wall mirror looked outdoorsy and unbearably cozy. She also looked warm for the first time in weeks.

"We'll take it," Savannah told the hovering sales clerk, who despite her beliefs about Vermont hadn't taken his faintly shocked eyes off her face since they'd entered the store. Brynn pulled at the price tag on the sleeve to look at the figure, a protest already on her lips. Savannah snatched her hand away, carefully tugging the tag loose. "For god's sake, Brynn," she said in a low voice. "I could buy you a house and my accountant would barely notice. Now come and try on some boots."

"Wow," observed Brynn trailing behind her. "Rich *and* bossy." Savannah shot her a look and saw her eyes were twinkling. She had to wrestle her son away from pulling all the boots to the ground and Brynn thankfully behaved like a sensible adult and picked out her own pair of waterproof snow boots. She kept them on her feet and let Savannah grab her some gloves for good measure before handing over her credit card. "My toes had just about dropped off," she admitted.

They exited the store together, all three finally clad properly for the winter. Brynn lifted her head as they stepped into the icy wind. She stopped still in the middle of the street, wrapping her arms around her body, clearly enjoying being weatherproof for a change.

"Thank you," she said, her eyes meeting Savannah's. "I appreciate you, Richard Gere." Savannah spluttered out a laugh. "Can you please buy me an overpriced hot chocolate now?" She gestured to a picturesque cafe across the street.

They sat in the window with their hot chocolates, rich and thick with real chocolate for the adults and sweet and milky for Tucker, who, as per usual, managed to spread the milk far and wide. It was Brynn who gently mopped him up and Savannah watched her long elegant fingers with affection instead of desire for a change.

"Can I ask you a question?" she found herself asking.

"Shoot," replied Brynn easily.

"After what you told me about med school... why on earth are you thinking of going back?"

Brynn looked down at the remains of her hot chocolate and picked up her spoon and stirred.

"Well," she said lightly, concentrating on the foam in the bottom of her cup, "I don't know what else to do. I don't want to fish people out of the sea forever. I need a change. A... well, I mean, a *career* sounds so cheesy, but I just need something that gives me more meaning. Something that pushes my boundaries, makes me grow. What better than the thing that nearly killed me?" she said wryly.

Savannah felt cold inside.

"I don't know," she said. "Pretty much anything? The world is big. There are so many other options. I mean, look at you right now: did you ever think you'd work with children?"

Brynn snorted.

"Childcare or teaching? Heaven forbid. My mother would never speak to me again. I know-" she warded off Savannah's indignation, "she's a horrible snob."

"Does it matter? What she thinks?"

"It's not so much whether it matters, it's more that she's been the voice in my head for so long, it's hard to separate what she wants for me and what I want for myself, you know?"

Savannah didn't know what that would feel like, but she nodded anyway.

"It's just that when I feel lost, med school - being a doctor - it's at least a familiar beacon I can recognize," Brynn said, her tone a little defeated.

"You feel lost?"

Brynn contemplated this for a moment.

"Right now? Here with you and Tucker, in a beautiful place? No. I don't." Savannah smiled at that. "The rest of the time? Absolutely."

"It's hard for me to imagine you feeling lost," she said. "You seem so sure of yourself. Like you're just confident in your skin."

Brynn chuckled.

"Oh honey," she said warmly, "it's all - what's the phrase? Piss and vinegar. Bravado covering up my true self: all insecure and wounded on the inside."

"I don't know." Savannah couldn't stop herself. "I still happen to think you might just be kind of wonderful in there."

"Wonnerful!!!" Tucker echoed.

"See?" Savannah raised an eyebrow.

Brynn shook her head.

"Fools, the pair of you," she said with a smile.

Back outdoors they wandered amongst the early Christmas shoppers, the bare trees all along the street lit up with gold fairy lights under the slowly darkening afternoon sky. Savannah spotted a shop window and asked Brynn to mind Tucker while she slipped inside. When she returned, she held a soft cashmere scarf in a gleaming burned gold.

"Here," she said to Brynn, reaching up to wrap it around her neck and tucking the ends into her jacket. "Now you're perfect." She didn't mean it to sound as sultry as it came out, but it didn't seem to matter. Brynn's gaze glowed into hers, her dark hair and eyes offset by the bright scarf, and everything around them faded to black. They stood smiling at each other under the fairy lights for a moment.

"Oh my god," Brynn breathed, looking up. "It's actually snowing."

Large, soft, fluffy snowflakes drifted lazily from the sky and everywhere people paused to look up, flooding out from the shops to stand in the street and gaze up at the first snow of the winter. Kids ran around them, trying to catch snowflakes on their tongues and Savannah boosted Tucker up onto her hip to see.

"Look!" she told him. "Snow!" He blinked up at it, unimpressed, as the snow hit his nose and eyelashes and pushed his face into her shoulder to hide from it instead. Brynn was gazing around her in wonder. Bright white flakes nestled in her dark hair like jewels.

"It's like a fairytale," she murmured. "I can't believe it's real."

"Snow, it turns out, is in fact real," Savannah agreed, and Brynn huffed.

"No, look-" she insisted. "Look at all of this." She took in the beautiful street, the gold lit trees, the gathering people. "Look at you," she whispered, her eyes soft as she gazed at Savannah and Tucker in

178

her arms. She reached out and brushed snowflakes out of the little boy's dark hair, then gently touched Savannah's own snowy hair, making her want to melt. "It's like a fucking fairytale," she murmured.

Savannah could only stare back, drinking in the sight of Brynn in the falling snow, looking at her with such wonder. *Nothing can happen,* she reminded herself, a twist of pain shooting through the sweetness. *I can't have her.* But she imprinted the moment in her brain all the same, as a postcard to look back on after she'd gone. She took Brynn's hand - they were both wearing woolen gloves so for some reason that seemed to make it okay - and pulled her further into the street. Brynn turned them slowly around in a full circle, smiling up at the sky.

"Oh, what a beautiful family you are!" An older woman standing nearby in an expensive wool coat and oversized beanie leaned in to tell them. "Just gorgeous."

"Oh, we're not-" Brynn started.

"Thank you," Savannah interrupted with a smile.

"Oh, my goodness!" The woman did a double take. "You're her... the singer, Savannah Grace, aren't you? Oh, forgive me, my daughter would never speak to me again if I didn't-" she pulled out her phone. "Would you please?"

"Sure," Savannah smiled, transferring Tucker over to Brynn so she could put her arm around the woman's waist as she took a selfie.

"Thank you," the woman bubbled. "If you don't mind me saying, I'm glad you got rid of that man. You've definitely upgraded there," she nodded approvingly towards Brynn, who was standing with Tucker in her arms, and looking like a very attractive deer in the headlights.

Savannah quickly made her excuses and turned to Brynn, who was now looking steadily away, carefully gazing up at the sky again, blinking at the increasingly heavy snow.

"You're in Vermont for winter," Savannah informed her. "You're about to meet a whole boatload of snow. Shall we get this kid out of the weather, *babe?*"

Brynn's mouth quirked.

"Sure thing, sugartits."

Savannah nearly tripped into the snow, and Brynn laughed out loud.

———

The snow fell fast that night and all into the next day. Savannah skipped the morning in the band room to join Brynn and Tucker outside on the lawn, showing them both how to make snow angels. Tucker was teething - his back molars making him miserable and neither of them had gotten much sleep - but even he cheered up in the face of hoards of adult attention and the novelty of snow.

Brynn caught onto snow quickly too, gleefully and athletically pelting Savannah with snowballs, but Savannah had two years of Vermont winters behind her, so she retaliated by dumping snow down the back of the Californian's jacket. Brynn shrieked and immediately tripped Savannah flat on her back into the snow, laughing uproariously at her shock and making her wait far too long before helping her back to her feet.

With great reluctance, she left them to warm up indoors while she headed in to work with Noah. Her heart was both in the *longing song* this morning and outside it, specifically, hovering somewhere in Church Street where Brynn shone with snowflakes and gazed deep into her eyes.

"This is driving you nuts," observed Noah, after she'd let both her notebook and her guitar slide to the floor and was staring at the walls in some kind of fugue state. He was not wrong.

So when she finally gave in and headed back out for the day, she opened the door of her private wing and wondered momentarily if she had indeed gone mad. A piano was playing, and it was playing the *longing song*. She stopped still, just inside the door, listening, the hair standing up on the back of her neck.

It wasn't a hallucination. Her piano - not the grand one downstairs, but the old one, the first she'd ever owned - was being played in her living room. And the melody was the same one she and Noah had been working on all week. Only this time it was a little slower, like it was being caressed out of the keys. She tiptoed further down the hall before freezing still, as a woman's voice, low and sweet, began to sing the lyrics. It was not quite verbatim, transitioning frequently from words to humming and back again, but the voice was beautiful and the *feeling,* the one she'd tried so hard to capture, was right *there.*

She crept in through the kitchen and hung back, staring, a tremor starting up in her chest. Brynn was at the piano, her back to Savannah, Tucker curled on her lap, nestled between her arms, her hands softly stoking along the ivory. Then the key changed, and the song transitioned exactly where Savannah and Noah had been stalled. The chorus. Brynn's voice arched from low and throaty to aching and beautiful, words Savannah hadn't written falling from her lips.

It's only when I'm alone that you're in my arms
Whenever we're together we're far apart
Every word you say gets written on my heart
Each time I look at you you look away
I see you every... single... day
But I'm in love with your ghost

Savannah's pounding heart was in her throat.

"Wh-what..." she choked out and the music died instantly. "What the fuck, Brynn?"

Chapter Thirteen

"What the *fuck,* Brynn?"

Brynn jumped as if she'd been shot, wrenching her hands back from the keys. Savannah was standing behind her, looking like she'd seen a ghost. Brynn had never been so embarrassed in her whole life.

"Oh my god, I'm sorry-" she was already apologizing, letting Tucker wriggle down and run to his mama. He hugged her legs, but Savannah didn't seem to even notice.

"Mama, mama!" he cried, and she picked him up like an automaton, her eyes never leaving Brynn's. She seemed to be in some kind of shock or a cold rage, Brynn wasn't sure. Perhaps the piano was precious?

"I shouldn't have touched it," Brynn apologized awkwardly. "Tucker was miserable and the music seemed to soothe him, so-"

"Why are you... how did you know that song?" Savannah sounded accusing, and Brynn frowned.

"Uh, you literally never stop singing or humming it?" She pointed out, and Savannah blinked. "You and Noah both. It's prettier when you do it," she admitted. "I'm sorry, it was just stuck in my head. I didn't mean to upset you-"

Tucker started complaining loudly, and Savannah did something Brynn had never, ever seen her do. She carried him over to the far corner, plunked him in an armchair, and switched on the television. Gazing up as the *Bluey* theme song played, Tucker looked like all his Christmases had come at once. Then Savannah walked into the kitchen, pulled out a bottle of red wine and poured herself a very large glass. Brynn got up to come join her, and Savannah stopped her with a strong gesture.

"*No,*" she said firmly. "Stay."

With a gulp, Brynn backed away and sat back down on the piano bench. She'd stepped on something here and she had no idea how to fix it. She felt terrible, not to mention humiliated. Savannah walked back into the room, gripping her wine glass like a lifeline. She walked all the way over to Brynn and took a seat right next to her on the piano bench.

"Play that again," she said. It wasn't a request. Brynn flinched.

"I mean, I don't really know it, I just- "

"*Play* it, please."

Brynn swallowed hard and rested her hands on the old, worn keys. She began to coax out the by now familiar melody.

"You're the singer, you should- "

"Brynn... just sing. Pretend I'm not here," Savannah interrupted. Well, that was pretty much impossible. Brynn could feel the heat of her body almost touching her own as she played. She closed her eyes tightly and did the best she could to sing without straight up dying of embarrassment. She got to the end of the melody she knew and stopped. "Keep going, please," Savannah murmured.

Brynn wanted to shrink into the floor. The words had been sneaking up in her for weeks, until they rang in her head every time she looked at Savannah. To sing them in her presence felt nauseating, especially in her amateur voice. Her voice cracked, but she scrunched her eyes closed even harder, feeling her way back through the lines. She thought of Savannah, in the snow, looking like a stupid, ridiculous goddamn angel from heaven, her golden hair flecked with stars, blue eyes gazing back at her, where just for a moment, Brynn wondered-

The song finished and she left her hands on the keys, her eyes closed, for just a moment longer. Then she slowly opened her eyes and looked at Savannah. She was crying.

Brynn took her hands off the keys fast.

"God, I'm sorry," she flailed. "I'm- "

"Where did that come from?" Savannah asked plainly, as if tears weren't streaming down her cheeks. "That sound, those... words?"

"Oh." Brynn faltered. "Noah called it the *longing song*. I mean... we've all been there, right?" Savannah didn't answer. She nodded, then swiped at her face roughly.

"Do you normally write songs?"

"Oh, god no. It was just sort of in my head? I mean, I write stuff sometimes, like... I don't know, verse. Just words, mostly. But I usually throw it out; it's embarrassing."

"Why didn't you tell me you were a musician?" Savannah's blue gaze was intense and accusatory. Brynn pulled back.

"I mean, I'm not?" she pointed out.

"Except that you very clearly are." Savannah gestured to the piano. Brynn chuckled, trying to break the tension.

"My parents made me learn classical piano all the way from kindergarten through high school. It was supposed to help me become a surgeon, somehow. Look, I can play Chopin!" She smirked and let her hands remember the opening bars of *Nocturne, Opus 27*. Savannah gaped at her for a long moment, then reached out and pulled Brynn's hands off the keys. She didn't let go of Brynn's fingers, pulling them into her lap and squeezing them. It made her pleasantly dizzy.

"And that voice? Is it trained too?"

Brynn snorted with embarrassment.

"I mean, obviously not. I did singing lessons for a bit as a kid, but the teacher didn't keep me on. My mom said he'd told her I didn't have the talent and it wouldn't be worth keeping going with it."

"Someone lied," Savannah said flatly. "Brynn," she squeezed her hand tightly, making her go light-headed again, "your voice is..." she turned to check Tucker was absorbed and far away then met her eyes, "*fucking* stunning."

"Oh." Brynn felt her stomach flip-flop. "Thank you, that's nice of you to say. I'm glad you like it."

"*No.*" Savannah looked at her fiercely. "I'm not nice and I don't *like* it. I'm *blown away* by it. Sing me something else," she said. "Anything at all." She let go of Brynn's fingers and waved her hand impatiently when she hesitated.

Brynn didn't have to think too hard. She placed her hands on the keys and began to sing the song Savannah had played to Tucker to send him off to sleep. After she'd remembered a few lyrics from it and asked Noah the name of the artist, she'd been playing the song non-stop until she'd absorbed it, accidentally learning it by heart. This afternoon she's started tinkering through it on the piano, hoping to soothe Tucker's crankiness. Without realizing it now, she'd closed her eyes again to get through the song and when she opened them, Savannah was sitting completely still, her mouth ajar.

"Do you-" she started, then swallowed audibly. "Do you even know how hard that song is to sing? Brandi Carlile herself practically panics when she sings it live. Your range, Brynn, it's...wild. And you made me *feel* it." She searched her eyes hard, then suddenly stood up, abruptly grabbing her wineglass and taking a big swig.

"I think I'm in some kind of shock." She began to pace back and forward. She turned and pointed at Brynn, her mood unreadable, still almost angry. "I just walked into my own damn living room to discover this incredible musician, singer and songwriter. Why didn't you *say* something? Why aren't you writing with us?"

Brynn flinched.

"I'm not. I'm not any of those things. Not like you or Noah. I'm not the creative *type*, I'm... I've never-" she stuttered.

"I've been working on that song for weeks. Every spare moment. Noah and I, both two experienced professional musicians. And you just completed it without even trying. You made it better than I ever dreamed it could be and you just *got* it. You got the feeling, exactly." Her eyes flooded with tears again. Brynn swallowed.

"Well, I've got all the feelings," she said quietly, far more honestly than she should.

"Stay," said Savannah abruptly, even though Brynn hadn't moved. "Can you...please just *stay*?" Her tone was pleading and Brynn nodded, unsure what she was agreeing to. The singer stared at her for a beat longer, as though assuring herself Brynn wouldn't disappear, then walked over to where Tucker sat. Brynn realized the tired little boy had passed out. Savannah gently scooped him up and left the room.

Brynn got to her feet. She felt hazy and confused and a little resistant. It had been a long day, and now she was exhausted and discombobulated. She didn't like feeling this exposed; honestly, Savannah was acting slightly bananas.

When Savannah returned from putting Tucker to bed, she found Brynn lying on the floor, looking up at the ceiling.

"Get up," she said, tapping her fingers on a battered notebook. "We have work to do."

———

"You're going to have to excuse me," Savannah said about an hour and a half later, "but I think I'm about to have to get quite drunk." Brynn laughed. Savannah was already a little tipsy and frankly Brynn was enjoying it. The singer's limbs were loose and she was alarmingly cute. "Is that okay? I'm not quite coping right now," she said, pointing her finger accusingly at Brynn.

"It's fine," she allowed. "Just know I'll be annoyingly smug in the morning when you're feeling sorry for yourself." Savannah pointed at her again, knocked back the remainder of her wineglass in one big gulp then put it aside.

"You're right. I'm done. This buzz will have to see me through. What the *fuck*, Brynn, how did you - how did we do this? Are you hearing this?"

Brynn was. The *longing song* was complete. They'd sung each other snippets, finished each other's lines, Brynn had played the melody and they'd just now sung it through once from the top, together. Mostly she'd been gobsmacked by how it felt to sing with Savannah, their voices intertwined, singing of desire, of want, of deep, ragged longing. They didn't look at each other as they sang, Brynn couldn't, not yet - maybe not ever. She felt like she was confessing her feelings over and over until it was dizzying. But as for the song? Even an amateur like Brynn could hear it was devastating.

190

"It's... beautiful," she said, inadequately.

Savannah looked her square in the eye.

"It's the best song I've ever written. And it's mostly you. Your first songwriting credit! What the fuck, Brynn?" She shook her head again in disbelief.

"Can we... eat?" Brynn replied, feeling overwhelmed. "I'm starving."

Savannah stared at her, like she couldn't believe the mundanity of Brynn's needs at a time like this.

"Of course," she said after a beat. "You're right. We need fuel."

Brynn groaned.

"You're planning to work me hard all night, aren't you?" She mentally kicked herself a she replayed the sentence back.

Savannah's eyes widened slightly.

"I sure am," she recovered, heading over toward the kitchen. "I guess I better hope that if I feed you first, I won't wear you out too fast." This she threw with a smile over her shoulder, and Brynn tried extremely hard not to blush. She drifted over to take a seat at the kitchen island, watching as Savannah pulled things out of the fridge.

After eating big bowls of Luis's thick rustic tomato soup with oven-warmed bread rolls in more or less companionable silence - both women deep in their own thoughts - Savannah cleared the table and cocked her head back toward the living room.

"Are you coming?" she asked when Brynn stayed where she was. Brynn turned sideways in her chair to face her.

"I don't really know what you want from me," she admitted.

"I want you to write with me," Savannah told her, as if it should be obvious. "We just made something like... magic." She puffed her fingers out like an explosion. "I want to know what else we can do."

"No pressure then," said Brynn, wincing. "I don't really even know how to start."

"Then let's figure it out together," Savannah came over and took her hand, pulling her up from her seat. Brynn let herself be dragged back to the piano.

The hours seemed to disappear. Savannah gave her starters, little things she'd been percolating and Brynn felt out sounds on the keys. Savannah sang the beginnings of lyrics in her ridiculous sexy voice and Brynn let herself feel it, through and through, until she found a response to sing, sometimes teasing, sometimes aching, and watched when her input landed. Savannah's eyes would sometimes widen, sometimes slide closed, a little breath escaping her. Brynn was already worried she was getting a little bit addicted to making Savannah look that way.

Shortly before midnight, she remembered to text Noah so he didn't send out a search party. Looking at her phone she saw a couple of messages, checking in. Feeling oddly guilty, she fired off a reply.

Staying late at Savannah's, all good x

Almost immediately, he responded.

Is that a good idea?

She frowned.

It's not like that. I'm working.

The three little dots appeared, disappeared, then reappeared.

Be careful x

"Is that Noah?" Savannah asked her, from where she'd curled into an armchair, sipping tea, her ever-present notebook on her lap.

"Yeah. Just making sure I'm still alive."

"He's getting a piece of my mind in the morning." Savannah frowned. "He never once mentioned how talented you are."

"Savannah." Brynn dropped her phone and slumped into the other armchair. "You're the only person who thinks this way. I'm actually kind of worried you're having some kind of psychotic break."

Savannah rolled her eyes.

"So you keep saying. What's actually happening is that I get to hear you first, but the whole world is going to collectively lose their minds about you."

"So *you* keep saying." Brynn wasn't about to entertain Savannah's uncharacteristic nonsense speak.

"What does Noah say? I mean, how has he not told you about your voice?"

"I don't think he's ever heard me sing," Brynn mused.

Savannah sat up straight.

"What?"

"I don't really sing around other people. Ever since my mom told me I wasn't talented, I don't know. I don't like people witnessing me sucking at something."

"If I hadn't walked in on you, I'd never have heard you sing?"

"Probably not."

"But Noah's your husband! You don't sing in the car, or the shower or something?"

Brynn did, in fact, sing in the car, and in the shower, when she was in her own home - the one she lived in without Noah - but she couldn't exactly own up to that. Not wanting to lie she just shrugged.

"How long have you been married?"

"Four years," Brynn blurted the first number that came to mind, starting to hate herself. Songwriting felt so close and intimate. Lying to Savannah was feeling increasingly fucked up.

"What was your wedding like?" There was an odd, sad note in Savannah's voice. Brynn guessed she was probably remembering her own wedding. For a moment, she decided to confess all and fuck the consequences. Then she thought of Noah, his care in taking her here, the fact it was a risk he'd taken for her. She thought of his concerns for Savannah herself, if the truth came out now, right in the middle of their writing process. She thought fast.

"My mom wouldn't let me get away without a big, fancy wedding," she said truthfully. "Hundreds of guests, in a giant church, with a ridiculous designer white dress."

She was essentially describing both her siblings' weddings, the opposite of what she herself would ever want if she ever did it. An image flashed in her mind, of Savannah in a field, flowers in her hair, smiling into their kiss, and she felt it like a punch in the guts.

Back in reality, Savannah was nodding, her face glum. She seemed to be elsewhere. Her gaze zeroed in on Brynn's hands.

"You don't wear a ring," she observed. Brynn went cold. She and Noah had never even considered that. She imagined the two of them shopping for cheap rings somewhere to complete the illusion and it felt psychopathic. Who would do that? What were they *doing*? She stared at Savannah, her mouth opening to say, *we are idiots, we are dumb, dumb idiots,* but Savannah already looked glum. To throw out her focus, or maybe even her trust, right in the middle of a writing breakthrough... well, now Brynn understood exactly why Noah didn't want to shatter the process for her.

"We're not really jewellery people," she managed. "Do you want to...?" Brynn asked, gesturing back to the piano. They were so close to finishing another song and she wanted desperately to get out of this train of conversation and get that look off Savannah's face.

"Yes," sighed Savannah, her gaze swinging back to Brynn, a tired smile tracing back onto her features. "I'm not done with you yet."

By two a.m. Brynn was woozy. Savannah was next to her on the piano bench, and she very slowly rested her heavy head on Brynn's shoulder. It took all of her strength not to wrap her arms around her waist and sink into her body.

"Is that Tucker?" Brynn pricked up her ears and Savannah jumped up, dashing off out of the room to the sound of her son's cries.

Brynn quietly tinkled the keys a moment longer. They'd completed the love song and - to Brynn's shock and Savannah's glee - almost completed a whole-ass *second* song. This one felt less of a love song and more of an internal battle, Savannah's lines a pull and Brynn's the push, all temptation and guilt. They seemed to have an unspoken agreement not to speak about what they were writing, instead just letting the songs be.

The minutes ticked away and Brynn began to realize Savannah probably wasn't coming back. Just to be sure, she tiptoed down to Tucker's room, only to find it empty. The door to the master suite was open and in the low glow of the nightlight, she could just make out Savannah lying in bed holding her sleeping son. Just as she was about to creep away, Savannah said her name in a low tone and gestured for her to come in.

She approached the bed, to say goodnight, feeling impossibly drawn to the cozy scene. Tucker was curled into his mama, fast asleep and assured by her presence. Savannah lay facing the door, half covered by the soft cushy blankets. Brynn couldn't remember ever feeling this tired.

"Stay," Savannah murmured softly, her eyes barely flickering open, and Brynn wanted to crumble into her arms. "We'll write again in the morning." Oh my god, the woman was mad. Brynn carefully sat on the edge of the bed, trying to figure out how to explain this to her without waking the child. God, the bed was soft. "Please don't go," came the whisper again, and as she watched, Savannah's eyes drifted closed. She'd stay until they were both asleep and slip out. She rested her head on the pillow, just for a moment.

———

There was something warm and heavy on her chest. It constricted her breathing slightly, but she was so sleepy she didn't mind. Then the weight jumped up and smashed back down and Brynn's eyes flew open, her breath crushed out with an *oof!*

Tucker looked down at her with delight from his perch, straddling her sternum.

"Wake!" he shouted. Brynn groaned and scrunched her eyes closed. She heard a chuckle and turned her head to see Savannah sitting on top of the bed a few feet away, looking far too bright and amused for her liking.

"Whassatime?" Brynn croaked, blinking blearily in the soft lamplight. As far as she could tell, it was still dark outside. Savannah picked up her phone to check.

"Six-fifteen," she announced. "What a sleep-in." She smiled wryly, hugging one knee and wriggling her bare toes on top of the comforter. "Tucker's been dying to wake you since five."

This explained why Savannah and Tucker were both fresh and fully dressed while Brynn felt like a barely alive human. She grumbled exhaustedly and tried to hide her face in the pillow.

"Hug!" Tucker bounced again and then squished down her body to give her a full body embrace with his hands around the back of her neck. Grunting, she rolled on her side so he was no longer crushing her and cuddled him into her side, resting her face in his soft curls. He giggled happily.

"There's coffee on the bedside," Savannah told her, "if that helps at all." Brynn cracked open her right eye to see the other woman was watching them with a soft expression. Slowly, she disentangled herself from the squirming toddler and sat up, running her hand ineffectually through her bed hair. "Thought that might rouse you." Savannah beamed, getting up off the bed. Her jeans were tight and Brynn wasn't alert enough to avert her eyes from the sight just yet.

"How are you so cheerful?" Brynn reached for the coffee after a beat and settled back against the bedhead, taking a sip. "We got essentially no sleep last night."

"Yes, but you were amazing." Savannah threw a coy smile over her shoulder on her way out the door, happily exiting before she witnessed Brynn choke on her coffee. "At song-writing, I mean," she called on her way down the hallway, and Brynn could envisage the pleased smirk on her face.

"Your mama," she pointed at Tucker, "is trouble."

Savannah had toasted bagels, orange juice, and more coffee on the way when Brynn padded into the kitchen. She was humming something.

"What's that tune?" Brynn asked, snatching a bagel. Savannah looked up.

"Another song." She met Brynn's eyes. "It just came to me right now. We'll work it out in the band room this morning."

A strange pang hit her as she thought of Savannah taking her fledgling songs back to Noah. Her face must have fallen, because Savannah stepped closer to her.

"You know I mean with you, don't you? You're not getting out of it this lightly. Not now I know what you can do."

"What about Tucker?" Brynn asked, trying not to show exactly how excited and nervous she was to keep trying to flex this new song-writing muscle in the light of day.

"It's Take Your Kid to Work Day," Savannah announced perkily. She was in the sunniest mood Brynn had ever witnessed, flitting around the kitchen, piling up their plates and refilling their coffee. Brynn had to force herself to stand stock still because she kept getting the urge to smack Savannah's extremely tempting ass in those jeans, or press her back against the bench and kiss her, as if waking up in the same bed had somehow made them lovers.

They made it through breakfast without incident and all three of them tumbled into the band room where Noah was sitting on a stool, strumming a guitar and looking worried.

"Good *morning*," he said, his tone loaded as he looked up at Brynn's tired features and yesterday's clothes.

"You," announced Savannah in lieu of a greeting, "have no idea what's coming for you this morning." She shepherded Tucker over into a corner and set him up with a pile of toys, a children's story playing on her phone. While she fussed around him, Brynn and Noah had a complicated conversation with their eyes. Noah's eyebrows were raised, his stare hard, while Brynn shook her head and held up her hands.

Savannah extricated herself and joined them.

"I have no idea how to explain this," she said, taking Brynn's hand in her own and Noah's eyebrows nearly shot off the top of his head, "so I think we're just going to show you."

She towed Brynn toward the piano in the corner and made her sit. Brynn had never felt more like a performing monkey in her life. She stared down at the keys, exhausted from the night before, and already worried she was going to embarrass herself and let everyone down. Then Savannah laid a gentle hand on her shoulder and made her look up.

"You okay?" she whispered.

Brynn searched her eyes. What she saw in them made her feel eight feet tall. She nodded and raised her hands to the keys. And then they both began to sing.

When the final notes faded out, Brynn turned to look at Noah. He was her best friend. He'd be sure to tell her if Savannah was simply deranged. Before she could glimpse his face, he spun on his heel, turning his back and walking away. Her heart sank. And then he turned around.

Chapter Fourteen

Noah seemed to have imploded. His face was doing all kinds of contortions. He kept turning around in circles like a broken spinning top. Savannah told him the story of walking in and hearing her, and thinking she'd lost her own mind. The two of them got so hyped up at the craziness and the potential of it all, they almost forgot Brynn existed.

Finally, she spoke up.

"So she's not crazy?" she interrupted. "You think I have a good voice too?"

Noah looked at her for a long moment. Then he took a leaf out of Brynn's own playbook and made a show of his legs giving way as he crumpled to the floor. Brynn snorted as he did a dying-man crawl to where she still sat at the piano bench and clutched at her ankles.

"You're a fucking *god*," he said and she laughed and kicked him away. He hauled himself up and hugged her to his chest tightly. "You're out of this world," he told her. "What," he looked up at Savannah, who was watching him hold her with unreadable eyes, "are we going to do with her?"

"I mean, first of all, I guess I'm going to have to get a new nanny," she said with an exasperated laugh.

———

The next few weeks passed in a strange kind of haze for Brynn. She'd never in her life been so immersed in something; music seemed to just pour through the three of them like a river. It took time, of course. For all Savannah's hype and excitement, Brynn was *not* a professional musician. She had two patient and invested teachers though, coaxing her through both her lack of technical skills and confidence.

Noah and Savannah, for their part, never seemed to lose their unflagging enthusiasm towards her contributions. She'd catch them staring at her, at each other, in a way that filled her all the way up to the brim. Whatever had been sparking between Savannah and Noah or between Savannah and Brynn seemed to blaze into fire when all three of them were in the room, like a match to gasoline.

The three of them worked and wrote in all kinds of combinations: Noah and Savannah working out the knots of a riff, Brynn and Noah arguing over piano arrangements and verse, Savannah and Brynn squeezed next to each on the sofa so they could scrawl their own lines in the same notebook.

Tucker lived wild: the band room his playroom, the playroom their band room. He ran between all three adults for hugs and games and meals. He passed out for naps to the sounds of the piano playing; Brynn had never seen him so happy.

Suddenly, her days were filled to the brim. She and Noah ate breakfast together most mornings in their own suite - quick bowls of cereal or a plate of toast, washed down with coffee - anything just to get on with the real day. They'd meet Savannah and Tucker in the band room before it even hit eight o'clock. Usually Brynn and Noah got there first and Brynn would always feel a prickle up her spine as Savannah walked in and smiled at her, like every part of her night and early morning was just waiting for this moment. The moment where everything would begin, all over again.

Was it songwriting, or was it Savannah? Brynn couldn't tell which came first, only that the two were wrapped up together for her, in a tangle of desire and creativity, like nothing she'd ever known before. She craved the moment a song began to come together, when a new line or a key change made the whole thing click. And she equally craved the joy blooming in Savannah's eyes, the sound of their voices mingling, the heat of her body next to hers on the piano bench.

They spent hours and hours together every day. It was the four of them, but the addition of Noah and Tucker didn't detract from the intimacy. In a way, it almost enhanced it. Sometimes they felt like a family. Other times, the way Savannah caught her eye and something private passed between them - despite the presence of others - felt so intense it was almost sacred.

Often the two of them would end up going for long walks during Tucker's nap time, sometimes swapping song lyrics, other times just walking side by side through the hushed snowy woods, talking at length or in sweet silence. It felt on the tip of her tongue at all times: *Am I crazy? Do you feel this?*

Any barriers or safeguards Brynn had held onto to protect her heart were pulverized into dust as the two of them scribbled their innermost thoughts together on the page. She ached with her intense and growing feelings, and the ache turned into music.

Her conversation with Noah loomed large in her mind at all times. She remembered him asking if her feelings for Savannah were serious, and she knew that if he asked her now, her answer would be very different. But every time she thought about telling him the truth - that her heart was on the line now - she thought of the fall-out. She imagined exploding the sweet bubble they were all in - losing the trust of Noah or Savannah, or most likely both - and she shrank from the conversation, just a little longer.

Would it really change anything, anyway? Yeah, sometimes the way Savannah looked at her made her wonder, but she also knew there was a strong likelihood she was tumbling head over heels for an oblivious straight woman and amplifying every glance in her mind with desperate, wishful thinking.

Embarrassingly, Brynn had caved into an urge she'd been fighting for far too long and straight up googled the woman she was so wrapped up in. Amongst a thousand photos of Savannah looking gorgeous - all the way from an adorably fresh-faced twenty-three-year-old and growing increasingly sexy with every year - she saw at least half of them featured a staggeringly good-looking man - tall, handsome, strong - the heat between him and Savannah jumping right off the screen. There was not a thing in any bio that she could see that hinted anything other than clear heterosexuality.

The closest she came were a couple of articles where Savannah professed her strong support for the LGBTQI+ community, of her band who included an out gay man and an out trans woman. This, as per the articles, was adamantly not the norm in country music, Coral in particular being singled out as if she were some kind of novelty instead of just a talented musician and successful artist. But as for Savannah herself? Just *husband husband husband* was all Brynn could see. That and a clear reminder of Savannah's staggering success that only reminded her of the immense gap between their worlds. She wished she hadn't looked at all.

She reminded herself that what was important right now was the music. Not the feelings she had all but given up fighting. The music that just seemed to grow and grow, every time they were in the same space as each other. *That* was what she needed to focus on.

Brynn had never felt so at home. She found she loved playing piano again, letting the years of rigid formal training slip away like sand, instead feeling out pure *sound*. She quickly went from extremely uncomfortable singing in front of her friends to hearing her own voice just as another instrument in a room full of instruments. When she viewed it that way, discomfort no longer felt applicable. And there was something incredible about joining her voices with theirs. It felt as close to holy as Brynn had ever experienced.

As for everything else? The heartbreak she was clearly headed for? Brynn wondered if that was the price she'd just have to suffer; losing her heart to gain her voice.

They ate dinner together every night now, either after Savannah had settled Tucker for the evening, or sometimes all four together, if it was early and they were all starving. Brynn realized she lived for the evenings when Savannah lingered by the fireside, her sweet boy in bed, a glass of wine in her hand, and the three of them talked about anything and everything.

Thanksgiving passed by in a quick blaze of warmth, the three of them only barely remembering to press pause on their creative endeavours long enough to eat themselves into food comas. That night after dinner, as they took turns around the table saying what they were most grateful for, every single answer was the same: *the music*. The music, and each other.

Brynn was grateful for Noah's presence for another reason; without him there, she knew she could all too easily cave in to her desire to reach out and touch Savannah as she laughed and glowed before her in the firelight. Thank god she didn't drink any more; her willpower was shaky enough with her inhibitions intact.

"You know, Christmas is only three weeks away," Savannah remarked as another evening passed, all three of them sprawled around on couches. The living room was increasingly cozy from the heat of the log fire; three minutes ago Savannah had arched her spine luxuriously as she'd peeled off her sweater and Brynn *still* couldn't drag her eyes off all that silky skin.

"Whaaaaat?" drawled Noah, deep in his third whisky now he'd finally acquired a taste for it.

"I honestly forgot to even mention it. Time seems to have lost all meaning." Savannah smiled. "But I won't hold you captive. Surely the two of you have family that will be missing you this time of year."

Brynn and Noah looked at each other. Brynn was not a fan of family Christmases, and Noah's parents were relatively indifferent to the holiday. They both shrugged.

"Nah," said Noah simply. "But wait, what are your plans?"

"I'm just staying here," said Savannah. "Tucker and I usually have a quiet one."

"You don't go to family?" Brynn asked curiously. Savannah almost never spoke of them, she realized.

"No."

It sounded like a closed subject.

"So... will you have us?" Noah looked at her.

"Please?" Brynn added, with a probably unnecessary flutter of her eyelashes.

Savannah straight up glowed.

———

And then, that Sunday at dinner, Chester had news.

"The label called," he said, in the tones of an announcement. He had flown in that evening but so far hadn't said a word about the state of affairs in Nashville. There were clinks as everyone put down their forks and turned to look at him. He looked them all in the eye, then addressed Savannah. "They love the demos."

"Yes!" Noah fist pumped.

Savannah let her head fall back to stare at the ceiling, some kind of complicated emotion crossing her face.

"They're getting antsy though," Chester warned. "They want you to lay down a couple of studio tracks, ASAP," he continued.

A silence fell around the table and everyone looked to Savannah.

"The band?" she asked.

"I managed to find a couple of clear days in between everyone's day jobs, tour dates and the holidays," he replied, then paused, looking worried, "...starting this Thursday."

"Well," Savannah breathed in. "Looks like we're going to Nashville."

Chapter Fifteen

"Jesus," whispered Brynn as they stepped out the doors of a small wing of the Burlington airport to find a private jet waiting. Noah grinned and nudged her.

"What did you expect?" he asked, readjusting his duffel bag on his shoulder and hunching against the icy wind.

"I mean, I'd had hopes for first class tickets..." she trailed off. Savannah and Tucker were ten steps ahead of them, climbing the stairs into the jet like they did it all the time, which, Brynn suddenly realized, they probably did.

Onboard, everything was spacious, pale earth tones, and big white comfortable armchair sized seats. Savannah met her eye and smiled from her seat at the front of the plane as she passed by. Brynn smiled back, somewhat queasily.

After a couple of months of just the four of them hanging out in the woods, Brynn - despite her brief foray into Google, and the reality of the incredible house they were in - had almost entirely lost sight of the fact that she was in the presence of a huge star. It was impossible to hold that in her mind when Savannah was always just *there,* in jeans and bare feet, the tired mama of a small child, making everyone coffees, being sweet, casual, and very vulnerably human. It side-swiped her to remember she was also the *private jet owner* level of famous.

A sinking feeling entered her gut as she took her seat a little further down the plane. It was ridiculous imagining any hope of her feelings being returned when Savannah Grace had the whole damn world at her feet. Brynn, on the other hand? Brynn didn't even have an apart-ment over her head or a plan for her life. She felt slightly sick.

Noah took a seat facing her own. "You good?" He frowned as he caught her expression.

"Yeah." She nodded. "This is the smallest damn plane I've ever flown on. Just getting my rich people legs on," she told him, trying for levity.

He grinned.

"I think you'll find you catch on quite nicely." He pulled his headphones on and gazed out the window, his eyelids already starting to droop.

The jet took off smoothly. Almost as soon as they reached their cruising height and Brynn felt comfortable to cautiously take off her seatbelt, Tucker came flying and landed in her lap.

"Hey buddy!" Brynn hugged him as he bounced on her.

"Apparently we couldn't wait any longer to come see you." Savannah smiled down at her. A small air bump hit and Savannah grabbed for the seat back to stabilize herself.

"Not to worry," came the pilot's voice, "just a little pocket of turbulence on the way; we'll be out of it in a minute or two."

Brynn wrapped her arms tightly around Tucker. Another bump hit and the plane wobbled.

"Oops." Savannah swayed and smiled at her son, who didn't seem at all fazed.

"You couldn't afford a bigger plane?" Brynn complained, her free hand gripping tightly to the armrest.

Savannah laughed.

"You're not a good flyer?" The plane did a small hop that made Brynn scrunch her eyes shut and suddenly Savannah was squeezing herself into the seat next to her and Tucker. The seat was big and roomy, but not *that* roomy. The whole sides of their bodies were pressed together and Savannah's hand was laid on her knee, in a way Brynn supposed was meant to feel reassuring. The turbulence eased, or perhaps it didn't. Brynn was only aware of two things: the heat of Savannah's body pressed against hers and her own internal turbulence.

Between them, Savannah and Tucker kept up a light, playful conversation, clearly aimed at keeping her distracted. It worked. By the time Tucker grew restless, pulling his mama up to go look out the window across the aisle, Brynn had relaxed. Savannah squeezed her shoulder and smiled back at her as she left and all of Brynn felt like jelly. This woman, the one with the world at her feet, still took the time to care for her. To treat her like she was the only person who mattered.

"*Fuck,*" she muttered. "Fuck! Noah!" She kicked at his foot until he groaned and sat up straight, pulling off his headphones and rubbing his eyes.

"What?"

"We have to tell her." Brynn leaned forward, her stomach tight as she prepared to plead with him. "We have to tell Savannah the truth about us."

Noah blanched.

"Brynn, no," he said urgently. "She's going to hate us."

"I don't care," she said. "I can't keep this up any more. She deserves to know. I *need* her to know."

Noah stared at her.

"Brynn." His voice was flat and as close to angry as Noah ever got. "I *told* you not to catch feelings for her. I went out on a limb for you... I'm risking a lot here to help you out. I don't want to fuck up all we've worked for just because you can't keep it in your pants. We're going to get through this, and we're going to be professionals, and then we're going to *leave*."

"Noah." Her voice was hoarse. "I don't want to screw anything up for you. But I can't lie to her anymore. And you can't either. It was one thing when we didn't even know her, but now we both care about her. I know it's a risk, but she deserves better. You know she does."

He looked her in the eyes for a long minute. Then he sighed.

"Shit. This is serious for you, isn't it?" He kept his voice low, glancing over to where Savannah knelt at the window, smiling down at her son who was chatting and pointing at the clouds.

"I'm... I'm beyond falling for her," Brynn admitted softly. "I *know* - I don't have a chance with her, but- "

"Brynn," sighed Noah. "You absolutely have a chance with her."

Brynn bit her lip, staring down at her hands. She wished she shared Noah's conviction. For all she knew, Savannah was in fact what she appeared on paper to be: a straight woman who enjoyed teasing another woman who she also thought was straight. Maybe what Brynn was interpreting as crackling chemistry and a deeper connection between them was all coming from her own desperate *want*.

But, a little voice nagged at her, the way Savannah occasionally blushed around her, the immensely soft look in her eyes she got sometimes? The way she let her gaze drill into Brynn when she sang that unbearably sexy song, rocking her hips forward just so? There was always just enough hope to keep her tantalized.

"Look," Noah said, spreading out his hands. "You're right. Of course you're right. We should tell her. But not today, okay? She's about to head into the studio to record her first solo tracks. She's pumped. She's happy. She's in the right headspace. We can't fuck with that. As soon as recording is over, if you're sure you want to go ahead with it, we'll sit her down and tell her," he promised. "Or, I guess maybe you should tell her yourself, depending on what you're planning to say." He raised his eyebrows.

Brynn considered it. The idea of keeping the stupid pretense up of being Noah's wife for even an hour longer seemed terrible. Not when Savannah was being so... *Savannah* all the time. She thought of her teasing glance and flirty remarks in the bedroom the morning after they'd first written together. Of Savannah offering warmth and courage, her body pressed up against Brynn's only minutes ago. *Did*

Brynn have a chance? She was terrified to find out, but she desperately wanted the freedom to make a move if she could ever get up the courage.

But Noah was right. Brynn would never forgive herself if the confession went badly and the news threw Savannah off her game right when she needed to be focused.

"Okay," she agreed. "Not until after the recording is over."

At that moment Savannah looked over and caught her eye and smiled. Brynn's breath caught.

"Oh dude," Noah whispered. "You're so fucked."

———

From the airport, a limo whisked them away to Savannah's compound on the outskirts of Nashville. The grounds that awaited them made Vermont look practically quaint in comparison. Brynn squinted at the expansive, lush green surrounds and the huge modern mansion, a glamorous feat of polished concrete and spectacular plate glass.

Discreet staff arrived, as if by magic, transporting baggage and guitar cases and ushering Brynn and Noah to their very own extensive guesthouse beyond the gigantic blue swimming pool. Nashville was significantly less freezing than Vermont. What would have felt like a solid winter to her once was practically balmy in comparison to where they'd been. Brynn was almost sad to leave her new winter jacket in the closet.

For the next three days, she barely saw Savannah at all. Savannah had abruptly dismissed her from her nannying duties for a couple of days, with the instruction just to relax and enjoy exploring Nashville. Noah took her downtown, where they ate amazing ribs in famous restaurants, drank - or didn't drink - in famous bars and listened to up-and-comers playing on every damn street corner. Brynn had never in her life even thought about the city before and she felt half in love with it already. Almost everyone spoke in the same soft, woozy accent Savannah had, and that in itself was almost enough to make her want to move in for good.

But also... the *music*. She'd walk into a bar and get blown away by someone on a tiny stage with more talent in their pinky finger than Brynn could hope for in her entire life, and they were just the opening act. She felt like an unbearable pretender taking out the little blue notebook Savannah had given her, but still, lyrics kept pouring out of her. Some wall that had held back a dam within her had burst, and there was no going back.

She missed having a piano, but she strummed things out sufficiently enough on Noah's guitar, sitting on the side of the bed back in the guesthouse and staring out at the pool. She recorded snippets on her phone just to stop them escaping. She wanted, as always, to share them with Savannah, but other than brief text messages checking in, it was like she'd disappeared entirely. Tomorrow was Thursday, and Brynn expected she'd be even less available, now the band was arriving and recording was set to begin.

"Knock knock." As if her longing were a prayer, all of a sudden Savannah was standing right there at the bedroom door. Brynn scrambled to her feet, dislodging the guitar.

"Hey!" she said, drinking her in. It felt unbelievably good to lay eyes on her after days apart. Savannah's hair was scooped up in a messy bun, a soft black designer sweater exposed her delicate collarbones and half a bare shoulder, while tight ripped black jeans showed tiny glimpses of skin. A rose gold necklace with a tiny matching pendant glistened in the hollow of her throat. She wore makeup for the first time in Brynn's presence, her eyeliner a perfect winged cat-eye. She looked beautiful, sophisticated and rock'n'roll all at once. So this was Nashville Savannah. Brynn wanted to touch the nape of her neck, tuck back a golden strand of her hair, thread a finger through the belt loop of her jeans, anything, everything to casually and explicitly claim her.

"Brynn." Savannah was shaking her head. "Are you for real?" Brynn blinked, suddenly worried her desires were screamingly obvious. "You play guitar as well?" She was looking over at the discarded guitar on the bed.

"Oh, barely," she denied. "Just enough."

"I'm starting to realize that you understate pretty much everything about yourself," Savannah leaned against the doorframe, "so I suspect you're actually pretty good at that, too."

"I'm afraid I'm going to disappoint you there." Brynn shifted her weight on each foot, shaking out her aching muscles. She'd been writing longer than she'd thought.

"Nothing about you has ever disappointed me," Savannah said softly, and Brynn swallowed.

"I've-" she started and then stopped herself. She'd been about to tell Savannah she'd *missed* her. "How have you been?" she asked instead.

"Good," Savannah said. "Busy," she exhaled. Then she straightened. "Which reminds me, I've got someone I want you to meet."

Brynn followed her out to the living room. She didn't remember the sun setting, but Savannah must have turned the lights on on her way through. Standing looking out toward the pool was a skinny white person with short lavender hair, mostly shaved on one side but flopping over the top in a bright swoop. They turned and Brynn saw fine features, a strong, angular jaw, olive skin and big golden-brown eyes fixed on her with a bright, interested gaze.

"This is Lane," Savannah introduced them. "Lane, Brynn." Brynn reached out to shake their hand. "Are you guys okay to share your pronouns?"

"Oh, sure," Brynn said. "I'm she/her."

"They/them." Lane gave her a little backward '*sup* nod.

That was easy and seamless. Brynn couldn't help but tuck into her brain this new knowledge of the clear comfort and ease Savannah had with queer etiquette. But then again, it was just *human* etiquette, after all, and she was always an immaculate hostess.

"Lane is our new nanny," Savannah explained to her.

Brynn blanched.

"*What?* You're firing me? But I love looking after Tucker." She was shocked by the level of sadness she felt.

"You can still hang out with Tucker whenever you want," Savannah reassured her with a smile. "And you're not being *fired*. We're just going to be so busy recording the next few days that I'm going to need childcare. And then after that, well... I don't know how much more time we're going to have left." Brynn swallowed hard at that as Savannah looked away, her eyes unreadable. She turned back to Brynn and shrugged. "I want as much songwriting time with you as possible."

"At least let me look after him while you record," Brynn tried. "He doesn't need to be left with a stranger - no offense." She glanced at Lane, who shrugged. "Not if I'm here."

"Brynn." Savannah cocked her head, a trace of concern in her eyes. "You know you're recording with us, don't you?"

"Me?" Brynn was so shocked, she looked behind her as if a different Brynn might be standing there.

Savannah bit back a smile.

"We're doing the *longing song* this week. It's written as a duet. Who did you think was going to be singing it with me?"

"Someone professional?" Brynn's voice cracked. Savannah stepped closer to her.

"I don't want to sing it with anyone other than you," she murmured, looking up into her eyes. Brynn swallowed. A long moment passed as they gazed at each other.

"Okay," she croaked. She was far from sure, but she couldn't say anything other than yes when Savannah was looking at her that way. "Are you sure they're qualified, though?" she whispered, making one last attempt to wriggle out of it. "They look about twelve." She glanced over at Lane.

Savannah laughed.

"I told you Brynn would want to vet you too," she told Lane. "Can you reassure her, please?"

Lane grinned.

"I've been a nanny for three years and I'm studying to be a kindergarten teacher. *Oh,*" they looked up at Savannah's gesture, "and my first job was as a kid's swimming instructor so I'm CPR qualified."

Brynn looked hard at them. "Okay, young grasshopper," she said. "I guess I can hand on the baton."

————

That night, the band arrived and everyone gathered for a big reunion, pre-recording dinner party. The atmosphere was raucous, the band reunited, their stories and fond ribbing all tumbling over each other. Savannah sparkled in the middle of it - the other band members all seemed to take great joy in teasing her - and she absorbed it all with happiness. She was also a great host, making sure Noah and Brynn were included, throwing to them both regularly, her eyes flicking up to Brynn's enough times to induce a warm glow in her chest.

Conversation turned to the planned recording session. Everyone seemed beyond excited to record the new tracks. The way they talked it was as if they were about to embark on a new odyssey, one that included epic tours on the road, press junkets, parties and *music music music*, and all of it hinged on recording one hell of an album.

"I'm not remotely nervous anymore," declared Savannah after her second glass of red wine. "I have my secret weapons, after all." She nodded over at Noah and Brynn. "Everything we write turns to gold." There was a raucous cheer at that. "And wait until you hear her *sing*." She pointed at Brynn. "You've only heard a crappy demo. To be in the room with her: it's going to blow your minds."

"Oh, please, no-" Brynn did not want to be hyped, but she was drowned out as everyone raised their glasses and toasted to her noisily. She went scarlet. Savannah caught her eye and gave her a private, pretty smirk, and raised her glass one more time.

Brynn lay awake, staring at the ceiling for what felt like the entire night. In the morning, they were all chauffeured to Music Row and into a vast recording studio. It was a sign of the massive clout Savannah's name held that space had been made for the sessions at such short notice. Some lesser known artist would have been turfed out to make way for them today, and that knowledge hung over Brynn as she traipsed in behind the band. This was the big leagues. The fact that she was here at all was bordering on an absurd joke.

The first song to be recorded was *Make Me Wonder*. Neither Noah nor Brynn were required for the recording, but after being introduced to Greta McCafferty, Savannah's producer, they were both allowed into the sound room to observe through the glass. Greta was intimidating as hell, a six foot white woman with a shaved head and hipster spectacles, and who, despite her surname, was extremely German. Brynn could not tell when she was joking or when she was serious because her tone stayed flat and her eyes unflinching. Mostly she just tried to stay out of her way, which was easy enough, since while Noah got a solid nod from her, Greta ignored Brynn's existence in light of the nobody she was.

The band all took their places behind the glass with supreme comfort and confidence. Savannah stood in the middle of the room, an extremely large and overly technical looking microphone extending down before her. She looked at each member of her band to share a smile. Brynn remembered, all of a sudden, the nervous woman in the band room the first time she'd heard ever her sing. Savannah had a hell of a lot riding on these songs. Today, though, she looked transformed.

She stepped up to the mic, her face and body in profile to the sound room. For once, she held no instrument. The band was supplemented with additional recording musicians and right now it was all about her voice. Brynn had heard the demo of course, had even played and sung through the song herself, but when Travis stroked the first notes on his electric guitar, Jed strummed the bass and Coral kicked in the beat, she got chills. Savannah sang the opening lines and she found herself grabbing hold of Noah's hand. They gripped onto each other and listened as the string section joined in and the whole thing soared.

The song was nothing like the stripped back sound of Savannah and Noah, and yet Brynn could still remember the feeling of hearing it for the first time. She watched Savannah, no longer barefoot in a basement in Vermont, but belting out the high notes in the very epicenter of Nashville. She looked beautiful and powerful and very much in her element.

The final notes faded and everyone broke into a cheer. It sounded incredible.

Greta pressed a button and spoke into her mic. "Again," was her only comment. Without even blinking, the band took their places again. Savannah smiled into her mic. They played the track another twenty-three times.

———

The following morning, Brynn stood with her back against the wall in the recording studio hallway. For the second night in a row, she'd barely slept. She'd barely eaten breakfast. There was no room in her stomach since her pounding heart seemed to have taken up her whole body. Today was the *longing song*. Brynn's turn had arrived to walk through those doors and perform in that hallowed, big league, professional recording studio, in front of Savannah, the band, the session musicians, the sound techs, Chester and the terrifying Greta.

Coral appeared beside her.

"You got this?" she asked.

Brynn could hardly turn her head to look at her, she was so focussed on not throwing up.

"Mm-hmm," she replied, the sound barely exiting her lips. Her fingers felt a little numb. She felt Coral examine her more closely.

"Are you sure?" she asked. "Cos... you know who that is, right?" She gestured to a tall white guy with an elaborate belt buckle around his middle who'd just entered the sound room. Brynn shook her head mutely. "Bryce Campbell," Coral told her. "Head of the label." Brynn let her head fall back, staring up at the ceiling, trying to slow her breath. Trying to remember how to breathe at all.

All of a sudden, the studio door flung open, and Savannah's voice rang out, calling them in. Brynn moved on wobbly legs into the bright room, feeling like she was having an out-of-body experience. The band were all taking their places, while Savannah was over by the piano, giving the session musician some last-minute instructions. Brynn had been told ahead of time they were going to use a professional pianist to play her composition and she'd agreed in theory that it would be better for her just to have one job to focus on. Now, however, looking around at the room, all she wanted was a piano to stare down at. She felt insanely exposed as she took her place at the mic the sound tech directed her to.

To her horror, she realized the sound room was visible. From the other side she had imagined it was one-way glass. She could clearly see Greta's serious face at the decks and more than one guy in a suit - including the fucking *head of the label* - standing behind her. She began to sweat. Her entire hands went numb. Savannah stepped up to her own mic about six feet away and looked up. She did a double take.

"Brynn," she said. "You got this. We got this. Okay?"

Brynn nodded dumbly. Her thoughts were whirling. Savannah's boss watching, the real musicians all around her, all about to see her unmasked as a fraud, Tucker's new nanny replacing her, her mother's voice telling her she had no talent, lying to Savannah, *falling* for Savannah, potentially ruining everything in the entire world for Savannah. Before she knew it, the opening chords were playing and Savannah was singing the first lines. The drum beat kicked in. Brynn missed her cue. The music petered out.

"Okay, let's go again," came Greta's stern voice over the speaker.

"Don't worry about it, Brynn," Savannah reassured her, her voice calm. "Let's start it again, nice and easy."

This time, she made her cue, but her voice died two words in. She was struggling to breathe. The music cut out again.

"Are we doing this or what?" Greta's disembodied voice snapped. Brynn saw her behind the glass, looking irritated. The label head had his arms folded across his chest. Brynn's stomach lurched.

"*Give her a fucking minute.*" Savannah whirled around and glared at the sound room. Brynn had never seen her look this furious. "She's new at this, but she is worth every second of your time."

When silence rang out from the sound room, Savannah stepped back from her mic and walked all the way over to Brynn.

"I'm sorry," Brynn croaked quietly. "I can't do this. I'm sorry. I should go-" she turned, dying to get out of there, but Savannah grabbed both her cold numb hands.

"No," Savannah stopped her, her voice soft. "Listen to me. Forget them," she gestured toward the sound room, the band, the other musicians. "It's just me and you."

She stepped in closer until she was all Brynn could see. Her blue eyes were steady and her lips slightly parted. Her hair was up in some kind of complicated braided knot and soft loose strands fell around her face. Up this close, Brynn could see the gray swirls in her blue irises and the faint lines around her eyes. She was still holding both Brynn's hands, but now she pulled them up and back towards her, so they were resting on her upper chest, clasped between her own warm fingers until Brynn could feel the steady rise and fall of her breath.

"Just me and you," Savannah repeated. "We're going to share this mic, and I'm going to sing to you and you're going to sing to me. That's all."

Brynn sucked in short, hard breaths for a moment and Savannah kept holding her hands, breathing slowly with her.

"Is it always so hot in here?" Brynn managed after half a minute, her voice sounding almost normal.

"Take your shirt off?" Savannah suggested, and Brynn gaped at her. Savannah giggled at her response and gestured at her until Brynn saw the logic and unbuttoned her lucky plaid shirt and flung it aside, so she stood there in just her dark green tank top. "Can we get the lights down a bit?" Savannah called out and the blazing lights dimmed to a warm glow. "Better?" she asked, her eyes flickering down Brynn's body, her bare shoulders and arms. Brynn nodded. "Mm. You *look* better." Savannah let just enough innuendo into her voice that Brynn realized she was being flirted into feeling better.

"Greta, I'm on the mic with Brynn," Savannah's voice broached no argument, her eyes still on Brynn's. There was a pause.

"Okay. We might need some extra vocals later, but we can work with that."

Savannah took her hand and pulled her back to the mic. It was fixed down from the ceiling to sit at Brynn's head height. Savannah stood on the other side, maybe six inches away, their height difference causing her to look up, just slightly.

"Brynn," she whispered again, her gaze soft. "Just you and me."

Brynn nodded. She kept her eyes on Savannah's as the piano began.

"*You make my knees weak,*" Savannah's low warm vocal began, her eyes never leaving Brynn's. "*You steal all my sleep,*" her honeyed voice nearly moaned.

"Your lips keep me captive," Brynn's vocal was husky but at least in key, *"your eyes lock the doors."* The words escaped her like a confession. *"Your body could free me,"* Savannah took a ragged breath as Brynn's voice climbed *"why aren't I yours?"*

"You draw me in closer," Savannah's eyes had gotten wide, *"but I can't make you stay. You render me breathless and just walk away."* Her chest was rising and falling erratically, but her voice stayed miraculously steady. They'd never looked each other in the eye while singing this song and right now it was becoming adamantly clear why. Singing this song to Savannah felt like getting naked with her.

"If I could just touch you," Brynn begged, *"I'd heal all your pain. I'd make you my own, again and again."*

Savannah's pupils dilated and she gave Brynn a look of such ferocious, unmistakable want that Brynn gasped into the chorus as the drumbeat competed with her pounding heart.

"It's only when I'm alone that you're in my arms." Her voice cracked with emotion, while Savannah's soared. The chorus climbed and their voices intertwined. Brynn had no control over her facial expression anymore, helpless to the want and fear bleeding out absolutely everywhere, while Savannah's eyes reflected hunger and pain of such magnitude that Brynn's every breath was ragged. When they reached the final line of the chorus, Brynn felt with aching clarity that it wasn't just the song; this was real, for both of them. It had to be. *"I'm in love with your ghost,"* she almost whispered, feeling tears stinging her eyes as she gazed at Savannah, whose neck was flushed a mottled red with emotion.

The rest of the song passed in a shocked blur as their gazes locked, finally utterly bare. Their eyes practically dared the other to look away, the lyrics almost beside the point as their mutual revelation unraveled. And then, there was silence. Savannah dropped back down on her heels, and only then did Brynn realize she'd sung the whole song on her tiptoes. They were both breathing like they'd run a marathon. For a solid fifteen seconds, you could have heard a pin drop.

"Fuck *me*," breathed Coral and the entire room erupted in furious applause, the band getting to their feet, quickly followed by the session musicians: a standing ovation accompanied by whistles and exclamations. Brynn dragged her eyes from Savannah's to see that Greta was standing up too, her face close to the glass, stock still and staring, while the label execs joined in the applause, giving each other high-fives and back-slaps. The voice came over the speaker.

"That was perfect," Greta said. "Now let's go again."

Chapter Sixteen

Brynn paced around the darkened guesthouse. Noah was out having drinks with the band. She'd been invited along too, but she had far too much adrenaline to shake out to sit there sober all night, around a bunch of drunk musicians. Savannah was nowhere to be seen. After they'd sung to each other for three long, intense, intimate takes, Greta had set them free and Savannah had all but fled the room. Brynn had turned, wanting urgently to follow her, but the band had surrounded her, showering her with praise and questions and the label head had wanted to shake her hand. When she'd finally escaped, Savannah had disappeared.

She'd glimpsed her briefly at dinner, everyone rowdy with the glow of a successful day of recording, Savannah down the other end of the table from her, avoiding eye contact with her entirely. Then she'd pulled the vanishing act again. Brynn told herself to give her space. Recording would be over in another two days, after which they'd return to Vermont to finish writing, and there, Brynn could finally tell her the truth - all of it - and see where they landed.

Which was how she'd ended up wearing holes in the floor of the guesthouse. She was arguing herself in circles. Savannah had feelings for her; Savannah just had feelings for the music. Savannah wanted her; Savannah would be horrified to know that Brynn was straight up falling in love with her. She was on the brink of being the happiest she'd ever imagined being; she was on the brink of heartbreak.

She was staring out over the pool toward the darkened main house when a light snapped on on the ground floor. Brynn saw a silhouette clearly illuminated in the distant window. Savannah was not only home, she was right there, in the kitchen, just off the main living room. Without pausing to reconsider, Brynn pushed her way out the door, past the pool, and into the house. By the time she got there, Savannah was just switching off the light and turning to go. She gasped when Brynn entered the room.

"Oh god," she said, "you gave me a fright." She put the bottle of water back down on the counter and straightened her spine. Her eyes were slightly wide. "What are you doing here?"

Brynn swallowed. She didn't have a good answer for that. She drifted closer, her eyes adjusting to the dim room. Savannah was dressed for bed in a small pale cotton camisole and tiny matching shorts. Her hair was loose and her shoulders, her arms and her thighs were all bare. Brynn had never seen so much of her skin and she was... not coping.

"I need to talk to you," she said, trying to make her voice firmer than she felt. Savannah stood still.

"I don't think that's a good idea." She raised her chin and looked away. Brynn took a step closer.

"Why not?"

Savannah kept her gaze averted, so Brynn stepped closer again, trying to get her to meet her eye. Savannah stepped back until her back hit the counter and then, finally, with nowhere further to go, she looked up.

"I think you know why," she whispered.

Brynn's heart began to pound. It was an admission, but it wasn't enough.

"I need to hear you say it." She stopped just in front of her, almost close enough to touch. Savannah bit her lip and didn't speak, her blue eyes almost begging. "Why can't I be here?" Brynn pressed.

"It's late," Savannah tried, her gaze darting sideways.

"So?"

"I..." her voice petered out. Her chest rose and fell the same way it had in the studio, and Brynn found herself drawn unstoppably closer, stepping all the way in until their bodies were only inches apart.

"Savannah," she whispered, putting her hands lightly on the counter, effectively trapping her between them, nowhere left to go but where they'd been headed the whole time. "Did you write that song about me?"

"Don't *ask* me that," Savannah implored, her tone desperate and her eyes down; Brynn's heartbeat pounded in her ears. That was a yes if she'd ever heard one.

"Because I wrote it about you," she admitted quietly, and the ragged breath that escaped Savannah made her body clench, low and tight.

"We can't do this," Savannah whispered, finally raising her head, her pupils blown, the tops of her breasts rising and falling rapidly above her camisole. Brynn could see the shape of her nipples, hard beneath the thin cotton. She felt like she was going to come out of her own skin if she didn't touch her.

"I can't *not*," she murmured, her voice cracking as she crossed the last inch between them to brush her lips just barely against Savannah's own. She made herself pull back, almost in shock at what she'd just managed to do, and the moment hung suspended, both women breathing hard, their mouths close.

Her hand came up to cup Savannah's body, sliding around her rib cage just below her left breast. She could feel the heat of Savannah's skin through the thin cotton.

"Your heart is *pounding*," she whispered, desire and awe thrumming through her. Savannah whimpered, head tilting up, lips parting and this time Brynn kissed her fully, their mouths open and soft, then desperate and heated, Savannah licking into her mouth like she would die if she didn't taste her.

Brynn pressed in all the way in against the soft curves of the body she'd been longing for, her nerve endings lit up like wildfire at the sensation of Savannah, almost bare, in her arms. She ran her hands up Savannah's neck and into her hair, holding her still to kiss her more firmly, feeling her limbs tremble and the moan that escaped the other woman made her feel savage. Savannah kissed like Brynn was the oxygen she needed to breathe. Her breasts were pushed up against Brynn's, her hips fitting up against her own, the kiss ferociously hot, the sound of her gasp inflaming Brynn, when all of a sudden Savannah wrenched away and pushed her back.

"*Fuck*," Savannah cried out, wiping her mouth with her hand. "Oh god. I didn't mean to-" she looked frantic.

"Savannah-"

"Let me go." Savannah shied away from her outstretched hands, and Brynn dropped them instantly. "This isn't *happening*."

"Wait-" she tried, but Savannah had already fled.

———

After a restless night, burning and tossing between the sheets, Savannah ignoring her texts and calls, Brynn was desperate to get into the studio. At least there Savannah couldn't hide from her. She'd already resolved she'd have to change the plan and tell Savannah the truth as soon as possible. Even if it knocked her off her stride, she couldn't possibly be more distressed by the news than she'd looked by what she thought to be their illicit kiss last night.

But it turned out that Savannah could and would avoid her. She finally arrived only moments before the session was due to start, striding in the door only after all the musicians had taken their places. Noah was playing lead guitar for the track, but Brynn was so far surplus to requirement, so was positioned just out of Greta's way. Savannah stepped up to the mic, her game face on, impossibly beautiful in a short white shift dress and her hair loose. She did not once look toward the sound room.

The guitar squealed, and Savannah straight up wailed into the microphone. *Beware the Fury.* Her small body arched back as her crackling voice climbed into a fierce roar. Brynn was both slightly terrified and extremely turned on. She remembered the ragged gasps and hungry whimpers Savannah had breathed into her the night before and her body burned. The drums smashed, and the guitars shrieked and Savannah was one with a wall of sound. At the end of the song, she was panting for breath and everyone screamed in shocked delight. The queen of country music had just smashed her crown like it was a guitar at a death metal concert.

Brynn was relieved to see Savannah break into a smile at the reception to her song, picking up a bottle of water and taking a long drink. Her eyes skated past the sound room and she flinched, just barely, when she saw Brynn, before turning away for the next take.

When they broke for lunch, Savannah of course disappeared, and Brynn hung around trying to figure out where the hell she was hiding. She sent her a couple of text messages, both congratulating her on the track and asking her to please, please talk. There was no reply. With a sigh, she returned to the sound room, only for Greta to all but push her back out.

"You're not required for the rest of the day," she said shortly. "Savannah sent a car for you and said to give you the day off." Brynn felt mutinous, but Greta didn't budge. She frowned out the car window all the way back to the compound, worry and annoyance battling it out within her. If Savannah would just *talk* to her...

Hanging around the guesthouse made her feel like she was going to climb out of her skin. Going into the main house felt like an invasion of Savannah's boundaries, even though the band were all bunking there. Then she heard a bright, cheerful voice and a splash. Heading out to the living room, she looked out over the pool to see Tucker excitedly bobbing about in Lane's arms. She rushed for her swimsuit.

"Hey buddy!" she called out, stepping out onto the stone tiles.

"Fwimming!" Tucker yelled out gleefully, and Brynn did a dive bomb into the deep end. The water was warm despite the coolness of the air. She swam up and scooped him up away from his new nanny and back into her arms and whirled him around while he giggled. Lane relinquished him with a grin and swam around them in a circle.

They all splashed and played and goofed around and for a moment Brynn felt like everything in the world was going to be okay.

"Alright, kiddo, you're shivering." Lane pulled themself out of the water and grabbed a couple of towels. Brynn reluctantly handed the toddler back up.

"That's because someone thought a mid-winter swim was a good idea," she couldn't help admonishing as Lane stripped him of his wet bathing suit and wrapped him in a towel like a burrito.

"You weren't complaining a minute ago," Lane gave her an easygoing shrug.

"I was just making sure you weren't going to let him drown," she dug back, hauling herself out of the pool.

"Are you always this much of an ass- I mean, this much of a jerk?" Lane asked curiously. "Or just when you're fighting with Savannah?"

Brynn's jaw dropped. She wrapped her towel around her body.

"What makes you think I'm fighting with her?"

"Because she looked like hell this morning and you're back here on your own, moping around. Considering the vibes between you two, it's pretty easy to work out."

"I'm not moping," Brynn denied. "And there's no vibes. Stay out of the grownups' business."

"You're so condescending," Lane's grin was irrepressible as they towel-dried Tucker's hair affectionately. "First up, I'm twenty-two. Secondly, you're being suspiciously defensive."

"Are you always this annoying?"

"Totally! Want to come eat pizza with us?"

"Yeah!" enthused Tucker.

Savannah's Nashville chef was even better than Luis, Brynn realized, as the three of them mopped up melted mozzarella with perfect crusts in the sheltered courtyard beyond the formal dining room.

The view was expansive; rolling green hills and what looked like pedigree horses galloping through neatly fenced paddocks, then the private vineyard she'd long suspected. Noah was right: you really could acclimatize to this kind of wealth very damn easily. She remembered her old tiny apartment back in LA with a pang. She didn't need this kind of lifestyle, but wow, it would be nice to know she had a roof of her own to call home. Her medical textbook had been abandoned when she'd started songwriting, and now she was even more confused about her future plans.

"So what's the deal with you and Savannah, anyway?" Lane asked her when Tucker had jumped off their lap to run his greasy hands and little toy digger through the small stones edging the gardens.

"You do not give up, do you?"

"Nope," they said easily. "Come on, spill, I'm discreet."

"You can't use the word *spill* and then claim discretion," Brynn informed them. "It's really none of your business."

Lane was quiet for a while as they watched Tucker play.

"You're in love with her, though, right?"

"Honestly, what would it take to make you shut up about this already?" Despite all odds, Brynn found herself smiling.

"That's a yes."

"I'm not talking to you anymore."

"I hope you work it out," Lane mused. "She's *so* fucking hot. And you're fucking hot. It's like the law of physics that two people that hot should be together."

Brynn shook her head.

"Such deep wisdom, in one so young," she said drily. "And you're not allowed to think of her as hot; she's your boss."

"And off limits," Lane said slyly. "Clearly."

Brynn laughed out loud.

"You're not a threat, young grasshopper," she informed them. Instead of being offended, Lane looked delighted.

"You're *so* into her, they could see it from space."

"Fuck off, kid." Brynn elbowed them. "Can we go watch some Disney or something now?"

———

The afternoon spent with Lane and Tucker had settled her for a while, but back in the guesthouse as the sun began to fade, the stony silence of her phone made her stomach clench all over again. When it suddenly rang, she nearly fell off the couch to answer it.

"Mom?" she frowned as she picked it up. "Is everything okay?"

"I was just going to ask you that," her mother's patrician voice came down the line. "You haven't answered my call in months."

"Oh," she scrunched up her nose, feeling guilty. "I'm sorry. I thought I told you I was going away with Noah for a while."

"Yes darling, but for *months*? Honestly, Brynn, I know lifeguarding isn't any kind of serious career, but what are you thinking, just swanning off like that? I feel like you're not taking your own life seriously and it's becoming concerning to me."

Brynn felt a headache coming on.

"I'm..." she paused. What *was* she even doing with her life? "I'm recording some music, Mom."

Predictably, the phone went dead silent.

"Music," her mother spoke the word in the same tone she'd say *dog shit*.

"Yes, mom, music," she said firmly. "I'm in Nashville with Savannah Grace, recording, and-"

"Savannah Grace?" her mom said. "Oh my goodness! How's she doing?"

"Uh... ...what?"

"How is she doing? That dreadful man, I don't know how he could do such a thing. And her baby was so young," she tutted.

"Mom? How... do you know this stuff?"

"Unfortunately, everyone knows this 'stuff', Brynn. I don't live under a rock."

"I thought you always said reading celebrity gossip was for idiots and troglodytes."

"It's not celebrity *gossip*," her mom sounded offended. "It's Savannah Grace. She's a supreme talent. I can care about art and artists without being a troglodyte, thank you very much."

Brynn pulled the phone away from her ear and stared at it for a moment.

"I didn't realize you liked country music," she said, unsure what had happened to her mother and who this woman was.

"Well then, there's a lot you don't know about me," her mother huffed.

"I'm singing with her," Brynn said, uncertain of where the ground was anymore. "I'm on the album."

Her mother was silent for a long time.

"Well," she said, "that is rather surprising. Then again, you always did have a lovely voice, I suppose."

Brynn jumped to her feet.

"What are you *talking* about?"

"You had voice lessons, remember?" her mother replied. "That odious man. He wanted to put you on stages, take you on as some kind of protégé. He practically begged us. It was really quite improper."

"Mom," Brynn gripped the phone so tightly her fingers went white. "You told me Mr Abram didn't want me as a student. You *told* me that he said I wasn't talented."

"I did no such thing," her mother denied.

"You absolutely did. You made me think I *sucked* at singing."

Her mother was silent.

"You were so excited about it," she said after a long moment had passed. "Too excited. The lessons, the practice, the talk about shows and rehearsals, it was eating into the time you needed for serious things, like study. You were getting sidetracked from your path."

"You don't get to decide what my path is!" Brynn exploded. "*I* get to decide that, mom, *me*. You crushed me. You made me think I was no good at the one thing that actually might be special about me."

"Brynn-"

"Mom, when I dropped out of med school, it was because I tried to kill myself." The words were out before she could stop them. Her mother sucked in a shocked breath. "Then I drank myself into a stupor every day for a year. Because I thought the only path that was possible was the one *you'd* picked for me."

"Brynn, darling, *no*, oh my god. You always wanted to be a doctor-"

"I *never* did. You just wouldn't accept anything else and I wanted-" she was crying now, clutching the phone and sobbing. "I just wanted you to love me."

"Baby girl," her mother's voice broke. "I have *always* loved you. I just want you to have a good life."

"Then let me decide what that looks like, mom." Brynn wiped her eyes, trying to still her shuddering breath.

"But- no, okay, let me finish darling - music? That isn't a steady option, or something you can make a solid life from-"

"Some people do." Brynn rolled her eyes as she took in her opulent surroundings.

"Yes, some very exceptional people do, that is true."

"Is it so hard to think I might be exceptional?" Brynn whispered, speaking out her deepest fear. "After all," she said, "Savannah thinks I am."

She thought of the look on Greta's face after the recording session, of the standing ovation from the band. She thought of Noah looking at her like his head might explode; of Savannah grabbing for her like Brynn might evaporate in front of her like a hallucination; Savannah telling everyone in the studio that Brynn was worth the wait; Savannah's eyes when Brynn sang. She straightened her spine and took a breath. Maybe she did have a plan for her life after all.

"Well darling, that is a very high compliment indeed," her mother acknowledged. "I look forward to seeing what you can achieve."

"Yeah... me too, mom."

———

That night at dinner, Brynn was determined not to let Savannah slip away on her without at least the promise of a conversation. If the singer needed time, that was okay by Brynn, but she at least wanted her to have all the relevant information.

As the band and all the other musicians and industry friends of Savannah all piled into the dining room, Brynn expertly finagled her way to a seat that was not exactly opposite Savannah, but not far off it either. She saw the singer wince slightly as she found herself in close proximity to Brynn, which hurt more than she cared to admit. But like the star she was, Savannah turned on her practiced charm and sparkled and shone throughout the dinner, all the while carefully ensuring to avoid Brynn's eyes.

The dinner was exuberant as always and the talk on everyone's tongues was the new album and tracks. There were many toasts to Savannah's beyond rock'n'roll performance today and excited exclamations about what it would sound like belted out live in a sold-out stadium.

"And then this one over here," Travis pointed his finger at Brynn. Every head swiveled her way and glasses were raised again. "What a fucking *voice*. You're a dark horse, Brynn, why the hell did you keep that on the down low?"

Brynn hesitated. This was normally the point Savannah would jump in, glowing and telling and retelling the story of her discovery, but tonight Savannah stayed quiet.

"I, uh, I never really sang much in front of anyone," Brynn told them again. "I didn't think my voice was anything all that special to tell you the truth."

"That's *insane*." Coral shook her head. "I've played in a lot of bands, heard a hell of a lot of music… and there's just nothing like you." She waved her wine glass around in emphasis.

"Why didn't *you* point it out?" Travis swiveled to look over at Noah, who was sitting next to her. "You're her husband, and presumably you have ears," he ribbed him.

Noah scratched the back of his neck. He'd been taking a lot of heat for this the last few days.

"I mean, she doesn't really sing around me," he said truthfully. "I swear to god, I didn't know," he gave her a rueful glance.

"Never?" asked Coral incredulously. "How the hell long have you been married?"

"Just over a year," Noah said awkwardly. All of a sudden Savannah looked up at him, a strange expression on her face. She looked from him to Brynn and all the blood rushed from Brynn's face.

"A year?" Savannah spoke up for the first time. "I thought it was four years."

Noah looked confused and then worried.

"Oh yeah." He tried for a chuckle. "It only feels like a year, you know how it is."

Coral made an *aww* noise that might have been sarcastic, but Savannah just looked bewildered. She looked at Brynn and saw the panic in her face and a muscle ticked in her jaw.

"What was your wedding like?" Her voice sounded tight. Brynn tipped over her soda water, both in panic and in the hopes of a diversion, but sensing the odd tension, no one looked away.

"Savannah-" she tried, but the singer ignored her. Noah seemed uncomfortable but somewhat oblivious, already blurting out his story even as Brynn whacked him with her elbow, trying to get him to stop.

"Ouch!" he exclaimed. "It was pretty casual," he went on quickly, "just the two of us and a couple of friends, down on the beach. We're pretty down-low, you know."

Savannah stared at him, then at Brynn, heat rushing up her neck.

"Why are you lying?" Her voice was small. "What's even happening right now?"

"Savannah," Brynn said urgently, "can I please talk to you outside?"

"No." Savannah looked at her like she was a total stranger. "You can tell me what the hell is going on right now. Please."

"Oh man," Noah said, his face crumpling. "I fucked up. I'm sorry-" he looked horrified. This was his worst nightmare, and it was happening right there in front of everyone. "Savannah, it's my fault. It was my idea. We're not married at all, Brynn and I," he hesitated as the singer shook her head in confusion, her blue eyes incredulous. "We're not even together," he continued, and Savannah's mouth fell open. The bewildered look in her eyes as she turned her head to stare at her made Brynn feel sick.

"Why?" Savannah managed. "Why would you lie about something like that?" She was asking Brynn, but as she opened her mouth to speak, Noah jumped in nervously.

"It was my idea," he said again. "Brynn's my best friend. I wanted her to come with me - she was having a crappy time of it - and I just figured you wouldn't question it if I said I wanted to bring my wife."

Savannah blinked slowly.

"You *lied* so she could come with you? Why wouldn't you have just told me you wanted to bring a friend?"

"I don't know, it seems stupid now," admitted Noah. "I'm so sorry. You just... we didn't know you, you were like this random celebrity, we weren't yet-"

"Friends," Savannah said flatly. "I wasn't your friend; I was just a rich, dumb celebrity that came with lots of perks, right?"

"*No-*" Noah and Brynn protested in unison, each of them burning with shame. The room was silent, the rest of the table hanging on every word, electrified. Savannah kept staring with that terrible look in her eyes.

"And then - stupid me - I thought we actually did become friends, but you just kept lying to me?"

"Brynn wanted to tell you," Noah fell on his sword. "I stopped her. I didn't want to fuck up the recording session, so I stopped her, I'm sorry."

"Brynn is a goddamned adult," Savannah snapped. She took a breath and visibly tried to settle herself, looking around at the large audience. "You know what? Sorry, everyone, please, go on without me," she stood up. "I'm just not really in the mood and it's been a long day. Excuse me." She strode out from the room. Brynn shoved her way back from the table and raced after her.

Chapter Seventeen

"Savannah!" Brynn tried to slow her exit from the house, but Savannah didn't even pause. Brynn caught the door on the backswing as Savannah flung it wide open and kept striding out into the dark. "I'm not going to leave you alone until you let me explain," she warned her, following as Savannah stormed across the dimly lit courtyard.

"Oh, you're going to explain?" Savannah whirled around and stared at her. "Please, explain it to me, Brynn. Tell me how you lied to me, made me think that you were completely unavailable and yet you *flirted* with me every single day. Explain it to me, Brynn! Make it make sense."

"I'm *sorry*." Brynn knew better than to reach for her. She stood as close as she dared, hating herself for the look on Savannah's face. "I should have done everything differently from the very beginning. I didn't know that I was going to..." she sucked in a breath and threw herself over the cliff edge she'd been teetering on, "...fall in love with you." Her voice cracked.

Savannah looked like she'd been slapped.

"You... lied to me." Her voice was small. "You lied to me and for no good reason. I trusted you with my *child*." Brynn's chest felt like it was about to cave in. "You made me think I could never have you, that I was standing on the outside looking in, never able to have the person I desperately wanted because she was already taken. Maybe that doesn't mean anything to you, but I have been alone for a long time, and I have *suffered,* Brynn."

Tears were coursing down her cheeks. She looked small. Brynn broke at the sight and reached out for her, but Savannah dodged her hands.

"And then, last night... for you, I betrayed myself, my morals. For you, I proved that I'm no better than *Cole.*" She threw up her hands, before hugging herself tightly as if trying to physically keep herself from falling apart, her eyes aching. "When I could have just been... kissing you. Without compromising myself. All of that, for *what?* That's not *love,* Brynn, that's just fucking with my head."

"Savannah." She felt sick. Her hands started shaking. "All of that, it's *true.* I've behaved like the biggest asshole on the planet. I have fucked this up, so spectacularly and I am so desperately sorry. But it was just that one stupid lie. Everything else between us was the truth. You have to understand that," she begged. "I have *never* felt this way about anyone... it blindsided me. And if I'd honestly been able to believe that maybe you felt for me what I felt for you I would have told you everything, in a heartbeat."

"Is that the real problem here, Brynn?" Savannah's voice was low. "That you don't believe you're lovable? Because if you wanted to know, all you had to do was look at me. I am a *mess* for you and you refused to see the blindingly obvious."

They both fell silent. Brynn had no comeback for the truth. Finally, she raised her eyes.

"I regret every bit of pain I've caused you, more than I can stand," her voice broke. "But Savannah, hear me when I say that I will do anything, whatever it takes, however *long* it takes, to show you that you can trust me."

"*I was married to an addict!*" Savannah all but shouted at her. Her cheeks were wet with tears. "To a serial cheater, okay, Brynn? I have been lied to by the person who was supposed to love me, more times than I've taken breath."

"And I am not *Cole!*" Brynn's voice was vehement. "I mean it, Savannah. Whatever you need from me to make this right, I will do it."

"I want you to leave," Savannah's voice was low and unbearably sad. "I want you to go, tonight, and I don't ever want to see you again."

"Savannah, please-"

"You asked me what I need and I'm telling you."

Brynn's heart cracked in two. She gazed at Savannah, both of them crying. All she wanted in the entire world was to pull her into her arms, stroke her hair, soothe her tears, promise her she'd fix everything, to kiss her, hold her tight and never let her go.

"Okay," she whispered instead.

Savannah nodded, her eyes on Brynn's face. Then she turned on her heel and walked away.

———

Brynn was packing when Noah came in. He took one look at her face and crumpled.

"I'm so sorry, Brynn," he said shamefacedly, sinking down on the bed next to her open suitcase. "I should have listened to you."

"No." She looked at her feet. "Savannah was right. I made my own choices. And you only ever did this for me. I'm sorry I'm such a fuckup."

"You're not a fuckup." Noah nudged her foot with his own. "Or rather, we both are, it turns out." He stood up and walked over toward the wardrobe before pulling out his own suitcase.

"Noah, no," she protested. "I'll be okay. You don't have to leave as well."

"Actually," he announced, "I do. Savannah kicked me out too."

Brynn didn't think anything could make her feel worse, but now she found it could.

"I'm so sorry," she whispered, sitting down on the bed with a thump. He looked up.

"Don't look like that." He gave her a wry smile. "We did what we came for. We wrote some killer tracks with a killer artist. It might have all imploded in a trash fire at the end," he shrugged, "but those songs are forever."

She nodded slowly, thinking about that for a moment. Their songs - theirs and Savannah's - out there for the rest of time. She didn't know if that made it better or worse. She stood up again and started to pack. She drifted around the guesthouse, picking up shirts and socks. As she lifted up her sweater, a tiny yellow digger fell out and her heart broke all over again.

———

Her knock was tentative, but it didn't take long for the upstairs suite's door to swing open. Savannah stood there, her hair mussed and her eyes red. She looked confused and then outraged.

"I thought I told you-"

"Please let me say goodbye to him," Brynn was trying but failing not to weep. Savannah stared at her, speechless.

"He's asleep," she said finally. "I don't want you upsetting him."

"I won't," she promised. "I won't wake him. Please don't make me leave without saying goodbye." She stared fiercely down at the digger clutched between her fingers. Savannah followed her eyes and then nodded briefly.

Brynn followed the woman she loved and couldn't have, down the hall to the room of the child she loved and couldn't have. Savannah opened the door and peeked in at her sleeping son.

"Be quick," was all she said. "Please don't be here when I come back." Her shoulders were tense as she walked across the hall and closed the door behind her with a solid click.

Brynn crept in. Tucker was asleep on his side. In the dim light she could see the soft tangle of his curly hair, the snub of his tiny nose, his sweet pout. His little pudgy hand lay relaxed beside him. She stood there, wishing she could snuggle him up, trying to comprehend that she was never going to see him again.

"Goodbye, little buddy," she whispered into the darkness, placing his digger beside his pillow where he'd see it when he woke up. "I'll... miss you. Be good for your mama."

She walked to the doorway where she just barely held back a sob, then carefully closed his bedroom door.

She turned as she heard a movement behind her and saw Lane step out from their own bedroom partway down the hall. They were wearing Shrek-themed flannel pajama pants and a baggy black t-shirt and had never looked so young. Their face regarded her with absolute sorrow.

Brynn paused as she passed their room.

"I fucked it up," she confirmed quietly as Lane watched her.

"Damn," they said with proper feeling. "I thought so."

"Look after him?" She gestured towards Tucker's room. "And her, please."

Lane straightened their spine, raised their chin and looked at her seriously.

"I will. Don't worry." Then they paused. "Are we hugging friends yet?

Brynn cry-laughed and nodded and Lane wrapped their arms around her and gave her a fierce hug. And then, she left.

Chapter Eighteen

Is this rock bottom... again? Brynn wondered, as she woke up, her whole body stiff from Noah's couch, late the next morning. And if so, what part? The part where she had ended up right where she'd started - in LA, without a home or job - or the part where she'd met what could have been the love of her life and ruined it before they'd even gotten started?

She felt a savage pain that winded her every time she thought of the night before, of everything she'd just lost. Lost on her own, by her own actions, choices and inactions. She winced at the savagely bright sunshine coming through the living room window and pulled the blanket over her head.

The days only got worse from there. Noah had reassured her she could stay as long as she needed, but his passive aggressive housemate Dan and his obnoxious girlfriend clearly felt otherwise. The crash to earth from living in Nashville's biggest star's guesthouse to existing out of a suitcase in a cramped, hostile living room was one Brynn experienced with a thump.

She'd schlepped out to the beach at the end of her first week to ask for her old job back, but her position had been filled and there was a backlog of young, eager, wannabe lifeguards across the city beaches. She needed a Plan B, and fast.

After a day of pounding the pavement with her resume, Brynn came home feeling very small. Her mom had called, "just to check in," she said, and Brynn couldn't bear to tell her she'd already screwed up her start in the music business that she'd only just talked up. She pretended her battery was about to die and hung up quickly, hating herself.

When she arrived back at Noah's, he was out living whatever version of landing on his feet he always seemed to manage. There was a note from Dan asking her to please start storing her suitcase in Noah's room and not to keep her cosmetics case in the bathroom as the 'clutter' was 'killing the vibe'. She sighed and sat down on the damn couch, the one that was her bed only as long as no one wanted to stay up late watching Netflix.

On the coffee table, a newly opened bottle of whisky had appeared. Brynn stared at it. She thought about all her failures, all her other rock bottoms and concluded that this one really was, in fact, the worst. This time, she was a fully formed, fully independent adult. The world had been handed to her on a silver platter: a beautiful, talented, strong woman who wanted her, an adorable child who made her world light up, and a golden spectacular chance at a music career. And she'd dropped it *all*. Her hand reached out for the bottle. Honestly, at this point, who cared what she did?

In her mind's eye she saw Savannah's face, heard her shouting, *I was married to an addict!* She dropped her hand like it had been burned and sank back on the couch, overcome with shame. She, of all people, knew exactly what Savannah had gone through. She couldn't face the idea that she, too, could burn through people, through supports, through love, through family and choose obliteration. She hated the idea that Savannah had immediately linked Brynn's stupid lie to her ex-husband. They shared a disease, but they were *not* the same.

Right then, her phone rang. It was a FaceTime request from an unknown number. For a second, she thought to decline the call. Then a wild thought that maybe, somehow, Savannah- she pressed accept.

"Well, you look like shit," Lane looked delighted, and an unexpected laugh bubbled up from Brynn's chest.

"Why does that make you so happy?"

"Oh, it doesn't! Sorry. *So* sorry you're sad and wallowing and miserable, that your hair is flat and you're wearing what looks like pajamas in the middle of the afternoon."

"Wow, thanks," Brynn looked at them incredulously. "I'm really feeling your sympathy."

"Well, don't," Lane retorted sharply. "I'm fucking mad at you," they added. Brynn could see the outside wall of Savannah's winter home behind them, a brilliant Vermont winter sky overhead. "She's beyond miserable." Lane shook their head in clear disapproval, obviously referencing their boss. "You weren't kidding when you said you fucked up. What the hell did you *do?*"

"Does it matter?" Brynn felt incredibly tired. "She doesn't want to see me ever again. And tell me, why is this your business, exactly?"

"Because I feel like my mommies have broken up!" Lane huffed. "Savannah looks like this beautiful broken-winged bird and you look like a hot mess and-" they paused, "someone wants to say hello to you!"

"Hullow to you!" Tucker's bright face appeared on the screen, his big woolen beanie with the gigantic pom-pom on his head, and Brynn gasped and grinned in shocked delight.

"Tucker! Hi! Hey, buddy, hi!"

"Rainbow ice cream," he informed her, looking shy but pleased.

"I'm picking the menu now that Savannah has been crushed into a barely functional heap of misery that you inflicted," Lane explained, swinging the screen back to their face momentarily.

"Yeah... that's great, thank you." Brynn winced. "Hey Tucker," she called, and he jumped into Lane's lap with a bounce that made them wince. "Eat some carrots, okay?" she instructed. "Or some apple. Maybe some broccoli - yum yum!"

"Yummy!" he squeaked, then jumped up again out of view.

"How exactly did you get this number?"

"Chester," Lane said with a shrug. "Oh, that reminds me, he said to check your bank account and let him know if there were any problems."

"Uh. Yeah. Right. Pretty sure that message wasn't for me?"

"Okay?" Lane didn't care. "Probably. Anyway, talk tomorrow," they said brightly. "Go have, like, a shower or something. Say goodbye Tucker!"

"Byeeee!" Tucker's face filled the screen before suddenly it flicked to a view of the snow underfoot and Lane hung up.

Brynn scratched the back of her neck. She lay down on the couch and looked up at the ceiling for a while. Then she sat up, picked up the bottle of whisky and marched over to Dan's bedroom, tossed it onto his bed and closed the door. She decided Lane's advice was actually on point, and went and took a shower and washed her hair.

As she was blow drying, her phone rang again. Brynn steeled herself to answer it.

"Hi Mom."

"Hi darling. How's Nashville?"

"I'm actually back in LA." Brynn swallowed, feeling lower than low. "Things didn't work out." She stared at herself in the mirror, telling herself she could cope, that she was more than her mother's estimation of her.

"Oh." There was silence down the line. "I'm sorry to hear that. You'll have another opportunity though, if it's what you truly want to pursue."

"Thanks... Mom." Brynn's reflection looked somewhat startled.

"Do you want to talk about it?"

"No, I'm good. Thanks though." Was her mom *dying?* "Is everything okay?"

"Everything's fine. I was just calling to see if I could entice you home for Christmas, after all. The whole family will be there and we'd love it if you'd join us."

Brynn paused. Christmas with her family was never her favorite time of year. It wasn't exactly that her siblings bragged, they were simply confident and successful doctors, just like their family wanted. Not to mention with picture perfect spouses and children. And it wasn't that her parents nagged her... no, it actually really was that they nagged her. Another year of Brynn sitting around the table, feeling like a failure.

And yet, couch surfing alone in LA, heartbroken with a bottle of whisky calling her name?

"Sure, that sounds great. I'll drive up and see you on Christmas Eve." Jesus, if she had enough money left for fuel for a twelve-hour return trip to Palo Alto.

"Don't be silly, darling, I'll book it now and send you your flight details."

"Oh. Thanks." Her parents had enough money, they'd barely notice the cost of a fare, but it still rankled to accept their support; she was supposed to be a damn adult. After she'd dropped out of med school, her parents had retaliated by insisting she repay them the college fees they'd covered for her, in full. It had hurt in more ways than one, but this weird reversal felt strangely even lower. She wondered if her parents paid for things routinely with her siblings or if it was just her. She told herself to be grateful for their generosity. She needed to save every penny she could while she had no income coming in.

After she hung up with her mother, another anxiety hit her. Her mom and dad, grandma, her two siblings and their spouses, two nephews and a niece. She had to buy gifts. Last time she'd checked her bank account she had around $350 left to her name. She was just hoping to keep herself in food and fuel until she got a new job. Feeling nauseated, she opened her banking app.

She blinked at the screen. The balance now read $20,346.50. A business named SG Domestic had deposited $20,000 into her account yesterday afternoon. She remembered Lane's weird comment about money and scratched the back of her neck again and searched her contacts.

"Chester?" She reached him. She heard a guitar and the kick of a drum in the background, and she wondered with a pang if he was in the same room as Savannah.

"Hello, Ms. Marshall," he said neatly, walking away from the music, and Brynn let her head fall back for a moment. She wasn't imagining his tone as he called her by her real name. "What can I do for you?"

"Did... did someone put money in my bank account?" she asked, feeling very uneasy.

"Oh good, it arrived," he noted. "No problems then?"

"Um, yeah, one. What the hell's it for?"

"It's your back pay," he said, like it was obvious. "For the nannying job. Savannah said to make sure you got paid for all your work."

Brynn sat down with a thump.

"Well, I don't want it," she said roughly.

"I'm afraid that's no concern of mine," Chester said politely. "I just pay the bills, and Savannah's instructions were quite clear."

Brynn swallowed. She had been relegated to Savannah's paid staff. Ex-staff.

"What kind of nanny earns 20K for a couple of months' work?" she asked, still reeling.

"A valued one," Chester said shortly, "as I think is clearly evident."

She was mulling over the meaning of that statement and just about to hang up when Chester spoke up again.

"You should probably get used to it, Ms. Marshall." His voice was a fraction warmer. "The album's on its way. You co-wrote what looks to be a smash-hit with a major recording artist; the royalties on that are nothing to be sneezed at. Merry Christmas."

Leaving Brynn flabbergasted, he said goodbye and disconnected the call.

Chapter Nineteen

It had been a long, black night.

The morning after she sent Brynn away, Savannah awoke feeling like she had the flu, her bones aching, her eyes swollen. She showered and dressed, feeling brittle and wishing for nothing more than to swap lives with a wild woodland creature, with no one to see today but the grass and the trees. Instead, she had a full house of people - all of whom depended on her keeping her shit together - and a recording studio to get to.

She knew how enormously privileged she was, with her wealth, her success and her fame. But at that moment, she would have traded all of it for just a moment of true privacy. After she'd left Brynn, she'd had to skirt the dinner party of musicians and other employees she was hosting, then bumped blindly into both Chester and her startled housekeeper, when all she'd wanted to do was hide. She'd blurted to Chester to fire Noah and waved off her housekeeper's concern, desperately wishing for invisibility so no one would witness her breaking apart. And that was before she'd fled past her startled new nanny at the top of the stairs, already a crying wreck of a human being.

She took a deep breath. Everyone was depending on her, from her tiny son to her long-suffering manager. She'd come from too humble beginnings to ever entertain behaving like a brat or a diva, but more than that, she prided herself on being a professional. After all, she'd had plenty of experience over the years at putting on a brave face while her heart was cracking into pieces. She was already dreading having to face everyone after the mess of the night that had been, but the whole damn show had to go on. She would hold it together. *She* would not be a mess.

At her bedroom door she stopped still, frowning when she saw a note had been slid underneath. Surely Brynn hadn't-

Tucker and I have gone out for an early walk for a couple hours. I asked Annabelle to deliver breakfast upstairs for you.
   Lane

Savannah tiptoed out and found that not only was her space quiet and blessedly empty, but there was a bagel with the works, a fruit salad and fresh pot of coffee waiting on the table. In grateful silence, she sat, sipping coffee and forcing herself to nibble on enough food to settle her stomach, where it sat like lead.

By the time she arrived at the recording studio, she'd had ninety minutes to steady herself. Her game face was back in place.

"Morning y'all," she'd greeted her band, arriving just in time to sweep in the doors with them when Greta gave the green light.

"You good?" Coral asked her, her eyes dark with concern. Savannah waved her hand.

"Fine. Let's get this in the can," she said with as much cheer as she could muster. "What are we doing today, again?" She tried to gather herself. Despite her efforts, her brain still felt filled with soggy cotton wool.

"*Looking Back,*" Coral reminded her and Savannah went cold. She and Brynn had written the song together. It was, of all things, a love song - one she herself had adored up until right this very minute - and she remembered the writing of it like it was yesterday.

It had been mid-way through their writing streak, during that incredible time where no one could so much as sneeze without a song getting written. She, Brynn, and Noah had been in the band room all morning, Tucker running wild around them and by late morning, Savannah and Noah were starting to bicker and Brynn got cabin fever.

"I'm not like you mad musicians," she'd stood up, stretching her long limbs. "I usually work outdoors all day. I need some fresh air."

Noah and Savannah had protested - they were right on the verge of something good, they were sure - but Brynn was insistent. Tucker was napping on the band room sofa and as Savannah's eyes followed Brynn out the room, Noah had shrugged.

'I'll watch him," he volunteered, so Savannah had caught up with her at the back door. Brynn had tossed her a blinding smile.

"Aha, *gotcha*," she said, pulling on her winter jacket and slipping into her boots. "You need this too, you know," Brynn told her as they both padded out into the snow

"Maybe," Savannah allowed. The day was blue and cloudless, and the snow lay soft and ankle deep, squeaking under their boots.

"You start to look like a caged creature without your time outdoors," Brynn told her. "Like a little squirrel who needs a tree to climb or something."

Savannah's head jerked up and she stared at her. Then she sputtered a laugh, which she tried to turn into a glare.

"You couldn't have said like a majestic mountain lion, or an eagle that needs to soar?"

"Nope," Brynn said smugly. "Like a tiny, adorable, angry squirrel-" she ducked and laughed as Savannah flicked a snowy branch towards her, flinging snow at her face like a slingshot.

They trudged through the snow together, down to the edge of the lake. The water lapped on the shore, breaking up shards of ice where it had frozen in the night. Savannah brushed snow off the top of the large boulder near the water's edge and boosted herself up. Brynn joined her. Her face glowed with the cold and her eyes were bright above the burnt gold of her scarf.

"You know, this is where you first broke my writing block," Savannah said after a while. Brynn smiled.

"I'm a genius," she shrugged. Savannah rolled her eyes, though secretly she thought that actually probably was, in fact, true. "You literally looked for a second like you were going to kiss me on the mouth that day," Brynn said casually, and Savannah swallowed.

"You wish," she scoffed. They both kicked their heels against the rock and watched the icy lake. Savannah found herself imagining a world where kissing Brynn was a thing she could do and no one would get hurt by it, where it had been her that had been rescued from the surf in Malibu and gotten to fall in love.

"Hey," Brynn interrupted her thoughts a few minutes later. "Did you bring your notebook?"

Savannah smiled.

"You know I did." She reached into her pocket and pulled it out, followed by a pen. Brynn shifted up further on the boulder and turned her back, pulling off her gloves to pick up the notebook and scribble a few lines, before putting it back down beside them.

Savannah picked it up and turned her body away too, so the two of them were back to back. Facing away from each other was their unspoken song-writing rule. She read the words.

I want to feel your heartbeat
Your warmth inside the cold

Savannah gazed down at the messy swooping handwriting and wished with all her heart that Brynn was writing about her, and not either some amorphous inspiration because of the icy lake, or her handsome husband back at home. Again, she let herself fall into the fantasy that she'd been the one to meet Brynn first. She picked up the pen.

Through ice and snow
I'll always know
Your hand is mine to hold

She put down the notebook and again Brynn picked it up. There was a pause while she read Savannah's addition and then she shuffled back just slightly so they were resting against each other, back to back. She leaned on Savannah as she tapped the pen on the page, thinking.

They wrote lines this way for over half an hour, the firm press of Brynn's back warming her even through their layers of winter clothing, as they gazed in opposite directions upon the snow and wrote a love song together.

Now, in the recording studio, Savannah felt the rush of understanding that Brynn *had* been writing her lines to her, that right in that moment on the snowy lake edge, her aching daydream could have been a reality if not for Brynn and Noah's stupid lie.

She stepped up to the mic, listened for her cue, got two lines in, and in front of the whole studio - her band, the session musicians, the sound techs, Greta and god knows who else - she burst into tears.

———

"So," said Coral softly, as they sat outside the studio in a quiet nook and Savannah told her everything, "you caught feelings for her after all."

"I can't tell you how much I wish I hadn't." Savannah pulled her knees up to her chest, laying her head on them. "I wish I had some magic way to just switch off my feelings for her, now that I know who she really is."

280

"And who's that?"

"A *liar*. She lied the whole time, to my face, for months, even though we got so close." She scrubbed at her face. "I feel so stupid, like how could I *possibly* have not learned any better by now? After everything!" She angrily scrubbed away another tear.

"Woah," Coral looked at her. "I mean, first up, this is kind of a different situation, don't you think?"

"I don't see how. A lie is a lie is a lie."

"I mean, some lies are the lies of someone who doesn't give a fuck if they hurt you, and some lies are just a stupid mistake that got out of hand. It doesn't sound like either Brynn or Noah intended you any harm."

"It doesn't matter what they intended! The harm happened anyway. I was the butt of the joke, while the whole time I was... really falling for her." She covered her face with her hands. "Oh god, what do I *do*?"

"Can you just... talk to her? You might get a little more clarity on the situation-"

"I have more than enough clarity," Savannah raised her head, fingernails biting into her palms. "And talking to her is out of the question. It's done, Coral, it's over. I just have to find a way to move through this. Move through it so I can just get to the part where I grow old and die alone because I am so *done*."

"Okay. Sure. Good. But before you sign yourself up for a nunnery - Sister Savannah, my love - how about you try working through it in the traditional way?"

"Which is?"

"Channelling all that into your absolutely killer voice, recording one hell of a song, then putting out the album of a career, showing them for once and for all, who's the fucking *boss bitch?*"

Savannah sniffled a laugh and blew her nose.

Back in the studio, as the last notes of the song faded, Savannah wrapped her arms around her midsection and tried as hard as she could to shove the feelings the song had flung her into as far away as possible. Greta nodded to her through the glass.

"That was wonderful," she said crisply. "Let's go again."

Savannah stepped back from the mic.

"Greta." She shook her head. "If it's great, it's great. Let's just use the raw vocals, because I am *through* with this song."

———

Two days later, they'd recorded what they'd come to do, and Savannah was due to fly back to Vermont. She felt sick at the thought. The plan had been for Noah and Brynn to fly back with her, for the three of them to re-enter their close, intimate world of song-writing to finish up the album. Now she was facing the trip - and the writing - alone.

She thought about delaying it - giving herself a day or two's grace to gather herself - but the solitude called to her. Her Nashville home was still full of people - the band weren't heading out for another day or two - and Savannah felt like she couldn't stand literally another moment being surrounded by humans. In the end, she, Tucker and Lane headed back first thing the next morning.

They'd been lucky to make it in at all. The runway and the roads had been plowed, but several feet of snow surrounded them. Lane's eyes were enormous as they surveyed the immense walls of white every-where, the snowcapped forest, the house looking like something out of a winter fairytale.

"Tucker!" they enthused as the car pulled up at the front door. "We can build a snowman! We can figure out how to do - what are they called - snow angels?"

Savannah bit her lip hard. Would the whole time they were in Vermont feel like this? Just one Brynn-related memory socking her in the guts after another?

Inside the living room was the ten-foot blue spruce they'd decorated together, Brynn holding Tucker on her shoulders so he could shove ornaments precariously into the higher branches. Beside the tree and the piled presents was a large new gift - one that Savannah had arranged after seeing Brynn writing songs on Noah's guitar - a beautiful acoustic in its own case.

"Can you please... get rid of that?" she asked a confused Lucille, who'd only just had the damn thing wrapped. The housekeeper nodded a little curtly, then took Lane to go and see their rooms.

Savannah sank down onto the couch by the fire, finally almost alone. Tucker climbed up and nestled himself into her lap, clearly tired and disoriented. She cuddled him close and let his soft chatter and the hypnotic pull of the fire lull her into a little bit of warmth. This was her home, her haven. She'd lick her wounds and recoup. Her album depended on it.

The following day, she gritted her teeth and walked down into the band room. Her chest seized. Every instrument, every piece of furniture, every viewpoint - the air itself - felt infused with the three of them. The low three-legged stool Noah always picked to work from, despite the comfy couches. The sofa Brynn had watched them perform from, where they'd been tucked close to each other as they wrote. The piano in the corner, coming alive under Brynn's fingertips. Sadness overwhelmed her.

She sat down on the other stool and picked up her acoustic guitar. She stared hopelessly at the floor. Her writing had been ferociously blocked until Noah and Brynn came along. And now, three songs from finishing her solo album, she was alone and far from feeling her best. Anger grew within her, replacing the sadness. The shame at being a dupe all over again, at being just a dumb rich symbol to Noah and Brynn instead of a real person. She squeezed the neck of her guitar tightly and began to strum.

———

Less than a week later, it was Christmas. Savannah sent her staff home to their families, Luis having left behind a beautiful spread. Her band were all with their own loved ones and Rosalie was always married to her job at this time of year. So it was just Savannah, Tucker and Lane around the tree on Christmas morning. She made her absolute best effort to make it a warm, sweet experience for the two young people in the room. There was Christmas music playing, hot chocolate and croissants for breakfast, a pile of gifts to unwrap and Savannah was doing a stellar impression of a human with an intact heart.

Tucker was more excited by the wrapping than any of the actual gifts they contained, chanting *"present present present"* as he shredded the paper with glee. Of course, the only present he really got excited over was the one Brynn had left for him: a little construction set complete with yellow hardhat. Hat wobbling over his eye, he shouted *"bang bang"* with glee, smashing the little hammer against the couch arm. Savannah withheld her sigh and celebrated his joy with him.

Lane looked straight up surprised when Savannah gave them their own small stack of gifts to open, but the truth was that even though they'd been in her employ for just a few weeks, they were already indispensable.

"Jeez, Santa, thank you," they said to Savannah, running their fingers over the high quality headphones they'd opened last and clasped to their chest with a grin. "I wasn't sure what to get my boss who has literally everything, so-" they handed over a small flat gift. Savannah, touched, opened it to find a soft, brown, leather-bound notebook, the spine tooled with an intricate design that when she looked closer read *Savannah's Songs*.

"It's beautiful," she said. "Thank you."

"You're welcome." They shrugged. "It took me until yesterday to finish. It would have been easier if your name was shorter, to be honest."

"You made this?" Savannah ran her fingers along the spine. "You're talented," she said. Lane made a face, their cheeks pink.

"Oh, you know, random shit I learned at the center." It was the first mention Lane had made about where they'd found each other. Savannah smiled at them. "What's that one?" They pointed for distraction at a small, brown-paper-wrapped gift half hidden behind the tree.

Savannah picked it up with a frown. The gift was heavy, with a tiny gift tag: *To Savannah, from Brynn.* Her stomach dropped. Lane saw her face.

"Ohhh," they said. "Pretty sure I can guess who that's from. Are you going to open it?" they asked when she didn't put it down.

Savannah wasn't sure what motivated her to do it, especially with an interested audience, but she pulled the paper off to find a plain card-board box. Inside the box was more brown paper stuffing, protecting something delicate. She reached in and pulled out the strangest contraption she'd ever seen.

It was a small glass globe set on a brass base, housing an array of burnished brass instruments, with multiple dials and what at first looked like analogue clock faces. She looked closer. *Hydro,* read one, *Celsius/Fahrenheit* read another. It was an antique weather device, with a thermometer, barometer and something labeled a hygrometer. It was strange and beautiful and she wanted to spend hours under-standing how it worked.

"Damnit." Her vision went hazy. Lane tactfully turned to Tucker and gave him unneeded help assembling his tool box. Brynn had gotten her a perfect gift: unique and meaningful, not only tailored perfectly to Savannah, but to *them.* She remembered the conversation at the window, their bodies close, watching the frozen rain, Brynn's tease about Savannah's weather facts, but even more importantly her response to Savannah's revelations about her childhood, the vulnera-bility as she'd shared her own life back. That day had been - for

Savannah anyway - the moment she had first started to fall into what could have, one day, been love.

Now, looking down at the soft glow of the brass, she wondered if it had been the same for Brynn. The gift felt like a message, perfectly clear only to the two people who'd been in the room that morning: *remember that time when we first started to truly see each other?* Brynn had lied about something critical, but Savannah knew she hadn't lied about her feelings for her.

"Are you going to forgive her?" Lane was inspecting her face and looking hopeful.

Savannah blanched. She'd never said a word to Lane about what had happened between her and Brynn. Unfortunately, Savannah had apparently been so damn transparent they'd been able to read the situation like a book. Her first instinct was to snap that it wasn't their business, but, after all, it was Christmas and Lane was spending it with her.

"It's not a matter of forgiveness," she said instead, carefully putting down the weather station. "It's that we're over for a good reason, and that reason isn't going to go away."

"Man," Lane said reflectively. "That really sucks."

"Yeah," Savannah agreed, flatly. "It really does."

The rest of the day crawled. The three of them only took up one small corner of the big dining table, but they all played their parts in making things merry. When Savannah put Tucker down for his nap, she stayed and cuddled next to his soft, warm body for a while, immensely grateful for the love she did have in her life.

That thought was what stirred her to go back downstairs where Lane was sitting on the couch, an old Christmas rom com playing quietly.

"I never get this stuff," Lane said after a while as they sat and watched together. "Does Christmas really look like that for some people?"

On screen, a large family of attractive white people in neat sweaters were dining around a loaded table, laughing and smiling, clearly all adoring each other while beautifully tasteful Christmas decorations lit the scene.

"It's not how I've ever experienced it," Savannah agreed. Once, when she was a kid, her mom had served up yogurt as a Christmas treat. There'd been barely any food in the house for weeks, but she'd hoarded it so they'd have something special. Neither Savannah nor her younger siblings had mentioned that she'd kept it so long that the yogurt had spoiled.

She considered Lane beside her, the basic facts she knew about their life.

"Do you ever talk to your family?" She wasn't sure if this was out of bounds, but Lane only shrugged, their eyes on the television.

"Nah," they said. "Not since I was thirteen."

Savannah's heart ached a little.

"Well, thank you," she said, "for being here with me. Fucking Christmas, you know?"

"Fucking Christmas," they agreed.

Chapter Twenty

Brynn stared out the tiny window of the plane. She thought of the flight she'd taken to Nashville, not the unspeakable luxury of the private jet so much as the press of Savannah's body alongside her own, Tucker nestled warmly in her lap. She blinked back tears. She wondered if it would have made a difference if she'd just said it then, turned to Savannah and told her, *I made a stupid mistake, Noah and I are just friends, please understand how much you mean to me.* She could only imagine Savannah's face falling, but maybe, if-

It was useless to try to rewrite things.

To her immense surprise, her little brother Stephen was at the arrivals gate to meet her. His tall, rangy frame had filled out and instead of the little nerd she still thought of him as, he looked like the adult, physician and dad that he was. She tried to noogie him anyway.

"Little bro."

"Middle sis." He hugged her. "Man, it's good to see you."

It was nice to have a warm welcome and they chatted easily enough on the drive to her parent's home. The ease was due mostly to Brynn keeping up a stream of questions about his job, his wife and his young daughter, and trying not to mind that his return questions were sparse and non-specific. She kept her own answers vague anyway.

She followed him through the door and was greeted in the entrance hall by her mom, who hugged her uncharacteristically tightly.

"My baby girl," her mom's voice sounded thick. "It's good to have you home."

Her mom looked put together as always, her thick dark hair where nary a gray dared to show its face, her features kept carefully smooth with subtle surgical nips and tucks and a skilful application of Botox. Her eyes were the same as Brynn's - dark and expressive - and Brynn caught a flicker of worry in them as she held her daughter at arm's length to examine her.

Brynn knew she could make things easier on herself by making the effort to dress less casually and more femininely, but the stubborn streak within her wouldn't let her deviate from her favorite jeans and flannel for her trip home. She was pretty sure her mom was wearing

Chanel. For once, however, her mother didn't comment on her appearance.

"Hello, Brynn." Both her parents were tall, but her father was, at sixty-eight, still a towering presence, with his neat salt-and-pepper hair and gray eyes surrounded in stately lines. Her father was never a hugger and so Brynn was completely taken aback when he pulled her into a stiff embrace.

"Hey Dad." Honestly, was someone dying?

The living room was tastefully decorated with a large Christmas tree and beautiful wreaths hanging in the picture windows, looking out on the lush, neatly tended garden. Waiting to greet her were her sister Anna, both her siblings' spouses and the three kids who were beautifully dressed but currently looking to be engaged in all out war as they squabbled over a small set of toy squirrels. Stephen stepped in to sort it out so Anna could come and give her an awkward hug hello. It was Anna who Brynn found most intimidating; her older sister was a younger, more disapproving version of their mother, and the most likely to deliberately show Brynn up.

"Still the same old Brynn." She smiled thinly as she looked Brynn up and down. Anna was - on vacation, at home, with family - wearing an outfit that likely cost about three times the price Brynn would get for her car. Her hair was expertly styled, and Brynn detected a new, intense smoothness between her brows. Anna was a Marshall through and through: never show a chink in your perfection.

"Sweetheart." The commanding voice came from an armchair by the window and she suddenly realized her grandmother, Thea, was watching her from just out of the action. Thea was almost ninety, but her posture remained ramrod straight, her bearing regal and her eyes piercing in her small, soft, wrinkled face. Brynn walked over, intending to bend down and kiss her cheek, but Thea had already struggled to her feet. She felt like a frail little bird in Brynn's embrace.

Thea was in every functional way the head of the family. Her father's mother was an early pioneer as a woman in medicine and had reached heights previously only reserved for men. She was the driving force for every member of the family to study medicine and it had been Thea that Brynn had feared most when she dropped out of med school. She'd stayed away from home for three years, battling for her sobriety and trying to find her way without her family's meddling.

When she had finally faced home, it had been as miserable as she'd expected, only as it turned out, Thea had been the least explosive. And yet - in the face of her father's anger, her mother's blind insistence that she *must* return to complete her studies and her siblings' discomfort at someone not toeing the party line - it had been Thea's quiet disappointment that had stung the most.

Now, feeling the frailty of the elderly lady, Brynn worried that she would die disappointed with her. Thea, though, was smiling at her.

"You get more beautiful every time I see you, Brynn Marshall." She reached up and patted Brynn's cheek.

"Grandma, are you okay standing up so long?" interrupted Anna. "Your hip-"

"My hip is healed quite nicely, *thank you*, Anna." Thea's voice was steely. She never did like being reminded of any weakness. Anna sat down, red blooming on her cheeks. "Come and sit with me, my darling, and tell me all about your life," she said to Brynn, and Brynn sat, her mother handing her an elegant crystal glass of eggnog, mouthing *non-alcoholic* as she walked away. Brynn stared. It was the first time her mother had acknowledged Brynn's alcoholism since their phone call in Nashville.

Away from the slowly resumed chatter of the rest of the family as the kids ran riot, Brynn gave her stately grandmother an edited version of the last year of her life.

"Well," said Thea as she rambled to a close. "You have been having an adventure. What do you plan to do next?"

"I don't know," Brynn said awkwardly. "I guess I'm going to find another job, see where I land."

"See where you land?" The steely tone returned. "That attitude will get you nowhere. If it's music you want to be doing, then you must work at it. It seems you've already been gifted a head start and if you don't follow it up with serious effort, you'll be a fool."

Brynn blinked.

"You don't think it would be a waste of time?"

"Of course not. If you're talented and driven, then you will succeed," she said declaratively, as if success in the music industry was ever that simple.

"I just figured that if it wasn't medicine..."

"You think I believe anything other than a career in medicine would be a waste of time?" Her grandmother sounded surprised, as if that assumption wasn't the bedrock of the entire family. Brynn raised her eyebrows at the old woman and nodded. "Medicine is a wonderful career - a calling, in fact - for those that actually want it." Thea looked at her pointedly. "But all I've ever wanted for you is to find your own calling."

"Grandma, forgive me, seriously," Brynn couldn't cope with this rewriting of history, "but you didn't exactly hide your disappointment when I quit med school. The whole family was horrified."

"I was disappointed with you, that's true." Thea glared at her. "But I was disappointed that you'd gone to damned med school in the first place when it was suddenly clear it was the last thing you'd ever wanted. What on earth were you thinking?"

Brynn gaped.

"I was thinking this family gave me no choice," she said, an old anger rising within her.

"So you just capitulated to what your parents wanted? To what I wanted? Were you not an adult who could make a rational choice? Where was your backbone, young lady?"

"Backbone?" she snapped. "I was trying to do the right thing. I wanted to make you all happy!"

"I will be happy when you stand up on your own two feet and say *this is what I want*, despite all the opposition, and then damn well do it! That's what I did and I would a thousand times rather that be the legacy I leave my grandchildren than bloody medicine!"

Brynn was aware the room had fallen silent, as everyone gave up pretending not to listen in on the heated conversation.

"Mother," her dad interjected. "Do you think it's wise to let yourself get worked up? Your heart–"

"Oh, for god's sake, Phillip, calm yourself. I'm not about to fall into cardiac arrest because I'm debating my favorite grandchild." Her voice was haughty. "Let me have this one joy instead of sitting around being stuffy and boring for the entire Christmas season."

Her father fell quiet. Thea looked her in the eye, challenge sparking off of her.

"So, Brynn, if I live to see you next Christmas, who am I going to see? A scared girl in her thirties who's *just seeing where they'll land* or a goddamned rock star?"

———

That evening, after everyone had gone to bed, Brynn sat out in the cool night air in her parent's garden. She remembered when this - Palo Alto in winter - had been her idea of cold.

She thought about seeing snow for the first time in Vermont and wondered how Savannah and Tucker's Christmas was going. They'd planned to spend the holiday together, before their little bubble had been horribly burst, and Brynn grieved the cozy day they'd have created. She hoped the band were making up for it, gathering around her, filling her world with raucous dinner parties, cheer and laughter. She hoped Tucker was excited about Santa and that he'd let his mother sleep in past five a.m.

In her longing for the two people she missed the most, she returned to the daydream that had been keeping her going since she'd left them: imagining she'd gone to Vermont with Noah and done things right. Maybe they'd never lied in the first place, or maybe they'd fessed up in the first week. There were so many things she would have done differently.

She'd have told Savannah how damn hot she looked behind a guitar, just for a start. She'd have let her gaze linger as Savannah had sat on her living room floor, pizza in hand, gesticulating wildly and teaching her to love country music. She'd have returned that burning gaze that day in the band room, not let go when Savannah took her hand beneath the freezing, rainy window. She'd have kissed her for the first time on one of their walks in the forest, tilting Savannah's face up to her own and letting all the feelings for her she'd held back spill out in her eyes before she kissed her warm mouth.

Perhaps if she had then that day in Burlington with the snow falling, Tucker's small hand in hers, she could have told Savannah - as she stood there, snowflakes sparkling in her hair and eyelashes - that she was the most beautiful sight Brynn had ever seen in her life. That she never wanted to stop looking at her.

She brushed back a tear. It was all pointless, magical thinking. She could not undo what she had done. Savannah had been perfectly clear: what she wanted was for Brynn to leave her alone. And so she would. But somehow, despite this, she found that here, in the quiet darkness on Christmas Eve, she could not quite bring herself to give up hope.

"Oh lord, sorry," a voice rang out behind her. She turned to see Anna standing half in and half out the back door in what were probably Gucci pajamas. "I didn't realize you were out here moping."

Brynn sighed and scrubbed her face.

"It's okay, there's plenty of room to mope if you need to join me."

To her surprise, Anna closed the door behind her and came and sat in the outdoor chair beside hers.

"Aren't you freezing?" she said after a moment.

"Not really," Brynn told her. "I came from Vermont." She felt Anna turn and look at her.

"I thought you were in Nashville singing country music," she said accusingly. Brynn found she couldn't help a small smile at how horrified her older sister sounded.

"Sort of," she said. "I was in Nashville, but it wasn't country music. Before that we were in Vermont, writing."

"So it's true," Anna said. "You were literally doing music with Savannah Grace."

"Yeah."

"*Fuuuuuuuck,*" Anna groaned, tipping her head back to the sky and slumping in her chair.

"Excuse me?" Brynn was shocked. Her sister's facade never cracked, and she'd told Brynn off for swearing more times than she could remember. Anna seemed to be struggling for words for once.

"You just... you just do whatever the hell you want, don't you?" she said. "You swan off to LA, literally get employed to hang out on the beach in a bikini all day and then - bam! - you're a musician and recording with a massive star. What even *is* your life?"

"That's not exactly accurate-"

"Bullshit! And then you act like being around your family is literally the worst thing you could ever imagine and you mope around as if you're some kind of victim."

"Oh wow, Anna, tell me how you really feel."

"I will! Some of us work our asses off, okay? We do exactly what is expected of us and we *excel* at it, and it's still not enough! You get to live this insane, exciting, spontaneous, adventurous life while we're *trapped* and you're still the one with a chip on your shoulder."

Brynn was about to bite back when her argument died. Her life did sound amazing, when she viewed it through Anna's eyes.

"Are you... okay?" she asked, suddenly seeing her sister in a new light. Her rigidly perfect veneer, her slightly too thin body, her brittle asides. Anna crumpled. "Oh, honey, no." Brynn leapt out of her chair and crouched in front of her, her hands resting on her sister's knees.

"No," her sister wept. "I'm not. I want to leave Bradley. I'm just holding it together until the kids are back in school, so they're not there when it all falls apart. And I'm burnt out, but I can't take a break because the department needs me and what if Bradley uses my burnout against me in a custody battle?"

"Oh shit," Brynn whispered.

"Oh shit is right." Anna raised her head and looked at her miserably.

"You're as fucked up as I am," Brynn breathed and Anna spluttered out a laugh.

"Of course I am," she agreed. "We're from the same family, asswipe."

"Ooh, Stanford teach you those insults, Ms. Head of Department?"

"Can you stop being a smart-ass and just give me an actual hug, please?"

Brynn hugged her sister. She went inside and made two big hot chocolates and they sat up in the garden for hours, making plans and strategizing. To ease Anna's rambling over-thinking once they had a workable plan, she confessed her own life disasters, including the long-held secret of her alcoholism and her recent struggle not to drink. Anna took it all in with no more comment than a hand squeeze between their two chairs.

"Okay, let me get this straight," she said eventually. "You fell in love with *Savannah Grace?*"

Brynn snorted out a small laugh. Of all the revelations, that was the one Anna was most taken by.

"Yeah."

"And *she* was smitten with *you* - my gangly annoying little sister - until you fucked it up?"

"Incredibly, yes."

"Wow."

"Yeah. I know."

They were silent for a moment.

"You have to get her back," Anna sat up straight. "What are we going to do?"

Brynn's heart warmed at the *we,* but she sighed.

"She said she wanted me out of her life. I have to respect that."

"Ugh," said Anna. They sat in silence for a while. "You know how they say that living well is the best revenge?" she asked a few minutes later. Brynn frowned. She had no desire for revenge. She was the one in the wrong, after all. "Maybe living well is also the best way to win her back. She saw the one shitty thing you did and made a judgment call. Maybe you just need to prove her wrong."

"I mean, it's a nice theory, but it doesn't mean much if she's busy pretending I don't exist. I can be as great as I want, but it's not like she's going to notice from all the way up there in the world she lives."

"Brynn, even in this family - honestly whose heads are up their asses most of the time - you shine the brightest. I think if you try hard enough - and if she really does love you - you could shine hard enough she'd see it from space."

Chapter Twenty-One

To Brynn's surprise, her mom insisted on driving her back to the airport herself, once Christmas was over.

"How are you doing, Mom?" she asked, still wondering if someone was dying. Both her parents had been uncharacteristically soft with her the entire visit. It was actually pretty nice, if somewhat uncomfortable.

"Oh, fine, darling," she said distractedly, as she navigated her way through the streets.

"Is something wrong?" Brynn pressed, worriedly.

"Why do you ask?" Her mother merged into traffic, her steely confidence as clear in her driving as it was in every realm of her life.

"You and Dad are being weird," she pointed out.

"I'm sorry. How exactly are we being 'weird'?" Her mother sounded offended.

"Just... no one has told me off for wearing the wrong thing or asked when I'm going back to med school or told me I'm off track or... *anything*. You're being conspicuously extra nice to me and I'm not sure why."

"Brynn Marshall!" Her mother took her eyes off the road to glare at her. "Your father and I are nice people. And we love you. I don't know what's *weird* about that."

"So no one is dying?"

"What? Goodness no. What rubbish you speak sometimes, darling."

Brynn fell silent. She watched the road go by. They passed the rest of the short trip with barely a word. When they pulled up at the airport, she undid her seatbelt and went to open the door, when suddenly her mother's hand reached out to stop her. She looked over and her mom's face was red with emotion.

"We nearly lost you," she said. "I can't stop replaying our conversation where you told me you tried to... that you wanted to die.

And I can't - your father and I - we can't forgive ourselves for the fact you couldn't come to us."

"Oh, Mom-"

"And that you had to cope with all of that... that you were struggling with alcohol.... that you fought all that without us. And you kept it a secret all these years."

"I'm sorry, Mom-"

"No." Her mom was crying. "*I'm* sorry. *We* are sorry. You dropped out of contact, would barely speak to us and we just... let you. I was angry and confused and I thought if you understood what you were losing that maybe you'd try harder." She took in a breath. "It was the wrong thing to do. We should have checked on you. We should have told you that we love you, no matter what."

"I love you too, Mom. And Dad." Brynn was crying now, too. "I'm sorry I shut you out."

"We didn't give you much choice," her mom said shakily. "And I'm... I'm sorry I lied to you about your singing. You had the most beautiful voice, even as a small child. And afterward... well, I never heard you sing again. I told myself it was for the best, but I missed hearing your voice. It was a terrible thing to do to a child."

"Thanks, Mom." Brynn felt about eight years old, as she reached out to hug her mom over the gear stick. They hugged tightly, then her mother pulled back.

"Listen to me," she said fiercely. "Thea is right. Chase your own damn dream, okay? Don't you ever try to please us, ever again."

"Uh, sure, no problem." Brynn managed a smile.

————

"Nice digs," Lane's voice crackled from her phone a week later, as Brynn gave them a video tour of her new rental. It was just one bedroom and nothing particularly beautiful, but the light was nice and it featured a complete lack of roommates. Brynn loved it.

"What do you reckon?" Brynn asked Tucker as he popped his face into the screen.

"Reckon!" he replied.

"Do you just copy everything we say now?" she asked with a grin.

"Evwything we say now," he confirmed.

"Let me tell you, as a paid employee, that is *very* unfortunate at times." Lane shook their head.

Brynn was about to push them for an example to highlight exactly where they were falling down as a nanny when another call came in.

"Gotta take this." She hung up. Ever since Savannah had broken off contact she'd gotten superstitious about unknown numbers. As a result, she seemed to be a wildly popular target from cold-calling sales lines, scams and political surveys.

"Hello?" she answered.

"Brynn Marshall?"

"Yeah, who is this?" It was a woman's voice, but not one she recognised.

"Jennifer Landry, Sony Records."

"Oh, uh... hi?" Brynn wasn't sure she was ever going to be in the right place for whatever discussions about Savannah's album had to eventually happen.

"Listen, I'm just walking into another meeting, so I've got to keep this brief. Bryce Campbell gave me a call. He had some pretty interesting things to say about you and told me to set up a meeting."

"I'm sorry.... Bryce?" Brynn was unsure.

"Bryce Campbell." The woman sounded mildly incredulous. "The head of the label? He saw you during recording with Savannah Grace in Nashville?"

"Oh! That Bryce Campbell." Brynn smacked her forehead, embarrassed.

"I understand you're LA based? I'm there on Tuesday with a free spot in the afternoon if you can make it." Her tone was breezy, but at the same time absolutely assumed that Brynn would be there. "Do you have representation?"

"Representation? *No.* Do I need it?"

"I'd recommend arranging someone right away. I can send you some names if you need some?"

"I don't understand." Brynn's brain was slowly catching up with her in a spiral of worry. Savannah's boss, formal meetings, representation required. "Am I... being sued or something?"

There was a pause.

"No, Ms. Marshall." Rebecca Landry sounded amused. "We want to offer you a recording contract."

———

In the end, Brynn took Noah with her, and his agent, Bella. Bella was Korean and no more than five feet tall and between her casual sneakers and unassuming smile she didn't seem like much of a threat, but Noah assured her that Bella was cut-throat.

"So," Jennifer Landry said, as they all sat around a boardroom table. "The story goes that you're getting a co-writing credit on four songs on Savannah Grace's upcoming solo album and you're a featured vocalist on what will likely be her first single." Brynn swallowed. It was a lot to take in. Even just attending a business meeting where Savannah's name was casually thrown around was a lot.

Jennifer was a glamorous red-head somewhere in her late forties, with striking green eyes and impressively sculpted arms. Brynn wasn't sure if she was attracted to her or mildly terrified of her, or both.

"There's a lot of hype for this album," she continued. "Between Savannah already being a significant artist and the fact that it's her first solo work... all early indications report it's going to be an incredible hit. So there's a supernova of publicity coming your way, Ms. Marshall, and as of right now, you're not even a newcomer; you're a ghost."

Brynn blinked at that.

"We know you've got the voice for it," Jennifer continued, "and it seems you've got the writing chops, too. But time is incredibly short if we're going to introduce you to the market at the right time, when the public are looking to find out who you are." She fixed Brynn with a hard stare. "What I want to know is, are you hungry for it? Have you got the drive to buckle down and write harder than you've ever written in your life? Have you got the desire to work day and night to record an album in record time? Are you ready to perform night after night and turn this into your whole world? Because that's what it's going to need to be if you want to make this your reality."

Brynn took a deep breath. She thought of her life. She thought of her dreams. She thought of the textbooks gathering dust on her shelf. She thought of her mother. And she thought of those weeks in the band room, with Noah and Savannah, the creativity that poured through them all, the haze of it, the heat of it; it was the happiest she'd ever been in her life, she realized that now.

"Yeah." She met Jennifer's eyes. "I am."

She and Noah took seats outside as Bella rolled up her sleeves and faced down Jennifer, two legal reps and a stack of paper nine miles high. Brynn took a breath.

"Do you think I can do this?" she asked Noah.

He turned to look at her, his hands clasped loosely in his lap.

"Hell yeah," he told her, his face serious. Then he grinned. "Brynn Marshall, you absolute animal. I've been working my ass off for decades, finally climbing into a little recognition and here you swan into a major label record deal without even trying. I think I'd hate you if I didn't love you."

"Noah," she tried. She'd been working up to this since almost the moment she'd gotten off the phone from Jennifer. "You're on a hiatus right now. Would you... would you do this with me?"

He stared at her.

"How so?"

"I mean, like all of it. Write with me, record with me, tour with me, if it gets that far... You don't have to-" she hastened to add.

"Are you for real? Fuck yeah, Brynn, of course I will. I'd be honored."

He wrapped his arm around her shoulders and gave her a sideways hug. An hour later, his arm was still there, when Bella opened the door smiling and Jennifer called them in to tell them that Brynn had a record deal.

Chapter Twenty-Two

Savannah's first album as a solo artist was finally finished. The previous night the band had all gone out to celebrate, piling into Tootsie's, Savannah creating an accidental furor by getting drunk with the excited revelers and dancing in the crowd to the live music, security keeping a close eye and more or less succeeding in keeping the paparazzi at bay.

It was her first real return in years to the scene that had nurtured her into stardom. The early days of celebrity had been completely overwhelming and Savannah had hated the loss of anonymity, with what felt like crowds of eyes on her every move. She hated even more the infamy that came with Cole's excesses and for a time avoided going out at all unless she had to. Then, she became a perpetually tired mom whose every foray into a public space involved expressions of sympathy or enthusiastic offers to punch her ex-husband in the face, even long after the dust had settled.

But the night the album wrapped, Savannah found for the first time in years that she wanted to *dance*. She got tipsy enough to welcome the enthusiastic interactions with fans and she shrugged off the occasional ex-husband-related comment with a smile and a lazy "Cole *who?*" to great delight.

Soon enough she would no longer be known as Cole Corbin's jilted wife, nor one half of Twice Struck. Once the album dropped, she'd finally get to be Savannah Grace, for once and for all. She danced with abandon and when the performers on stage got wind that she was there, she got hauled up to join them and - at first, reluctantly and then with laughter - lent her vocals to an enthusiastic rendition of one of her old hits.

The next morning, she awoke with her first hangover in almost half a decade, her head aching, her stomach churning and a desperate yearning for someone to hold her. And not just any someone, she admitted to herself. She felt filled with a deep sadness, that for a moment, overshadowed the elation of what she'd just achieved. Her anger at Brynn renewed itself, and she pulled the pillow over her head and groaned.

Her phone buzzed and when she squinted at the screen, she saw Coral had sent through a link to a TMZ article showing Savannah staggering out of the bar in the early morning hours, laughing and leaning on Jed's arm. *Savannah's Hot Night with Mystery Lover,* the title read. Coral followed the text with about forty laughing face emojis.

"Am I going to need to send his wife a gift basket?" she asked wryly when Coral picked up.

"Depends," Coral considered. "How was he in bed?" They both erupted into laughter. "Who do you think sent me the article? Lucinda loves it. She's going to dine out on that for months."

"Maybe it's Jed who's going to need the gift basket," Savannah giggled. "I'm not sure he's going to cope with being described as a *mystery* after being on stage with me for the last twelve years."

"At least you look hot in the photos," Coral commiserated. After they'd hung up, Savannah took a closer look. The Savannah of last night did look surprisingly great considering how worse for wear she'd been. Her hair had been curled before going out and it somehow just looked artfully mussed, while her favorite red lipstick was thankfully still on her lips. But more than that, she looked happy. The Savannah of this morning looked decidedly less glamorous and felt significantly less bright.

It had been over three months since she'd last seen Brynn. The first few nights had been the worst, Savannah waiting for Tucker to fall asleep so she could curl in a heap and cry until she exhausted herself into a fitful sleep, finally sure that she wouldn't cave and try to call Brynn.

She missed her and raged at her all in the same moment and - even worse - she longed desperately for all that had never happened between them. She recalled the heat of their bodies as they almost touched, felt the way she'd trembled into Brynn's arms, relived the desperate ache of her kisses. It still made her feel weak and Savannah never wanted to be weak over anyone ever again.

She'd mistaken weakness for strength the whole time she'd been with Cole, convinced she could carry them both through his tribulations, steeling herself against his transgressions and taking him back each and every time he fell to his knees, begging for her forgiveness. She'd clutched tight to his increasingly short-lived periods of sweetness and held herself up by sheer force when instead he made damn sure she suffered.

She'd never make that mistake again, drawing a boundary with Brynn so severe that she'd have no choice but to stand strong. If she didn't see her or speak to her, then she couldn't possibly crumble. And yet here she was, three months later, still feeling a bit like she'd been torn in two.

Here, in the privacy of her bedroom, hiding beneath the bedsheets, she could admit something dark: deep down, she'd never expected Brynn to adhere to the line she'd drawn. Cole had always campaigned to wear her down with flowers, jewelry, love songs and heartfelt speeches. At the time, Savannah had believed it was because despite everything, he just loved her so much. Now all she saw were her boundaries being trampled.

Brynn, however, appeared to be taking her at her word. No lavish flowers arrived, no tearful letters. There were no grand gestures, not one single attempt to win her back. There was only silence, and a void in her life where Brynn had once almost been. She hated herself a little for the realization that part of her was aggrieved by this. At times, she would have done anything for one more word from Brynn, to open her front door to find her standing there, ready to fight. But at the same time, she felt the full impact of the respect Brynn was showing her. One thing she'd said seemed true: she wasn't behaving like Cole at all.

———

The night at Tootsie's was only a couple of weeks after her return from Vermont. Being back home in Nashville again always gave her a slight head spin. Gone was the immense peace and isolation of the snowy forest, her days instead beginning to get filled again. There were meetings, dress fittings, beauty appointments, photoshoots, and the ceaseless buzz of the city. Thank god Nashville also contained two other things that kept her sane: the quiet green compound she called home, and Rosalie Carlson.

"I'm sorry," Rosalie greeted her when Savannah arrived on her doorstep for dinner, "you look kind of familiar, but I just can't quite seem to place you?"

Savannah rolled her eyes and pulled her oldest friend into her arms to hug her. Rosalie hugged her back and for a long moment Savannah did not want to let go.

"I'm sorry," she said when she finally pulled back. "Shit got real."

Rosalie observed her closely for a moment, her sea-green eyes filled with softness.

"So it would seem," she said, giving her shoulders a quick squeeze before turning to walk into her kitchen, where something smelled absolutely delicious.

Savannah loved Rosalie's home. It was a fraction the size of any of the properties she owned and sometimes she hated herself for what had become a weird inability to live like a damn normal person.

Rosalie didn't have to worry about paparazzi or stalkers, however, and her lovely Victorian cottage on a quiet leafy street just off downtown was about the most beautiful place Savannah knew, for all her own wealth and luxury. There was something about the warmth of the gleaming floorboards, the quiet collection of books, the shining cookware and the beautiful tangled flower garden outside the french doors that always felt like home. If anyone had asked her where on the planet she felt safest, it would be curled up on a sofa in her oldest friend's living room. Walking in through the front door made her feel like she could breathe out properly for the first time in months.

Savannah had finally called her, just after Christmas; Coral's accusation about their friendship ringing in her ears. Still, when her heart was fracturing there was only one person on the planet she wanted to talk to. Rosalie's combination of over-protective love, deep understanding and a light scolding was exactly what she'd craved.

She looked at Rosalie now where she stood in her kitchen, pouring them both a glass of wine, and as always had the strangest sensation of seeing double. Rosalie looked casually lovely, the way she always did, with her auburn hair and creamy skin, and yet still within the grown woman Savannah could always see her as she'd looked the very first time she'd laid eyes on her: a wide-eyed sixteen-year-old in boy's pajamas.

"Savannah Grace," Rosalie said now, handing her the glass of wine. "If you don't sit down and tell me literally everything, I swear to god, I will never speak to you again for as long as we both shall live."

Dying of gratitude, Savannah sat.

———

"So," Bryce Campbell looked at her steadily across the desk in his enormous corner office at the label's lavish Nashville complex, six weeks later. "How are you feeling?"

"Pumped," Savannah admitted, reaching out and snagging a candy from the big bowl that perpetually appeared wherever the label head arrived. "I'm beyond ready."

"We all are." Bryce stretched back in his executive chair. "I have to admit Savannah, this album was worth the wait, and then some."

She glowed at him smugly, and he laughed.

"*Longing* is the first single, of course." He lifted his finger to tap off his agenda items. Savannah frowned.

"I think it should be *Beware the Fury,*" she argued. "I like the idea of arriving back with a blaze."

Bryce considered her.

"It's the least Savannah Grace that Savannah Grace has ever sounded," he said thoughtfully. "And it's a hell of a track. It's going to get people talking, that's for sure." She nodded, happy he was taking her view of things, until he continued. "Here's the thing. That song is a fuck you to Cole Corbin, and I'm not saying the man doesn't have it coming. Part of me wants to give the punters what they want: Cole's long-suffering, country music darling, ex-wife finally venting her righteous rage and kicking his ass from here to kingdom come."

"Does sound good, doesn't it?" Savannah smiled.

"Sure. But it's also exactly what the world expects of you right now." Her smile faded. "*Longing,* on the other hand, well that's more of a wild card. Savannah Grace is back, and Cole Corbin is nothing but a blip in her rearview mirror. Savannah Grace has forgotten the man even existed. Savannah Grace is, in fact, singing love songs to and with a beautiful woman."

Savannah stood up sharply, her heart pounding.

"Don't you *dare,* Bryce." She felt the blood drain from her face. "Don't you fucking dare turn my life into a marketing gimmick." She glared at him and he spread out his hands, gesturing for her to sit

321

back down. Eventually she did, albeit reluctantly, tense and ready to fight.

"That's not what I'm proposing," he said calmly. "Your business is your business, and you know the amount of respect I have for you. I'm simply proposing the song standing on its own and speaking for itself. You didn't record it with a male vocalist after all," he pointed out and she blinked. She hadn't even considered it. "It's your finest work, Savannah. It's passionate, it's heartbreaking and it's sexy. It'll be the hit of the year, if not the next five years."

She breathed in a deep breath and looked down at her hands, considering. Even the very fact of his insinuation had thrown her; this would *not* fly with the establishment if she was still firmly inside country music. Instead, it appeared she really was entering a whole new world. She'd lived in the old one so long she had no idea how to feel.

"Fine," she said shortly. "We'll do it your way."

"That's great," he relaxed back in his chair. "Next thing on the agenda then, is the music video." He rattled off a couple of big name directors and potential filming dates, all of which she had thoughts on. "Alright, done," he said once they'd come to an agreement. "I'll get Jen to clear Ms. Marshall's schedule that week too and we'll get it in the can so it can all be wrapped up well before the album launch."

"What do you mean, Brynn's schedule?" Savannah asked, a sinking feeling in her chest.

"Well, of course, since you're both singing on the track, we're going to need you both in the video. And Jen wants things lined up so that her album launches six weeks after yours."

Savannah stared at him.

"*Her* album?" she asked.

He nodded, looking pleased with himself.

"We signed her the second we could get hold of her," he told her. Then he looked perturbed. "She didn't tell you?"

Savannah felt dizzy. The primary feeling in her gut was all out pride. Brynn had a major record deal. She wasn't going to waste her talent or force herself into med school. She was going straight to the big leagues, where she belonged. The next wave of feeling was grief that Brynn couldn't tell her, that they couldn't celebrate together the way this should be celebrated.

"Bryce," she sighed. "I know you just said my business was my business, but you probably need to hear that Brynn and I don't speak anymore. And that there is no way in *hell* that we're going to make a music video together. If you try to insist on that, then I will fire the director myself and find someone to make some arthouse feature short film where no one has to lip sync to the camera and that's my final word on the subject."

"I see," was all he said.

Which was how a month later, Savannah found herself swanning dramatically around wheat fields, gazing tearfully out car windows and lip synching into the wind at a cliff's edge, with the knowledge that Brynn was being flown in to film the counterpart the following week so they'd appear in the same music video without ever having to cross paths at all.

Chapter Twenty-Three

Of all the things that had flabbergasted Brynn over the last year of her life, it was the *Longing* music video that almost broke her brain. She'd turned up as requested, submitted herself to the hair, makeup and wardrobe departments and been introduced to Hans, the director. Then she'd completed a bewildering process of being thrust into weird locations to sing along to the backing track of her own vocals, then was shoved in front of a green screen and assisted to emote and cry and rage, which luckily wasn't very hard for her those days, considering her intense schedule and immense exhaustion as she battled to complete her album.

She'd been disorientated and uncomfortable, only hoping she hadn't screwed it up too badly and that was the last she'd thought of it, until months later when Bella had called to give her the heads up that Savannah's first single was landing, and congratulated her on a job well done. She struggled internally for the rest of the day before she finally lay on her bed, put on her headphones and listened for the first time to the fully mixed and engineered recording of *Longing*. She'd cried, burned, glowed and missed the hell out of Savannah, wishing she could call her. With a slight hit of weirdness - considering the nature of the song - she sent the Spotify track to her mom, and then she'd gone on with her life.

The real event came late that evening, in the form of a text from Lane that confusingly just read *MOMMIES!!!! OH MY GOD* followed by a link. Within seconds of clicking it, Brynn realized she'd entirely forgotten that the music video would exist at all. She didn't have time to prepare herself before Savannah's face appeared on screen.

The film was black and white, and there, posed in a short white dress, Savannah looked like the classic and timeless blonde beauty that she was. Her face looked wistful, sitting alone in an old school diner, an empty coffee cup beside her. She gazed out the window, her full lips parting over the opening lines to *Longing*. Then Brynn jolted as she saw herself on screen strolling past the same window dressed in black motorcycle boots and skintight black jeans, her real life leather jacket suddenly immortalized. The Brynn on screen paused to tuck a lock of her hair behind her ear as the wind machine tousled her, the camera zeroing in on her face as her mouth moved to sing.

She had just about enough time to cringe with embarrassment when Savannah got to her feet and all but pressed herself against the window watching her go. The Brynn of real life fumbled with her phone, her jaw dropping as the video showed the two of them exchanging heated glances from their opposite seats at a bar before losing each other in the crowd, then inexplicably cutting to the pair of them arguing passionately in a car before Savannah cried prettily, looking out the window and Brynn stormed off through a field.

She couldn't believe her eyes. Was this really what she thought it was? Was the video for Savannah's first single actually portraying them as star-crossed lovers? All doubt was swept away by a shot of Savannah's nude back, her tousled hair tumbling down her spine, sitting up in an artfully unmade bed, wearing understated lingerie with a black leather jacket strewn beside her, a closeup of her delicate fingers running over the sleeve.

The video had no real storyline, just the two of them gazing heatedly, fighting furiously or weeping stormily, Savannah in her white dress all heavy lidded with desire and Brynn in her black leather, moody and brooding. By the time the video ended, she was the very definition of head-fucked.

She was beyond angry. At no point had the plan for the video ever been clearly explained to her, and she would be damned if her sexuality was going to be used to boost record sales. She was also aggravatingly turned on, aching at the sight of Savannah performing a show of lust for her. Given that they'd never actually made love it was beyond Brynn's ability to cope with the vision of an imaginary post-coital Savannah in bed, presumably after Brynn had had her way with her. It was all so outrageous she was almost at the point of breaking her hard and fast rule by texting Savannah to ask her what the hell she was playing at, when Noah called.

"Have you seen it?" she demanded instantly.

"Yeah," he said slowly. "About that. Coral just called me. She told me to tell you that Savannah didn't know either. That they sold her a much vaguer version. That she's furious and apologizes for not being more thorough in her vetting. She said that she's normally a control freak about this kind of thing but that, I don't know, I guess she's been focused on other things. She said to tell you that Savannah's going to try to fix it."

"Oh," Brynn said. It wasn't a conversation with Savannah exactly, but it was an indirect communication from her and for a moment all she felt was relief that Savannah cared enough to get the message to her. It felt, after eight months of silence, almost like a thaw.

———

Autostraddle: Savannah Grace is queer! The gay internet explodes!

Country music superstar Savannah Grace sat down for a profile piece in the New York Times this week and confirmed a very publicly speculated on rumor.

"Traditionally I'm a very private person," she told the Times. "I prefer to let my music say anything I have to say and I don't think I owe it to anyone to share my personal life. But recent events have caused me to realize that's not always the case. I think it's important for me to share something that's always been who I am: I don't identify as heterosexual and I've always been attracted to people of all genders."

Last week saw the release of Savannah's first single since her divorce from longtime collaborator, Cole Corbin. The music video for Longing *raised eyebrows and temperatures across the globe as the much crowned queen of country music Savannah Grace sang a sultry duet with broodingly attractive singer-songwriter Brynn Marshall. The two engaged in such intense eye-sex and mutual thirst that it induced a level of keyboard mashing by the queer community unseen since KStew was first spotted gal palling around town.*

Accusations of queer-baiting were initially rife in the media, yet again misusing the term to place undue pressure on an individual celebrity to publicly explain their own sexuality. While it's disappointing to see this process play out for the hundredth time, Savannah herself appeared philosophical about the experience.

"Listen," she told the reporter for the Times, "if we're honest, it's about damn time. I've been in the public eye for well over a decade and there's been many occasions that I've wanted to be out, that I've feared being out, that I've wondered whether I'd still have been awarded the accolades and given the radio play I've achieved if the fullness of my identity was known. And I hate that. At least now I'll know that any success I have in the future will be as myself."

She went on to describe the numerous constraints placed on country artists by the industry itself and the silencing impact of the overt misogyny, homophobia and racism that has, at times, seemed intractable.

"I love country music," she told the Times. "It's my heart and my soul. But do you think it's a coincidence that I'm here, getting to tell the world I'm bisexual on the eve of an album release that's not in the genre?"

Savannah has been somewhat absent from the public eye since her divorce and the subsequent breakup of her band, but as publicity ramps up for her impending solo album Beware the Fury, *it's exciting to see her appearing so relaxed and free, and more than ready to conquer the mainstream charts.*

As for Brynn Marshall, little is yet publicly known about the stunning singer bringing out the sapphic thirst in Savannah Grace, but we bring you this very important piece of reporting from her Instagram account:

1) She can rock a flannel shirt to the point we had no choice but to reproduce the compelling evidence here, here and here, just in case you needed to stare at it intensely for any length of time.

[photo caption: this is gay]

2) She's previously attended Pride events in LA.

[photo caption: being eaten alive by rainbows]

3) There is more than one past picture of her canoodling with what can only be described as gal pals.

[photo caption: roommates for life and in bed probably.]

Savannah and Brynn are more than just duet partners; they wrote the romantic song together after Savannah reportedly discovered Brynn's considerable talents while they were cozily on vacation together in Vermont and staying in Savannah's home. Listen, we just report the news, people! *But when the NYT tried to probe her on this point, Savannah poured cold water over that particular daydream.*

"No, Brynn and I are not in a relationship. Due to scheduling clashes, we actually didn't even film the video at the same time, but we're obviously thrilled our green screen acting was so successful!"

Will this stop us from hitting repeat to see Savannah Grace practically making out with a window - in a gay way - to our heart's content? Definitely not.

———

Interview with Savannah Grace
Transcript excerpt

NPR: You mentioned earlier that part of what prompted you to come out at this point in your life and career was to make yourself visible as a representation of a publicly queer person from Tennessee. You've discussed the impact of the current political landscape and increased targeting of queer people across the United States and it's very clear the concern you hold for queer and gender diverse youth in our country, particularly in conservative states. What was your experience like, as a young queer person in Tennessee? Did you identify as such?

Savannah: Well...

NPR: This sounds difficult for you to talk about. Would you prefer we moved on?

Savannah: No, I think it's important to talk about. [Pause] I grew up in a very small rural town in Tennessee, you know, the kind where everyone went to the same two churches. My mom got married when I was eleven and my stepfather was very religious. We didn't have a lot - well, we didn't have anything! - but my parents were very proud and the church was a big part of that, I guess, projection at wanting to be respectable.

I first realized I liked a girl when I was almost seventeen and I didn't know what to do with that information. I was just trying to sort of... process it. My mom found out and threw me out of the house. In a way, I like to think she was maybe trying to protect me? My stepfather's views were strong and he could be very violent towards us as his step-children, and I have no doubt as to what he would have done had I stayed.

NPR: Were you able to return to the family home?

Savannah: No, from then on, I had to find my own way in the world. It was incredibly frightening, but it was also the greatest thing that ever happened to me. I made my way to Nashville. I had to grow up, fast. I found amazing friendships. I found myself surrounded in music. If I'd stayed where I was, I'm not sure what would have happened to me. Certainly not the life I have now!

NPR: Can I ask, as time has passed, have you and your family been able to repair the relationship?

Savannah: Short story... no. We've both tried, in our own ways. My mother decided when I married a man that I was acceptable in the family fold again, but I knew this was a false kind of acceptance. I knew who I was on the inside, and to be only seen as worthy of their love if my partner was a man... well that hurt. At a certain point in time, I realized that I didn't want that kind of relationship with my family. I have made sure that they are set up and that if they ever need anything I can help, but we don't have close contact.

NPR: What I'm hearing is that despite your family's rejection of you, you financially support them?

Savannah: Of course. They're my family.

NPR: I also understand that you fund services for queer and homeless youth in your home state. Is that, in a way, what you wished the young Savannah Grace had access to when you found yourself alone?

Savannah: No. Because I didn't find myself alone. I was incredibly fortunate to find both friends and supports when I needed them. I think that sometimes people in liberal states have this naïve idea that queer people living in conservative areas should just get the hell out. But it's our *home*. It's my home. And I want to do whatever I can to make it a safe place for everyone.

NPR: Tell me about Brynn Marshall.

Savannah: Brynn is an incredibly talented musician. Everyone should listen to her upcoming album.

NPR: She's also a queer musician herself, who you discovered?

Savannah: Yes, as you saw from her publicist's response, she's out from the beginning, which is a strong, brave move.

NPR: After *Longing,* which the two of you co-wrote and performed, the question on everyone's lips is of course-

Savannah: No. We are not in a relationship. But thanks for asking!

Chapter Twenty-Four

The week Savannah's album dropped, Brynn was almost comatose with relief. Somehow she'd done the impossible, and both written and recorded *her own album* under immense pressure and time constraints and seen it through to completion. In a way, the crushing deadline was the best thing that could have happened to her. There'd been no time to overthink what she was doing, and no time to do anything other than live and breathe music.

She and Noah had hunkered down in a rented cabin in the Nevada mountains and written hard. At first, it was an incredibly strange experience to write songs without Savannah; to write songs for herself and not *for* Savannah.

"Brynn," Noah had said one morning, as they sat out on the porch with a view out over the valley. "I think you need to just give up pretending this whole thing isn't about Savannah."

"Ugh..." Brynn all but flung her guitar down. "Am I that obvious?"

"Duh."

"I can't write a whole album of songs about her. That's way too tragic, even for me."

"Or it's just absolutely musical tradition," Noah shrugged. "Love, loss, heartbreak: it's every great song ever. Look," he continued when she sighed. "Not to put too fine a point on it, but we have an incredibly limited amount of time. And every time you try to write something generic... well, that's how it comes out sounding."

"Great..." groaned Brynn. "This is a great pep talk."

"Yeah, but then you write something about Savannah and it's..." he made little explosion gestures with his hands. "I say lean into it. Write it all out. Only you and I need to know that it's essentially a concept album."

Brynn looked at him flatly.

"What if *she* ever listens to it?"

"Yeah," he said, looking her in the eye. "What if she does?"

Brynn had to admit that had worked on her. The writing had been at worst an incredible catharsis, Brynn allowing herself to absolutely drown in her own feelings, and now she was out the other side she found she could experience some level of peace with her loss of Savannah.

Mostly.

It took her another full week to get to it, but her first runthrough of Savannah's album was her last. She lay on her living room floor with the record playing and found herself ravaged by emotion as it played. The songs felt like a journey through everything she loved about Savannah, as well as everything that had grown and then shattered between them. She was so damn proud of her, of the absolute work of art she'd achieved and unbelievably honored to see her own name in the song-writing credits - and, even thanked in the liner notes - and yet she found she almost mourned the fact that now it was out in the world. Savannah was singing these songs to millions, when once, in a basement band room, she'd sung them just to Brynn.

She lay there, long after the final notes had faded, wishing like she'd never wished before, for a drink. Afterward, she'd gently returned the vinyl into its sleeve and hid the album behind the back of her collection. And then she'd rung her sponsor.

The aftermath of the album release had been out of this world. She couldn't get in an Uber or through the grocery store without hearing the two of them serenade each other. Even worse was the wall-to-wall PR and media coverage. Not only did Brynn pass billboards of Savannah's face and body plastered across the city but she couldn't turn on the TV, scroll through the news or flick through social media without her being everywhere, glowing with professionally put together beauty, though seeming to Brynn's eyes a little too thin. She'd worried. Was the pressure getting to her? Was she getting any rest?

While she'd shopped for dinner ingredients on Friday evening, she'd dialed in for her daily FaceTime with Lane and Tucker, but when she'd tried, subtly, to check in on Savannah's wellbeing Lane refused to play ball.

"She's great," they'd said noncommittally. "Hey Tucker, tell Brynn your new word!"

Tucker had grinned and stayed silent despite Lane's encouragement, prodding and whispering, until they'd finally blurted, "he can say brontosaurus!"

"Sure he can," Brynn needled but she'd felt distracted. In the early days of their conversations, Lane had gone to great pains to detail exactly how crushed Brynn had left Savannah, but for months now, they hadn't volunteered a single word. She wondered if Savannah had moved on with someone new and Lane was being deliberately evasive to spare her feelings.

She'd looked up as she passed the magazine rack, and raised her eyes skyward for strength. Savannah was on the cover of *Rolling Stone* in black leather skintight pants and looking like a quintessential rock-star. The gossip mag next to it also featured her name, with a grainy paparazzi shot of Savannah laughing with her hand on the arm of a striking brunette runway model as they dined in a restaurant together, the headline salivating. Brynn squeezed her eyes tight and turned away.

"You know when you drop the phone like that all Tucker and I can see is your left boob." Lane's voice had pulled her back to reality. She'd jerked the phone back up.

"Did Savannah ask you not to talk to me about her?" Brynn had blurted. "Because I'm not after any details - ever - I just want to know that she's okay."

"Or what? You'll swoop in and rescue her?" Brynn had fallen silent. They had a point.

———

Rolling Stone
   Cover story: *Savannah Grace is Taking No Prisoners*

Words by Sam Chaoudry
   Pictures by Huma Jordan

In person, Savannah Grace is smaller than you'd imagine. To see the country crossover megastar perform live is to get run through by a tornado, from her storms of passionately devoted fans to her golden voice that varies from intimate to brutal to sexy, often within the same song. But here in her hotel room in Chicago in the maelstrom of a press junket, Grace appears startlingly like a mere mortal, no more than 5'2" in her bare feet, tiredness marking her undoubtedly lovely features. She remains, however, every inch the star. She deftly fields questions from the gathered journalists that range from borderline worship to invasive and misogynist and she doesn't suffer any fools.

Later that evening, as we share a quiet dinner at Oriole before her performance at Soldier Field, she reflects on the last three years of her life. At the height of Twice Struck's fame, there came the birth of her beloved first child, Tucker (now aged three) the drawn out and public breakup of her marriage to collaborator Cole Corbin and the ensuing period of depression she entered where she couldn't even listen to music, let alone pick up her guitar

Contrast that to the second half of the year when her first, critically acclaimed, genre-defying solo album exploded, going triple platinum in just six weeks and beating streaming records internationally. Then last week - just four weeks into a grueling eight-month sold out stadium tour across the US - she received news of her nine Grammy nominations, including Best Album, Best Record, Best Song (*Longing*), Best Songwriting, and Best Female Artist.

So, what was the turning point?

"The turning point for me is always music," she says. "Noah Lyman's *Dead Star Ballads* was the first music I could listen to when I had spiraled out. It reminded me why I started writing songs in the first place."

At first glance, the LA-based, underground, alternative music darling Lyman and the queen of country music might seem like strange bedfellows, but it was a collaboration that thrust Grace out of her comfort zone and helped produce her best work yet.

"This album is what I'm most proud of in my life," Grace tells me, her eyes suddenly misting with tears. "It came about from a period of both incredible healing and unexpected turbulence and what I can only conceptualize now as a kind of magical alchemy. I think that all shows through in the music."

A secondary collaboration arose with astonishing newcomer Brynn Marshall, whose own debut album is now causing waves.

"Brynn is a super talent," Grace says of the singer-songwriter. "She's going to set the world alight. I'm in awe of her work."

The lead single - Marshall and Grace's duet *Longing* - features two astounding vocalists whose seamless connection (not harmed by the sensual gazes the two share in the Hans East directed music video) sent sales into the stratosphere, but when I ask Savannah to describe the inspiration for the passionate song, she's unwilling to be pressed.

"If I've learned anything in the last ten years, it's that my life needs to remain my own and that the music can stand on its own," she responds shortly, making clear the subject is over.

Continued on Page 18.

Pitchfork Review

Artist: Brynn Marshall
   Album: Jane

As the legend has it, Brynn Marshall was discovered by chance by Savannah Grace, on a visit to the country singer's vacation home in Vermont. Ears pricked up around the world when Grace's single Longing *hit the airwaves, featuring the duet with the as yet unknown artist. Who exactly was Brynn Marshall? Now signed as a label mate* to Grace with a three album deal with Sony, the answer has finally arrived in the form of Marshall's debut album, Jane. It's not a straightforward answer, however; instead, Jane lures you in with Marshall's otherworldly voice only to trip you up with lyrics that both hide and reveal the artist behind it. Marshall has been tight-lipped with the press thus far, leaving the songs up to the interpretation of the listener.

The titular track is a reimagining of Charlotte Bronte's Jane Eyre, though in Marshall's interpretation it is Jane who is responsible for any and all demons in the attic. The result - like the novel - is an unsettling breakdown of desire versus morality, detailing love laid to wreck by a lie.

The theme of lost love is the thread that runs through the album, laid perhaps most bare by the lead single Without where Marshall breaks down everything she's lost, her voice hushing into benediction as she turns everything from a cup of coffee to her lover's cold feet into sacrament. Snow Day is a poignant exploration of the fleeting nature of happiness, while Buddy reveals a sweeter side as Marshall sings a small boy through to adulthood. Mid-album comes the stonking Dropout, a slammer of a song that will have crowds on their feet when Marshall tours this summer.

Where the album really becomes sublime is the penultimate track Rock Bottom. A vividly painful self-evisceration that turns at the three-quarter mark into crackling tormented hope, her devastation giving way to a promise of a steadfast and lifelong devotion. It's a staggeringly ambitious and sprawling seven minute track that - assisted by friend and collaborator Noah Lyman's blistering guitar - grabs you by the throat and doesn't let you go. In contrast, the album finale Frozen Rain is a tender paean to watching a lover sleep. What could otherwise be a mundane love song is, in Marshall's hands - and raw, cracked voice - staggeringly heartbreaking.

Jane is an astonishing debut, a masterclass in songwriting and performance from a newly discovered virtuoso.

Rating: 8.4/10

———

When her own album dropped, Brynn had curled up inside her apartment for a week, overcome with anxiety and avoiding everyone's texts and calls. Finally, Noah had all but hammered down her door and forced her to sit and listen as he'd read the critic's reviews, practically bleeding with pride as he did. A slow, permanent shift took place within her as he read. Her dreams became plans.

"*Fuck,* Noah," she jumped up off her sofa. "What were you thinking? We need to rehearse!"

They'd played a handful of small-time gigs well before the album release, mostly just to give Brynn the confidence to see if she could, in fact, perform live. It had given her the jitters, made her knees shake and made her wonder if she was a fraud, however the reception they received in small bars and tiny side stages had given her enough of a boost to keep going. But this Friday night, they would play an official album release show, which had originally been booked in a small theater in front of a crowd of seven hundred people. Two weeks out, Bella had passed on the news that due to the demand - Brynn's profile since the release of *Longing* had jumped dramatically - they were moving to another venue.

"Where?" she'd asked. Bella had paused.

"The Wiltern," she'd told her. Brynn had attended gigs there before. It was an ornate art déco theater, and it seemed monstrously big.

"How... many people?"

"It's just two thousand," Bella had downplayed, "-three hundred." Brynn had thrown up twice since she'd heard the news. Now, though, she suddenly felt like she could do it. That maybe she even wanted to.

That Friday night, she stood in the wings, hearing the buzz of the crowd. Her hands were shaking, her fingertips felt numb, her stomach whirled. Noah clapped her on the shoulder, hard, giving her a reassuring grin, stepping out on the stage first and waving to the crowd, their cheers increasing. She remembered Savannah, stepping right up into her face, telling her to *forget them, just sing it to me.* She breathed deeply, then stepped out onto the stage and the crowd roared.

Afterwards, she'd been on a high beyond any drunken bender of her life. Backstage, after the encore was over, she and Noah kept grabbing each other's arms and shouting. The experience was already a blur of adrenaline, but she'd learned one new thing about herself she would never unlearn: she *loved* performing. She would chase this feeling for the rest of her damn life.

The band that had slowly grown around them as they'd recorded were equally hyped; they milled around high-fiving and shrieking their excitement. Various industry insiders and the technical support crew all joined to gather around, chatting animatedly and congratulating them. Suddenly, a particularly stunning face Brynn recognised broke through the clamor.

"Congratulations," greeted Coral, and Brynn forced herself to smile, her brain in total shock. "No, she's not here," Coral said drily at the look on her face. "But we had a few nights off and I wanted to come see what you were made of."

"And?" demanded Noah at her side, his eyes fixed on her face.

Coral considered him. Their eyes seemed to lock.

"You're living up to the hype, and then some." She paused, taking them both in. "Keep this up and you're going to be legendary."

It was high praise from such an industry stalwart as Coral; Brynn and Noah high-fived like idiots.

"So," Coral said as they regained their dignity, "interestingly enough, it turns out you're not married."

This was ostensibly addressed at both of them, but it was Noah she was looking at from under her lush lashes.

"We're *so* not." He dropped Brynn like a hot potato.

Brynn knew when to make herself scarce.

As the after party continued to blaze, drinks were poured liberally and Brynn had to keep waving away offered glasses of celebratory champagne, sipping on soda water and trying to keep names straight as she was more or less mobbed.

She fielded questions from music journalists, smiled and played nice with various senior record executives with big egos and wandering, proprietary eyes, found herself bluntly propositioned by both men and women, then declining two separate and completely random offers of a congratulatory hit of cocaine. After pretending to consider the options she headed where she'd always been headed, over to the woman she'd seen earlier propping up the bar - with a champagne glass filled with what looked like orange juice - who'd had her eyes on Brynn the whole night. She took a seat next to her, turning her head to smile.

"How're you holding up, kiddo?" Laura asked.

Brynn just shook her head, her eyes wide.

"Thank you for being here," she said quietly. "This shit is wild."

"No problem," said her sponsor.

Chapter Twenty-Five

Savannah's hands were shaking. This was ridiculous. She'd been minding her own business: getting on with the exhausting work of touring, press, parenting her son - on a tour bus, airports and in hotel rooms - then pulling out all the stops on a ninety-minute show three to five nights a week. Then, immediately after checking in at their hotel in Manhattan, amongst the usual flowers, gourmet gift baskets and fancy wine, there'd been a brown paper-wrapped vinyl album for her. It wasn't uncommon for artists to send her their work, as a gift or as part of a request. But the moment she saw it, she knew what it was going to be.

Ripping open the paper, she saw Brynn's face, close up, in profile. The lighting was dark, a dim forest green overlay that offset the usually warm olive of her skin. Whatever makeup artist they'd used had been genius; while her lips were full and warm, her eyelashes lush and her brows sleek, they hadn't covered her freckles. Before she knew what she was doing, she was tracing them with her fingers. Then she laughed. Brynn's dark hair tumbled down her back under a perfectly serious, dark brown, motherfucking cowboy hat. And holy god did it suit her.

Savannah had two hours to herself before it was time to help get Tucker fed and to bed, before heading down to Madison Square Garden. It was the first of three consecutive shows at the massive venue, and she had to be at her best. What she absolutely should do was nap. But the album beckoned to her and when she flipped over the album to the back and read the song titles, she gasped. So many related to her that there was no way she'd ever sleep again without knowing what Brynn had written. She felt lightheaded and incredibly stressed all of a sudden.

Her rooms were always set up to play music; it was on her rider. So she walked over to the record player and, with shaking fingers, let the needle drop. Forty-five minutes later, sobbing, she played it again.

That night she walked on stage, her own makeup artist having had a job to do to make her look like a rockstar instead of a puffy mess, and played what everyone told her later was her best show of the tour so far. She had never thrown herself harder into her songs, and when - as she always did live - she ached through both parts of *Longing*, the crowd lost their minds.

This tour was a dream come true - her songs, her comeback album - but it was also, at times, a goddamned nightmare. She was wildly proud of the songs, thrilled to be performing again, but there was not one that Brynn had not touched in some way. There were the songs Brynn had literally co-written, then the songs she'd inspired, songs Savannah had written in response to her betrayal, and the songs that she'd sung to her first. And now, every stop on the tour meant a sold-out stadium packed to the rafters with fans singing those words right along with her.

That night she completed her encore, thoroughly farewelled the crowd, briefly celebrated with the band, then greeted, shook hands and exchanged air kisses with the various establishment figures, before fleeing as soon as humanly possible. She wanted to be alone, with *Jane*.

This time, in her pajamas, she sat on the floor and, as the music played, she allowed herself one choke of laughter and a jolt of unbelievable warmth. Brynn Marshall, Californian lifeguard, med school drop-out and absolute philistine, had written one hell of an alt country album.

She looked at the liner notes. The lyrics were superb and devastating. The artwork understated and beautiful. And after all the acknowledgements, where her name was listed right after Noah's with no elaboration except a thank you, there was a dedication. She sucked in a breath.

To the Rochester to my Jane. Everything I have and everything I do is because of you and for you, always.

Savannah fell asleep with the album cover beside her.

―――

348

They played two more epic nights at Madison, performed on Good Morning America and did their press circuit, Savannah pretty much running on fumes. They took a long weekend off, and Savannah and Lane - along with the now requisite security again - took Tucker to Central Park to let him run wild. It was here that Lane's phone lit up with a FaceTime request and they looked sideways at Savannah in askance.

"Go on." Savannah walked away to let Tucker have his moment. She felt a familiar knot in her chest. It had only been a little more than a couple of weeks after she'd sent Brynn packing that Lane had come to her, admitting they'd called Brynn first, but now Brynn wanted Savannah's express permission to be in phone contact with her son.

Her first instinct had been to refuse it. She was still so angry and anyway, what was the point of dragging things out for Tucker? But she knew how much her son adored Brynn and the amount of joy and fun she'd brought to him, and besides, she figured, one of them would tire of the contact soon enough and it would trail off, perhaps softening the blow of Brynn's abrupt disappearance for him. She would never have believed that nearly ten months later, they were still chatting almost every day.

Lane swore blue that Brynn almost never asked about Savannah and that when she did it was only in broad strokes about her wellbeing. Savannah felt both relieved and confused by this. Brynn wasn't using Tucker as an excuse to be in her life, which was good, and yet... and yet, what? Did she want Brynn to be chasing after her?

Over the last several months she'd caught tiny snatches of their chats on the tour bus, or when she walked in the door back home in Nashville and the sound of Brynn's voice had always made her throat catch. She made sure never to linger long enough to listen, knowing nothing could make her crumble faster than hearing Brynn's goofy tenderness with her child.

She sat on a park bench ten feet away and watched as Tucker's face lit up and he spun in circles, showing off, Lane working hard to keep him upright, just barely. When the call ended, they took Tucker's hand and shepherded him back to his mama, where he jumped into her arms, still hyped.

"Well?" she asked Lane, who shrugged annoyingly.

"She's good," they said. "Looks good, sounds good, probably is good." There was a tone of mild exasperation in their voice and Savannah shot them a look. "You could always ask her yourself if you care so much?" they pointed out, eyebrows raised, playing their usual part in the ritual. Savannah, as always, ignored this suggestion.

By Monday, she felt almost rested and keen to get back on the road. There was a rhythm to tour life and after years away, she was finally hitting her stride.

Coral made it back to New York, just in time to board the bus to Philadelphia. Tucker was practicing his coloring in his designated play space near the back of the bus, Lane taking the role of chief crayon wrangler, trying to prevent his exuberant drawings marking everything and everyone in a five-foot radius. Coral slipped into the seat next to Savannah who was lounging halfway down the bus, and yawned.

"So?" asked Savannah.

"Good morning to you too," replied Coral. "My flight was fine, thanks for asking."

Savannah glanced out the window, gathering herself while trying not to worry about why her friend was stalling. Coral relented.

"She was amazing," she told her with a slow, wondering shake of her head. "Absolutely killed it; the crowd couldn't get enough of her."

"And the after party?" Savannah got to the real point.

"Was a blast," Coral grinned, "You'll never guess who I spent the whole evening with -" she trailed out when she saw the anxious look on her friend's face and answered the real question. "She wasn't drinking, honey. I watched her like a hawk. She turned down about twelve offers of champagne without hesitation and necked nothing stronger than soda water all night."

Savannah breathed a sigh of extreme relief, a weight she'd been carrying ever since she'd heard the news that Brynn had signed a record deal lifting ever so slightly. Success in the music industry could be a real mixed blessing and Savannah knew better than anyone the impact it could have when everyone around you treated you like you were special, as if the ordinary rules didn't apply to you anymore. The free alcohol and drugs, the parties every night. Add that to any residual impact that might have lingered from the distress she'd seen in Brynn's eyes the night she'd told her she never wanted to see her again, well... she'd been worried.

Of course, there was still plenty of time for it all to go to hell, but it felt like a good start hearing that so far Brynn was resisting temptation despite her recent lows and highs.

"There's something else," Coral told her, and her stomach clenched. She knew it was only a matter of time until Brynn moved on, and it was right, it was good, and it didn't matter to her, but god she didn't want to hear it. "I met her band." She met Savannah's eye. Oh great, Brynn had moved on with a sexy musician, how extremely perfect for her. "They're all sober, too."

"What?"She backtracked her racing thoughts.

"Yeah. I noticed they were all on the damn soda water, so I asked her drummer. Apparently, sobriety was a condition of joining the band and going on the road with her. I mean, aside from Noah, but he barely drinks anyway and he knows how important Brynn's sobriety is to her."

"Oh."

Warmth flared in her chest. Brynn was not only smart about her sobriety, she was dead serious. Savannah smiled.

"Ugh, when you smile like that, I realize I probably shouldn't tell you the next part."

"What next part?" She turned to look at Coral who was shaking her head and looking... something.

"Well, then I cornered Brynn to congratulate her on her choices and she told me, and I quote: 'I know it's stupid because I'm not even a part of her orbit anymore but I feel like Savannah would somehow manage to find a way to blame herself if I fell off the wagon right now, so you know, just to be clear.... I won't.'"

"Oh."

For some inexplicable reason, this made her cheeks warm.

"Yeah, oh."

Savannah went back to gazing out the window with her thoughts.

"Savannah!"

"What?!" she jumped.

"I know we're smack in the middle of your own personal romantic drama, but would you get your head out of your ass for two seconds and listen to what I've been up to?"

"Oh my god yes," breathed Savannah, turning her whole body to look at Coral, who she belatedly realized was straight up glowing with glee. "Tell me everything."

"You so don't deserve it," Coral side-eyed her. But she spilled anyway.

———

The tour stretched on. It was a disorientating way to move through the world and before she went on stage each night, Savannah had to check eight times the name of the city they were in, just to make sure she didn't greet the wrong crowd.

She'd worried about Tucker - this was her first time touring as a mom - but her son seemed to be having a blast. He loved the intensive mama time with her in the mornings, climbing all over her in bed as she recovered from her late night, sipping coffee and playing peek-a-boo with the covers. The rest of the time, he and Lane were thick as thieves. Somehow her nanny managed to keep Tucker safe and in line, with good boundaries, and yet behaved more like an older sibling. They played for hours, Lane's energy almost as boundless as his own, and he'd run to them for comfort as willingly as he did his mama. Lane was a goddamn dream come true.

The tour was going brilliantly, the album sales and streaming data were beyond her wildest dreams, and she'd been nominated for more Grammies for this one album than Twice Struck had gathered across their whole run. Despite her sharp left turn from country music - and her coming out as queer - her fans had not deserted her. Oh, there was some predictable fury in the conservative media and some nasty tweets, but any losses she'd made there, she didn't grieve. If homophobes and the religious right didn't like her, she knew she was living her life right. Besides, the unexpected gift of her own freedom after all these years still brought tears to her eyes; there was no sacrifice here.

On top of that, her new album had garnered a massive swathe of new listeners outside of the genre. She and the band were having an absolute ball performing the new tracks.

And yet.

Despite the incredible upwards trajectory her life was on, she couldn't fight the feeling that at her core, there was still something... unresolved. That despite her success, she wasn't really quite what she could describe as fully happy. When she tried to pinpoint the feeling, it most arose the moment she walked off stage, hyped up and sweating, into no one's arms. It stirred its head when her own hit the pillow each night, in bed after unfamiliar bed, alone. It struck her when they piled off the bus in Portland to find Jed's wife Lucinda waiting in the hotel foyer to surprise him and he swept her into his arms, spinning her in a circle, his normally reticent features bright with joy.

She started listening to *Jane* through her headphones on the bus. It might not have been healthy exactly, but some of her loneliness eased as she listened to Brynn's voice soaring through all the ways they'd fallen apart. She accepted a handful of dates she got asked out on - a gorgeous model, a rapper with a reputation as a ladykiller, a movie star or two and she'd had a great time, even a couple of great kisses. She'd never been single as a star before, and it had some serious perks. But to her even greater melancholy, nothing broke her from her unrelenting desire for the woman whose body she'd never quite had and whose voice was still in her head.

The Seattle shows were great fun, but despite losing herself in the music the way she always did when she performed, she arrived into her dressing room feeling an ache in her chest and her lower belly she just couldn't shake. She remembered her first ever tour, the way she and Cole would run off stage, laughing and swilling whisky and barely making it back to their low budget motel room to make love. She shook her head. Exhaustion was making her maudlin.

A knock came on the door.

"Come in," she called, leaning in towards the mirror, about to remove her eyelashes.

"Hey there, darlin'," came the slow drawl and she froze still. As if she'd conjured up the devil by thinking about him, there in the doorway stood Cole. "Miss me?" he grinned at her stupefied expression, stepping into the room and closing the door behind him.

"No." She recovered, getting quickly to her feet as he pretended she'd shot him in the heart. He was as towering and handsome as he'd always been, the growing lines around his eyes only adding to his appeal like it always was allowed to do for men; his plain white t-shirt and day old stubble still sexy rather than slovenly. She hated him for it.

"Great show out there," he told her. "I was dubious when I heard you were going out on your own, but you proved me wrong, sweetheart."

"What do you want, Cole?" Her hands were trembling and she fought hard to hide it.

"Come on, you haven't forgiven me yet? It's been years. Water under the bridge by now, surely. What do you want me to do, Savannah? Get down on my knees? You always did like it when I did that..."

Savannah stared him down.

"I want you to listen, when I tell you - *again* - that I don't want you anywhere near me. I want you to leave."

"Still singing that tune, are we?" he persisted. He moved closer and she backed away, not quite fast enough. His huge hands came down to cup her hips, making her feel tiny between them, and for one single second, she remembered what they'd been like together and her body wavered. He saw it in an instant and grinned, tipping his face down toward hers. She jerked out of the way and moved back three feet.

"Fuck off, Cole," she said, forcing her voice to be even. "We don't do this anymore."

She saw his face change.

"You look good, Savannah," he said, and she braced herself. "Now you've finally lost all that baby weight." He puffed out his cheeks and rounded his hands out around his body, miming a blimp. She waited for the sting to land, but to her surprise, this time, it didn't. All she felt was contempt and a little sorrow for him.

"You aren't going to even ask about Tucker, are you?" she said softly. "You don't even have that within you."

"Oh, come on, darlin', you know I don't even know if he's mine."

The cruelty and unfairness of the accusation hit its mark, but only briefly. She raised her head, looking at her ex-husband with the exact dark curls and deep brown eyes of her child, the argument that had already been resolved with a court-ordered paternity test, after a decade of fidelity to this same fucking man.

She thought of how he'd sent Tucker one gift after they'd split - a lousy bicycle that was about five years too old for him - and then never tried again. He never called. He never... FaceTimed.

"You know what, Cole? You're absolutely right," she said. "He isn't yours."

That same old fury she remembered flashed on his face, but Savannah had zero interest in playing the part he'd turned up to try to make her play. She wasn't going to be his fix ever again.

"We're done here." She turned her back on him, peering into the mirror to remove her lashes, before he could get started. "Don't make me call security to throw you out." She kept a wary eye on him in the reflection, until he flung the door open, bouncing it on its hinges and stormed away, flinging a disgusting word at her in his wake that he was too chickenshit to say while looking her in the eye.

She locked the door behind him, still trembling, but when she raised her head and met her own gaze in the mirror, she felt *clear*.

The next day, back on the bus, Coral was beyond pissed that Cole had turned up without her being there to "punch him in the dick. Was he high?"

"I don't think so, but it doesn't matter. These days he's just an asshole whether he's high or not."

"The man is jealous, baby girl. His solo album turned out average, and his tour? Well, he's sure as hell not playing stadiums. Turns out he's nothing real special without you."

Once, beating Cole so comprehensively would have given her a charge. But Savannah found she truly didn't care anymore. She couldn't stop replaying the contrast in her mind between Tucker's literal blood parent's total disinterest and Brynn's ongoing investment in his life. She pulled on her headphones and listened again, to *Jane*.

Chapter Twenty-Six

Four months into the tour, they took a two-week hiatus. Savannah, Tucker and Lane flew back to Nashville. It was both luxurious and disorientating to find herself back there. Coral had flown to the Bahamas, Travis to Ibiza and Jed and Lucinda to Mexico, but Savannah craved no holiday more than her own peaceful, private home. She rode horses, played with Tucker in the pool, went on long runs through the hills, cooked her own meals and slept in her own bed.

Rosalie came over for lunch after Savannah had called to say she was home. It wasn't unusual for them to swing between long gaps in contact followed by moments of living in each other's pockets if Savannah was home in Nashville but still, the second she walked in the door and pulled back from their hug, Rosalie's eyes narrowed, assessing her.

"What's up with you?" she asked immediately.

Savannah looked at her flatly before turning and leading the way out to the back patio for a glass of wine. They took their glasses and wound up lounging side by side on the lawn under the dappled shade of the willow tree.

"Huh," Rosalie said, after Savannah had admitted how incredibly hung up she still found herself on Brynn Marshall, despite every single sensible reason she had not to be. "It sucks for Brynn that you're so perfect and blameless in every way yourself." Rosalie smiled, giving her the kind of look that let her know there was a whole movie reel of Savannah's life happening behind her green eyes.

Savannah let her empty glass slip from her fingers as she lay back on the grass and gazed up into the branches above her head, trying not to think about that for a while.

They had a long lazy lunch, catching up on events at Rosalie's job, running their joint not-for-profit, leading Savannah to immediately text her accountant to send through what more or less equated to a blank check. She trusted - and had always trusted - Rosalie with her life, after all.

Still, despite all the things she did to try to fill her days, every evening she found she struggled to sleep. She tossed and turned and stared at the ceiling, until eventually she'd quit even trying, instead getting up to play music or bake cookies that the next morning Lane would happily devour.

Some nights she lay in bed and just listened to Brynn serenade her. She couldn't stop turning the whole thing over in her mind. Brynn was respecting her boundaries. Brynn offered no grand gestures. Brynn had written a beautiful, brutal, deeply loving album about her, but both dedicated it and delivered it without demand or expectation. Brynn was investing in her child, with not even a chance of a pay-off. Brynn was safeguarding her sobriety, not only for herself, but a little bit for Savannah, too.

When Savannah had caught Brynn in her lie, she'd instantly seen it as the lie of an addict. No matter that Brynn was at the time - and apparently remained to this day - sober. She'd automatically linked the lie to Cole and to all of Cole's many lies, and certain she was about to get emotionally abused all over again, she'd thrown up her walls and banished Brynn before that could happen. What kept Savannah awake at night was this thought: had she been wrong?

I am not Cole, Brynn had told her, fiercely, her chin held high, but had Savannah really truly been able to hear that? Because every one of Brynn's actions since that night had only proven beyond a doubt that she wasn't. Savannah lay rigid in bed. What if Brynn was actually what she appeared to be: a good (kind, beautiful, talented) person who'd made a dumb mistake? She thought of Rosalie's blunt observation. Was it a worse mistake than kissing someone you thought was married? Worse than freaking out and locking out someone who might actually love you, just because you were afraid? Savannah lay there and stared at the ceiling, and stared and stared some more.

———

At almost exactly the halfway mark of their vacation, Chester called her with the news that their support act had had to pull out of the tour after the lead singer had perforated her appendix. Savannah walked aimlessly as they spoke, ambling through the courtyard.

"That's a shame," she said, making a mental note to get her assistant to send extravagant flowers. "They've been amazing. But it's no problem for us, we'll be able to find a replacement easily enough."

There was a pause.

"Here's the thing," Chester hedged. "I've been tasked with telling you - since you're still not exactly talking to Bryce - that they've picked another act to join the tour already."

"Who?" she snapped. She wasn't keen on any more meddling by the label at this point in time. She stood still, waiting to hear the response as she stared down into the blue of the swimming pool.

"It's...well, actually, it's um...Brynn Marshall," he told her. Savannah's head snapped up. She was, for once, quite lost for words. "Savannah? Look, I know, it's not what you want. The thing is, the label is promoting her, too - her album is selling quite well - and what with the duet, well, to them it's a match made in heaven."

Savannah sat down hard on the pool tiles. She could hear Chester coughing slightly with discomfort and trying to gauge just how extreme her response was going to be.

"They'll want us to sing the duet, won't they?" she said flatly. Her heart was in knots in her chest at the thought of not only seeing Brynn, but singing together - especially that song.

"Yes," Chester confirmed.   .

"I don't know if I can do it," she confessed quietly. It clearly wasn't the fireworks her manager had been expecting because instead of arguing with her, he went quiet too.

"Well," he said eventually. "You're the best judge of that. Look, Brynn's an untested performer, in that she's never played a venue even a shadow the size of a stadium. She's had a short tour as they work out exactly where they want to pitch her and she's apparently been knocking it out of the park. Now they want to sign her up for the LA shows next week since it's already her home turf and you're in need of a starting act, but it's a trial, nothing more."

"I don't know, Chester," she said. "We...that is, *I* didn't leave things well. I don't see how this could possibly be good for the tour."

"You know, you could actually just choose to forgive her?" Chester was rarely ever directive with her and she blinked. "But if you decide you want us to fight it, then we'll fight it. The label won't be happy, but of course you have the clout to say no if that's what you really want to do. Just... let me know by tomorrow, because I'll need to pedal as fast as I can to sort this out."

They hung up the phone and Savannah flung herself, fully dressed, into the pool.

———

That evening, after she'd finally succeeded in getting Tucker to sleep in his own bed, she sat out on the second-floor balcony gazing out over the dark land. It was so quiet that when her phone pinged with a message tone, she jumped like a startled rabbit. The name on the screen made her jolt a second time, and she stared at her phone like it might bite. *Brynn Marshall was texting her.* She stabbed her finger at the screen and read the message.

> I just got told the label wants me on your tour. If you're not comfortable with me being there, just say the word and I will tell Jen I refuse the offer, no questions asked x

Savannah sat with her mouth hanging open for far too long. Brynn had been so scrupulous about not contacting her that it felt surreal to suddenly see her name on the screen, like she was just *there,* like Savannah could practically touch her.

She also knew Jennifer Landry well, and the idea of Brynn telling her anything made her want to laugh. It meant a lot that Brynn would consider refusing the tour; it was an enormous deal for an up-and-coming artist. But she found she wasn't surprised. Of course Brynn would respect Savannah's boundaries. Of course she would refuse to leave the burden of refusal all up to her. Savannah wasn't sure if Brynn quite understood the shitstorm she would be bringing down on her own head if she defied the label on such a level, but she appreciated the offer more than she could say.

If she was honest, though, it was the x at the end of the text that made her decision for her.

She picked up the phone, ready to text back. Then she stopped. She knew if she let herself get into a text exchange with Brynn, she might not want to stop. Instead, she rang Chester and spoke without preamble.

"Tell Brynn she's on for the LA shows."

Chapter Twenty-Seven

Brynn was in a head-spin. She'd been handed the biggest shot of a lifetime, playing stadiums across the whole country... if she could pull off the LA shows. The SoFi stadium held 70,000. Her biggest gig so far had been 3000 people, and that had felt intense. If she choked, her failure would be beyond epic.

And that was less than half of the noise that was happening in her head. It was *Savannah's tour.* She would *see* Savannah, with her own eyeballs, literally next week, for the first time in almost a year. Savannah Grace herself had given it the green light. Brynn had no idea what to make of that. Was it forgiveness? Another shot? Or was it merely being professional? And not only that, but toward the end of Savannah's set Brynn was scheduled to join her on stage to sing *Longing* together, for the first time since the day she'd blown it all up and kissed her. Was this what having a heart attack felt like?

She and the band were practicing their set day and night. She'd been sent the arrangement for the live version of the duet, and ran through that, over and over, Noah singing a somewhat less dulcet and distracting version of Savannah's part. She'd scheduled two damn sessions with the therapist she'd started seeing on her return to LA to try to get her head in shape. It was *so* much pressure. Between her dreams of a serious career in the music industry and the woman her heart still beat like crazy over, it was all one big stress ball of a nightmare-slash-dream come true.

She'd hit the gym hard that morning, trying to get the nervous energy out of her body, then showered and walked back toward home, stopping at her favorite coffee shop on the way home, unsure if caffeine would help or make things worse. It was late fall in LA, but she was still pretty damn warm in her maroon zip-up hoodie, so she sat down at a little outdoor table to drink her coffee. She calculated the time it would be in Nashville and hit dial to FaceTime Lane.

The phone rang out for so long that she was about to hang up, when suddenly Tucker's face filled the screen. He broke into a grin.

"Hey buddy!" she said. "Whatchu doing?"

"Am going swimming!" he exclaimed.

"Oh man, listen to you. I miss how you used to say 'fwimming,'" she told him. "You're growing up so fast! Are you tall? You look tall."

"So tall," he agreed.

"What's Lane thinking, letting you swim this time of year, anyway? They trying to freeze your butt off or what?"

Lane predictably ignored her, still holding the phone so that only Tucker could be seen. Tucker giggled, "butt!" Then he started prattling lines from his current favorite story, like he was quoting great literature. Brynn had bought her own copy when he'd gotten obsessed with it to read him over the phone, so she knew the lines too and chanted them with him, making him jump up and down with glee.

"Everything okay, Lane?" she asked, her routine, every day, don't-ask-for-details check in, but Lane ignored that too. "Are you avoiding my face?" she asked, fighting a grin. "Does that mean you stayed up late cutting your own hair again? Is it that dramatically bad?" Lane still refused to speak or appear in view, and Brynn sighed. "Tucker, don't tell Lane I said they were a noodlehead, okay? *Don't tell them.*"

Tucker giggled and chanted *noodlehead, noodlehead.*

"Okay, kid, I guess we'll chat soon. Eat all the veggies. Be good for your mama and Lane. Bye!"

"Byeeee!" Tucker shouted. She was just about to hang up when the phone swiveled and suddenly she was face to face, not with Lane but

Savannah, in a white bikini top, her blue eyes meeting Brynn's in the screen. Her lips moved.

"Bye," she said softly and disconnected the call. Brynn sat there like a gaping goldfish.

———

The days counted down to SoFi stadium. Time moved fast in a haze of activity and anxiety, but something had shifted inside of Brynn. The last time she'd been under anything like this kind of pressure, it had been the final weeks of med school. Only this time, older, sober, in therapy and chasing the right dreams, Brynn had made one very clear decision: she was going to stop thinking of failure and give it her all.

If everything that mattered to her in the world was all going to come to a head in one damn night, then she was going to throw everything she had at it. She would end tonight knowing that she had done absolutely everything in her power she could.

Which meant walking onto the biggest goddamn stage she'd ever seen in her life, for a rehearsal at four o'clock on the afternoon of the show, and not instantly passing out at the unbelievable sight of 70,000 empty places that would soon be filled. It meant not freaking out that she'd briefly forgotten the lines to *Snow Day* and hit a flat note in *Real Estate* as they marked out their paces and trusting she'd get it right when the whole damn world would be watching.

It meant stopping her brain in its tracks - as the day grew dark and the time ticked down closer to showtime - from gasping on loop: *Savannah is here, somewhere in this building Savannah is here,* and wondering at what point she'd suddenly run into her and need to somehow say actual words.

It meant locking herself alone in her dressing room, after her hair and makeup had been done, pacing around in her tailored goddamn *sequined suit* and talking herself down from hyperventilating.

Brynn finally stopped turning in circles and stared at herself in the mirror. The woman that looked back at her startled her. The insanely expensive suit was black and sparkled in the light, the jacket cut to show bare skin and cleavage. Her hair was professionally tousled, her eyes extra dark under the liner and lashes. She looked hot as fuck. She looked like a goddamn *star.* But it was the look in her eyes that shocked her. She'd thought she was barely a minute from losing her shit, and yet the woman in the mirror looked confident as hell. She nodded at herself.

When the knock on the door finally came, Brynn strode out. She could already hear the roar of the immense crowd and the feeling swept her up like a tidal wave as she joined her band in the wings of the enormous stage. The piped in music went quiet, the stage lights went dark and the crowd screamed in anticipation.

Noah turned to her. There were no words left; they'd been saying them to each other all week. Instead, he just grinned at her, his eyes blazing absolute adrenaline and joy, and swaggered out on stage, in view of 70,000 people, who sent another wave of overwhelming noise at the sight of the opening band beginning to take their spots. Brynn counted down another 15 seconds, her life flashing before her eyes. Then she strode out onto the stage to a deafening roar and picked up her guitar to sing.

Chapter Twenty-Eight

Savannah locked herself in her dressing room. She looked in the mirror and despite all the regular trappings, tonight, instead of a rockstar, all she saw was a small and extremely anxious looking woman. The knock on her door came.

"It's time," came the voice, and Savannah made herself cross the room to open the door. Coral straight up choked back a laugh when she saw her face. "Oh honey." She grabbed her hand. "I've got you."

They made it to the wings just in time for her to see Brynn, less than ten feet away, striding out in front of tens of thousands of screaming fans, like she'd done it a hundred times. Her suit sparkled as the lights came up, guitar in her hands, her chin held high, and Savannah wondered if this was what it felt like to have a heart attack. Then Brynn's voice rang out across the gigantic arena in a husky rasp.

"Your heart is my only home and I've been evicted," she sang the opening line to *Real Estate,* then the guitars, bass and drums all smashed in at once and the crowd went wild. Through Savannah's headphones on the bus and in hotel rooms, the song had been a devastated howl, but here, storming a stadium, it sounded glorious. She was squeezing Coral's hand so hard her best friend turned to stare at her, and they both burst into massive grins.

Brynn looked and sounded like a fucking superstar. The outfit, the hard strum of her guitar - which, if she'd only been *passable* at like she'd claimed, she'd done a hell of a lot of work on - the rhythmic bounce in her body; Savannah could not stop staring at her. She was so different to the woman she'd been curled up with at home in Vermont, and yet somehow, Savannah realized, Brynn had always carried herself exactly like a rockstar, with her artful slouch and confident movements. It was one of the first things that had attracted Savannah to her. And here it was now, fully realized.

When the song ended, the crowd's applause was rowdy and Savannah was just close enough to see the wide-eyed grin that Brynn threw to Noah as he caught her eye, in reality as well as on the huge screen behind her, projecting her beautiful face in LED out over the massive crowd. She was clearly having an incredible time.

"Hello, Los Angeles," she said easily into the mic. "You're looking fucking beautiful tonight." The crowd roared as she flirted with them, and Savannah couldn't blame them for it one bit. The opening notes to *Jane* rang out, a band pianist playing the first ominous chords, then Brynn all up wailed her temptation, her remorse, her demons and Savannah found she was shivering like she had a fever. Coral felt it and kept gripping her hand. When the song hit the intense musical bridge, Brynn casually bumped the pianist off the bench and took over, smashing out the notes herself to the absolute delight of the crowd, her body arching back and forth as she played, before letting him swap back in as she returned to her mic for the song's dark conclusion.

Her set was tight, all hungry and dramatic alongside Brynn's comfortable showmanship. She made soft songs like *Buddy* and *Frozen Rain* epically beautiful in the huge cavernous space, her voice soaring out into the night sky, Savannah weeping helplessly at hearing what had once been their private heartbreak hit the mark with 70,000 people.

The band smashed through *Dropout* and Savannah lost Coral, who was straight up jumping up and down and dancing along with Jed and Travis in the wings. Then, as the final notes faded out, a small rowdy group of fans at the front started shouting, *"Savannah! Savannah! Savannah!"* impatient for the main act to start and Savannah cringed.

On hearing it, Brynn cupped her ear toward the crowd.

"Who's getting excited to see Savannah Grace tonight?" She smiled widely into the mic. Oh my god, Brynn was pumping the crowd for her. Okay, well, that was just adorable. "Do you love her?" she continued, waiting for the crowd to finish screaming their enthusiastic response. "I know you do. Not like I love her, though," she said with a flirtatious smirk. Savannah went still. The crowd loved it: it was a clear reference to their duet and famous video, or was it? Brynn had to know she was there, watching. Her heart was pounding in her chest. Did Brynn just use the present tense despite this long, drawn out year of silence?

"This song is for Savannah," Brynn said, simply. Then she launched into *Rock Bottom,* the blast of her and Noah's guitars drowning out the crowd's excited response.

Of all the songs to dedicate to her. If Brynn had wanted to deliver a grand gesture she could have picked the romantic, heartbreaking *Without,* or the melancholy, sweeping beauty of *Snow Day,* songs Savannah quietly adored. But this song? She stood in the wings and could only watch as Brynn tore herself to shreds, exposed all her faults and scars, her face contorting with pain and rage at herself. And then the key change, that devastating, hopeful key change and Brynn's voice soared.

I'll warm your feet, I'll hold your nights,
I'll be your home, I'll fight your fights
I'll kiss your scars, I'll heat your bed
I'll be the place for your weary head
I'll keep your heart safe, I'll keep your heart safe
I'll keep your heart safe, I'll be your saving, Grace.

The song wasn't asking forgiveness. It wasn't begging for a chance. It was a promise.

Coral came and wrapped her arms around her from behind and held her tight as she sobbed. As the song reached its epic conclusion, the final chords sounding, Coral grabbed her arm to turn her.

"Come on," she said gently. "You cannot be here looking this soggy when she walks off stage feeling eight feet tall." Savannah let herself be pulled away into the corridors backstage. "Besides, we go on in half an hour, so you're going to have to get your shit together."

Before she knew it, Coral was ushering her back into the dressing room, where her concerned looking makeup artist was waiting. Jon's eyes went wide when he saw Savannah's face. "Don't mind her," said Coral. "She's having a *lot* of feelings."

Chapter Twenty-Nine

When Brynn walked off stage, she was practically attacked. Noah flung his arms around her and ruffled her hair and she clung to him, both of them laughing. The second he pulled back, the rest of the band were on them, everyone wild-eyed and thrilled to the point of prattling incoherently at each other, all at once. Jen appeared, a wide satisfied smile on her face, her strong handshake accompanied by a warm arm squeeze.

"Well done, Brynn."

"You crushed it!"

"Way to destroy a stadium, you animal!"

Amongst the congratulations and compliments, Brynn looked around her. Savannah was nowhere to be seen. Had she seen any of Brynn's set? Or was she too busy avoiding her, or even just getting ready for her own show? Anything seemed possible.

"You're the real thing, Brynn Marshall," came a voice to her left and there was Coral looking glamorous in her on stage ensemble. She thanked her and tried to find a way to ask that wasn't too desperate, but even as she opened her mouth Coral responded. "Yes, she was here. Yes, she watched the whole thing. But we're on in fifteen, so you're going to have to leave her alone." Her tone was a warning, and Brynn wondered what the hell that meant.

Before she could ask, more well-wishers swept in and Coral melted back into the crowd. Another of the label executives pulled her aside, talking excitedly about sales and strategies and plans, and she nodded in what she hoped were the right places, but she could barely hear them, let alone listen.

"I'm your new biggest fan!" piped up one of the guitar techs as he rushed back and forth onto the stage and she smiled at him gratefully. The pace on the empty stage was increasingly frenetic as what seemed like a hundred people scurried around moving gear. There was a slow drum beat happening to hype up the crowd who were already howling Savannah's name.

A bottle of cold water was shoved into her hand and she looked up gratefully to see Noah beside her as he towed her to a better spot to see the set. He nodded over to the very edge of the wings and she saw with a shock, that there in the dark, Savannah was standing, alone, her head bowed. She almost looked like she was praying. Brynn felt electricity jolt through her at the proximity. After all this time, suddenly there she was, eight feet away at most.

Brynn went lightheaded with the realization that any second Savannah could look up and meet her eye. But then Coral strolled out on stage like it was a catwalk and the crowd went nuts. The band all took their spots, strumming out noise, the atmosphere in the stadium on a knife edge. Then Savannah lifted her head and walked out and the roar hit the stratosphere.

She was smiling, her charm at a million watts, wearing a very short gold sparkly dress that made her look like she was drenched in a thousand tiny lights, her limbs and shoulders bare and gleaming, standing taller in dangerous stilettos. Brynn wanted to bite her, she looked that good. She lifted the mic off the stand and the wall of sound morphed into the opening bars of their second single, *Dumb and Rich.* Brynn was in knots. If there was a more effective way to be reminded of the stupidest thing she'd ever done than having it blasted over a stadium with 70,000 people chanting the chorus, then she didn't want to know about it. But god did Savannah look and sound incredible while she destroyed her.

When the song faded out, Savannah greeted the crowd, her banter warm and easy. Then Coral spoke up into her mic, her tone both sultry and teasing.

"You know I get this feeling, Savannah, honey, that tonight you've got a little *extra* steam built up, am I right?"

The crowd screamed for it. There was a tiny fraction of a pause, long enough that Brynn wondered if Coral had gone off script. But Savannah raised her head, her smile a straight up tease.

"I think you might be right," she said warmly into the mic.

She reached down and picked up a bright red electric guitar and pulled it onto her body. Then she lowered her lashes.

"Don't look at me with eyes like that," she began, her voice every bit as sultry as Brynn remembered it the first time when Savannah had fixed her eyes on her in the band room and taken her apart, line by sexy line. Only this time the crowd made sure to scream the hinted word *wet* and Brynn's teeth nearly went through her bottom lip. Savannah writhed and rocked her hips into the guitar, dropping words like *splayed, helpless,* and *honey.* Brynn was not even sure if she was breathing anymore.

Brynn found herself unprepared when the band followed this up with *Looking Back* and her eyes filled with tears, remembering so clearly that day by the snowy lake, how badly she'd wanted *everything*, even the simplest of pleasures, like holding Savannah's hand in the cold. It felt like ten years ago. It felt like yesterday.

The rest of the set raced by, everything from pyrotechnics to lights that could give you a damn seizure, incredible, unbeatable music and in the center of all of it was Savannah Grace. Tonight, though, it wasn't just Brynn losing her mind at the sight of her, it was 70,000 other people too. Every single pair of eyes in the stadium were fixed with admiration, heat and adoration for the woman projected out on the massive screen, her voice filling up the whole damn world.

Brynn felt incredibly small all of a sudden. She'd had one chance with Savannah, who somehow, miraculously, had seen her and wanted her, and she'd fucked it up. And now, here she was, just one of the millions with a crush.

And then, "you're up next," came the prompt from a stagehand. Just like that, Brynn straightened her spine. She was not just one of millions, after all. She'd tasted the mouth of the golden-voiced woman singing on stage. She'd had her right there in her arms, gazing into her eyes like she'd never want to look away.

All of a sudden, a hundred tiny moments rushed over her. Savannah, blushing and staring at her in a blanket fort, lit up by fairy lights. Savannah teasing her with a coy glance over her shoulder on her way out of the bedroom in the early morning light. Savannah dumped in a snowdrift, her laughing accusatory eyes looking like she couldn't pick between yelling at Brynn and kissing her.

Distantly, Brynn could hear Coral hyping her, announcing her name. It took everything she had, but Brynn stepped out, to deafening applause, just managing to remember to smile and wave at the crowd as she walked all the way up to Savannah Grace herself, who stood waiting for her at the front and center of the stage. Savannah was smiling back at her, all golden and beautiful and twinkling with practiced charm. They hugged, as had been literally choreographed, but on feeling Savannah's body finally in her arms it was all she could do to remember to draw back. She stepped up to the mic stand, feeling lightheaded, and the music kicked in.

"You make my knees weak…you steal all my sleep." Savannah's moan was addressed to the audience. She could do it that way if that's what got her through. Brynn wasn't going to play it that way though.

She turned her body fully as she watched Savannah sing, then locked her eyes on her face, the first lines tumbling out of her mouth like a prayer.

Savannah felt the look and turned too. Brynn blazed with instant heat as their eyes met. Savannah sighed out the next words, her eyes on Brynn's face. She was performing for the crowd, but there was something there in her eyes that snagged on Brynn's heart.

Gripping tight to the microphone, she moved, ridding the distance between them. She was dimly aware of the crowd losing their minds, but all she could see was the fast rise and fall of Savannah's chest and her red painted lips parting, as Brynn lifted the mic to sing to her, their bodies only inches apart.

"If I could just touch you-" Brynn let all the want inside her spill out into her features as she sang through her lines and she saw the exact moment Savannah's game face slipped, with a small, fast intake of breath.

The chorus hit and Savannah didn't look away from her face as their heated, longing lyrics spilled from them before a crowd of tens of thousands. Their lower bodies were just about touching, Brynn's thigh almost between Savannah's. They were so close she could smell the soft hit of perfume on her skin and her knees almost gave way. The minutes of the song slipped away, Brynn drinking in the sight she'd been longing for, for almost a year: Savannah looking back at her with all-out desire.

For a moment, she forgot it was a performance, until all of a sudden the music was fading out. It was over. Their farewell hug was choreographed too, though not the part where she leaned in close and murmured into her ear above the roar, the last move she would ever make for Savannah Grace.

"I will be sorry for the rest of my life. And I will love you for the rest of my life." Savannah jerked slightly at her words. "If you need to take until we're seventy to forgive me, I will drop everything and everyone to be with you when you do. But jesus, Savannah, I hope you don't wait that long."

She slipped out of Savannah's arms and left the stage, waving to the crowd and fighting sudden tears. She could still see Savannah's face on the big screen staring out over the crowd, her eyes wide and unreadable, her lips parted.

She returned to the wings, her hands trembling. She'd left Savannah with no doubts whatsoever as to her ongoing feelings and intentions toward her. She'd given it her absolute best shot. But while she'd seen unmistakable yearning in Savannah's eyes when they sang, she had no idea if her feelings made one speck of difference.

On stage, as the cheers finally died down, Savannah stood absolutely still. The intensity in the crowd began to grow the longer she stood in silence. The stage lights dropped down to black for several long seconds, then a light slowly grew up around her. When she began to sing, her voice was brittle with a cold rage. The hair on the back of Brynn's neck stood on end. *Beware The Fury* grew louder, more frenetic, and Savannah howled with more desperate *fury* than Brynn had ever seen her. Her body bent and quivered with it, her voice contorting until the song hit its peak and she screamed herself ragged.

The lights shut out at the end of the song with a bang. It was the end of the set and the crowd collectively lost their minds. Savannah stalked off stage and stormed straight past her without sparing her a single glance.

Brynn stood there for an unknowable amount of time - the crowd chanting *Savannah! Savannah! Savannah!* - and felt icy cold. Savannah was furious with her. She'd crossed a boundary - using a professional moment to push a very personal agenda. She'd given it her all, but all she'd managed was to succeed in fucking it all up, all over again. Her chest felt like it was caving in. She suddenly realized she couldn't stand there and watch for another second. She slunk off out of the wings, only - to her horror - to pass by Savannah herself, heading back to the stage for her encore. Their eyes met and Savannah's gaze blazed into hers for a split second before they passed each other, and Brynn fled for her dressing room.

She could dimly hear the encore - a raucous performance of a song she somewhat recognised from the one and only time she'd played the album - followed by more crowd noise and then, eventually, relative quiet, before the corridor outside filled with noise, people's voices, doors slamming, laughter, back slaps, high fives.

Brynn stayed slumped in her chair, avoiding her own gaze in the mirror. She'd never felt such a consuming mixture of emotions. On the one hand, she'd played the show of a lifetime and had smashed it. From here, the world was hers and a big part of her was over the moon. On the other hand, she'd lost Savannah for good this time. There was no more chance of redemption. She felt sick and immensely sad.

Someone knocked on the door. She stayed still, hoping that Noah or whatever industry type who wanted to talk to her would go away. They knocked again, insistent. Brynn sighed and tried to rearrange her face to look mildly less devastated.

"Come in." Her voice sounded tired, even to her. She looked up as the door opened to see a sparkle of gold as Savannah slipped inside. She froze still. Savannah closed the door behind her and then, with her eyes on Brynn's, she reached over and slowly clicked the lock.

She stepped out of her towering heels and sauntered in bare feet all the way over to Brynn's chair. Brynn stopped breathing altogether, staring up at her as Savannah slipped in front of her and pushed herself up on the dressing room bench before her, her bare legs almost touching Brynn's knees. She looked back down at Brynn sitting before her. Her gaze looked dangerous. Brynn stared at her like an apparition.

"Savannah..." Her voice came out husky, her heart pounding at how close she was. "What are you doing?"

Savannah leaned back on her hands and looked at her from under her long lashes.

"I'm alone with you in your dressing room, in a very tiny sexy dress, and I just locked the door," she emphasized, her voice low. "What do you think I'm doing?"

Brynn's brain short-circuited.

For three whole seconds, she just stared, her eyes wide. Then a sound escaped her that was almost a growl as she pushed herself up out of her chair and slid her hands into Savannah's hair and kissed her hot mouth desperately. Savannah drew her in with a gasp, arching against her, wrapping her legs around Brynn's hips and pulling her in hard, kissing her back with ferocity. They kissed each other roughly, wildly, until Brynn pulled back to bend her head and taste the salt of Savannah's skin, hungrily kissing and licking at her throat, breathing in the sweat of her body post performance and biting down on her gleaming shoulder. Savannah whimpered and bucked.

"Don't make me wait," she begged, lifting her hips, and Brynn's vision went white for a moment before her hands slipped under the sparkle of the dress to tug the scrap of silk that passed as Savannah's underwear down and off. Savannah moaned with approval and pulled her in hard again, their mouths a clash of wet heat.

"I've waited a *year* for this." Brynn pulled back, her heart going a million miles an hour, her breathing erratic. "You can wait another damn minute, so I can have you the way I want you." She roughly tugged the top of the golden dress down until suddenly Savannah's breasts were bare before her.

Savannah gasped and Brynn moaned at the sight, burying her face in the feverishly hot skin before her, licking, sucking then biting at one hard nipple and then the other, making Savannah cry out and arch her back, pressing herself desperately against Brynn's mouth for more.

Savannah pulled back with a ragged gasp and her fingers grappled with the button that held Brynn's suit jacket together, the expensive garment hitting the floor as Savannah stared at her in the skimpy black lace bra the stylist had given her. Her pupils dilated as her eyes raked down her torso, her gaze hungry, her lips parting.

"Oh god, I need you *now*," she whimpered, pulling Brynn back in close, raking her fingernails hard into her naked back. Brynn let her own fingers trace slowly, disbelievingly, up the insides of Savannah's smooth thighs, feeling her convulse in anticipation. Brynn wanted her desperately - had wanted her for so long - and having her like this was beyond her wildest dreams, but-

"Are you here to hate-fuck me?" The words fell out her mouth, even as her hands stayed where they were. Savannah gaped at her, her thighs trembling.

"Actually," she said slowly, "I was under the impression we were making love."

Now it was Brynn's turn to gape. Her hands slipped higher.

"But," she couldn't comprehend it, "right after our duet you sang *Beware the Fury* like you wanted to murder somebody."

Savannah looked at her with what suddenly seemed like incredible affection.

"Because that was the set list?" she pointed out. "Besides, I needed somewhere to put all that pent up energy after you *eye-fucked* me on stage in front of a stadium crowd."

Brynn's fingers moved again, tracing the crease where her thighs met her body and Savannah shuddered.

"Then you stormed right past me in the wings like you couldn't stand to look at me," she reminded her.

Savannah's voice was trembling with barely held together tension as she responded.

"I didn't *see* you. I'd just come from blinding stage lighting into forty different people in the dark. I did see you when I came back for the encore though, and I couldn't understand why you were running away so fast."

"Then you... you don't hate me," Brynn whispered, her fingers slipping further, caressing unbearably soft skin.

"Right *now* I kind of hate you," Savannah's hips bucked, "*Please, Brynn-*"

"Because you came here to make love." Brynn's fingers didn't budge.

"*Yes.* Although, I can't believe you were going to let me hate-fuck-" her voice stuttered out as Brynn's hand cupped her right where she was ferociously hot and wet.

"You were saying?" Brynn whispered, moving her fingers in a slow, wet circle.

"Nothing-" Savannah choked out, and Brynn watched her in fascination as red heat mottled her neck and her head fell back. "Oh god, *Brynn-*"

"You're so beautiful like this," she murmured wonderingly, keeping up the slow movement until Savannah lifted her head to gaze at her. Brynn felt her own body clench at the absolutely dazed desire in those blue eyes. She kept stroking her, watching Savannah shiver with pleasure, her lips parting, wordless with want. It felt, for a second, like an out-of-body experience, touching Savannah the way she'd always longed to.

"Please-" Savannah begged, and Brynn would have given her anything - the world if she could - with that look in her eyes. "More," she whimpered, "I need *more."*

Brynn slipped two fingers inside her and Savannah cried out and arched her back, her legs wrapping tighter around Brynn's hips. Brynn pushed a third finger inside her and Savannah cursed, digging her fingernails into her shoulders, spreading her thighs wider for Brynn to fuck her.

Brynn's bicep burned as she pushed hard into Savannah's molten hot body, but there was nothing on this planet that would make her stop. She found the angle that made Savannah's moans turn to ragged, short gasps and used her thumb to lightly slip against the bundle of nerves where she was needed most and Savannah's jaw dropped, her face almost shocked as she was wracked with pleasure, her hips furiously riding Brynn's fingers.

"Fuck *yes,"* Brynn gasped, thrusting harder, watching Savannah start to lose it. She'd never seen a hotter sight in all her life.

"Brynn," Savannah's voice came out a breathless stutter. *"Kiss me,"* she begged. Brynn did. Savannah gasped into her mouth and Brynn felt her whole body convulse, clenching down on her fingers. She pulled back just enough to see Savannah's eyes squeezed tight, her face flushed red, her body trembling like a leaf as she rolled her hips, riding out the sensation. Heat suffused Brynn's whole body as she watched Savannah come for her.

When her blue eyes opened again, Brynn felt her heart crack at the rawness of the expression on her face. She slowly slipped her fingers out, making Savannah moan, then pulled her in close and held her tightly while she regained her breath, tipping her face back for Brynn's kiss. They kissed for a long time, Brynn cupping her hot face and Savannah clutching her hips to keep her close. Eventually, Brynn found herself smiling into the kiss.

"What?" Savannah murmured against her lips.

"I actually think you made my back bleed," she accused, feeling the intense sting in her skin. Savannah pulled back and looked down at her hands.

"Oh my god, I forgot about these!" She held up her dainty fingers, each tipped with an expertly applied acrylic nail. Brynn grabbed her hand and looked at the extremely hard polished tips, built for beauty, but also to withstand guitar playing.

"I notice that wasn't an apology." She rolled her shoulders with a pointed wince.

Savannah just smiled.

"I'm not apologizing. It's the least that you deserve. Although," she paused, looking at Brynn through lowered lashes, "I suppose it means I'll just have to use my mouth on you instead." Brynn stopped breathing altogether and Savannah straight up smirked at her expression. "Oh," she noted, "I think you'll cope."

She slipped off the bench and switched them, so Brynn leaned against it, her hands already gripping it for strength. Without looking away from Brynn's eyes, Savannah reached down and slowly undid her pants. Brynn went dizzy. Between them, they got her out of them and Savannah tossed them aside.

"Shall I leave these out?" she asked, her voice a soft tease, looking down at her breasts, still bared above her dress and Brynn made a strangled sound in her throat, nodding adamantly. "You want to watch me get down on my knees for you?" Savannah asked. Her voice was low and sultry - as if that was a real question - and Brynn nearly came right then and there.

Savannah slid to her knees and tugged off Brynn's soaked panties, kissing her way up her thighs before giving her a long, lazy, sinful lick from bottom to top, and Brynn almost blacked out. Her mouth was hot and her tongue soft. She looked down to see Savannah raise her lashes and make eye contact with her as she slowly swirled her tongue. She made little hums of pleasure as she worked Brynn up, making almost embarrassingly short work of her, teasing and slipping her tongue against her and into her, her fingers caressing Brynn's ass and making her legs quiver until she slowly lapped her tongue and didn't stop, her satisfied eyes watching Brynn absolutely come apart at her touch.

Brynn had *never* come that hard. Savannah moaned with pleasure as Brynn ground against her mouth, making a show of wiping her chin as she stood. She melded her body into Brynn's as Brynn trembled with aftershocks, breathing hard.

"That," Savannah murmured into her ear, "is for assuming I was a straight girl."

Brynn gripped her tight, her knees still shaking.

"I mean, I-"

"You did."

"I did."

"You were wrong."

"I see that now."

They stood, holding each other for a long time, breathing each other in.

"Savannah." Brynn didn't want to break the spell but she couldn't cope a moment longer without knowing. "What happens now?" she asked. "Because you *know* how I feel about you... you know that I want to be with you."

Savannah stilled in her arms and then pulled back. Brynn swallowed, watching her.

"I don't know, Brynn," she said softly, and Brynn just tried to keep breathing.

Savannah took another step back and pulled the front of her dress back up, covering her half bared body. She moved away from her, pushing herself back to sit on the bench again.

"I think it depends," she said, finally meeting Brynn's eyes. "What would that even look like, to you? I mean, we live in different states. I have a *child*. Not to mention our lives are completely insane. Do you have a plan here exactly?"

Brynn paused to find her panties, needing some kind of dignity for this conversation, even if that meant sitting there in nothing but fancy lingerie. She pushed herself up to sit next to her.

"I do," she said, firmly.

"You... have a plan?" Savannah looked surprised. It clearly wasn't what she'd expected. A realization hit Brynn all of a sudden, of exactly how many people probably propositioned this woman on a daily basis.

"Yeah, I absolutely do." She raised her chin and met her eyes.

"Care to share it?" There was a disbelieving note in Savannah's voice.

"Sure," Brynn told her. "It goes like this. First, you take me home with you to whatever luxury hotel room you've got going on and I'm going to lay you out in those fancy sheets and make you come all night long."

Savannah drew in a quick breath, letting that hit. Her eyes flickered down Brynn's body just for a second.

"Well, I can see how that would be a given," she acknowledged. "But then what?"

"Then you invite me on your tour."

"Are you seriously using this as a career conversation right now?" Savannah spluttered a laugh, turning to her with both eyebrows sky high, her eyes amused rather than offended. Brynn shook her head.

"No, I'm being pragmatic. You're on a massive tour. The label wants to send me on a less massive, but still extensive tour. We can go on separate tours where I never ever get to see you, or you can invite me on your tour and I'll be right here to hold you every night."

Savannah sucked in a breath at that. Her eyelashes flickered.

"I see your point," she murmured. "And then what? What do our lives look like after that?"

"After the tour? We pick one of your ridiculously over the top properties and spend time getting to know each other off the road. We write incredible songs together, make love, hang out with Tucker and you can finally take me on one of those terrifying hikes in the forest you once promised me."

"That... doesn't sound terrible," allowed Savannah.

"I'm not finished."

"Please, continue." Savannah rolled out her hand elaborately, her eyebrows raised.

"By then an appropriate amount of time has gone by and I've saved enough in royalty checks and merch sales to buy the prettiest damn ring you've ever worn in your life and put it here," Brynn reached over and toyed with her bare left ring finger.

Savannah gaped at her, her blue eyes gone wide and her mouth opening to speak, but Brynn got to her feet, standing in front of her, with one finger raised to stop her. She reached down and curved her hands over Savannah's ass and squeezed.

"Then," she added, working hard to keep her face as serious as possible,"I want to get you pregnant." She pulled Savannah in, hips first, against her body, making her breath escape in a gasp as her jaw dropped.

"*Excuse* me?" Savannah looked up at her like she'd lost her mind.

"At least once," she continued, not wanting to let go of the luscious ass in her hands. "Maybe twice. I bet you're fucking hot when you're knocked up." She bit her lip, trying not to laugh as Savannah tried to kick her. She grabbed her leg to stop her. "Tucker needs a sibling," she argued. "And besides, I think you should get to do it right this time, where I'm there to rub your back and bring you weird snacks, and I'm right there with you to catch our babies and hold them when they cry so you can rest."

Savannah's eyes were wet. Brynn came and sat next to her again.

"I want Tucker to grow up knowing he has a mama *and* a mom." Her eyes started to mist too, so she swallowed, then rushed on. "I mean, the next part is a bit less planned out, it's just a general blur of parenting and writing music and going on tour and honestly we're going to need to pay Lane a stack more money to make them stay because it all sounds like a *lot* to manage. But it goes on like that for a while, then at some point we become the kind of people who gross out our grandchildren because we still make out a lot and then eventually we get really, really old and preferably die on the same day," she shrugged. "Anyway," she told her, all cards on the table. "That's my plan."

Savannah looked at her for a long moment, her face flushed and tear streaked. Brynn gazed steadily back. There was not a single doubt in her mind of what she wanted for her life. Everything was in this woman's hands.

"Brynn," she whispered slowly. "I was just hoping to hear you say you'd consider moving to Nashville."

"Oh," she said. "For sure. In a heartbeat."

They smiled at each other. Savannah was quiet for what felt like forever.

"Okay."

"Okay?" Brynn's heart pounded.

"Okay, as in, let's start with the first step and see how it goes from there." Savannah's eyes were achingly soft. Brynn managed not to burst into happy tears. She swallowed and nodded.

"Oh shit," she said, making her voice level with some effort. "I forgot the first, first step."

She got to her feet.

"And what's that?" Savannah looked slightly dizzy. There was a light in her eyes that Brynn had never seen before. It thrilled her.

"It's where I take you over to that couch over there and make you lift your dress so I can give you the best head you've ever had in your life," she announced, biting her lip against her smile.

"You're extremely cocky," Savannah considered her, but Brynn could already see the decision flaring in her eyes.

"Actually," she said, taking her by the hand, "you once told me that I understate everything about myself." She led her across the room.

"I did, didn't I?" Savannah bit her lip as she followed.

"Mmhmm," Brynn settled back on the couch, pulling up a cushion and resting her arm behind her head. "So I'd suggest it's in your best interest right now to come here and sit on my face."

Savannah gazed down at her, lust and amusement making her glow. Slowly, she pulled her dress all the way up and over her head, letting it fall to the floor. Brynn's teeth nearly went through her lip.

"How are you real?" she breathed. She wanted her in every possible way, all at once, right now. She was also dying to prove to Savannah that everything she had to offer was *everything* she could ever want. God, would she ever take care of this woman.

"I'm definitely real." Savannah looked at her from under her lashes.

"I also can't believe you manage to wear that insanely tiny dress on stage without a bra," Brynn breathed, as reality caught up to her. Savannah laughed, her eyes lighting up.

"There was some strategic boob tape," she confessed, straddling Brynn's lap. "I ripped it off on my way to your door."

"That might be the sexiest thing I've ever heard." Brynn was definitely imagining it.

"Shut up."

"Make me."

Savannah did. She tasted so good Brynn wanted to die. A few moments in, muffled between Savannah's thighs, she heard a knock at the door. She didn't stop moving her tongue and Savannah squeaked, her hips rolling.

"Brynn?" came the voice, sounding concerned.

"She's indisposed at the moment," Savannah called out, and Brynn licked her harder.

"Oh." There was a long pause. "Hey, Savannah, you're not, like, murdering her or anything, are you?" Noah asked tentatively.

"If I am, I promise you she's enjoying it," Savannah replied wryly, her breath hitching and there was a splutter of a woman's laugh from outside the door.

"Noah, they're *fucking*," Coral's voice came. "Now, are you going to come home with me tonight or not?"

Brynn laughed too, making Savannah jump, and she tugged on her thighs to pull her back against her mouth, swirling her tongue so softly that Savannah moaned and chased the sensation. She pulled back further, her tongue just a tease, and Savannah cried out in frustration. Brynn kept her just on the brink, the feather light promise of more until Savannah convulsed, cried out and convulsed again, still chasing the friction. When she felt Savannah's thighs tense up she knew she had her where she wanted her, and kept up the same impossibly light flicker as Savannah started to come. And then come. And then come some more. Brynn didn't let up until Savannah cried out in exhausted surrender and pulled away, collapsing on top of her, limp, trembling and breathless.

"Are you finally ready to take me home with you?" Brynn whispered as she held her tightly. "Because this couch is small and we have a *lot* of catching up to do."

Chapter Thirty

Savannah's back hit the inside of her hotel room door as Brynn kissed her. Brynn kissed like she did everything else - with intense passion and skill - and Savannah was overwhelmed with sensation. It was such a shift, from steely silence and sharp absence to *this* - Brynn's firm body holding her pinned - that Savannah almost expected her to melt into an apparition, leaving her alone and bereft like she was before.

"I can't believe this is real," Brynn murmured into her skin, apparently reading her mind. "I've never stopped wanting you," she whispered and Savannah got goosebumps. Brynn's strong thigh slipped between hers and she ground against her, already wet and needy all over again. Suddenly, Brynn sprang back in the dim light.

"Holy shit, where does Tucker sleep?"

"Relax," Savannah smiled. "He's in the adjoining room with Lane."

Brynn stayed ramrod straight.

"And the door locks?"

"Yes, Brynn," she pushed herself up off the door, stepping closer, "it locks."

"Thank god," Brynn sighed, taking her by the hand and pulling her back in to kiss. "In that case..." she unzipped Savannah's dress, letting the gold pool on the floor around her feet, her eyes dark with hunger.

Savannah shivered, pulling at Brynn's clothes until she had her back down to the black lace she'd been mesmerized by back in the dressing room. She cupped Brynn's breast with her hand, feeling the hard nipple pebble, then bent her head to bite her through the lace. Brynn was here, real, her skin warm, her scent heady and even though she'd already made Savannah come harder than she'd come in *years* - twice in fact - she was nowhere near sated.

It had been a long damn time.

Brynn's breath was short, her hands gripping tight to her bare hips as Savannah undid the scrap of lace that was in her damn way, her lips slipping around a firm nipple, feeling Brynn jolt with pleasure. Her body was lean, tanned and strong and Savannah felt lightheaded with the potential that had been sparking between them for so long. How had she ever resisted this?

"Bed," Brynn gasped, apparently of the same mind, *"now."*

It felt so incredibly indulgent to have Brynn in her bed that it was almost wicked. Savannah pulled her on top, luxuriating in her long, muscular body, her smooth skin, the heat of her and they writhed together, thighs intertwined, hips pressing, kissing breathlessly. God, she was so *warm,* Savannah could die, already desperate for her touch.

"Wait," said Brynn, pulling away, despite Savannah's protest. She backed away from the bed, her eyes on Savannah's, teeth sunk deep into her lower lip. "Listen, I don't know how you feel about this, but..."

She left the words hanging as she crossed the room to go and unzip her overnight bag. Savannah propped herself up on her elbows to watch, as Brynn pulled out a smaller silk bag. She found herself entirely distracted by the unbeatable sight of Brynn Marshall in nothing but a pair of black lace panties, so it took a moment for her brain to catch up. Brynn was almost back to bed, her eyebrows raised in question, watching her where she lay - naked and extremely ready - when Savannah finally clocked the black leather harness and sizable strap-on in Brynn's hand.

She sat up abruptly.

"You came prepared," she said, trying extremely hard to sound offended. "You were *that* sure you would manage to seduce me."

Brynn laughed.

"I absolutely was not." She cocked her head questioningly, watching closely as Savannah nodded fast and adamant. She stood up to fit the harness. "I knew being with you tonight was a hell of a long shot. But on the off-chance I got what I wanted... it's been a fucking *year*, Savannah." She fitted the cock into place and stood up. Savannah lay back. She bit her lip, hard, at how Brynn looked with it on: intent and dangerous and very fucking sexy. "I've had far too long to think about all the ways I want you."

"And?" The word came out more breath than sound.

Brynn looked down at her, her eyes raking her body hungrily.

"Put your arms above your head," she said quietly, and Savannah whimpered. Biting her lip, she surrendered like she'd been told. Brynn took in a sharp breath as she looked at her. She took her time. There was lube - entirely unnecessarily, of that Savannah was sure - Brynn's body holding her thighs wide. As she pushed inside her agonizingly slowly, she watched Savannah's face intently as she gasped. "Fuck, you're so goddamn pretty like this," she murmured, her hips pressing in and Savannah struggled to breathe.

"You know you've got... *quite* the opinion of yourself," she managed, looking down toward the thick toy being pushed inside her and spasmed at the erotic sight.

"Mmm," Brynn was looking too, her gaze hazy with sex. "I think you can take it for me, baby."

Savannah made an embarrassing sound at the soft word dropped from Brynn's full lips with such heat. She wrapped her legs around Brynn's waist and pulled her all the way home, her hips bucking in greedy demand.

"Oh good *girl*," Brynn hissed and Savannah forgot herself, lifting her hands off the bed to dig her fingernails into Brynn's back as she began to thrust.

Oh god, Brynn had stamina. Savannah arched her back in desperate appreciation, her eyes squeezing shut, then fluttering open as her hips rolled to meet her. Brynn was gazing down at her with a focus and hungry determination that made her ache even harder.

"Touch yourself," Brynn whispered, and her dark eyes burned as Savannah slipped her hand between them and began to stroke, her mouth falling open at all the sensation as Brynn shifted her hips to thrust deeper. Oh *god,* she was not going to last.

After she'd come, helplessly hard, crying out so loudly she only hoped the rest of the hotel was sleeping deeply, she pushed Brynn onto her back and sat astride her, writhing her hips and pushing the base of the dildo up against her in slow, rhythmic pressure, watching Brynn's eyes go wide and then slam shut as the friction pushed her over the edge, gasping as she rocked up into Savannah's body.

"Just wait," Savannah leaned down and murmured in her ear, "until I can use my fingers on you properly."

Brynn convulsed.

The goal to make love all night was admittedly grandiose mid-tour right after a stadium show. It was close to three a.m., and Savannah curled into Brynn's body, her desire momentarily sated and her heart incredibly full. Her eyes began to drift shut, despite herself. Brynn lightly brushed her fingers over her cheek, making her smile, then slipped away, freeing herself from the harness. Then she was back, her naked body incredibly warm, kissing the nape of her neck and making her shiver before pulling her in to spoon her, strong arms around her body.

Savannah could only imagine how exhausted Brynn too must be after the adrenaline of the night and her first ever stadium show. To still have the energy to *fuck* Savannah the way she just had, well... Savannah smiled as she thought about how confused Chester would be when she called to all but beg the label to book Brynn Marshall for the entire rest of the tour. She reached out and snapped off the bedside lamp.

"I cannot tell you how glad I am we didn't wait until we were seventy," Savannah whispered into the dark with a smug grin.

Brynn laughed softly.

"That would have been a long damn wait." She felt Brynn's smile against her skin, another kiss finding the nape of her neck.

"Slightly less so for me," Savannah mused sleepily. "I'm four years older than you. I learned that from your NPR bio."

"You read my press?" Brynn's husky voice in the darkness sounded incredulous.

"Sometimes," she admitted. She stroked the arm slung around her, remembering the long days and immensely long nights without *this*. "I missed you," she whispered into the darkness. It felt like an understatement. She'd *longed* for her. "Even when I was angry, I still wanted whatever I could have of you."

Brynn tugged her onto her back and cupped her face.

"I missed you too," she whispered, then kissed her with immense care, like Savannah was breakable. The sweetness of it made her gasp, and they found they were not so tired after all.

———

"Savannah," the voice was insistent, intruding on her wonderful dreams. She snuggled deeper into the pillow. "Savannah!" Someone was gently shaking her and her eyes cracked open on an incredible sight: Brynn Marshall, stark naked, in her bed, in the golden morning light. Looking... wide eyed and panicked? Finally, Savannah heard the knocking on the internal door from the adjoining suite. "Oh my god, what do we do?" Brynn jumped up, still naked, and Savannah paused for a moment to fully appreciate the sight. "*Savannah.*" She grabbed the quilt from the bed to wrap around herself.

"Two seconds," Savannah called, belatedly jumping into action. She stepped equally naked to the wardrobe and opened it, pulling out the complimentary robes, smirking when she realized that despite her panic, Brynn's eyes were solidly on her ass. She turned and raised an eyebrow, until Brynn blinked, and they were both rapidly clothed in white, fluffy hotel robes.

Savannah went over and opened the door and in rushed Tucker, jumping into her arms.

"Mama!"

"Hey baby! How'd you sleep?"

Tucker just smooshed his face into her shoulder and clung on like a baby monkey the way he always did in the mornings. He was getting heavy, but Savannah found she still hoped he'd never stop.

"Holy shi- sugar," said Lane from the doorway. They pushed into the room and pointed at Brynn, who was trying her best to look natural in her robe, and not like she'd just about been sprung naked in Savannah's bed. Savannah couldn't wait until she found out about the serious sex hair she was sporting. "*Yes!*" Lane cried, pumping their fist like they were at a sports match. "How *long* did it take you to finally do something right for a change?" they accused Brynn, who laughed even as she rolled her eyes.

"I did it all for you, Lane," she said. The two of them hugged like they'd been parted for a decade, Brynn ruffling Lane's hair until they ducked out, batting her hand away. Savannah laughed.

"I didn't realize you two had become such good friends."

"Oh, we're not," Lane denied, making a disgusted face. "I've just been tolerating her presence in the hopes she'll stop flailing around and make good with her life."

"Totally." Brynn looked appalled. "If anyone asked me, I would definitely not say they were basically like my best friend other than Noah. Because that would just be all the constant annoying contact talking."

Lane looked genuinely moved for a second.

"That's so embarrassing for you," they said, biting back a grin. "I'm basically a kid."

Tucker pulled back from Savannah's shoulder and wriggled to be put down. He saw Brynn in the room and did a visible double take.

"Hey buddy," Brynn knelt down on the floor, smiling at him. He stared at her in confusion.

"Not on the phone," he tried to work it out.

"She doesn't actually live in the phone," Savannah told her befuddled son.

"You're here," Tucker said.

"Yeah buddy, I'm here." Brynn's eyes were bright with unshed tears. Tucker marched up to her and grabbed a lock of her hair, smooshing it slightly in her face. It almost looked like he was suffering from cuteness aggression.

"Hi!"

"Hi!"

They grinned at each other, and Tucker jumped on her lap.

"Read a story," he instructed her, and Brynn held him tight and laughed.

———

The tour had booked out a private dining room on the third floor of the hotel and eventually the four of them had made it down for breakfast. Brynn found she was absolutely ravenous after being too nervous to eat the night before, followed by some serious exertion, and she piled her plate up high at the buffet. When she made it to the table, she found they weren't eating alone.

"Good morning, *Brynn*," Coral's tone was smug and teasing. "Fancy seeing you here." Savannah looked up from her plate and rolled her eyes, but the happiness in her smile was obvious. Brynn just grinned.

"I could say the same to you, *Noah*," she shifted her attention to where her best friend lounged comfortably next to Coral. "Seems like half the band had trouble finding their way home last night." The four of them exchanged smug grins and Lane made a gagging sound beside her as they helped Tucker with his toast.

"Mommy looks happy," they said in a low voice, looking over at Savannah, who was laughing as Coral continued to tease her. "Does that mean you're going to be sticking around?"

"I am. And you *have* to stop calling her that, it's so wrong."

"Stop calling me what?" Savannah overheard. Brynn shot Lane a look, and they looked up, wide-eyed and wholesome.

"They like to stir me by calling you 'Mommy,'" Brynn explained. Savannah tilted her head and examined them.

"That's kind of sweet, I guess, in a weird way?"

"No, Savannah, it's not sweet. Not the way they're using it," Brynn told her. "They're calling you hot, which is *totally* inappropriate." She shot Lane a look.

"Am I not hot?" Savannah asked her innocently. All eyes were suddenly on Brynn with interest. She groaned.

"Yes, you're hot," she relented. "Everyone at this table knows I think you're beyond hot. I'm just trying to protect you from sexual harassment by your extremely junior *employee*."

"How chivalrous." Savannah smirked.

"She's cute when she's feeling threatened," Lane piped up.

"For the last time, you're not a *threat*," Brynn corrected them.

"I don't know," mused Savannah. "Don't forget, I've fallen for my nanny once before."

Lane cackled, though they also went noticeably pink. Brynn shot a dirty look at Savannah who just smiled at her sweetly.

"You're trouble," she observed, picking up Savannah's hand and kissing her fingers.

"Y'all are good together," Coral was smiling widely, her expression soft. "I'm glad you finally got your head out of your ass." Brynn fully expected this to be addressed to her, but her eyebrows shot up when she realized Coral was talking to Savannah. Coral caught her stare. "This one," she explained to Brynn, "is stubborn. Here she is winning Grammies and smashing stadium tours and all she does is sit on the bus looking mournful and playing your record day and night."

"That is an inaccurate characterization-" Savannah objected, her face flushing.

"Oh, it's accurate," Coral interrupted her. "She might have gone on a little date here and there, but she's been in knots about you forever. She's the one who sent me to your gig, did you know that? Wouldn't go herself, but she still had to know you were doing okay."

Brynn looked at Savannah, who was definitely pink in the face. Warmth spread throughout her body.

"She also asked me about you literally every time you called," Lane announced, looking thrilled at the pile-on.

"I'm allowed to *care*," Savannah interjected. "Everyone at this table clearly knows I care-"

"Care?" scoffed Coral. "You broke your own damn heart."

"Oh, you *loooooove* me," Brynn sang under her breath, letting Savannah off the hook and teasing her all at the same time. She tugged Savannah's face toward her and kissed her to whistles all around the table.

———

TMZ: Savannah Grace frolics with new lady love in the waves!

Country crossover musical icon Savannah Grace was spotted at Malibu Beach this weekend with hot new beau, musician Brynn Marshall. The previous night, the two had set tongues wagging with a steamy performance of their hit duet *Longing* at the SoFi stadium, leaving concert goers stunned. "They were so into each other," described one attendee on social media, "I don't think they even knew the audience was there #Bravannah"

Suspicions were confirmed the following day as the pair were seen playing happy families in the sand with Grace's young son Tucker, looking for all the world to be a well-established couple, in contrast to Grace's statement back in April and again in May, where she denied the pair were an item, despite their obvious chemistry.

Later, leaving her son in the care of his nanny, the two frolicked in the waves, embracing and exchanging steamy kisses, before walking out of the water holding hands, leaving no doubt as to the nature of their relationship status.

The singer - whose multi-Grammy-winning album *Beware the Fury* has dominated the charts since its release - is overdue for some happiness in her romantic life after the public meltdown of her previous marriage to professional womanizer Cole Corbin.

Wearing a stunning white swimsuit and a beaming smile, Savannah looked over the moon with her lady love. One bystander described how the loved up pair "couldn't keep their hands off each other. They make a beautiful couple."

Savannah Grace finally lucky in love? We love to see it.

———

Oblivious to the long-lens camera they'd later learn about, Brynn wrapped her arm around Savannah on the seashore. Tucker and Lane were building a sandcastle a hundred yards away, and Brynn's heart was full. The fall day was unseasonably warm, even for California, and she had sun, sand, surf and a beautiful woman in her arms.

Savannah pulled slowly back from the kiss and smiled. She looked like a million bucks in a swimsuit, her hair tangled and her skin salty.

"Brynn." She looked out at the waves. "Did you know it's twice now, that you've told me you loved me? Three times, perhaps, if you count to the crowd?"

Brynn gazed at her steadily.

"Yeah," she said softly. "Because I do."

Savannah smiled and looked down at the sand.

"Does it not worry you that I've never said it back?"

Brynn watched her for a moment.

"No," she said, "I figure that after everything you've been through, it might take a while for you to feel safe." The gentle breeze tousled her hair, and she tucked it back out of the way.

"And you're okay with that." Savannah was still watching the waves. She was so beautiful, Brynn's chest ached.

"I'm okay with that," she said. "I know when you're ready you'll fall in love with me, *hard.*"

Savannah turned to look at her, amusement and something else shining in her eyes.

"So confident," she observed.

Brynn shrugged, and Savannah rested her head on her shoulder. They watched the waves together as they rolled and crashed against the sand.

"I've always been safe with you," Savannah said softly. Brynn turned to look at her. "You probably should know that I'm terribly in love with you," she let her eyelashes fall, "and I have been for some time."

Brynn's heart exploded. She tried and failed to push down her grin.

"I know," she said. Savannah burst out laughing, and Brynn pulled her into her lap to kiss her again.

The End

Bonus Story

If you'd like a free bonus epilogue novella about Savannah and Brynn's journey sign up on my website at www.rubylandersbook s.com

Grace Notes Trilogy

The Grace Notes Trilogy explores three separate sapphic romances while following the story of country star Savannah Grace.

Falls From Grace

Grace Notes: Book One

Savannah Grace is a huge star in Nashville. At least, she was. Her hit band *Twice Struck* topped the country music charts for almost a decade until her high profile marriage to her bandmate and co-writer publicly exploded. Now she's fading from the spotlight and her own life, just trying to keep her head above water.

Brynn Marshall is a little lost. Dropping out of med school made her the black sheep of the family and now she's floating around LA trying to find a sense of purpose. When she falls down on her luck, her best friend - indie musician Noah Lyman - refuses to let her wallow. After all, he's just got his big break: co-writing with a megastar!

When Savannah enlists Noah to help her break out of country music and make a name for herself for once and for all, what better way to do it than to spend the winter in her secluded vacation home in the woods of Vermont? And what better way for Noah to help out a friend than to pretend he's bringing along his wife?

After all, what could possibly go wrong?

Graceless

Grace Notes: Book Two

Savannah Grace is on top of the world. She's back to selling out stadium tours and winning Grammies and she's just arrived home from her honeymoon after marrying the love of her life...nothing could burst this bubble.

Except, of course, her estranged family.

When her younger sister Cassidy shows up on her doorstep, in need of help and thoroughly - inexplicably - pissed off, the whole household gets turned on its end. Where did she spring from and why the heck is she so damn *mad?*

Savannah's nanny Lane has grown all the way up, from a cute punk kid to a classic heartbreaker, a long trail of short flings in their wake. They don't have a second to waste on Cassidy; after all she's rude, ignorant, hot-tempered and kind of a brat. It's just...does their boss's little sister have to be so *hot?*

Of course things could always get worse. Cassidy has one plan and one plan only: for her sister to turn her into a star.

Saving Graces

Rosalie Carlson is the person everyone turns to in a crisis. She's kind, calm, caring, and a social worker, after all. She's got it all together... except that her personal life is kind of a disaster. Things can get a little hectic when your complicated best-friendship is with a megastar like Savannah Grace.

When twenty-six year old Kinsey moved to Nashville, it was in the hopes of finding a creative partner and making it big. When she meets Cassidy Carver, musical sparks fly. It's a chance meeting with a beautiful older woman however, that truly knocks her off her feet.

Rosalie's gorgeous - and there's no denying the intense chemistry between them - but she refuses to consider even a single date with a young musician. Besides, Rosalie's given up on love altogether, so what would be the point?

Fighting this level of temptation is always a losing battle, but after one red hot minute they go their separate ways. It's just lucky there's no connection between their different worlds and no way they'll ever cross paths again...

Acknowledgements

The Grace Notes Trilogy was born out of the desire for some delicious escapism during a period of darkness, in both the world and in my own life. I hope it gives you some warmth and light, some love and heat, and the occasional urge to yell *you idiots, just fucking kiss already!*

Writing this series really saved me. When things got bleak, I got to fall in love... three times! I hope it does the same for you.

Me, writing again at all would not exist without the encouragement and support of Moira.K. Thank you for 150,000 years of friendship, for being a goddamned inspiration and for explaining the dream-world of indie authorship to me in a hundred infinitely patient messages, FaceTimes and windswept walks on the beach. This is all your fault.

To Melissa.H, always. You're my one call from jail, bury a body with no questions asked, risk our credit scores for each other in a heartbeat, phone call where there's no words just crying, do you need a kidney cos I have a spare, code red best friend. Gratitude doesn't cover it. Without you my life would be infinitely greyer without the love and smarts, chaos and joy that you bring to it.

To my son. You recently explained to me that you are no longer a baby but a big boy. We cut your curls and we both cried. You have long legs and a wild heart and actually, my beloved creature, you're always going to be my baby, even when you eventually outgrow me. You will never read this, thank god, but I can't not thank you because you are *always* my reason.

To my own mama and my sisters who I also probably won't let read this? But because we're all the same you will understand why and also be secretly relieved. I love you to the moon and back and your support has been everything to me, always, but this past year in particular.

This series would not exist in its current form without Evren.D, Mary.S, Sarah.G, Karen.F, Bancy.P, Jerica.T, Kate.J and the team of beta readers and critique partners who generously gave me their time and feedback, fixed my dialogue tags and explained to me that mysteriously, Americans do not use the words 'fortnight', 'grizzle' or 'road verge'? (Guys, *why?*) Your early support and encouragement have been critical. When my Australian romance comes out this year you will get to see the choice I finally made between "ass" and "arse" and for that, I thank you from the *bottom* of my heart.

Thank you to the entire community of sapphic authors who I am rapidly finding out are the kindest people on earth. In particular, thank you to Elizabeth Luly, Jo Havens and J.E. Leak for early support and advice, you are all wonderful humans and I really appreciate your time and kindness to a newbie! Thank you also to iHeartSapphic - I love what you do and you are so appreciated! Thank you also to The Lesbian Review for early reviewing.

Thank you to Cath Grace for her absolutely stunning cover design, you are a total star.

To the readers of indie authors and sapphic romance fans: thank you for reading me! Ultimately, all of this is about you and for you. Thank you for reading, for reviewing, for purchasing and for posting about it. It's that stuff that allows us to keep going and literally every single one of you is a gift.

Also? Queer people? We're the best people. (What? I'm just *saying!*) I see you, the thousand daily acts of bravery, joy, resilience and resistance. Please go and look in a mirror right now and say *I am fucking loved.*

All my love

x *Ruby*

Author

Ruby Landers lives in Meanjin (Brisbane) Australia. As you're reading this she is either typing a million daydreamy words a minute, giving someone a thousand-yard stare while secretly working out a plot twist, having a deep conversation with anyone four-legged, bargaining with an expert toddler negotiator, or dreaming of quitting her day job. Either way, there'll be coffee.

You can follow her at

Instagram @rubylandersauthor

Graceless (Sneak Peek)

Cassidy felt sick. Behind her lay everything she knew. Ahead of her lay an unknown world. She hunched her shoulders, feeling the backpack shift against her hot, damp dress: everything she now owned she carried on her back. The sun beat down as she blindly navigated the back roads, her hair sticking to her neck, her shoes already rubbing. Her feet moved by instinct. Her stomach ached. She did not know where she was going.

Her mind raced with furious words: the things she'd said, the things she should have said. The rage had sideswiped her with its suddenness. One minute she was quietly washing the breakfast dishes; the next, she was blowing up her entire life. She hadn't even been aware of the fury building within her, but now, as she marched grimly along the road, sweat beading on her brow, she could see the way its roots had spread throughout her life, angry tentacles that strangled everything in its path.

The counter-reaction had been swift and merciless.

Panting, she struggled up the incline and found herself at the edge of the highway. In one direction lay the Appalachian foothills; in the other... well, there was only one way to go. She dropped her backpack onto the path beside her and stared into the distance, where the asphalt seemed to wave and shimmer in the heat.

She took a swig of her water bottle and cursed herself as only a couple of drops fell into her dry mouth. Her arm dropped, the useless bottle mocking her thirst. The air around her was like breathing in hot soup. A truck appeared on the horizon and her decision was made. As if she'd done it a thousand times before, instead of never once having crossed the border of her tiny hometown, Cassidy extended her arm, her thumb raised.

The truck screeched to a halt ten feet past her, its engine idling and the window rolling down. A shot of fear ran through her, chased equally by a blaze of incandescent rage. This was what she'd been reduced to: a frightened girl, with no one left to turn to for help but a total stranger on a deserted strip of highway. If her body were to end up tossed on the side of the road, there was only one person to blame: Savannah Grace.

Printed in Great Britain
by Amazon

54571765R00249